A Murder for the Books

A Murder for the Books

A BLUE RIDGE LIBRARY MYSTERY

Victoria Gilbert

CROOKED
LANE

NEW YORK

Copyright © 2017 by Vicki L. Weavil

Published in the United States by Crooked Lane Books, an imprint of The Quick Brown Fox & Company LLC.

Crooked Lane Books and its logo are trademarks of The Quick Brown Fox & Company LLC.

Library of Congress Catalog-in-Publication data available upon request.

ISBN (hardcover): 978-1-68331-439-4
ISBN (ePub): 978-1-68331-440-0
ISBN (ePDF): 978-1-68331-441-7

Cover illustration by Cheryl Martucci
Book design by Jennifer Canzone

Printed in the United States.

www.crookedlanebooks.com

Crooked Lane Books
34 West 27th St., 10th Floor
New York, NY 10001

First Edition: December 2017

10 9 8 7 6 5 4 3 2 1

For my mother,
Barbara King Lemp

Chapter One

A nyone who claims there are no stupid questions has never worked in a public library.

"So what do you think? Hemlock or cyanide?"

I allowed this query to bounce around my mind, recalling what little I knew about poisons. Cyanide would be quicker, but there was a certain philosophical charm associated with hemlock . . .

I shook my head to silence this amusing diversion. It really didn't matter. My answer would be ignored. The woman blocking my passage through one of the library aisles had been writing a mystery—and asking similar questions—for the last ten years.

Not that I'd known her that long. I'd only started work at the Taylorsford Public Library a year ago, but fortunately my predecessor, Ralph Harrison, now living happily patron-free with his family in Georgia, had left behind a list detailing the eccentricities of the library "regulars." I'd thought this in poor taste when I'd found it stuffed in a file, but I soon realized that he'd bequeathed me a great treasure. Without those notes, I would have undoubtedly done something extremely foolish. Something even worse than asking the mayor if he had a local address. Of course he did. He couldn't be the mayor if he didn't live in town. In fact, without Ralph Harrison's list, I probably would've been dismissed from this job months ago.

Although keeping my position as library director was still touch and go as far as I was concerned.

The patron wagged her finger at me. "Excuse me, Ms. Webber, I asked you a question. Cyanide or hemlock?"

"You can call me Amy, and I think that depends on the effect you're trying to achieve." I flipped a fallen volume upright on the shelf. "If you want, I can show you some books that discuss . . ."

The patron flapped her hands. "No, no, I've read all that stuff. I just want your opinion."

"You know I can't give you that. Librarians can help you find information or provide books that might assist you, but we can't make decisions for you."

The woman snorted. "You're just as useless as the last one, making me do all the work. I need an answer, not a scavenger hunt. Do they teach you those tactics in library school?"

"Actually, they do. Watch your step, by the way." I pointed at a strategically placed bucket, one of many that were collecting drips from the leaky roof. At least the brightly colored pails weren't as unattractive as the blue plastic tarps that were draped over the top of some of the bookstacks, ready to be deployed to cover an entire range of shelves during heavy downpours. Unfortunately, both were a necessity despite looking distinctly out of place in the historic building.

The Taylorsford Public Library, with its thick fieldstone walls, deep windowsills, and vaulted ceiling, exuded an air of elegance only slightly undercut by the modern addition housing the children's room. It was a Carnegie library, built in 1919 with a grant from industrialist Andrew Carnegie. I appreciated its historical significance while bemoaning its disintegrating roof and the rivers of wiring hidden beneath rubber conduits. Although they certainly had known how to build beautiful libraries, no one in 1919 had envisioned the current demand for network cabling.

As if echoing my thoughts, the lights flickered. One of the volunteers must have heated something in the break-room microwave. I sighed and made a mental note to speak to the town council, once again, about upgrading the wiring throughout the library.

"Guess I'll just have to manage on my own." The patron flounced off in the direction of the reading room, a collection of sturdy wooden tables and chairs separated from the bookstacks by a decorative mahogany arch.

One more person dissatisfied with my job performance. What had convinced me that academic library experience would translate to the public library sphere? If only I could've stayed in my university job . . . but Charles had made that impossible. As long as he remained on the faculty at Clarion University, I could never work there again.

I flushed, recalling our final encounter. It had been at a formal reception following the debut of Charles's new music group, the Alma Viva Trio. I'd stumbled over Charles and his violinist, Marlis Dupre, in a back room and had discovered my boyfriend's fingers caressing Marlis instead of the ivories. Chasing them into the reception hall, I'd thrown a glass of champagne—aiming for Charles but hitting the dean of music instead.

Don't worry. Librarians are in demand, my friends had said when I'd given my two weeks' notice and fled, unwilling to face the constant looks of disapproval from the administration and faculty. But sadly, Clarion was the only college or university within commuting distance of Taylorsford. In fact, it was the only university in this part of Virginia. Although I was thirty-three and single and possessed enough library experience to work elsewhere, moving was out of the question. I couldn't leave Aunt Lydia alone, especially after her recent fall.

I spied a book sticking out at an odd angle and plucked it off the shelf to examine the call numbers on its spine. As I suspected, it had been shelved in the wrong location. Clutching the book to my chest, I marched up behind the walnut circulation desk.

"Looks like the Nightingale's been busy."

"Again?" Sunshine Fields, better known as "Sunny," was the library's only other paid employee. As she shoved her long blonde hair behind her shoulders, Sunny's stack of metal bracelets jangled from her wrist to her elbow. Raised on an organic farm by her grandparents, whom she affectionately called "the grands," Sunny was my best friend in Taylorsford. We'd met when I had started spending summers with my aunt at age fifteen. Sunny and I had been two of the few participants in a teen reading program at the library and had bonded over our mutual love of books.

"You didn't see her?"

"No, but she's a sneaky little thing." Sunny waved the book under the barcode reader before handing it back to me. "Not checked out. So at least she hasn't been raiding the book drop again."

The Nightingale—named in honor of the famous nurse—was another regular, whose attempts to be "helpful" included reshelving books. Unfortunately, she had no concept of the cataloging system and shoved car-repair manuals between young adult titles.

"Thank heavens for small blessings." I flipped through the book before placing it on the shelving cart. "And she didn't leave any notes about the dangers of reading fiction. Amazing."

Sunny lowered her head, causing her long hair to spill forward. "Oh, speaking of regulars, you missed all the excitement earlier."

"Something happened while I was leading story hour?" I wasn't surprised that I'd missed any commotion since I'd been reading *Where the Wild Things Are* to a bunch of preschoolers who'd demanded sound effects and contributed their own when my efforts didn't meet their expectations.

"Yeah." Sunny shuffled some flyers on the desk. "I caught Doris Virts cowering in the workroom, muttering about being followed."

I stared at Sunny's veiled profile. "I thought the family hired someone to accompany her when she left the house."

"They did, but Doris is apparently pretty good at giving the caregiver the slip." Sunny brushed back her hair. "Anyway, you may not know this, but Doris was a library volunteer until a year or so ago. I think she gets confused and still believes she should be working behind the desk or something."

"So where was her companion while all this was going on?"

"Just looking for some books that Doris requested." Sunny readjusted the placement of the bell on the desk. She was fidgeting, which meant something more had happened, but I decided to wait for the full story. "Doris can be quite clever when she wants. Anyway, she left the workroom meekly enough."

"She thinks she's being followed? Her paranoia must be working overtime these days."

"Yeah, it's gotten worse. Every time she visits the library, she claims someone's after her."

"Well, the caregiver has to trail her everywhere. I bet Doris doesn't really remember who she is sometimes. That could cause her delusion."

"Probably." Sunny frowned. "I sure hope the grands don't suffer anything like that. Poor Bethany, having to keep track of her mom and try to manage her diner at the same time. Don't know how she does it."

"With great difficulty, I imagine." *A lot tougher than your situation*, I reminded myself. Aunt Lydia might have a few physical problems, but her mind was still sharp. I knew Bethany Virts didn't like leaving her mom in the care of others, but she couldn't afford to give up the diner, which was her only source of income.

Sunny glanced at me. "Doris didn't mess with anything in the workroom as far as I can tell, but you should probably check it later. I only gave it a quick once-over 'cause there were patrons lined up at the desk."

"Sure, I'll do that."

"And"—Sunny shot me a concerned glance—"keep an eye out for Doris. Seems she escaped her caregiver again right after they left the library. Got a frantic call from Bethany and then another one from the aide. They're out looking for her now."

"Well, crap, that's awful." I pulled an upside-down picture book from the cart and immediately dropped it when my fingers stuck to the cover. Someone had decided to smear their bubble-gum across the face of a purple dinosaur. Great. I calculated how much it would cost to replace the book if it couldn't be properly cleaned. "Did they call the sheriff's office?"

"No, Bethany doesn't want to involve them if she doesn't have to. It's happened before, you know. She said they usually find Doris in the old Lutheran cemetery across the street, where her family's buried." Sunny's bracelets jingled as she lifted a stack of books from the inside drop box. "But I told Bethany we'd call immediately if Doris came back into the library, so if you see her . . ."

"I'll definitely give a call," I replied, yanking down the hem of my scoop-necked top. Every time I lifted my arms, the stupid blouse rumpled up to my waist. To be honest, if I were thin like Sunny, clothes wouldn't have been such a bother. But I was far too curvy for tops to fit smoothly.

"Curvy" was what Sunny and Aunt Lydia told me to say. Not plump—*curvy*.

Yeah, right. Tell that to the designers who create clothes for toothpicks.

I gave my top a final tug. A tearing sound was followed by a flap of material popping loose and hanging below the hem, frayed threads dangling.

"Shit," I said.

"Hello," said a deep male voice.

Although the man standing before me was of average height, his posture made him appear taller. I opened my mouth and shut it again as Sunny leaned over the desk and flashed a brilliant smile at the stranger.

"Can we help you?"

"I hope so." The man's gaze lingered on my body just long enough to make me question my choice of the low-necked top. "You look familiar. Do I know you?"

I shook my head. "Doubt it. I only moved here a year ago. Well, I've spent some summers and weekends here in the past, but I wasn't a full-time resident. I'm Amy Webber, the library director. And this is Sunshine Fields, my assistant."

The man cast Sunny an appreciative look, as most men did, but then turned his focus back on me. "Wait, did you ever work at the Clarion University library?"

I took a deep breath. There was no way to escape this question without lying. "Yes, up until about a year ago."

"Okay, that must be where I've seen you. I've only worked summers up to now, but . . ." He narrowed his gray eyes. "Of course it was in the library. I had to grab a few scores for my accompanist, and you were helping some conductor. I remember because I was impressed with how well you handled him. He was being a total jerk, demanding everything at the top of his lungs. I would've slugged him, but you were very patient."

"Was I?" As I examined the man's decidedly attractive face, a memory surfaced. Once, when we had been first dating, Charles had taken me to a contemporary dance recital. Part of his campaign to "sophisticate" me, I supposed. He had always been trying to do that, claiming that my knowledge of art and literature was adequate but my performing arts palate needed refinement.

Yeah, and you let him say that, Amy. What were you thinking?

I hadn't been thinking, of course. I'd been dazzled by his looks, talent, and fame.

Something about this guy recalled that date with Charles. It took only a second before I remembered that although the recital had featured students from the university's summer programs, one of their instructors had also performed a solo. It had been this man, whose breathtaking grace had been matched by his physical perfection. According to the program, he'd made quite a name for himself as a dancer and choreographer.

Another artistic guy. No, definitely not going there. I smiled coolly as I stepped around the desk to face him. "Oh, wait. I remember you from Clarion. You're Richard something, right?"

"Richard Muir. Dancer, choreographer, and instructor. Now primarily the latter, since I accepted a full-time teaching job this fall."

He smiled. Sunny grabbed a library brochure and fluttered it like a fan.

"I left Clarion to take the job here. I live with my aunt, you see, and she had a fall that injured her leg." I toyed with the loose edge of my shirt hem. Richard Muir seemed unaware of my real reasons for leaving my previous job, and I hoped I could keep it that way.

"Guess I can't count on your assistance at the university library, but I do need some historical information related to Taylorsford. Maybe you can help with that?" Richard Muir moved closer.

I stepped back. He was about to invade my personal space, and I was having none of that. He could keep his perfect body to himself. I'd had enough of handsome, artistic men.

"So what brings you to Taylorsford, Mr. Muir?" Sunny slid her tongue over her bottom lip.

I fought the desire to roll my eyes. It was Sunny's nature to flirt. She meant no harm.

"Actually, I've moved here. You know the old Cooper place?"

Sunny fluttered her golden lashes. "Of course. It's right next to Amy's house. Well, her aunt's place. The Litton house—the beautiful Queen Anne revival with the wraparound porch."

Richard Muir's gray eyes swept over me again. "You're my neighbor? I heard Lydia Talbot had a niece living with her, but I've never seen . . . no, wait—do you work in the garden in a floppy straw hat?"

I grabbed the picture book and stared at the damaged cover, keeping my head down to hide the flush rising in my face. Yes, I worked in my Aunt Lydia's garden—in shorts, a tattered T-shirt, and that stupid hat. If Richard Muir had spied me from his house, he undoubtedly had also garnered a lovely view of my backside as I bent over to weed the flowerbeds.

"Sometimes," I muttered, flipping the book over and studying it as if I'd never seen the damaged cover before. "It's a big garden, and my aunt can't get around so well these days."

"I have seen her out walking with a cane. Sorry I haven't come by to say hello, but I've been traveling until now. Choreography gigs here and there. Of course, I've stopped in to check on the renovations, but I only officially moved in a month ago."

"Oh, no problem." I laid the picture book on the counter, gum side up, and lifted my chin to meet his intense gaze. "Besides, my aunt and I should visit you first. That's how things are done, or so she tells me."

Richard raised his eyebrows. "Are those the town rules? You might have to help me with that. Been a city boy all my life."

Sunny leaned across the desk, causing her loose peasant blouse to slide off one shoulder. Slender as she was, she didn't have to wear a bra, something I envied even more than her lovely blue eyes. "So you're the brave soul who restored the Cooper place, Mr. Muir?"

"Richard. Yeah, although I didn't do the work. Not bad with a hammer, but I had no time, so I hired contractors." Richard looked Sunny up and down. "I bet you go by 'Sunny,' don't you?"

"How'd you guess?" Sunny straightened and flashed him another gleaming smile. "Are you psychic or something?"

"No, that name just fits you."

"Well, it's good you aren't a psychic, seeing as how your home is haunted," Sunny said.

"So I've heard." Richard turned back to me. "What do you think, Ms. Webber? Seen any ghosts flitting around my house?"

"It's Amy, and no." Forgetting the rip, I tugged on my blouse again, tearing loose another bit of hem. "But then, I don't believe in such things." I curled my fingers around the tattered edge of my shirt.

"Me either, although I like to keep an open mind. Anyway, now that I have some time, I'm interested in digging into the past. It was my great-uncle who last owned the place, you see."

So that was the other reason he looked so familiar. Aunt Lydia kept a framed photo of her former neighbor, novelist Paul Dassin, on a bookshelf in her library. "Paul Dassin was your great-uncle?"

"Yep. I inherited the house. Well, my parents did. They signed it over to me a few years ago, when I'd scraped together enough money for a decent restoration."

Sunny looked him over. "You're going to live here and work at Clarion? That's kind of a long commute every day, isn't it?"

"I used to do it," I said.

"But you were staying over at Charles's place half the time." Sunny tossed off this information as she stepped around the desk.

I wanted to clap my hand over her mouth, but Sunny was just telling the truth. I had lived with Charles when I worked at Clarion, although I had returned to Taylorsford on the weekends to help Aunt Lydia with the house and garden.

Richard cast me a sympathetic smile. "Well, that's the thing, I had a similar setup. I was living with my fiancée in an apartment near the university until she decided to run off to New York and marry someone else. So I thought, 'Why not move into my renovated house in Taylorsford instead of selling it?' I finally have the full-time position to make it affordable, so I can live here and fulfil a lifelong goal."

"Oh?" Intrigued by this proclamation, I decided my tattered hem was irrelevant and dropped my hand. "What's that?"

"Prove once and for all that Eleanora Cooper was innocent of her husband's death."

Sunny widened her blue eyes. "That's a tall order in this town, Richard. Everyone thinks Eleanora Cooper was guilty as sin even though she was acquitted. The old folks still say she got away with murder before she up and disappeared."

"I know, but my great-uncle never believed that, and I want to prove him right." Richard turned to me. "Thought I'd start by doing a little historical research. Someone told me the library held the town records. Is that right?"

"Yeah, in the archives. But we keep that material in a building out back. I'll have to get the key. Just a minute." I walked behind the circulation desk and into the workroom, leaving Sunny to chat with Richard.

She'll probably snag a date with him before I reappear. Not that she shouldn't. After the Charles debacle, I'd sworn off all men for a while, especially handsome men involved in the arts. But single men were few and far between in Taylorsford. If Sunny could start up something with Richard Muir, good for her.

In the workroom, I frowned as I rummaged through the key box. Designed to be locked, its own key had been lost long ago. I hadn't been particularly concerned when I'd discovered this situation, considering it unlikely that anyone would want to steal a key, especially since the workroom could only be accessed from behind the circulation desk.

But despite this precaution, the archives' key was missing.

We could still open the archives since I had personal copies of all essential library keys. But I couldn't allow a lost key to float about where anyone could find it. Especially not *that* key.

I strode out of the workroom. "The key's not there. Did somebody borrow it?"

"I haven't touched it in days." Sunny met my gaze and mouthed, *Doris?*

I bit my lower lip. If Doris had been a library volunteer, she probably knew where that key was kept. She could've swiped it before Sunny chased her from the workroom.

Not a bad hypothesis, Amy. Doris probably hoped to hide in the archive building to escape her phantom pursuer.

If that were the case, they'd find the key on Doris soon enough, and I wouldn't have to change the lock on the archives door, or—more important—explain the situation to the town council. Which would definitely make my life easier. I shook off my sense of foreboding and forced a cheerful tone. "Richard, it seems we've misplaced the extra key. I can let you in, but I'll have to accompany you."

"Don't you usually do that?" Richard asked as I stepped out from behind the desk.

"Not really, because there are only two of us working here most of the time. Oh, I know—valuable records and all that. But honestly, only a few people ask to visit the archives, and we usually know them pretty well." No use mentioning my theory about Doris stealing the key. Why cause an uproar when the problem might resolve itself? I shoved a straggling lock of my straight brown hair behind my ear. "Sunny, can you hold down the fort?"

"Sure, but would you do me a favor?"

"Of course, what do you need?"

"Just check to see if there's still a black car parked on the side of the road right outside our parking lot. It's snazzy and sleek like a sports car. I spied it when I ran to my car to grab my cell phone earlier. I forgot it again and needed to check for any messages from the grands."

Richard cast her a questioning glance. "Something unusual about a parked car?"

"On that road there is." Sunny crinkled her nose as she often did when she was puzzled. "It's really almost an alley, so most patrons park in our lot unless it's full. Which it wasn't. Maybe it was just some tourists, parking in the first place they could find so they could walk around town. But it was such an expensive-looking car. One of those with the big cat as a hood ornament."

"A Jaguar?" Richard raised his eyebrows. "That *is* a pricey ride."

"Yeah, not something you usually see around here. I thought it was weird, someone parking that sort of car in a spot where it might get sideswiped. And"—Sunny twisted her bangle around her wrist—"it almost looked like someone was sitting in the car. I guess I should've investigated further, but I didn't want to leave the desk unsupervised that long. Not to mention the whole thing made me a little nervous. So I just grabbed my phone and came back inside."

"Smart move," I said. "Don't worry. If we see the car, I'll give the sheriff's office a call. No one is supposed to park there anyway. Road's too narrow. Also, I don't like the idea of someone loitering out back for whatever reason. Okay?"

"Yep, sounds great. Well, don't let me keep Richard from his research. I'll take care of things while you're gone."

I flashed Sunny a grateful smile before heading for the back door. "This way, Richard. I can show you what type of records we keep, although you may want to come back another day to dig into them. It's Thursday, and we close at five on Thursdays and Fridays these days." I spread my hands wide. "Budget cuts."

"No problem. I don't really have much to do until the new academic year begins, so I can return easily enough." Richard gazed over the hedges that bordered the gravel lot separating the library and a small stone cottage. "No fancy black car that I can see."

"No, thank goodness." I shaded my eyes with one hand as I peered at the side street. "It is a little strange, someone choosing to park there, especially when the free town lot is rarely full."

14

"I agree. I usually use that one myself. It's more centrally located, but I guess tourists might not realize that and park here instead."

I headed for the archives' building without looking back at him. "Sometimes. We don't really mind, as our lot isn't often full, although it is needed for staff and volunteer parking too. The historical society prefers we not park on the street. Out front, I mean. 'Destroys the illusion of stepping back in time,' they say." I shrugged. "Always considering that tourism angle."

"Can't say I blame them. This part of Taylorsford is certainly quaint. Now, the strip mall and car dealerships as you approach town, on the other hand . . ."

"Not so quaint. But needed, I guess." I pulled my key ring from my pocket. "Just a second."

"Is this original to the site?" Richard pressed his hand against the oak doorframe.

"Yes, the library director used to live here. It was a necessary perk since the town couldn't pay much. Still can't, actually, but in the fifties, when the archives outgrew their alcove in the main building, the town took over this space." As I inserted the key in the lock, the door swung inward. "Wait, why is it unlocked?"

Doris must've let herself in. Which meant she could still be inside. I took a deep breath and considered how to deal with a confused, and possibly terrified, patron.

"Careful. Let me go first." Richard used his foot to push the door open wider.

"Not necessary. I'm sure everything's fine. I think one of our older patrons might have borrowed the key without asking, that's all." Not wanting to spook Doris any more than necessary, I crossed the threshold in front of Richard. I stopped short as sunlight glinted off an object lying on the wood-plank floor. "There's the key, but why would she toss it . . . ?"

I flicked on the light switch and peered into the shadowy interior.

The archive building was a single room with a large pitted-wood table situated under a dangling fluorescent light. The shuttered windows blocked any view of the outside. Old metal file cabinets lined three of the walls, while shelving stuffed with archival banker's boxes covered the fourth wall.

Everything looked perfectly normal.

Everything except for the body lying facedown on the floor with blood pooling around its head.

Chapter Two

I shrieked and dropped the key ring, which hit the floor with a clang like an old bell.

This can't be happening. It must be a hoax. It must be. I blinked rapidly and looked again, but the body was still there. Still motionless. Still haloed in blood spattered with what I could only assume was brain matter.

Richard grabbed me around the waist and pulled me backward with a grace that spoke of his experience partnering dancers. "We shouldn't disturb anything."

I pointed a shaking hand at the figure. "I know that outfit; she wears it all the time. That's Doris Virts."

Richard kept one arm around me as he slid his cell phone from his pocket. "I'll call nine-one-one."

"Shouldn't we help? She might still be alive."

"Doubtful."

I couldn't take my eyes off of the prone form. Yes, with all that blood, it was unlikely Doris was alive. The contents of my stomach sloshed like dirty water in a bucket.

"Dispatcher says the police will be here any minute." Richard pocketed his phone. "We'll need to answer questions. You okay with that?"

He still had his arm around my shoulders. A strong, well-muscled arm. I would've shaken off his hold except I was trembling so much I feared sliding to the ground. "Have to be, I guess."

"We shouldn't talk about it." Richard gave my shoulder a squeeze before guiding me to a concrete bench under a red-bud tree. "They'll want our stories, direct from each of us. No collaboration."

I eyed him as I sat down. All color had fled his face. "Sounds like you've done this before."

"Yes, unfortunately. Not a murder, but . . ." He shook his head. "Never mind. I'll tell you another time." He looked up and over the hedge. "Listen, there are the sirens."

I clasped my hands together until my knuckles blanched. "I can't understand this. Who'd want to hurt Doris Virts? She's a sweet old lady. I can't believe she has any enemies."

Richard glanced down at me. "Who knows? People keep secrets." He ran his hands through his short dark hair. "Just tell the police what we saw. Don't worry. I doubt they'll keep us long."

"Won't we have to go to the station or something?"

"Eventually. But hopefully they'll take statements now and ask us to come in later for a more formal report."

The back door of the library opened, and Sunny peeked out. "The sheriff just pulled up, and sirens are blasting. What's going on?"

I waved her back. "Stay where you are. Don't come out here."

"Why?" Sunny's eyes widened as she glanced toward the open door of the archives. "Is a patron ill? There's someone on the floor . . ."

"Just go inside. I don't want you caught up in this."

Obviously astonished at the sharpness of my tone, Sunny snapped her mouth shut. She backed through the door and closed it behind her.

Bradley Tucker, the county sheriff's chief deputy, dashed into the lot, barking orders. He was followed by two men in suits and an older officer whose uniform didn't quite fit. Probably a part-time deputy. Taylorsford couldn't afford a full-time police force, so the town deputized a few people with military or security backgrounds to assist the sheriff and his staff. I didn't recognize the older man, but that wasn't surprising. If he'd never visited the library, I wouldn't know him. I tended to spend most of my time either at work or at home, with occasional trips to buy food and other necessities.

I knew Brad, of course. He'd lived here all his life and, as chief deputy, covered most criminal activity in Taylorsford. Not murders, of course. There'd never been a murder except for that old Cooper incident, and that case was never solved.

Drug dealing, domestic disturbances, vandalism, and other crimes weren't uncommon. But not murder. Not until now.

Brad studied me and Richard, lines wrinkling his broad brow. "So these are our witnesses?" Although he now sported a slight paunch, Brad still resembled the football star he'd once been twenty-some years before. Now forty, he kept his blond hair short, his uniform neatly pressed, and his face shaved smooth as an egg.

He was examining us with displeasure. I thought I knew why.

Brad was considered one of Taylorsford's most eligible bachelors, at least according to Sunny, who'd dated him briefly before declaring his "red-meat attitude" bad for her aura. But I'd rebuffed his one and only attempt to ask me out—partially because I had still been too raw from Charles's betrayal to consider dating anyone, but primarily because I'd thought we would have little to talk about. Although Brad's obsession with sports occasionally brought him into the library to peruse magazines, I questioned whether he'd opened a book since high school.

Not used to being dismissed so coldly, he hadn't taken my rejection well.

Brad wasn't winded, although his fellow officer was puffing and clutching his side. "Where's the body?"

Richard pointed toward the archives' building.

Brad cast a sharp glance at me. "You stay put."

More people ran into the area, including the sheriff and a doctor who doubled as the local coroner. They swarmed the archives, examining the grisly scene.

The two suits approached us, and I realized they must be plainclothes detectives.

"You, come with me," one of them barked at Richard. "Miss, stay where you are."

As Richard walked off, the other detective sat down and bombarded me with questions.

I answered, fighting to keep a quaver out of my voice. But after detailing my actions for the fifth time, I doubled over, fighting off a wave of nausea. The vision of blood speckled with brain matter kept flooding my mind, no matter how I tried to suppress the image.

"Sorry. We just have to make sure we have all the facts." The detective twitched his lips, producing what he probably thought was a comforting smile. He was wrong. But then, very little could comfort me in that moment.

I swallowed the ball of bile that had rolled up my throat. "I understand. But really, there isn't any more to tell. I didn't see Mrs. Virts or hear anything. She was killed by a gunshot, I assume?"

The detective nodded.

I swallowed before I could continue speaking. "And you'll have to ask my assistant, Sunshine Fields, for the details about that fancy black car. She's the one who saw it. I only heard about it secondhand."

"Someone is questioning her right now, so we'll get to the bottom of that. As for noise from the gunshot, the thick stone walls of the archives' building and your library would muffle that. Or maybe the killer used a silencer." The detective's piercing gaze swept over me again. "So you believe the victim stole the key?"

"I expect so. My assistant said Mrs. Virts was in the work-room earlier, where the key was stored, talking about being followed." I rubbed at the back of my neck with one hand. My muscles felt as rigid as steel cables beneath my fingers. "Like I said, I think Doris took the key and came out here to hide in the archives' building because she thought someone was after her."

"But although Ms. Fields told you about sighting an unusual vehicle on the side street, you personally saw no one other than regular library patrons? No strangers or anyone behaving suspiciously?"

"No, and even that mystery car was gone before I came outside with Mr. Muir. Of course, if someone else was outside, waiting for Doris . . ." I gripped my upper arms with both hands to still my shivering. "Please understand—Mrs. Virts suffered from dementia, so it's hard to tell if what she said was real or just a delusion. It's likely no one was following her. Maybe she just came out here to hide and stumbled over someone looking to rob the closest vulnerable target."

I wanted to believe this. Although the outcome would remain the same, the thought of Doris being accidentally shot by a common thief was less frightening than someone I knew being stalked by a madman.

A madman who might still be at large in Taylorsford. I clutched my arms harder.

"Could be. We're well aware of Mrs. Virts's medical condition, but we'll still be investigating all possibilities." The detective continued to examine me as his partner strolled over, trailed by Richard. "We're done for now, I assume?"

His partner nodded. "But these two need to stay in town." He pointed his index finger at us. "We must be able to find you."

Richard looked as pale and drawn as I felt. "Not a problem. We live here, you know. Don't plan to move." As the detective seated next to me stood and offered me a hand, Richard waved him back. "Ms. Webber's my neighbor. I can escort her home if that's okay."

"I don't see why not. Your whereabouts have been confirmed for the suspected time of the attack, and we've recorded all your contact info."

"Then allow us to get out of your way." Richard held out his hand and helped me to my feet.

I pulled away to face the detectives. "My assistant, the patrons . . ."

"They've been questioned, and the building has been cleared and locked up. The library will have to remain closed for a few days, I'm afraid. Additional state investigators have to be called in for something like this."

Fabulous—that'll probably mean the end of my career here. The mayor will see to that. Library closed for days, lax security . . . I tightened my lips. What a jerk I could be sometimes. How could I think about myself when Doris had just lost her life?

Because it distracted me. Because thinking about that body lying in the archives was too painful.

Richard gently tapped my wrist. "I walked here from the house, but if you drove, we can take your car." He glanced around the lot with a puzzled frown. It was empty except for Sunny's canary-yellow Beetle.

I rubbed my free hand across my eyes in a futile attempt to erase the image of that still form surrounded by blood. "No, I walked too. It isn't that far."

Keeping my head turned to avoid glancing at the archives' building, I followed Richard out the back exit. But I could hear Brad Tucker on his cell phone, talking about a shot to the temple at close range and a missing murder weapon, which was "likely a pistol or revolver . . ."

Once we were completely beyond the parking lot, I stumbled a few feet to the right and threw up into a forsythia bush.

*　　*　　*

Richard didn't speak as we walked through the town, but he kept his hand hovering under my elbow.

"Sorry about that," I said after a few blocks. "The vomiting, I mean."

Richard patted my arm. "Don't worry. I feel the same. If I'd had anything in my stomach, I'm sure I'd have heaved it up too."

We lapsed into silence as we walked. Fortunately, although the Cooper place and my aunt's house sat at the edge of town, it wasn't a great distance. The central portion of Taylorsford was only ten blocks long.

Historic properties lined the main street. There were a few businesses housed in brick buildings that had been erected in the late 1930s or 1940s, but the town was mostly private homes, their small front yards separated from the road by a narrow sidewalk.

What there was left of a sidewalk, anyway. Taylorsford's former mayor, Lee Blackstone, had promised for years to replace the crumbling concrete with brick pavers, but the historic trust money had never materialized. Now Robert Blackstone, his son and the current mayor, promised the same thing.

I kicked at a clump of orchard grass sprouting up through one of the cracks in the concrete. It *would* be more in keeping with the historic nature of the town if they could replace the sidewalks. Maybe Bob Blackstone would make it happen. He was certainly more capable than his father, at least according to Aunt Lydia.

As I looked up, I noticed Richard studying the houses. They varied in style from plain two-story wooden structures with simple black shutters and stooped porches to elegant Victorians festooned with decorative gingerbread trim. One or two of the oldest were built from the fieldstone that had once been prevalent in the area. It was the same stone used in the low walls dividing up farm fields outside of town.

"How much do you know about Taylorsford?" I asked, hoping to divert my mind from that ghastly scene in the archives.

"Not too much. My parents occasionally visited my greatuncle, but they stopped coming when he died." Although it was a hot June day, Richard vigorously rubbed his upper arms as if he were freezing.

I understood. He was probably as traumatized by the sight of a brutal murder as I was. Most people would be unless they were psychopaths. I studied his face as we walked side by side. Handsome but not haughty. An unusual combination in my experience.

"He lived to be eighty-eight, you know. Died in 1985." Richard shot me a quick glance. "My parents brought me along on their visit the summer before he died, but I was only four and don't really remember anything. So I don't know that much."

"Well, Taylorsford is pretty old. For an American town, I mean. It was founded by English settlers in the early eighteenth century. The Germans showed up soon after." Yes, the bland conversation helped. I took a deep breath and uncurled my clenched fingers. "The name comes from a ferry that once crossed the nearby river. Operated by the Taylor family."

"Oh, I get it. *Ford*. Like fording a stream. Guess that's what made it an attractive location for a town too." Richard glanced across the street. "But most of these buildings aren't that old."

"No. Fire gutted the majority of the wooden buildings during the Civil War, and the blizzard of 1888 collapsed most of the remaining stone structures."

Richard looked over my head at one of the houses. "Not too many side streets, are there? But the valley is pretty narrow, so I guess that made it hard to expand. At least in the historic part of town."

I nodded. The houses had larger yards in the back. Beyond these lawns and gardens, groves of trees climbed the hills that rose to meet the Blue Ridge Mountains. Due to the steep rise, there'd never been much construction beyond the main road. "Not such a bad thing. You mentioned that mess on the eastern edge where the road crosses the foothills and spills into the wider valley. All that cheesy development. Discount stores and such."

Richard shrugged. "I know. I sort of hate it. But I really can't complain too much. I guarantee I'll still shop there. Got to get groceries and gas somewhere."

"True." I shot him a quick glance. Studying his rugged profile, I had to admit a grudging admiration. He'd neatly punctured my hypocrisy without a mean word. Despite my disdain for the unfettered development on that side of town, I also shopped in those stores.

We reached Aunt Lydia's house, which was separated from Richard's smaller farmhouse by a stretch of lawn and a picket fence bent under the weight of climbing roses. As I flipped up the latch on the front gate, Richard tilted his head back and gazed admiringly at the home's elegant lines. It was a stone structure like the original Taylorsford buildings, a vanity that had cost my ancestor, Albert Baker, dearly. By the time it had been built in 1900, fieldstone had no longer been readily available in the area and had to be imported from farther west.

A short flight of stone steps led to a wood-framed porch that stretched across the front and wrapped the left side of the house. The dark wood front door, with its heavy bronze knocker and stained-glass sidelights, was set off to the right side. Just off that edge of the porch, at the corner, the house bowed out in an attached tower—three-quarters of a circle where it rose with the house, then turning into a circular turret above the second-story roofline. The turret's wizard-hat roof was topped with a weathervane decorated with a blooming rose, its copper petals now colored with a green patina.

"It's stunning," Richard said. "I can see why your aunt wants to hang onto it."

It was the loveliest home in Taylorsford, according to most observers. But I noted paint flaking from the carved woodwork that decorated the edge of the porch roof. All the wood trim needed to be scraped and repainted, but that was an expense my aunt couldn't afford at the moment, and my meager salary certainly wasn't much help.

"Is it turn of the century? I know it's a bit older than my house."

"Yes," I replied automatically while I dug into my purse for my keys. I'd finally convinced Aunt Lydia to lock her doors during the day, but only after some recent break-ins had occurred down the street. "My great-great-grandfather, who had quite a fortune at the time, had it built."

As I gripped the wooden railing that flanked the front steps, a few white flakes fluttered to the ground. We couldn't postpone that paint job forever, but money was so tight . . . I could only afford the library job because I lived with my aunt. The salary certainly wouldn't allow me to live anywhere decent on my own.

If only I could've kept the university position, things would be so much easier. But no, I had to stop thinking like that. At least I had a job in my field and could still watch over Aunt Lydia.

"Now"—Richard turned to me with a serious expression—"how do you think your aunt is going to react to this? Did she know the woman?"

"Aunt Lydia knows everyone in town. I don't think she and Doris Virts were close friends, but they are around the same age, so they went to school together and all that."

"It's bound to be a shock. Perhaps you should break it to her gently?"

"Oh, Aunt Lydia will be okay. She's made of pretty stern stuff."

"Still, we'd better be prepared for her reaction."

"I am. Not quite sure you will be."

The front door swung open, and a tall, slender figure greeted us. My sixty-four-year-old aunt looked every inch the fine lady she was. She gazed down her slightly hooked, very English nose at us.

"Back so soon? I thought perhaps they might keep you at the sheriff's office longer."

"We didn't have to go there. They just questioned us at the library. And—you know everything already?"

"Yes, except who did it, of course. Assuming it wasn't either one of you." Her blue eyes sparkled with excitement. "It wasn't, was it? Although"—her gaze swept over the two of us—"I've never met a murderer that I know of. Could be rather interesting."

Chapter Three

Richard stared at Aunt Lydia, his gaze sliding from her perfectly coiffed cap of white hair to her elegant low-heeled pumps and back up to her fine-boned face. "Sorry, not a murderer, but still very happy to meet you."

I bit my lower lip to fight a smile. Richard had probably expected some frail old woman, overwhelmed by the news of a murder in her town. He was not expecting Aunt Lydia. No one ever did.

"You must be Richard Muir, our new neighbor." Aunt Lydia examined him for a second before offering a warm smile. "Yes, you look very much like your great-uncle. The spitting image, at least from early photos. I only knew him when he was quite a bit older, of course, but I can see the resemblance." She turned her sharp gaze on me and frowned. "Amy, I'm so sorry you had to be the one to discover the body. At least you aren't covered in blood. But what is going on with your blouse?"

I instinctively cupped my hand around the tattered hem of my top. "It's nothing. And how do you already know what happened?"

"Oh, Zelda called me, of course. Nothing gets by Zelda."

That was true. Zelda Shoemaker, who had recently retired from her job as town postmaster, was my aunt's best friend. She always seemed to know everything that went on in Taylorsford.

Sometimes, it seemed, before it even happened. "Aunt Lydia, Richard just moved in . . ."

"Yes, I know." Aunt Lydia's eyes narrowed as she looked Richard up and down. "Last month, wasn't it? But you've been traveling since, it seems. Anyway, did you bring that pretty fiancée of yours with you? I heard rumors there was one."

"Um, no." Richard sketched a circle against the porch floor with one foot. "Afraid you're misinformed. I am quite single at this point."

As Aunt Lydia clapped her hands together, her metal cane clanged against the heavy rings on her left hand. "How delightful! Taylorsford needs more single men, doesn't it, Amy?" She peered into Richard's face. "Unless, of course, you've decided you're gay?"

"Not the last time I checked," Richard said with a smile.

Aunt Lydia waved her hand. "Not that I care about that, but it would be a shame for the single ladies in town. I only asked because you *are* a dancer, right? I know the lifestyle's not unusual for people in that field."

"Aunt Lydia!" I fanned my heated face with my hand.

Richard shot me a look that said *help me* louder than any words could.

"Can we come in and, you know, sit down?" I tapped my aunt's shoulder. "I think Richard might appreciate something to drink, and I know I would."

"Of course. Come in, come in." Aunt Lydia ushered us into the entry hall, which ran the length of the house. The rarely used front parlor opened off from the turret side of the hall, its door standing ajar to allow a glimpse of velvet-cushioned settees and brocade-covered armchairs.

I looked away, focusing on the mahogany staircase that dominated the side of the hall beyond the parlor.

Ever since I'd started visiting Aunt Lydia when I was a teen, I'd shunned the parlor. It smelled like mothballs and dust and was stuffed full of uncomfortable furniture. Scarcely used, even by Aunt Lydia, something about it made me anxious even though I knew it was just an unused room, made uglier by the shadows cast by its heavy furniture. A room I disliked because it smelled odd.

But that isn't all, is it, Amy? It's also because it's the one space that's a perfect time capsule. The room that looks just like it did when the house was new. Back when Rose Baker Litton was alive.

My mother had shared too many unpleasant stories about her grandmother to make any room associated with Rose Litton feel inviting. So despite the allure of the curved window seat that filled the bowed-out turret section, I'd made a habit of avoiding that room.

On the other side of the hall, two more doors opened on the sitting room that we used as a living room and the library that Aunt Lydia used as an office. The sitting room, with its comfortable sofa, soft chairs, and large-screen television, shone in bright contrast to the rest of the house since Aunt Lydia had painted the dark wood trim a gleaming white.

Aunt Lydia led the way past the kitchen and dining room to the back of the house, her cane rhythmically tapping the hardwood floor. She moved quickly, not allowing for any examination of the myriad paintings covering the wall above an elaborately carved chair rail.

"You can check those out later," I whispered to Richard, noticing his interest.

"The paintings—are they all by the same artist?" Richard kept his voice low.

"Yes, my uncle. Her husband, Andrew Talbot."

"Who is, sadly, long dead." Of course Aunt Lydia had heard us. There was nothing wrong with her hearing. "Come, let's sit in the sun-room. Plenty of light to banish the dark deeds of this day." Aunt Lydia waved us toward a room at the end of the hall.

"Was this once a porch?" Richard glanced around as he entered the room, which spanned the entire back of the house. Tall windows lined three sides of the space, and the fourth wall was the same stone as the exterior of the house.

"Yes, Andrew had it enclosed to use as his studio." Aunt Lydia motioned toward a metal glider, its cushions covered in a paisley slipcover. "Have a seat."

As Richard sat on the glider, it swung back and clanged against the stone wall behind it. "Nice house," he said, stretching out his long legs to still the glider's motion.

"Thank you, although I can't claim credit. Haven't changed much since it was built except for adding the air conditioning and painting a few rooms."

"Your great-grandfather built it?"

"Yes. He left it to my grandmother, Rose Baker. Well, Rose Baker Litton as most folks around here would call her since she married Fairfax Litton, who ran the lumber mill for her father." Aunt Lydia leaned against one of the windowsills and ran a finger down the adjacent window frame. A fine white powder created by the flaking paint filled the air near her hand. "Unfortunately, Grandma Rose inherited the house but not the business. That went to her brother, William Baker, along with most of the money. She had enough to live well, but it dwindled over the years. Hard to live on that and still keep up the place these days."

"I imagine." Richard looked around the enclosed porch before his gaze settled on my face.

"But Amy helps tremendously." Aunt Lydia beamed at me. "Keeps my gardens in tip-top shape and cleans the house and paints and what not. She's a very hard worker, you know."

"I bet." Richard smiled at me.

I shot Aunt Lydia a sharp look.

"Now I'm sure you both are tired of talking about poor Doris, so I won't press you for any details."

"Which you probably already know." I sat in a high-backed wicker chair with cushions covered in rose-patterned chintz. "With Zelda as your source, you probably know more than we do."

Aunt Lydia fluttered her hands in a dismissive gesture. "Oh, I doubt that. Now where are my manners? I'm sure you're parched. Let me find something to drink. What would you like?"

"Water is fine. It's what I usually drink, anyway," Richard said.

Of course he did. You didn't maintain that physical tone slurping down wine like I was inclined to do after a hard day.

"Nonsense. Events like this require something stronger. And it's past five o'clock." Aunt Lydia headed back into the hallway, calling over her shoulder before she disappeared. "I'll bring a selection."

I cast Richard a quick smile. "She's going to bring food too, you know. No one comes to this house without being offered something to eat."

"I'm familiar with that habit." Richard sat back against the glider cushions. "My aunt's the same. My dad's sister, I mean. My mom is an only child. She was the one actually related to Paul Dassin. Only living relative when he died, although supposedly he had fostered a boy back in the 1950s. But that kid left town and disappeared at age eighteen. Since no one could track him down after Paul's death, and the will didn't mention him, the house came to my mom."

"I see." I sank into the cushions of the wicker chair. The sun spilling through the windows was filtered by wooden venetian blinds, painting the concrete floor with brushstrokes of light.

"It would make a nice studio," Richard observed before turning to look at me. "So your uncle died a while back?"

"Years ago. Before I was born, actually. I never met him."

Richard's gaze slid off me to focus on a battered wooden easel still occupying one corner of the room. "Was he a professional artist?"

"He was, although not famous. But he did sell some work here and there."

"Rather like my great-uncle, although he was an author. I guess since your uncle lived here in your aunt's home, her family money supported him?"

I nodded.

"That's not much different from Paul. He received an inheritance that allowed him to purchase the Cooper place and retire from journalism to write full time. Otherwise, I guess he would've gone back to the city and his newspaper work."

"Paul Dassin's a bit better known than my Uncle Andrew. At least around here. We have all his books in the library."

"Might be the only library that does. Only one book ever made him any real money." Richard lifted his arms in a graceful stretch. "Sorry, a bit tense. Need to loosen the muscles."

"No problem," I said, and it wasn't. Except for my stare, which might've lingered a bit too long on the elegant lines of his upper body. "That book about the Cooper case is the famous one, right?"

"Not famous exactly. In its day, maybe. But yeah, *A Fatal Falsehood*. He turned the true story into fiction, but everyone knew it was about the Coopers. He covered the trial as a journalist."

"And fell in love with Eleanora Cooper." Aunt Lydia entered the room, somehow managing to use her cane while carrying a large wicker basket filled with an assortment of bottles, glasses, and food. "No, no, don't get up. I'm going to set this down right here." She bustled over to a tall, narrow side table and pulled items out of the basket.

Richard studied Aunt Lydia as she uncorked a sherry bottle. "You seem pretty sure of that."

"Why, yes, I am. Now what would you like? Or don't you drink? I can fetch some water or lemonade if that's the case."

"I think I spy scotch. That will do," Richard said. "And just some of those grapes, if you don't mind."

Aunt Lydia poured him a glass of the amber liquid, then placed a few of her homemade cheese wafers on a plate along with some grapes. "You must try some of these," she said as she crossed to him. "I insist."

"Thank you." Richard took the proffered plate and glass and promptly placed them on the glass-topped end table beside the glider. "Now tell me, what makes you so certain my great-uncle was in love with Eleanora Cooper? That rumor's circulated in my family for years, but no one's ever been entirely sure it was true."

"Amy, you can get your own," Aunt Lydia said as she poured herself a full glass of sherry and sat in the wooden rocker near the side table.

I smiled, not offended by my aunt's order. It only meant I was family, not a guest. Visitors were to be pampered, but family, as she often told me, could take care of themselves.

Aunt Lydia studied Richard, her lips curving into a smile. She loved to tell stories from the past, especially if she could reveal something other people didn't know. "Well, you see, he told me so himself."

"Really?" Richard slid forward until he was perched on the edge of the glider. "When was this?"

"Often, actually." Aunt Lydia crossed her legs at the ankles and demurely sipped her sherry. "We were close. My father's father died when I was three, and my mother's folks lived in the Midwest, so we barely saw them. Paul Dassin was more like a grandfather to me than a neighbor. Although we had to keep our visits secret." She tilted her head and gave Richard a little smile. "Which just added to the charm, of course."

"Secret? Why?" I paused in pouring myself a tumbler of scotch to glance at my aunt. "You've talked about Paul Dassin as your neighbor but never mentioned this before."

Aunt Lydia shrugged. "Old habits die hard." She turned her brilliant gaze on Richard. "Poor Paul. So many people in town would never accept him. He was an outsider like Eleanora, so that was one strike against him. But the final straw was when his articles swayed public opinion outside town and helped Eleanora Cooper win an acquittal."

"He truly believed she was innocent." Richard picked up his tumbler and took a swallow of his scotch.

"But he was the only one who did. Of course, the case was tried in another town, since no one in Taylorsford could claim to be fair and impartial."

I clutched my drink. "But he was your neighbor. Why'd you have to sneak around to visit him?"

Aunt Lydia pursed her lips and sat in silence for a moment before speaking. "Because my grandmother hated him."

"Rose Litton?" Richard sat back, studying my aunt's stoic face. "My great-uncle included several mentions of her in his research for his book about the Cooper case, although he used her maiden name, Rose Baker. Guess she wasn't married at that point. I haven't examined all the papers carefully, but I remember that name."

I thought back on information I'd recently discovered in the library archives. "Yes, my Great-Grandmother Rose. She was involved in the trial, you know. Witness for the prosecution."

Richard sat up at that. "What? I knew she was a neighbor, but I'm surprised she testified during the trial. Wasn't she rather young at the time?"

"It's true she was only seventeen in 1925," I said, "but she was apparently a key witness."

Aunt Lydia pressed her back against the hard rungs of her rocking chair, her expression as shuttered as an abandoned house. "I didn't realize you knew that, Amy."

"Well, like Richard, I decided to do some historical research." I was confused by my aunt's reaction to this news. She was clutching her sherry glass so tightly I was afraid it would shatter.

"What brought that on?" my aunt asked, keeping her voice light.

"Oh, I don't know. Guess I realized how little I knew about my family history. Figured I might as well take advantage of my research skills during some slow times at the library."

"You could've just asked me." Aunt Lydia sat forward.

"Sure, but . . ." I polished off my drink, almost sputtering as too much of the scotch slid down my throat. Plunking my glass down next to my chair, I took a deep breath before speaking again. "I like to discover stuff for myself. Look through original documents and see if I can piece the story together. No offense, Aunt Lydia, but you would only provide your side of things. What you were told—not necessarily what actually happened. If I'm going to conduct proper research, I prefer to dig up the facts for myself."

Aunt Lydia placed her empty glass on the side table. "Fair enough."

Richard stood and crossed to stand near the windows, absently flexing one foot and then the other. "Now that's what I call research assistance. Seems you've already started compiling the information I need, Amy, even before my arrival. What else did you discover? Connected to Eleanora Cooper, I mean."

Richard exuded a physical energy that filled the room. I sank back against the chair cushions. "That Great-Grandmother supposedly saw stuff that made her suspicious. Some old herbal, for one thing. Apparently Rose spied Eleanora consulting it before Daniel fell sick and told the prosecution there were recipes for poisons in the book. In Eleanora's handwriting."

"An herbal?" Richard asked. "What's that?"

I met his interested gaze squarely. This was fortunately a topic I'd researched for a library patron recently. "A book containing information on plants, especially in relation to their medicinal properties. They were typically compiled by people who practiced herbal medicine. They can include a lot of folklore and even some references to magic, but there are legitimate treatments in them as well. I mean, like willow bark being used for fevers and such. A lot of herbalists wrote down their successful recipes and then eventually bound the loose pages into a type of book. Herbals in some form have been around forever—there are even examples from ancient Egypt and China. This one could've been in Eleanora's family for a long time, since supposedly her mother and grandmother were known as healers in their mountain community."

"Really?" Richard turned away to pace, making a circuit around the porch before speaking again. "So this herbal was part of the trial?"

"Yes, it was evidence," Aunt Lydia explained. "Like Amy said, Grandma Rose apparently found it after Eleanora was arrested and turned it over to the investigators. It was damaged, but Rose claimed the damning pages were missing because Eleanora had torn them out to cover her tracks. Rose testified she'd seen Eleanora writing the lost pages and swore they had detailed some type of herbal poison."

I slid to the edge of my chair. "But see, Richard, since the pages were missing, no one could prove Rose's claim. That was actually a factor in the acquittal. Because they only had my great-grandmother's word that such pages existed."

Aunt Lydia shrugged. "True, and I guess the testimony of a seventeen-year-old girl wasn't enough to convince the court."

"So what happened to the herbal after the trial?" Richard stopped pacing and leaned back against a window near the side table.

"I don't know. I didn't see anything about that in the archival documents," I said.

"It was lost?" Richard asked.

Aunt Lydia shook her head. "No, it wasn't lost. But it was also never returned to Eleanora."

A thought slid into my mind as if whispered by some phantom voice—something about the actual fate of the herbal. "They gave it back to Rose, didn't they?"

Aunt Lydia gasped and stood up so quickly that I feared her injured leg might give way and send her crashing to the floor.

Chapter Four

Richard closed the short distance to Aunt Lydia in two strides and offered her his arm.

"Thank you," she said, leaning against him. "I always forget about this bum leg of mine. So annoying." She straightened and waved him off. "I'm fine now. Just pour me another sherry, would you, Richard?"

He guided her back to the rocker before complying with her request. "So the herbal went to Rose Baker after the trial?"

"Yes, she kept it hidden in a trunk in the attic for many years." Aunt Lydia settled into the rocker before taking the drink from Richard's outstretched hand.

I gazed at my aunt's serious face. "But why?"

"I don't know. The authorities apparently thought they should return it to her since she had given it to them. Anyway, Eleanora Cooper had disappeared—some say she went back to the community she came from. She was never seen in Taylorsford again."

"Leaving behind the house and lands and mountain lumber lots everyone had claimed she killed Daniel for." Richard leaned back against one low windowsill, his leg stretched out in what looked like a habitual dancer's pose. "See, that part never made sense to my great-uncle, and it certainly seems strange to me."

"Well, as I said, Eleanora was an outsider. Daniel met her on one of his trips to oversee his lumber operations. She came from some isolated community up in the mountains." Aunt Lydia swirled the sherry in her glass.

Poor Eleanora. I knew what it was like to feel like an outsider in Taylorsford, and I had family connections even if I wasn't strictly a native. "So where is the herbal now? Still in the attic?"

"No." Aunt Lydia took a sip of her drink before setting it on the floor beside her chair. "I donated it to the town library. Mainly because I didn't want to burn it."

"Why would you ever consider destroying such a thing?" Richard flexed his extended foot.

"That's what Grandma Rose wanted." Aunt Lydia met my astonished gaze calmly, but I noticed her hands pleating the soft material of her blouse as it lay draped in her lap. "I didn't even know she had the thing, but when she was on her death-bed, she demanded I open an old trunk and bring her the book. When she saw it in my hands, she told me to burn it. Of course, Grandma was scarcely in her right mind by that point. She'd had serious dementia for almost twelve years—started showing signs of it in 1985, the year Paul Dassin died."

Richard stared intently at Aunt Lydia. "You were living here then and caring for her?"

"Yes." Aunt Lydia's hands stilled. "It was our home, you see. Our family home, anyway. Debbie, Amy's mother, and I lived with our parents a few blocks away but visited Grandma Rose often. My grandfather died right after I was born, and my dad was an only child, so he felt obligated to visit his mother almost every Sunday. Then when I was fourteen and Debbie was ten, our parents were killed in a car crash. Grandma Rose had been living all alone in this big house. So she took us in."

"My mother hated it," I said when Richard glanced in my direction. "Never liked this house. I don't really know why. She always claims Rose was mean and far too strict, but I don't think that was the only reason."

Aunt Lydia shrugged. "No, not the only one. Debbie was totally traumatized by the death of our parents, and I was not much help, being rather a mess myself. And Grandma Rose was no help at all. She thought Debbie was malingering, as she called it. Kept telling my poor grieving sister to buck up and get over her foolishness. Grandma Rose was never very warm and nurturing." Aunt Lydia's smile at this recollection resembled a grimace. "So Debbie grew up hating Taylorsford in general and this house in particular. She sent her daughter to visit me when Amy was old enough to travel on her own but wouldn't come back herself. I always have to make the trip to see her and the rest of the family."

"Did Rose say why she wanted you to burn the herbal?" Richard asked.

"Honestly, she was so confused at that point, I questioned the reasons for any of her demands. But she was pretty clear she wanted that book burned. So I said I'd do it."

I grabbed my tumbler and rose to my feet. "But you didn't."

"I hated the idea of burning any book—and a historical arti- fact? I just couldn't. Figured I'd donate it to the library after her death."

Richard caught my eye as I crossed to the side table. "That's the first thing I'd like to see in the archives for sure."

I shook my head. "I haven't come across it yet."

Aunt Lydia sighed. "And you won't. I asked the former direc- tor about it a few years back. Apparently the herbal went missing not long after I gave it to the library."

"Well, damn." Richard stepped aside as I reached for the scotch decanter. "I sure would've liked to inspect that book."

"But now"—Aunt Lydia looked up at Richard with a bright smile—"I think we've talked your ears off enough. You probably want to head home and relax after everything that's happened today. Don't let us keep you."

"Oh, that's all right. Just going home to an empty house."

Aunt Lydia tilted her head and stared up at the slowly spinning ceiling fan. "Poor Doris. It's so odd. Of all the people in town, I'd have said she was the least likely to be murdered."

Richard cast Aunt Lydia an inquisitive glance. "Did you know her well?"

"All my life, although we were never close. Doris Beckert, she was before her marriage. The Beckerts have lived here forever, so we couldn't help but be acquainted. And even though Doris was a year behind me in school, in a town like this, you tended to hang out with everyone around your age. She was always nice enough, although rather boy crazy. Married Peter Virts right out of high school. He joined the Navy, and they moved around until Don—that's their eldest—was born. Then Doris and the kids stayed here even while Peter was deployed."

Richard motioned toward the scotch decanter, which I was holding. "Think I'll grab a quick refill, if that's okay." He glanced at my empty glass.

Yeah, I know I shouldn't have more. I sighed and set down the scotch as the memory of Charles's many admonishments concerning excessive drinking or eating repeated in my head.

But Richard just motioned toward my glass as he picked up the decanter. "More? I wouldn't blame you for downing an entire bottle after the shock of today."

"No, thanks," I said but gave him a warm smile.

He smiled back before pouring a little scotch into his tumbler. "Donald Virts, that's the dentist, right? Has an office right outside of town?"

Aunt Lydia made a face. "That's him. Not as nice as his mother, I'm afraid. But then, his dad died when he was only seven, a year after Bethany was born. Killed in some action over there in the Persian Gulf. So Don grew up with just his mom and sister."

"He's not our dentist," I volunteered. "Aunt Lydia thinks he charges too much. And I think he's just . . . unpleasant." I frowned, remembering how Don had chewed out Bethany once in front of all her customers because she'd forgotten to pay some bill for their mother.

"Anyway"—Aunt Lydia shot me a stern look—"poor Doris was left with two little kids and nothing but her husband's pension, so she opened up a diner in town. You may have eaten there already. The Heapin' Plate?"

"Yeah, it's actually not bad," Richard said before taking a swig from his glass.

"Doris was always a great cook. Taught Bethany everything she knew, which was a blessing since Doris isn't . . . sorry, wasn't herself these days."

"She has early onset Alzheimer's," I told Richard, then bit my lip. "*Had*, I mean."

His gaze swept over me. "Hard to process, I know. You're going to think about it no matter what you do. You might want to talk to someone if you know a counselor." He finished off his drink and placed the glass back on the table.

"I'll be fine," I said, although I wasn't sure that was true.

"It really is peculiar unless Doris was just at the wrong place at the wrong time." Aunt Lydia stood. "Think I'll pack this stuff back up now if you've had enough." I moved toward her as she hobbled to the side table. Although she was usually able to walk easily with her cane, sitting for any length of time stiffened her bad leg.

Richard beat me to her side. "Here, let me help." He expertly repacked the basket while my aunt looked on with admiration. "I can carry this for you. Just point me toward the kitchen."

"I'll show you." Aunt Lydia glanced over at me as I stood, useless as a flat tire, beside the table. "Come along, Amy. You can escort Richard to the front porch and then lock the door behind him, as you always insist we do."

I wrinkled my nose at her. I knew her game—setting up a few more moments alone between me and an eligible man.

Aunt Lydia had only met Charles once and had instantly disliked him. Which was why she only met him once. Since our breakup, she'd been on the lookout for a replacement, which meant Richard was caught dead center in her matchmaking crosshairs.

But I was not going to play that game. Not even if I *did* think Richard Muir was rather nice and quite down-to-earth for a dancer.

Not all artistic guys are like Charles, Amy. I tossed my head, shaking errant thoughts about Richard's broad shoulders and slim waist from my mind as I followed him and Aunt Lydia into the kitchen. No, they probably weren't all like Charles. But I wasn't ready to get involved with another one just to test that theory.

After setting the basket on the large oak table that dominated the kitchen, Richard clasped Aunt Lydia's hand to thank her for the refreshments and say good-bye.

"You must come back very soon," she said. "For dinner, perhaps?"

Before he could reply, I headed for the hall, calling, "Come on, Richard, I'll walk you out."

He followed me but paused halfway to the front door to examine a few of the framed canvases hanging in the hall. "So all these are your Uncle Andrew's work? Very well done, from a technical standpoint, anyway."

"Yes. He was a great realistic painter. In a time when that style wasn't particularly valued, poor man." I moved swiftly toward the front door.

Richard caught up with me in two strides. "No kids? Your aunt and uncle, I mean."

"Sadly, no. Just a nephew and a niece. But my younger brother and Aunt Lydia aren't that close, so I guess I'm the nearest thing she has to a child."

"Not such a bad thing, I'd bet she'd say."

I was glad the light in the hall was dim so Richard couldn't spy my blush. "We get along."

"I can tell." He paused, one hand on the front door's crystal doorknob. "I'll just show myself out. Better follow your aunt's suggestion and lock the door behind me. We still don't know who shot that poor woman."

"Yes, you too. At your house, I mean."

Richard popped his hand up to his forehead in a mock salute. "I always lock my doors. City boy, remember?" He winked at me and stepped onto the porch.

I watched him gracefully take the stone steps two at a time, then closed and locked the front door, careful to throw the dead bolt. I flicked the switch for the hall chandelier and walked back toward the kitchen, where I suspected Aunt Lydia was washing up the drink glasses before starting supper.

I squared my shoulders and entered the kitchen. Before I could say anything, Aunt Lydia gave me a look—the appraising look she always gave when she thought I might be interested in some guy.

"Don't you dare start in on how perfect Richard Muir is," I said before she could speak a word.

Although she was elbow deep in soapsuds, the haughty look she gave me would have befitted a queen. "Now whatever gave you that idea? I know you have no interest in men right now."

"Right. So don't start matchmaking. Changing the subject, did you know Paul Dassin fostered a boy for a while?"

"Yes," she said in a tone so deliberately casual I was put on alert. "Karl Klass. He was brought to the orphanage when it opened in 1957. But he was a bit of hellion and got into hot water almost immediately." Aunt Lydia dipped a glass into the sink. "The orphanage board planned to ship him off to reform school until Paul intervened. Wanted to give Karl another chance, he said."

"How long did he live with Paul?"

"About six years."

"So you knew him?" I studied my aunt's perfectly composed face with interest. She had never mentioned this to me before, and I couldn't help but wonder why.

"I did. Although I was only five when Karl moved in next door, so I didn't have a lot of dealings with him." Aunt Lydia shot me a quick smile. "I only saw him when we visited Grandma Rose, and teenage boys don't have much use for little girls."

"But you must've been, what, about twelve when he left? Do you know what happened to him? Richard said his family tried to locate him after Paul died but had no luck."

"I have no idea." Aunt Lydia rubbed at a spot on the glass with her thumb before rinsing it again. "Honestly, I didn't much care for Karl. He was always so . . . domineering. A know-it-all who always wanted his own way. At least, that's how I felt as a child. But I do thank him for one thing."

"Oh, what is that?" I took the glass from her and placed it in the drying rack.

"He's the reason I met Andrew." Aunt Lydia met my astonished gaze with a smile. "They were friends from school, you see. Andrew was from Smithsburg on the other side of the county, but everyone went to the same high school back then."

"So you met Andrew when he was visiting Karl?"

"Yes. Of course, he cared nothing for me back then. I was just a kid. But Andrew continued to visit Paul from time to time even after Karl left."

"And at some point, he realized you weren't a child anymore."

A dreamy expression flitted across Aunt Lydia's face. "He did indeed."

She was obviously lost in the past, in happy memories of Andrew. I thought it best not to question her further about Paul Dassin's foster child and tapped her arm. "If you don't mind, I think I'll head out to the garden and do a little work before dinner. It'll help clear my head."

Aunt Lydia examined me, her gaze clear once again. "Okay, but don't overdo it."

"I won't. Just need some fresh air."

Outside, I surveyed the backyard from the porch stoop before taking the steps to the gravel path and grabbing my work gloves from the top of the workbench.

Aunt Lydia's garden was her pride and joy. Filling the entire backyard, the beds were laid out in a grid pattern, separated from one another by paths of white pea gravel. Vegetables filled the back beds, while those closest to the house alternated between flowers and herbs. On summer days, the mingled scents perfumed the air, and a low hum of bees emanated from the crimson monarda that overflowed one bed. A grove of trees and wild undergrowth provided a green backdrop to the garden, screening any view of the mountains. You could see the blue peaks ridging the treetops from the raised back porch but not from the ground.

Even though it demanded constant weeding and deadheading to look presentable, I loved the garden. Somehow the simple act of working among the colorful jumble of flowers and vegetables brought a peace I couldn't find anywhere else.

After pulling on my gloves, I headed straight for the rose bed. One of Aunt Lydia's antique rose bushes—which she claimed had been planted around 1926 by Great-Grandmother Rose—had died, leaving nothing but a grizzled husk. It stood out like a thorny weed amid the profusion of satiny emerald leaves and velvety crimson blossoms of the adjacent roses. I'd been eyeing it for days, hating the sight of its desiccated branches, longing to yank the entire plant from the ground.

It was old, though, and well entrenched. I had to run back to the garden bench to grab a shovel to loosen the soil around the bottom of the bush. Determined to accomplish my task, I attacked the base of the rose so viciously it broke off, leaving just a short section above the ground.

No stupid plant was going to defeat me. I reached down and pulled on the remaining stump, finally yanking the root ball from the ground with so much force it flew from hands and landed in the middle of one of the pea-gravel paths.

Great, now I had to clean up my mess before dinner. I sighed and scooped the exposed root ball and some of the dirt onto the shovel. I'd have to wash off the rest with the hose.

Something glinted against the white gravel. I bent down and stared at the object, which was tangled in a cluster of root tendrils.

It was a piece of jewelry. I freed it and stood with the object clutched in my palm. Uncurling my fingers, I swept grime from the still-gleaming surface. It looked like gold. Real gold, not just plated stuff. Something that could withstand the ravages of time and earth.

The fastening pin of the brooch was bent but still intact. I held it up to the fading sunlight. It was a simple oval with braided trim enclosing a flat surface engraved with florid initials. I squinted but couldn't make out the letters.

Now here was a puzzle that could distract me from thoughts of murder and imminent unemployment. I couldn't help but wonder who had owned the brooch and how it had been lost. Surely no one would have worn such a thing to work in the garden even in the good old days. And it had to be old since it had been buried under a rose bush planted over ninety years ago.

I should ask Aunt Lydia if she recognized it. But no . . . perhaps I'd do a bit of sleuthing first.

A sweep of wind rustled the leaves in the woods behind the garden. *Mystery, mystery,* they seemed to whisper.

Yes, Amy, something for you to research. See if you can tie this to one of your ancestors, and then present it along with that information to Aunt Lydia. Make good use of those library skills.

The thought filled me with excitement. I needed a distraction, and this could prove an interesting one.

I pocketed the brooch and washed off the path and my shovel with the garden hose before heading back into the house for dinner.

Chapter Five

With the library closed, I planned to spend most of Friday working in the garden. But as I threw on some shorts, a T-shirt, and a pair of battered sneakers, sunlight glinted off the gold brooch. I'd placed it on the top of my dresser the night before after soaking it in jewelry cleaner and rubbing it dry with a soft cloth. It was polished to a gleaming finish, but I still couldn't make out the faded inscription.

The brooch lay next to my work key ring. I studied both objects for a moment.

I'd become a librarian primarily due to my love of books but also because of my lifelong compulsion to find answers to questions or mysteries. Even as a child, whenever I'd heard or seen something I hadn't understood, I'd run to my books to research an answer or at least gather information. So of course, discovering who had once owned the brooch was haunting my mind.

You might be able to figure it out if you could use the resources at the library.

I picked up the brooch and balanced it in my open palm. There was never any certainty in such research, but I'd had success on similar hunts by sleuthing through old records and photographs. Although the building *was* still locked tight by order of the sheriff's department . . .

But I had keys.

I tossed my cell phone and key ring into my faded "I Heart Libraries" tote bag before tucking the brooch into one of its zippered side pockets. Hoisting the strap over my shoulder, I headed down the stairs, the bag banging against my hip.

In the kitchen, I discovered a note tacked to the refrigerator with a round magnet advertising Taylorsford's only pizza shop. "Gone to get groceries, see you later," the memo said.

So I didn't have a car and wouldn't for some time.

When I'd moved in with Aunt Lydia, I'd decided my old car was an unnecessary expense and sold it. I could walk to work, and on bad weather days, Aunt Lydia was happy to play chauffeur. Since she didn't use it much, I could also borrow her car whenever I needed it. I helped pay for gas, insurance, and repairs, which benefitted her financially.

But there were a few times when it was inconvenient to share a car, and this was one of them. Aunt Lydia's preferred grocery store was a thirty-minute drive from Taylorsford, and she liked to take her time, often stopping at a farmer's market for fresh produce before even reaching the store. So I knew she wouldn't return for some time.

Wait, this could actually play into your plans, Amy. Take a walk and end up at the library. If you happen to use your keys to enter through the staff door—well, if anyone discovers you, just claim you needed a restroom, and this was the closest one available.

My burning desire to learn more about the brooch convinced me this was a good plan. I didn't even bother with breakfast, just grabbed my house key from the ceramic bowl on the hall side table and headed for the front door.

I strode toward the library, confident I could conduct some research without getting caught by anyone from the sheriff's office. Knowing how short-staffed they were, I suspected the deputies wouldn't bother guarding the library itself. Someone was probably posted at the archives' building, but their view of the side entrance would be obscured by a thick wall of forsythia bushes.

Besides, I rationalized as I reached the library, *you're the director. Surely that gives you the right to enter the building even if it must remain closed to the public.* Anyway, that was a good excuse to offer if an officer challenged me.

Yeah, just play the confused professor type. It's what Brad Tucker will expect. I lowered my head and smiled as I realized the truth in that.

Preoccupied with my thoughts, I almost barged into someone running down the sidewalk.

"Amy!" the man called out.

Richard Muir. Of course I would stumble into him. I stopped short and took a couple of steps back.

"Out for a run?" I mentally kicked myself. It was a foolish remark, since sweat molded the thin fabric of his gray T-shirt to his chest.

"Yeah, trying to change up the exercise routine." Richard grabbed the hand towel tucked into the waistband of his gym shorts and wiped his brow. "Seems we had the same idea this morning."

I tried not to stare as he leaned forward and stretched out one well-muscled leg and then the other. Damn, the man was built. Yet he seemed as unconscious of the beauty of his body as a cat. I shook my head. "I'm just walking, not really exercising."

"Walking is movement, and all movement is good. That's what I tell my students, anyway." Richard tucked the towel back into his waistband. "So you're off today? Oh, wait, the library is locked down, I guess."

"Yeah, although I thought I might slip in and do a little investigating . . ." I snapped my mouth shut. Why was I telling him this? It was those friendly gray eyes, examining me with interest tinged with what looked strangely like admiration.

"Really? What's so pressing you have to dig into it today?"

Now you've done it, Amy. No way to lie your way out of this. No way that Richard Muir will believe, anyhow.

Because as pleasant as his gaze was, it was also obviously backed by a keen intelligence and, I suspected, a well-developed bullshit detector.

"Oh, I found something in the garden last night, and it's got me champing at the bit to do some research." I unzipped the side pocket on my bag and pulled out the gold brooch. "A piece of jewelry." I placed the pin in my palm and held out my hand.

Richard cradled my hand in his and lifted both closer to his eyes. "Looks old."

"It must be," I replied, curling my fingers around the brooch before sliding my hand away. "Found it tangled in the roots of a rose bush that was planted about ninety years ago. Figured it must've belonged to one of my ancestors."

"Rose?"

"Maybe, but I'm not sure. And for some reason, not knowing is driving me nuts." I slipped the brooch back into the bag.

"That's because you're a librarian."

"Could be. Now I should let you get on with your run."

"Oh, I'm done. So if you need some help with that research . . ."

I examined his expression, which displayed an eagerness matching my own. "I suppose it couldn't hurt. Maybe we'll find something that will aid your investigation into the Cooper trial. And it's nice to work in the library when it's quiet." I lifted my chin and met his intent gaze. "But we'll have to sneak in the staff door, and I suppose that isn't exactly legal."

Richard grinned. "An adventure? Sounds like fun." He peeled his damp shirt away from his torso and flapped the material with one hand. "But I might be in no condition to stand close to anyone."

I waved this off with one hand. "It's a big enough building. I think we can work together without getting too close."

"Damn, there goes my original plan," Richard said with a smile that reassured me he was only teasing.

"Well, research, unlike dancing, doesn't usually require physical contact." I slid past him, heading for the other side of the library building.

Richard jogged up beside me. "Depends on the research, doesn't it?"

I rolled my eyes before pressing my finger to my lips. "Hush. The law could be lurking."

"Ah," he whispered, following me around the side of the building, "so now we're *Spy vs. Spy*?"

I couldn't suppress a smile. "Something like that." I pulled my key ring from the tote bag and opened the staff door, which led directly into the workroom.

The library was dark and quiet—hushed as it only was without patrons. Although the media still liked to present libraries as bastions of silence, nothing could be further from the truth. With all the activity in modern libraries, silence was impossible and, actually, not that desirable. These days, there were so many group school assignments and cooperative research projects that keeping a library silent was neither useful nor practical. The age of shushing librarians had gone out with card catalogs, despite what popular culture might portray.

I flicked on the workroom lights, knowing its lack of windows wouldn't betray us, but didn't flip the switches for the main part of the library. There was enough sun spilling through the windows to light our way.

"So where do we start?" Richard asked as I turned on the computer at the circulation desk.

"Thinking," I replied. "Always start by thinking through the problem." I pulled the gold brooch from my bag and placed it on the circulation desk. "Try to figure out the best mode of attack."

"Because?"

"Because there are so many resources one can use and so many different ways to tackle any specific research question. You have to narrow it down." I stared at the brooch. "With this, for example, text materials might be useless, so I'm going to search images first."

Richard moved behind me. He was tall enough to view the computer monitor over my shoulder. "You mean old photos. Won't you need the archives for that?"

"Not necessarily. The county newspaper has been digitized, so I might find something if I search that resource. I assume the Cooper trial was big news, and if my great-grandmother was a major player for the prosecution, there might be a photo of her in the newspaper from around that time."

Richard leaned closer. "But wearing a specific piece of jewelry?"

"That's the fun part of research. It seems unlikely, but you never know. It's like a treasure hunt. You search and search and then sometimes—a discovery." I bent my head over the keyboard. It was true that I could smell the sweat on Richard's shirt, but strangely, it wasn't actually an unpleasant scent. Which was a bit unnerving, all in all.

"So you've pulled up the newspaper archive. Now what?"

"Now I have to figure out what terms to use to search." I turned my head to meet Richard's interested gaze. "That's one of the things a lot of people don't understand. They just type in stuff, and when no useful hits appear, they give up. 'Must not exist,' they say. But see, it all depends on how something was indexed. I mean, what title was given to an article, or what terms were used in it, or even how someone's name was spelled. Because if you search for a name with the wrong spelling, you might think there's no information available even if there is. And that works the opposite way too. Sometimes the article or report or whatever misspells names or other things. And then when you search with the correct spelling, you won't find that particular item."

"I see." Richard stepped to the side and looked me up and down. "So if I search Baryshnikov and spell his name wrong, I might not find all the articles or websites that reference him?"

"Right." I shot him a smile. "Of course, that brings in the whole language transliteration thing, which is another wrinkle. Translating from languages with their own alphabets is a real challenge. But the point is, despite what most people might think, everything in the digital world still goes back to human interaction."

Richard tilted his head and studied me. "What do you mean?"

"Well, even though we now have bots and spiders and things scanning the Internet and compiling information, they're still only searching what exists. At one point, somewhere, all that content was originally created by human hands. Stuff doesn't just get created on the web from thin air. Extracted, compiled, and perhaps reimagined, yes, but not entirely created. So somewhere along the line, it only exists because some human introduced the original content into the digital sphere."

"And humans are fallible."

"Yeah, and we all look at and comprehend things differently. I might use certain terms to describe something that you would label entirely differently. So even if we both enter the same information . . ."

Richard tapped the brooch with one finger. "You might call this a brooch and I might call it a pin? I see. Because if I only search under *pin*, I wouldn't necessarily find the information you wrote or uploaded."

I cast him a smile. "Correct. You must consider all the possible ways something could be indexed or described and all variations of names. Sometimes you have to take a leap of faith and try an entirely novel approach." I pointed at the computer screen. "See, I *have* found a picture of Great-Grandmother Rose, but it was listed under *Cooper Trial Witnesses*, not her name."

I moved aside so Richard could view the screen. "Didn't realize what a flapper she was," I said as we both examined the picture. "Kind of looks like that old movie star, Louise Brooks."

My great-grandmother was dressed in a sleeveless satin dress with a low-slung waist decorated with a jeweled band. Her silky dark hair was cut in a short bob, and her full lips were pursed into a pout. Her wide dark eyes stared out at the viewer as if daring them to take her for granted. Somehow, I doubted anyone ever could.

I peered at the label under the photo. "Rose Baker, age seventeen. Must've been taken around the time she testified at the trial."

Richard studied the digital photo for a moment. "She was quite a fox, wasn't she?" He glanced over at me. "You have her eyes."

"I suppose." Somehow, that thought didn't please me. "My mom inherited her dark hair and eyes. That's where I get it. Well, and my dad has dark hair too."

"So your mom resembles Rose? Obviously Lydia does not."

"Yeah, my aunt looks like her dad. I mean my grandfather, Randy, who looked like his dad, Fairfax Litton. All blue-eyed blonds." I stared at Rose's picture for another moment before stepping back from the computer. "Nothing showing the brooch yet, so maybe I need to reconsider my approach." I held up my hand as Richard opened his mouth. "I'm not giving up. I just need to try another tactic."

"Can I do something to help?"

"How about checking your great-uncle's book about the Cooper trial? I know it's fiction, but he used a lot of facts from real life. So maybe he mentioned the brooch when he described his Rose-based character?"

Richard, obviously lost in thought, rubbed his jawline. "That's a long shot, don't you think?"

"Typical of library research," I said, leaving the circulation desk and heading for the stacks. "Sometimes more art than science, to be honest. Here, I'll help you find the book, then you can dig into it while I sleuth on the computer."

Richard trailed me to the fiction section. "So this is all arranged by author's last name? I thought you always assigned specific call numbers."

"Academic libraries do, and they also typically use the Library of Congress classification system. Public libraries tend to use the Dewey Decimal system for nonfiction and then just shelve fiction alphabetically using the author's name. Makes it easier for patrons to browse." I reached the *D* section and scanned the book spines until I found the shelf holding Paul Dassin's novels.

"Here it is, *A Fatal Falsehood*." Richard reached over my shoulder and plucked the book from the shelf.

As he pulled his arm back, I spied an odd object pressed against the back of the shelf. "Wait, there's something stuffed behind Dassin's books." I slid my hand across the smooth metal shelf, reaching around the row of bound volumes. My fingers touched a worn binding, softer than our hardback library books. I pulled out the slim, battered volume and examined its stained leather cover. There was no title. I carefully opened the volume, noting that the pages were sewn together with linen thread, and stared at the spidery script that covered the top of the title page—"Eleanora Amaryllis Heron, 1916."

I gasped. "It's the herbal!"

"What?" Richard tucked his uncle's novel under his arm and leaned in to look at the book I held balanced between my palms.

"Eleanora's herbal. The one that disappeared right after Aunt Lydia donated it to the library." I stroked the heavy paper with my thumb. "But how did it show up here?"

"Could it have been stuck behind my great-uncle's books all this time?"

"Not possible. The shelves are straightened and dusted too regularly for that. Might've been the Nightingale."

"The what?"

"Oh, a patron who likes to help, as she calls it, by shelving loose books in wrong locations. I could see her shoving this in with Dassin's novels, but I wonder where she would have found it in the first place. Usually she just picks up things that are lying out on tables." I shook my head. "Well, that's one mystery we may never solve, but at least the herbal has turned up again. I was afraid it was lost forever."

Richard shifted position until his arm pressed against mine. "Heron? I guess that was her maiden name?"

"Must've been. And 1916." I did a mental calculation. "Means she was only fifteen when she got the herbal. I think it's older than that, though. Probably passed down through the family." I traced the spiky script of her signature. "Amaryllis. Pretty, but unusual."

"A flower," Richard said. "I bet her mother was an herbalist too. That would make sense. And you know"—he cast me a smile—"Amy could be short for that."

"Doubt that was my mom's intention. She's not very fanciful." I touched my fingertip to the rough edges of paper clinging to the interior spine at the back of the book. "Here's where the pages were torn out."

Richard leaned in and tapped the back of the opposite page. "You can also see where Eleanora wrote stuff. Pretty distinctive handwriting. Matches her signature."

"'A remedy for the colic,'" I read out. "Can't really decipher the rest, though. The ink has faded."

"I bet there won't be any recipes for poisons," Richard said, crossing to one of the nearby tables. "I can scan through that, along with Paul's book, if you want."

"Okay." I followed him and laid the old herbal on the table as he took a seat. "If you find anything interesting, just give me a shout."

Richard raised his eyebrows. "Shouting? In a library?" His grin faded as he picked up the herbal. "Shouldn't I be handling this with gloves?"

"Yeah, just a minute." I dashed back to the workroom and grabbed a pair of cotton gloves and carried them to Richard before I walked back to the circulation desk.

Using the computer at the desk, I ran several other searches in the newspaper digital archive before pausing to reconsider my approach.

Eleanora Amaryllis Heron. It was an unusual name. Certainly more so than Rose Baker. I decided I should conduct some searches using Eleanora's name, both before and after her marriage. Any hits on her unique name would undoubtedly lead back to the trial.

I entered the name several different ways, using quotation marks around each version to limit my search to hits including all of the terms. That was another research trick not everyone understood. Most search engines or databases included an implicit "or" between words. So looking up Eleanora Cooper would translate into Eleanora *or* Cooper and return all results that included any mention of an Eleanora *or* a Cooper. Enclosing the two words with quotation marks turned that search into Eleanora *and* Cooper, and only returned results that included both names. Much more precise.

After searching for some time, I finally discovered an article that mentioned both Eleanora and Rose. I scrolled to the bottom of the page, which merely reiterated what I already knew about the trial. But it did list an attached photo. I clicked on the link, and the photo came up in a new window.

It was a picture of Eleanora, at least according to the caption. I peered at it for a moment before releasing a loud and expletive-laced exclamation.

Richard stripped off the gloves and came running with the herbal balanced on top of his great-uncle's novel. "You found something? What is it?"

I pointed to the monitor, where the grainy black-and-white photo now filled the screen. A slender, stern-looking young woman with light eyes stared out at the viewer. Her dark hair was pulled into a tight bun, and she wore a simple dress with a white lace collar. Pinned to her collar was a brooch. "Eleanora Cooper."

Richard laid the books on the counter and lifted the brooch. He narrowed his eyes as he held the piece of jewelry up to the monitor. "It was *her* pin."

"Apparently." I grabbed Dassin's novel and flipped through it. "And listen," I said as I scanned a passage that described the protagonist of the novel. "Lily—that was the name he used for the Eleanora character, right?"

"Yeah." Richard glanced from me to the brooch nestled in his palm.

"'During her questioning'"—I read aloud—"'Lily wore a simple, understated dress of navy wool. Pinned to the white lace collar was a gold brooch given to her by her husband on their wedding day. Lily wore that piece of jewelry throughout the trial and was heard to say that she would wear it every day for the rest of her life.'" I snapped the book shut.

Richard curled his fingers about the brooch. "She always wore it? So why didn't she take it with her when she left town?"

"That's the million-dollar question." I placed *A Fatal Falsehood* on the reshelving cart. "She must've lost it in my great-grandmother's garden before she disappeared, but how?"

"They were neighbors. Perhaps it was during a visit after the trial when she was saying good-bye?"

"But Rose testified against her. Why would Eleanora have anything to do with my great-grandmother after that?"

Richard shrugged. "Those were politer times. I mean, people like Eleanora lived under different social constraints. Maybe she felt she had to be on good terms with her neighbors before she moved?"

I closed the link and cleared my search history before shutting down the computer. "Anyway, I guess that answers the question of who owned the brooch."

"And what happened to Eleanora's herbal. Well, not exactly where it's been hiding all this time, but at least we found it." Richard picked up the slim volume. "You want to put this in the archives?"

"Eventually, but I'll store it in the workroom for now." I met Richard's questioning gaze with a tilt of my head toward the back door. "There's a deputy out there right now."

"Oh, yeah, I forgot." Richard handed me the herbal as we walked into the workroom.

I laid the slim volume in the bookcase designated for my personal projects. No one else would mess with anything on those shelves.

When we reached the staff door, Richard turned to face me. "Sorry, forgot this." He uncurled the fingers of his right hand, revealing the gold brooch. "You probably want it back."

"No, you should keep it."

What are you saying, Amy? Why give it up, and to someone who is practically a stranger?

Because I must.

Honestly I didn't have idea why I felt that so strongly, but the moment Richard offered the pin, I knew with unwavering certainty that this was the right thing to do. "If it belongs anywhere, it belongs in your house. I mean, that was Eleanora's home, and the brooch was hers, after all. Nothing to do with my family."

Richard looked pleased. "Thank you. I felt the same way, but since you found it on your property, I hated to ask."

"Don't worry about it," I said, opening the door. "It just seems to me it should end up back at the Cooper house. I mean, since Eleanora was so attached to the thing. Now what do you say we get out of here? We've been fortunate so far, but I don't want to test my luck, which can be questionable."

"Or mine, which isn't always so great either." Richard slipped the brooch into his pocket before following me outside. "Once more unto the breach," he said after I locked up.

I shot him a surprised glance.

"Shocking, isn't it? But I do know a bit of Shakespeare," he said as we reached the sidewalk in front of the library. "Despite being a dancer, I'm not completely uneducated, you see."

So I wasn't the only one with some nagging insecurities. I pondered this as I struggled to keep pace with his longer strides. "Never thought you were."

Richard slowed his pace slightly. "Glad to hear it. Sometimes people think all dancers are stupid. Athletic but brainless."

"Some people think all librarians wear buns and cardigans and clutch their pearls."

Richard's lips quirked into a quick smile. "So they do," he said, "and obviously"—he looked over at me—"that isn't true."

"Nope. So why don't we ignore those stereotypes. Agreed?"

"Agreed," he said.

We spent the next few blocks talking about our favorite books and movies. Assuming he might be sensitive to any hint that he was one of those "brainless" types, I was careful to hide my surprise over Richard's interest in some rather esoteric foreign films.

As we paused in front of Aunt Lydia's house, Richard looked me in the eye. "We seem to share similar tastes, which is a nice surprise." He grinned. "The dancer and the librarian, who would've thought? Although I think we both break the mold for our professions quite a bit. You certainly don't fit the stereotype of the old maid librarian."

I unlatched the front gate and stepped into the yard. "I am thirty-three. Some people would call that an old maid."

Richard's gaze swept over me, taking in my short shorts and my T-shirt. Although loose elsewhere, it still hugged my breasts, as all blouses tended to do. "I can't imagine anyone saying that about you. Besides, not everyone needs to be married these days, do they?"

"Would you please repeat that sentiment in my aunt's hearing the next time you see her?"

"Sure, but I have a favor to ask in return."

"What's that?" Under his intent gaze, my fingers fumbled as I closed the latch.

"I'd like you to accompany me on a fishing expedition."

"Fishing? I must confess I'm not much of an outdoorsy type, except for walking or gardening."

Richard laughed. "No, not that kind of fishing. I mean a search for more information on my great-uncle. Remember how I mentioned a foster child from back in the fifties? Well, apparently the guy has resurfaced. In fact, he actually owns a historic house just outside town. A second home, I expect, because he said he was only there on weekends. Anyway, he called yesterday evening and invited me for a visit. I'd love to pick his brains about Paul, but it does sound a little odd. I'm worried he might be angling for a piece of Paul's property. I don't want to say the wrong thing and get myself in legal hot water, so I thought maybe an observant librarian companion could come in handy. What do you say?"

"A wealthy older man with an estate outside of town? You can't mean Kurt Kendrick."

"Yeah, that's the guy."

"But Kendrick never lived in Taylorsford before. Not from what I've heard. He's one of those überrich art collectors who has a gallery in DC and a townhouse in Georgetown. Only lives here part time and doesn't mingle with us lesser beings. I've never seen him, as a matter of fact. There was a photo in the paper once, when he donated money to fund a special exhibit at the National Gallery of Art, but otherwise he's as intangible as a ghost. Even Aunt Lydia has never met him."

"That's strange. He definitely said he was Paul's ward at one time. Although he did mention changing his name for professional reasons."

"Weird. But sure, I'd love to accompany you, if only to see the house."

Richard rubbed at his chin with the back of his hand. "Hmmm, not sure what that says about me."

I fought back a smile. "Nothing wrong with your company. I just meant I know I'll see you again since you live next door, while this might be my only chance to visit Kendrick's house. It's one of the oldest homes in the area, and rumor has it that the restoration is absolutely gorgeous. And I hear Kendrick keeps quite a collection of art there as well. I've been curious to see it for some time but never thought I'd get an invite."

"Then I'm happy to offer you this one. It will be useful for me as well, having someone along who knows a bit more about town history and the like. Anyway, thanks for the research lesson. And the brooch," he called out as he headed for his own house.

"No problem," I called after him.

But I was afraid that might be a lie. There could be a problem—a very big problem indeed—if he kept looking at me in that way with those sexy gray eyes.

Chapter Six

I received a phone call from Brad Tucker on Saturday, asking me to meet him at the archives' building. He said he wanted me to confirm whether anything was missing from the collections.

I didn't tell him I probably couldn't be sure since I hadn't personally inventoried the archives after taking my job. But I knew Sunny had completed an inventory right before Ralph Harrison retired, so I called and asked her to join us.

Brad was not pleased when the two of us showed up at the newly padlocked door.

"I didn't invite her." He pointed a finger at Sunny.

She simply squared her shoulders and tossed back her hair, a move that highlighted her long neck and thrust her breasts against her gauzy top.

The deputy guarding the door openly stared at her before stepping aside.

"Sunny knows more about the collections than I do." I snapped my fingers to draw Brad's gaze off my friend. "She conducted the last inventory, and we haven't gotten around to doing another one yet."

Brad muttered something under his breath before replying, "So you're telling me you might not know if anything *has* recently gone missing."

Poor Brad—facing two women who'd rejected him. No wonder he was rubbing at his jaw like someone with a toothache.

"Nope, not saying that." Sunny flashed a bright smile. "I always check after someone's been in the archives. I suppose a patron could sneak something out, but really, not that many people use the materials anyway. I actually think Doris Virts was the last person who even asked to look at anything in here, and I can't imagine her stealing old documents."

"But you don't know for sure. I mean, apparently she did steal the key out from under your nose." Brad tugged at the collar of his uniform. I wondered if it was the heat causing him to sweat or just his proximity to Sunny. "You can wait by the car if you want," he told the young deputy as he waved him off.

"No, not absolutely for certain." Sunny's voice conveyed no anger over Brad's jab. "But when she was in here before, she was just looking at old photos from the fifties. You know, back when her dad was on the town council and she was a little kid. It was one of those days when she seemed to be doing well, and I think recalling the past helps . . . helped keep her mind clear."

Brad leaned in with a key and released the new padlock. "You left her in here by herself?"

"No, I wouldn't do that, considering her health condition. Remember, Amy? I told you I had to stay with Doris that day. Although"—Sunny twitched her lips as she recalled the memory—"I did leave her for a few minutes because I had to use the restroom. But her son was with her 'cause he'd come to pick her up, so I thought it would be okay."

"Yeah, that was several months ago." As I followed Brad and Sunny into the archives, I forced myself the stare at the floor. It was scrubbed clean, but the bleach mixture had left a pale oval ring on the age-darkened pine planks.

"Well, take a look around. We've already dusted everything for fingerprints, so just let me know if you see anything out of place." Brad stepped back, his bulky body filling the open doorway.

I moved from file cabinet to file cabinet, opening drawers and peeking inside each one, while Sunny examined the items stacked on the metal shelves.

"These obviously haven't been touched," Sunny said, sliding her fingers over a row of archival boxes. She held up her fingers. "Still covered in dust."

"This is weird." I pulled an overstuffed file folder from one of the cabinets. "This folder's dated 1958."

I laid the folder on the table.

Brad strode back into the room, facing me across the worktable. "Weird how?"

I flipped open the file. "Because the folder was shoved in the front of a cabinet housing material from the 1930s, so it was seriously misfiled. Which might mean it was moved recently."

"Damn it," Brad stepped closer. "That needs to be checked for fingerprints, and now yours are all over it."

I held up my hands. "You already have them. Remember— our lovely town council requires all town employees to be fingerprinted before they start working in Taylorsford. So mine are on file at your office."

"Just don't touch it again." Brad glared at me before meeting Sunny's amused gaze. "You either."

I dropped my hands to my side and examined the top document, a yellowed newspaper clipping with a headline that screamed, "Five Children and Cook Dead, Others Sickened in Apparent Accidental Poisoning." "What the hell is this? I've never heard anything about an orphanage, much less people dying."

"Wow." Sunny crossed to stand beside me. "You haven't? It happened right next to your aunt's house—on the old Cooper farm. She never mentioned it?"

"No," I replied, drawing out the word as my mind processed this information. It seemed Aunt Lydia had kept some secrets from me over the years.

What else is she staying mum about? Maybe the real reason your mom won't return to the family home? I frowned and clasped my hands behind my back. "Never even heard a whisper about any such thing."

Brad shuffled his feet. "Well, people don't talk about it now. And your aunt was probably like, what—six or seven? So it makes sense you might not have heard of it, but it was a big scandal at the time, or so my folks say. Dad was in college, and Mom was working in DC when it happened. They were told not to come back to Taylorsford until the hysteria died down. Missed out on Thanksgiving, I remember them saying."

I stared at the brittle newspaper clipping topping the pile of mimeographed circulars and typed town council minutes. "Mushrooms?"

Brad scratched at his chin. "Yeah, supposedly the cook—Old Man Fowler's mom, by the way—mixed in some poisonous ones with other wild mushrooms she'd collected. She died too, so it was assumed to be an accident. That was the story I've been told, anyway. Damn shame."

"I didn't even know there *was* an orphanage." I glanced at Sunny, who shrugged.

"Even the grands have only mentioned it once in my hearing," she said.

"Nobody talks about it. Well, except Clark Fowler, and then only to spew conspiracy theories. I get it, he doesn't want his mom blamed, but he can turn overly aggressive. I've had to step in a few times when he's gone on a rant." Brad toyed with the gold badge pinned to his uniform. "Anyway, that Paul Dassin fellow who bought the Cooper place donated most of the land to the town for an orphanage where kids would be taught to farm. Named it after Daniel Cooper. Town said okay—mayor was thinking of running for state senate or some such thing and thought being charitable would help his chances, I guess."

I unclenched my hands and tapped the worktable with one finger. "You mean Lee Blackstone, the current mayor's dad?"

"That's the one. Never did get elected to any office higher than mayor of Taylorsford, though. After the deaths, the town sent the rest of the kids to other homes and razed the building to the ground. Luckily it never made the national news back then, so most people just pretended it never happened."

I examined Brad's troubled expression with interest. "Why be so secretive if it was just an accident?"

Brad wiped his damp brow with the back of his hand. "I dunno. Clark Fowler has these notions that there was some kind of cover-up. He says the kids and his mom were sick even before they ate those mushrooms. Claims the town didn't listen to his mom's complaints and waited too long to send in the doctor, or didn't provide the best care, or something. Seems to want to blame the Blackstone family, among others."

"Well, Bob Blackstone did purchase that land on the cheap. Before he became mayor, but still . . ." I said.

Sunny twisted her golden bangle around her wrist. "And now he's all set to sell it for that awful housing development. When his dad was mayor, the town put up all kinds of restrictions, and the land just sat empty for years and years, but all of a sudden, it can become a subdivision? I call that convenient."

"Don't you get started on that." Brad tugged on his collar again. No doubt he'd already heard Sunny's opinions on this deal. Bob Blackstone was in negotiations to sell the land adjacent to the Cooper farmhouse, which he'd bought a few years before, to some big developer. Sunny was part of a group opposing this move. She was prone to talking about the situation daily, so I was sure she'd bent Brad's ear about it when they were dating.

But she wasn't the only one upset about the possible sale—Aunt Lydia called the deal "a lot of shenanigans." Not just because the subdivision would be close to her house, but also because she was convinced that her second cousin, Sylvia Taylor Baker, was Bob Blackstone's silent partner.

Sunny and I quickly finished our examination of the rest of the archives while Brad looked on, but the folder was the only thing we discovered out of place.

"Well, if you're done, let me take that folder in to the office. Not sure what significance it has, but since it was misplaced . . ." Brad pulled a pair of blue nitrile gloves from his pocket as he stepped around the table. He picked up the file folder and held it away from his body. "Just gonna put this in the cruiser. I think I have a couple of evidence bags in the trunk. Lock up that door when you step out, would you?"

Sunny and I trailed him out of the archives' building. While Sunny walked with Brad to his car, I paused to latch the padlock.

"You'll be sure to bring that folder back when you're done with it?" I called out as I gave the padlock a tug to make sure it was secure.

"Sure, not like the department needs to store more paper files indefinitely." As Brad pulled a heavy plastic bag from his trunk and stuffed the file into it, a slight, dark-haired man dashed through the back gate. The deputy made a move to jump in front of Brad and Sunny, but Brad told him to stand back.

"You!" yelled the man. Shading my eyes with one hand as I crossed the parking lot, I realized it was the dentist, Donald Virts. I didn't run into him often since he never frequented the library. Which was fine by me.

Brad slammed down his trunk lid with the evidence bag stowed safely inside. "Hello, Dr. Virts. What can I do for you?"

"You can tell me how my mother died, for one thing. And who killed her." Don, who was a good foot shorter than Brad, stabbed his finger at the chief deputy.

"I can't, actually. You'll be getting the full report soon from the sheriff, just like we told you yesterday."

Don twitched his nose like an angry rodent. He was slender but wiry and had a wide mouth at odds with his sharp features and beady eyes. He wore his thick dark hair longer than was fashionable.

Probably because it's his only good feature except for his artificially perfect teeth, I thought, then chided myself for being mean.

But Don Virts was not a pleasant person. I'd once seen him humiliate his wife and children in public, not to mention his poor treatment of his sister.

"Very sorry for your loss, Dr. Virts," Sunny said.

"Yeah, sorry." I was certain my expression conveyed less compassion than Sunny's, but I didn't care. I'd save my real sympathy for Bethany.

Don waved off our condolences. "I just never thought I'd see the day when my innocent, addled mother was murdered. And in Taylorsford, of all places."

Brad leaned back against his car and crossed his arms over his broad chest. "Murders happen everywhere."

"Not when law enforcement is up to the mark." Don shoved his hands in the pockets of his khaki pants, as if he was afraid he might otherwise take a swing at Brad.

"I don't think that's quite accurate, but it's true we're not used to this sort of thing in these parts." Brad's eyes narrowed as he studied Don's belligerent face.

It's usually the family . . .

I shook my head. Despite my personal dislike of the man, it was hard to believe Don would kill his mother. It wouldn't be for money since, as far as I knew, he didn't stand to inherit anything. In fact, according to Bethany, Doris had had nothing but her social security checks and what little they shared from the diner's profits. And since Bethany often complained about her brother's lack of assistance, I was sure Don was not inconvenienced in that regard.

But you never knew. I examined Don, wondering if I was facing a murderer.

"So why are these two here?" Don stared pointedly at Sunny and me.

"Sheriff's office business," Brad replied.

I glanced up at his calm face, surprised that Don's aggressive attitude hadn't brought out any animosity in Brad. Perhaps he was less of a macho guy than I had thought.

"Is that right? Well, I'd take what they say with a bucket of salt. This one"—Don jerked his thumb toward Sunny—"is probably looking to throw the blame on me. Her and her bleeding-heart tree-hugging friends have it in for me anyway."

"That's not true." Sunny smoothed her silky hair with one hand. "I and my friends simply oppose Bob Blackstone's subdivision project. Didn't know you were that involved in it, actually."

"I just might be one of Bob's investors. Which is none of your business," snapped Don.

Brad rolled his eyes while I mentally filed this information away for later. Don's involvement in a lucrative land deal could be a motive, but only if Doris had had some connection to the sale. Which didn't seem likely. Still, it was worth investigating.

Sunny lifted her chin. "I'm sorry, but it is my business. Taylorsford doesn't have the infrastructure to support everything we have now, and you want to pile on more houses?"

Don's eyes narrowed to slits. "I've got Bob's promise that he'll personally pay for the wells and septic tanks that will be needed if we can't extend the town water and sewer system in time. And his guarantee that we will expand the town's services, eventually."

"Promises I've heard before." Sunny placed her hands on her hips and faced off with Don. "Just ask the Blackstones about those sidewalks. Yeah, I'll believe it when I see it."

"This is not the time or place. Dr. Virts just lost his mother," Brad said, shooting Sunny a sharp glance.

Sunny shrugged. "Doesn't act like it. But I suppose people have different reactions to grief."

Sarcasm dripped off this last statement. I slid my hand through Sunny's crooked elbow and pulled her two steps back. "Brad is right. This isn't the best time to bring up your opposition to the development." I eyed Don, whose lips curled into the semblance of a smile. It wasn't a pleasant expression.

"Anyway, I just wanted to see what was going on. Keep on top of things, you know," Don said, addressing Brad.

Murderers often return to the scene of their crimes . . .

I shook my head. Even if he could be considered a possible suspect, why would Don shoot his mother in a public place like the archives? Surely with his access to dental supplies, including drugs and anesthesia, he could have achieved the same result with less mess and little chance of discovery.

Brad cleared his throat before speaking again. "Like I said, you'll be one of the first people notified when we have more information. Right now there isn't any."

Don cast a glance back at the archives' building. "So you didn't find anything more in there?"

"Nothing significant, no," Brad said.

"Let's hope the other evidence will lead to an arrest, then."

In my opinion, Don looked far too pleased with Brad's comment. I noticed Brad studying Don intently and wondered if his thoughts matched mine.

It was possible that Don had killed his mother in a way that appeared far too messy and public just because it would seem stupid of him to do so. Maybe he wanted it to look like a theft gone wrong . . .

You're not a detective, Amy, even if you know some investigative techniques. You shouldn't be speculating on things without facts.

Which meant I needed to discover some actual information. For starters, I could check court records to see whether there were any lawsuits pending against Dr. Donald Virts or anything else that could be adversely affecting his finances. Of course, then I'd have to investigate whether there might be insurance policies or other hidden inheritances that could drive Don to murder Doris. All things I could probably find out with some carefully designed Internet searches and a few conversations.

I unlinked my arm from Sunny's and forced a smile. "Yes, let's hope the culprit is found soon. I hate to think of a murderer freely roaming the streets of Taylorsford."

"Great, hadn't thought of that," Sunny said with a shudder.

Brad tapped his chin with one finger. "I honestly doubt any-one else is in danger. This seems like a crime focused on one victim. Although why is baffling."

"That makes no sense. My mother had no enemies," Don said. "Maybe it was some nutjob passing through town or some-thing? I'm actually thinking Mom was just in the wrong place at the wrong time."

A convenient scenario to suggest if you were a murder. I uncurled my clenched fingers. I really had to stop thinking this way. Just because I didn't like Don didn't mean he was a killer.

But it did mean I needed to conduct that research.

"Unlikely." Brad straightened to his full impressive height. "Is that all you wanted, Dr. Virts? Because I really must ask you to leave now. I am heading out along with Sunny and Amy. My colleague here will guard the perimeter for a few more hours until his relief shows up. I really don't want him to have to deal with extra folks milling about."

Don threw up his hands. "All right, all right. I'll go. Just hope you people will have some real news for me soon."

"Like I said, you'll be the first to know."

"Guess that will have to do for now." Don turned on his heel and marched toward the parking lot exit. "But just remem-ber this"—he called over his shoulder—"I have plenty of lawyer friends who'd be happy to make a case against the town, the library, the sheriff's office, or whoever else."

"Jackass," Brad said under his breath as Don disappeared. He glanced at Sunny and me. "Now if you'll excuse me, I must get back to the office. I see Sunny's car, but do you need a ride home, Amy? I can easily drop you off."

"No, Sunny will take me home."

"It's the opposite direction."

"Sunny doesn't mind. She picked me up, and you know, 'Always go home with the one who brought you.'"

I could see my attempt at levity fell as flat as my attempts at biscuits. Hockey pucks were more appetizing. Apparently they would be more appealing than my jokes too, if Brad's expression was any indication.

"Fine. Good day, then. Thanks for your help." Brad turned away and began talking shop with the other deputy, leaving Sunny and me to share a conspiratorial glance.

"He wanted to drive you home," Sunny whispered as we reached her car.

"People in hell want ice water." I yanked open the passenger-side door.

"Poor guy. At least I gave him a chance." Sunny settled in behind the wheel. As she leaned forward, her hair veiled her profile but didn't quite hide her grin.

"And dumped him soon thereafter."

"True."

"So why push him on me? Besides, you know I've sworn off dating for the foreseeable future."

"Oh, I know"—Sunny fired up the ignition—"but I bet that's not going to last."

I shot her a sharp glance. "Why do you say that?"

Sunny skillfully maneuvered the car around Brad's cruiser, waving at him as we passed. "Your new neighbor is far too big a temptation."

"Hah—like he would look at me when you're available."

"He was certainly looking the other day."

"Nonsense." I stared down at my hands, which for some reason I had clenched in my lap.

"Just saying, you might need to save some of that ice water for yourself."

I didn't reply, preferring to flip on the radio and turn up the volume. Fortunately, it was preset to a station that played classic rock, which made Sunny sing along in her loud—and tuneless—voice.

But that was fine. I even joined in, happy to add some harmony even though Sunny kept changing the key.

Chapter Seven

On Sunday, Aunt Lydia always attended services at the local Episcopal church. I occasionally accompanied her but decided to stay home the Sunday after the murder, primarily because I couldn't face the curious stares and questions I was bound to receive.

Besides, the garden needed weeding.

Remembering Richard's view, I pulled on a pair of lightweight pants instead of shorts but still threw on a tattered T-shirt and my floppy straw hat.

It was quiet and warm in the garden, and I allowed my thoughts to wander as I pulled clumps of orchard grass from the iris bed. I'd spent much of the previous evening on my laptop, digging through layers of public court documents to see if I could find any evidence against Don Virts, but I had found nothing. As far as I could tell, there'd never been a lawsuit or any legal action leveled against him or his practice. Of course, that didn't mean he didn't need extra cash for other reasons, but it did puncture my first theory about why he might wish his own mother dead.

As I considered other avenues of research, I paused from time to time to wipe away the salty sweat that trickled from my damp hairline into my eyes. After a particularly stinging episode made me blink away tears, I shoved back my hat and straightened.

A robin, perched on the rim of the concrete birdbath that sat at the center of one of the crossed paths, dipped its beak into the water and flapped its wings before taking off toward the woods. I allowed my gaze to follow the bird's flight until it disappeared into the mosaic of leaves.

"Hello, Amy," said a voice off to my left.

I turned on my heel, causing my hat to sail off my head. Richard Muir stood behind the picket fence that separated his property from ours. He held back a spray of pale-pink roses with one hand and lifted his other hand in greeting.

"Richard—hello." I knelt down to retrieve my straw hat and swiftly stood back up, jamming the hat over my tangled hair.

"Sorry, didn't mean to startle you. I was just out doing yard work and saw you and thought . . . Well, I wondered if you might want to take a little break and see what I've done with the place." He motioned toward his house.

"Um, sure, I guess." I stared at my neighbor, who smiled in return.

"Thought you might be interested. Town history and all."

I dabbed at the sweat beading on my upper lip with a tissue. "Okay, just give me a minute to swing around to the front yard. No gate here," I said, pointing at the rose-draped fence before stuffing the tissue in my pants pocket.

"No, wait, I'll meet you in your garden." Richard headed for the back edge of his property, which was also swathed in trees.

"But there's no gate," I said as he disappeared into the woods.

He reappeared shortly, emerging from the trees on Aunt Lydia's side of the fence.

I took a few steps toward him. "How did you do that?"

He motioned for me to join him at the edge of the woods. "Didn't you know the properties are connected?"

"No. Never really wandered into the trees. Too much underbrush back there. But Aunt Lydia likes to allow the area to stay natural. Better for the wild creatures, she says."

"It is, but apparently at one time, someone tried to tame these woods." Richard waited until I reached him before turning and heading into the trees. "Watch your step. There is an old path, but it's pretty overgrown."

Entering the woods was like diving into deep water. I stumbled once as my eyes adjusted to the dim light filtered through layers of leaves.

"Just follow me." Richard batted aside a vine blocking the path.

There *was* a path, which surprised me. I'd visited Aunt Lydia for years, even before living with her, but had never realized the woods were anything but a refuge for the wild creatures who roamed in from the mountains.

"I think maybe this dates back to Daniel Cooper's time." Richard turned his head. The jade-tinged light gave his face a mysterious quality that suited his angular features.

"Oh, it's an arbor!" I exclaimed as I reached his side. Before us, an arched wooden lattice tunnel, silvered with age, groaned under the weight of wisteria.

"Ready to fall down, I'm afraid. I think the vines are the only thing holding it together at this point."

"It must've been beautiful back in the day." I glanced down the arbor, noticing that the beaten-earth path was clear beneath its vine-laden arched roof. "Look, there are even benches."

"Yeah, a romantic spot. Can't you just see Daniel and Eleanora Cooper spooning, as they called it, right here?" Richard's gray eyes were very bright.

I shook my head. "Maybe. But their story ended so sadly, I don't like to think about it."

"Not a fan of tragic love stories? That rules out a lot of ballet and a good bit of contemporary dance too." Richard grinned and pointed toward the other end of the arbor. "This way, then," he called out, passing through the arbor in a few long strides. "The path comes out in the woods behind my house. But watch your step." He turned at the other end of the arbor and held up one hand. "There's an old well along the path. Covered now, but the boards are rotten. Stay clear of that."

I walked under the arbor, glancing up once as a breeze stirred the wisteria and the old wood groaned. I quickened my pace to reach Richard.

"So where's this well?"

He pointed to his right. "Just off the path, there."

I glanced at what looked like pieces of weathered lumber. As I peered closer, I could tell the boards covered a short stack of stones poking out of the ground.

Something about that circle of stones covered by rotting planks made me shiver. I rubbed my upper arms. "That was Daniel Cooper's well?"

"No, older than that." Richard held back a spray of blackberry vines, his fingers carefully placed to avoid the thorns, so that I could walk out of the woods. "I'm using Daniel's newer well. Had the pump upgraded, of course."

"Can't you get town water service? Aunt Lydia does."

"I could, and actually Great-Uncle Paul had the house hooked up to the town system, but I decided if I had access to a well, why not use it? Why pay an extra bill?" Richard strode past me, crossing from the woods onto his short-cropped lawn.

I blinked rapidly and pulled my hat down on my forehead as I stepped out of the shady trees. The sudden blaze of sunlight was blinding. "Wait, you have another well? So what was that old one for?"

Richard waited for me to join him before walking toward the back of his house. "Not really sure. My well was apparently dug when the house was built back in 1923. That old one is dry, as far as I know. I need to have it filled in and permanently covered over." He lifted his hands. "It's on the never-ending list of things to do."

"I see." I stared at the back porch of the farmhouse. "You had that built, didn't you? I remember just a crumbling stoop."

"Yeah. Come, I'll show you the rest."

I trailed him up the few steps and onto the back porch, which was light and airy but devoid of any furniture.

"I need to buy some things," Richard said, opening the back door into the house. "I was thinking wicker."

"That would work." As I stepped through the door, a blast of cool air greeted me. "You put in central air?"

"Didn't care for those window units sticking out all over." Richard flicked on a light switch. "Kitchen," he said, although it was obvious.

He had opted for a style that paid homage to the farmhouse's roots—beadboard cabinetry with simple pewter pulls and built-ins that mimicked the stand-alone kitchen furniture of the early twentieth century. Soapstone countertops and an old oak kitchen table instead of an island completed the look.

"Nice." I pulled off my hat and gripped it with both hands. "Did you have a designer?"

"Nope, just me and Google"—he grinned—"and a library book or two."

"Well, good job." I bit the inside of my mouth. *Good job? Sounds like praising a dog, you idiot.*

But Richard didn't seem bothered by my flippant words. He led the way out of the kitchen. "Hall and staircase like in your house, only not quite so grand. A bathroom to your right. I had that added, of course. Back in the day, they seemed to think one per house was enough."

"Upgrade from an outhouse." I glanced into the simple but elegant half bath.

"True enough. On your left, storage closet with laundry—also added—and . . . now the front room. A little different, as you see."

I stepped into what had probably been a parlor and a bedroom separated by a continuation of the hall. But the hall had been obliterated. The front door opened immediately upon one large room.

"Very different," I said.

Part of the space was set up as a living room with the usual components—a sofa, some chairs and end tables, a bookcase, and a large television hanging on the wall above a rack of audiovisual equipment. But that only comprised one-third of the room. The rest was an area devoid of furniture with a floor of smooth wood planks. The one solid wall was covered with floor-to-ceiling mirrors. A ballet barre ran the entire length of the mirrors. On the far wall, under one of the windows, a sophisticated audio system was housed in a plain wooden rack.

"A dance studio?"

He shrugged. "I know it doesn't match the house, but I need a place to practice. I have a studio at the university, but as Sunny observed, it is a bit of a drive. I needed a place to dance every day whether I was teaching or not."

"It is unusual."

"But it works for me. Thank goodness for tall ceilings in these old houses. Wouldn't have been much use otherwise."

"So all the bedrooms are upstairs?"

"Yeah, would you like to see?"

Richard asked this quite innocently, but I took a step back. "Maybe some other time."

"Not that spectacular, really. Just three rooms and two bathrooms. I live here alone, so even that seemed excessive, but my contractor suggested it. Planning for the future and all that." He kicked off his sneakers and walked onto the gleaming wooden planks. "Of course, the biggest expense was the floor."

"A sprung dance floor?" I asked, remembering this detail from my time at Clarion.

"Cost a small fortune. But necessary if I want to do any real work in here." Richard executed a simple but elegant movement that brought to mind one of Charles's impromptu lectures while we had watched a dance performance on television. *Pas des cat* or something. No, *pas des chat*. That was it.

"You still dance?"

"Of course. I will always dance. I may not always *perform*, but I will always dance."

"You must love it."

"Always have." Richard smiled and turned in some sort of spin—a beautiful movement that made my mouth fall open.

"How the hell do you do that?"

"Practice. Lots of practice."

I shook my head. "I could practice from now to the end of days and not be able to do that. But then, I am the world's worst dancer."

"I doubt it," Richard said.

"Oh, trust me, it's true." I dropped my hat on a side table and leaned against the back of one of the living room armchairs. "So dance has always been your passion?"

Richard walked toward me. "Yeah, and the reason I need to prove Eleanora Cooper's innocence. For my great-uncle's sake."

"How are those two things connected?"

Richard moved next to me. "Well, without him, I'd never have become a dancer."

"Really?" I took two steps to the left and turned to face him. "But he didn't have anything to do with the dance world, did he?"

"No." A little smile tugged the corners of Richard's mouth as he met my gaze. "But you see, my parents never wanted me to study dance. My father thinks it isn't . . . 'manly' enough, and my mother always supports my father's opinions. Or says she does, anyway." He ran his fingers through his hair. "So they'd never have paid for lessons, or taken me to them, or anything, except they had to."

I raised my eyebrows. "Had to?"

"Remember me mentioning that I only visited Great-Uncle Paul once, right before he died? And I didn't recall much because I was only four? Well, my dad's sister, Carol, tagged along on the visit, and she told me all about it later. Apparently, Great-Uncle Paul put on some music during the visit, and while the adults were chatting, I started dancing. Jumping around like dancers I'd seen on TV, anyway." Richard smiled at this memory. "My mom loved old musicals and television variety shows, so I'd seen people dancing in those. Apparently I liked to imitate them. Drove my dad nuts. Anyway, Paul saw what I was doing and asked me if I wanted to be a dancer when I grew up, and Aunt Carol claims I very enthusiastically said I did."

"Your dad must've hated that."

"He did and, according to Aunt Carol, brushed the whole thing off. Until Paul's lawyers told him that Mom would only inherit her uncle's money and property if my parents followed certain stipulations in his will."

"He left money to you for dance lessons, I bet."

"And he left it in trust with Aunt Carol as the executor." Richard grinned. "He was a canny old devil. He read the whole situation like words in a book in that one afternoon."

"Your parents couldn't refuse, or they'd lose the inheritance?"

"Right. So they allowed Aunt Carol to enroll me in a local dance school, which led to me getting a scholarship for a university dance program, and, well . . . here I am."

"Hunting ghosts." I wrinkled my nose at him. "Well, researching the past, at least."

"With a handy librarian friend." Richard's merry expression sobered. "At least, I hope so."

"I'm quite willing to continue to help you in your investigations. It's actually very interesting, especially now that I know my family was involved."

Richard's smile made something in my chest flutter.

No, Amy, no. You can be friends, and that's all. I'm sure that's all he'll want, anyway. I twitched my lips to ease my frozen, no doubt odd-looking grin.

"Speaking of research," Richard said, "I want to show you something. Might add context to our investigations." He crossed over to the bookcase and grabbed a narrow gray box.

It was an acid-free storage box used for preserving old documents. I spied a few identical boxes lined up on the shelf. "Are those archival documents?" I asked, moving closer.

"My great-uncle's papers, or at least the research he did for *A Fatal Falsehood*. I suppose I ought to donate them to the archives, come to think of it." Richard sat on the sofa, placing the box on the coffee table in front of him.

I started to sink into one of the armchairs, but Richard waved me over to the sofa.

"No, sit here. You need to see this." He rifled through the files for a minute before pulling out a copy of a newspaper article.

"Check it out. It's one of the pieces Great-Uncle Paul wrote to demonstrate why he felt Eleanora was being unjustly accused."

I leaned in to get a closer look, ignoring that fact that my chest was pressed against Richard's arm, and quickly scanned the article. "So your great-uncle thought people were biased against Eleanora because she practiced herbal medicine?"

"Yeah, apparently some people called her a witch. Not to her face, of course, and not even in any trial testimony. I suppose, since it was 1925, such a claim would've been viewed as old-fashioned." Richard's head was close to mine. So close that if I turned slightly, our lips would meet.

I sat up straighter, shifting slightly so that there was more room between us. "But I bet a lot of people still thought she was engaged in unchristian practices. Which meant they wouldn't have had a hard time believing she could be a murderer."

"Right. That's one of the things a lot of town residents held against her, if Paul is to be believed. It may even have influenced your great-grandmother's testimony."

Richard slid the article back into the box and stretched his arms above his head before dropping them to his sides and leaning back against the sofa.

"It always amazes me how people allow superstitions to direct their actions," I said while trying not to stare at the rippling play of his arm muscles.

Fortunately Richard didn't seem to notice. He was gazing intently at the ceiling as if he could read runes in the uneven plaster. "It happens a lot. For years my parents had trouble renting this place because people claimed it was haunted."

"By what? Daniel Cooper's ghost?"

"I suppose." Richard tilted his head until he was looking right at me. "The irony is that the ghost thing apparently wasn't such a big deal at first. It only seemed to crop up when that article came out after Rose Litton passed away."

I fought my urge to slide closer. "The one about how my great-grandmother's death marked the end of an era?"

"So you've read it?"

"Saw it when I was digging into the archival files on my family. But if I recall correctly, it mainly talked about how Rose was the last direct connection to the infamous Cooper trial."

Richard studied me for a second as if also considering the proximity of our lips. Then he lifted his head and straightened until his gaze was fixed on the dark television screen on the opposite wall. "Sure, that was supposed to be the focus, but it came out around Halloween, so the magazine writer tossed in ghost story speculation as well."

"I vaguely remember some folklore thrown into the mix." I shrugged. "But I don't believe in ghosts, so I just blew it off."

"Well, you may not believe, but after that, lots of people did. In fact, every other tenant complained to my parents about strange stuff happening. Just a way to score a discount on the rent, if you ask me."

"You don't believe in ghosts either?"

Richard turned his head and met my gaze without blinking. "I've never seen any evidence to make me believe. I do like to keep an open mind, but so far"—he lifted his hands in a graceful arc—"I've lived in this house for over a month, off and on, and experienced no manifestations yet. What about you? Seen anything spooky at your aunt's house? It's even older than this one—although it wasn't the scene of a suspicious death, so maybe it's not really the right locale for a haunting."

I thought about my aversion to the front parlor. But that was ridiculous. It was just an unpleasant room. "No, not a single ghost that I'm aware of."

"Just a garden that spits up gold jewelry. At least into the hands of the resident sleuth." Richard grinned and tapped the side of his nose with two fingers. As he dropped his hand, he leaned in closer.

I scooted back against the sofa cushions. "Another mystery."

"And speaking of investigating curiosities, I told Kurt Kendrick we could come by for a visit next Saturday evening. Will that work for you?"

"That should be fine. I'm working at the library, but we close at five. Maybe you could just pick me up?"

"Always happy to do that," Richard said, his clear eyes examining my lips with interest.

I swiftly rose to my feet and moved to grab my hat. "Well, this is all fascinating, but I should go. I still need to finish weeding."

Richard stood to face me. "Okay, but feel free to drop by anytime. I have a few more files pertaining to my great-uncle's research on *A Fatal Falsehood*. Might be a good compliment to your library research. Oh, wait, before you go, just wanted you to know"—he pointed toward a photograph of an older man set inside one section of the bookcase—"I placed the brooch on the shelf there, next to Great-Uncle Paul's photo. I think he would've liked that."

"Very romantic," I said, keeping my tone light.

He took two steps closer to me. "I'm a romantic guy."

"Okay, well . . ." I spied humor sparking in Richard's eyes as I backed away. "Think I'll go out the front, if you don't mind. Rather not wander back through those woods."

"No problem. Let me get that." He strode past me and opened the front door.

"Thanks again for showing me your house," I said as I brushed past him.

"Hey, we're neighbors. I should actually give you and your aunt a key. In case of emergencies." Richard followed me onto the front porch, leaving the door ajar.

"If you want. I mean, we'd be happy to keep one for you." I put on my hat, pulling it down so that it shadowed my face. "Good-bye, Richard."

So impolite, I thought as I hurried to the stairs that led down to the front yard. I paused on the middle step and turned back to him. "I'll check with Aunt Lydia about that promised dinner and give you a call."

Richard's smile broadened. "Sounds great."

I, who never ran, practically jogged as I fled his yard and headed for my own.

I really did like him. Which was good since he was our neighbor.

And bad for many other reasons.

Chapter Eight

As I made my way back home, I noticed Aunt Lydia's car was parked in the detached garage that flanked the right side of the house. There was another car pulled up behind hers—a luxury-brand silver sedan.

I didn't recognize the car and couldn't imagine who we knew with the money to purchase such a vehicle. Taking the gravel path that skirted the garage, I heard voices and quickened my pace. Aunt Lydia was in the garden, talking to someone whose voice I didn't recognize.

"Amy, there you are! I was worried." Aunt Lydia was still dressed in her church clothes—a simple navy linen dress with a white bolero jacket and pearls. "I saw your clippers lying on the ground, and the back door was unlocked. I was about to call Brad Tucker."

"Oh, sorry." I hurried to her, bobbing my head at the other woman who stood nearby. Sylvia Taylor Baker, my aunt's second cousin.

What the hell was she doing here? She and my aunt were family but not friends.

"I was just next door. Richard Muir wanted to show me the work he'd had done on the Cooper place."

A bright smile replaced Aunt Lydia's concerned expression. I groaned internally. She probably thought her matchmaking efforts were paying off.

"Ah, yes," Sylvia said. "The great-nephew. Strange that he wants to live here after all these years."

Sylvia was tall and slender like my aunt, but her blue eyes were as steely as her expertly coiffed gray hair. She wore carefully applied makeup that made her look younger than her fifty-nine years. Her clothes exuded sophistication and wealth—a light-gray silk suit obviously tailored to fit her figure.

Sylvia's smile was cool. "Hello, Amy. How you've grown. But it's been years since I've seen you, hasn't it?"

"Yeah, I think so."

"Amy is living with me now, you know," Aunt Lydia said. "Such a help with the house and gardens. And she's the director of the town library too."

Sylvia looked me over. "So I heard. Left a position at Clarion, didn't you?"

"Yes," I muttered, bending down to pick up my clippers. When I straightened, I noticed Sylvia staring at me. "Needed a change."

"Yes, I heard that too."

I rubbed at the side of my nose as heat rose in my face. So Sylvia had somehow found out about my disgraceful exit. Of course she had. She was one of the university's biggest donors.

Sylvia Taylor Baker was the only child of Rose Baker's nephew, William Baker Jr. She'd inherited most of the Baker fortune—everything except the family home and a small legacy that had been bequeathed to Rose and her husband, Fairfax Litton.

Unlike my direct relations, Sylvia's father had turned his inheritance into a larger fortune, buying up real estate before the commuter rail took off and the area became a popular bedroom community for people working in Washington, DC. Sylvia, who'd never married, had built an elegant estate outside of town but rarely lived there. She spent most of her time traveling and managing her investment properties.

According to Aunt Lydia, Sylvia was not satisfied with her wealth, elegant estate, and various vacation properties. She'd always coveted the family home and had made numerous attempts to buy it.

Numerous unsuccessful attempts. I wondered if that was why she was here today. One more try.

"Sylvia was at church today . . ." Aunt Lydia shot me a conspiratorial glance. My aunt had often mentioned that Sylvia Baker only attended church services at Easter and Christmas. ". . . and asked if she could stop by to see the garden. So I invited her over."

"I see." I yanked off my straw hat and wiped my forehead with the back of my hand. "Sorry it isn't in perfect shape. Still need to finish the weeding."

"I suppose that is a never-ending chore." Sylvia's gaze swept over the expanse of flowers and vegetable plants.

I rolled the edge of my hat between my fingers. "Pretty much."

"Couldn't manage it without Amy," Aunt Lydia said. "Of course, it will all be hers someday, so she does have a vested interest."

"Yes, I suppose," said her cousin.

Aunt Lydia's smile shone in direct contrast to Sylvia's sour grimace. "And we're thrilled that Richard Muir has moved in next door. The Cooper place sat empty too long. I was afraid it would eventually fall to pieces and have to be torn down. Now with all the work Richard has put in, I'm sure the house will endure for many more years."

"Very nice," Sylvia said, although her expression did not match this pronouncement.

"Of course, we are concerned about the plans for the development Bob Blackstone is pushing. Have you heard anything about that?" Aunt Lydia said this in a perfectly innocent tone, but I knew she was fishing for confirmation that Sylvia was involved.

Sylvia thinned her lips and did not respond.

I cast her a broad, if insincere, smile. "Yes, it seems that Don Virts has invested some money in the deal. Guess Mayor Blackstone needed an infusion of extra cash to get the property into shape to sell. Heard he might have to put in a few wells and septic tanks if the town system can't be expanded soon enough."

"I really had no idea," Sylvia said shortly.

"No? I thought you knew everything that went on in town, especially where development was concerned. Aren't you on the zoning board?" I caught Aunt Lydia's warning frown out of the corner of my eye.

But if Sylvia Baker was involved in Bob Blackstone's land deal, along with Don Virts, she might know something useful about Don's finances. Not that she would be likely to tell me anything directly, but just knowing of her involvement could provide me with another avenue for research.

"I am, but I'm afraid I'm not at liberty to share the information from our meetings with outsiders." As Sylvia waved her hand in a dismissive gesture, a scent of flowery perfume wafted through the air.

It was enough to entice an inquisitive honeybee. The bee flew a circle about Sylvia's head.

"Get that thing away from me!" she shrieked.

"It won't hurt you if you just stand still," Aunt Lydia said after Sylvia batted at the bee furiously and jumped backward.

I covered my smile with one hand. The oh-so-elegant Sylvia was hopping on one foot like an angry crane. "Wait, let me shoo it away." I crossed to her and flapped my hand, and the bee took off, heading for the monarda bed.

Sylvia tugged down her jacket. "I hate those things."

"They're essential for the environment," I said. "We actually plant flowers to attract them."

Sylvia's lips twitched. "I never would. All that environmental stuff is mostly nonsense anyway."

"Oh, I can't agree with that," Aunt Lydia said. "We have to take care of the Earth. It would be a shame to leave a trashed planet to the next generation. Which is why"—she straightened and stopped smiling—"I don't agree with the plans for this development."

"Me either," I said.

Sylvia gazed at both of us, her expression once again haughty. "Progress is equally valuable. This town will die without an infusion of new blood. Just think of the businesses all those new households could support."

Aunt Lydia's slender fingers curled around her strand of pearls. "Yes, but where are those businesses going to be built? And when? You know how strict the zoning laws are here. Well, you should, since you had a hand in creating them."

"We will bring in the proper things at the proper time." Sylvia gave a little sniff. "Not that riffraff that's sprung up like mushrooms outside of town, either."

Some in buildings you own, I thought, fixing Sylvia with a fierce stare.

But . . . mushrooms. I looked from my aunt to her cousin and back again. "Funny thing, you mentioning mushrooms. Just uncovered an old article about that in the archives yesterday. It said something about an orphanage that used to be on the old Cooper land and people dying from eating bad mushrooms. Weird, because no one has ever mentioned that to me before."

Sylvia's face paled to match the white roses in the bed behind her.

"Oh, that was so long ago." Aunt Lydia, who had leaned over to deadhead a dried-up daylily, apparently did not notice Sylvia's reaction. Or, if she did, thought nothing of it.

But I did. I stared at my second cousin once removed with interest. Something about that old tragedy had touched a nerve.

I shoved my hat back on my head. "I just think it's strange that no one talks about it."

"It was rather a blot on the town's reputation," Aunt Lydia said. "Although it was no one's fault, really. Even poor Eloise Fowler wasn't truly to blame. I suspect she was distracted, dealing with feeding so many children, and just picked the wrong mushrooms accidentally. Or maybe one of the children did—they used to help her with the foraging, from what people said. Of course, I was only six at the time, so I wasn't told much directly. Just overheard stuff." She glanced at Sylvia, who had regained her composure. "And you were barely one, weren't you?"

"Yes," Sylvia replied tersely.

"Anyway, it broke Paul Dassin's heart. That's what he told me later. He'd so wanted to honor the Coopers with something positive, and then another tragedy occurs on the same land."

"It's just history now. No bearing on the present." Sylvia brushed an imaginary wrinkle from her slim skirt. "Which is why I support the development. Taylorsford has to move forward, not stay mired in the past."

That was rich, coming from a woman who practically worshiped at the altar of family history.

Aunt Lydia twirled the daylily blossom between her fingers as she studied her cousin. "But why not turn the land into a town park instead? That's what Amy's friend, Sunny, and her environmental group want to do. Which really makes sense to me. Let the development happen on the edge of town, where there's already a lot of modern construction. Preserve the historical nature of the town proper."

Sylvia lifted her sharp chin. "That environmental group, as you call it, primarily consists of young people from the city. Not true Taylorsford residents, except for Sunshine Fields. So why should they have any say in our town? And anyway, the type of people we want to move in have no desire to build where they'll be staring at car dealerships and grocery stores. They want the beautiful lots and views the old Cooper farm can provide."

I kicked some pea gravel with the toe of my sneaker. "The type of people you want? What does that mean?"

"People who can afford the best, of course. Educated people with good jobs in the city. People who can really contribute something to the town."

"People with money, you mean."

"Well, yes. Because those are the people who can support the things Taylorsford needs. Like the library." Sylvia cast me a pointed glare. "People more like our ancestors, if I'm honest."

"Oh, lumber barons? Not too many of those left."

Aunt Lydia dropped the daylily flower and gripped my wrist. "Now Amy, you know what Sylvia means."

"Yeah, I think I do." I eyed Sylvia with distaste. "She means people who can afford the rents she wants to charge for those buildings she owns in town. Driving out other people, like Bethany Virts, who can't."

"Speaking of Bethany Virts, I hope she's doing okay," Aunt Lydia said after squeezing my wrist rather hard. "Poor thing, losing her mother in such a fashion."

"A tragedy." Sylvia turned her cool gaze on me. "I understand you're the one who found the body. That must have been a shock."

I pulled free of Aunt Lydia's grasp. "Yes, it was."

"But I heard that you didn't see anything more? I mean, nothing that would help lead to the perpetrator? That's a shame."

"No, Richard and I just stumbled over the body. We didn't see anything else."

Sylvia's eyes were clear and cold as an icicle, and her gaze as sharp. "It's probably for the best. If you had seen the murderer, you might have been placed in danger as well."

I hadn't considered that aspect of the situation. I shivered. "I guess."

"I'm sure the sheriff's department and other investigators will find the monster who did this," Aunt Lydia said. "They always do."

"Not always. But I wouldn't worry. I agree with Don Virts—it was probably some vagrant passing through. High on meth or moonshine or some such thing. Maybe he'd broken into the archives to sleep off a binge, and Doris walked in on him, and"—Sylvia spread out her hands—"he was startled and attacked her. You know how those people can turn violent for no reason."

It was a clever hypothesis, I had to give her that. But also a good cover for a different type of murderer. I wondered if she or Don had come up with it and, if so, why Sylvia was willing to spread his theory. I wasn't aware they were friends.

But Don had money, and Sylvia was always seeking investors for her various real estate dealings. So there was one likely connection.

Or maybe they *were* joint investors in Bob Blackstone's pet project. I studied Sylvia's haughty face, which was surprisingly devoid of lines. No doubt she'd indulged in a bit of plastic surgery or Botox. Chasing youth the way she chased money.

Aunt Lydia looked thoughtful. "Maybe. That might explain it, because it certainly doesn't make sense otherwise. Doris Virts had no enemies as far as I know. And it's not like her children would kill her for their inheritance, because there isn't any."

Sylvia nodded. "That's why Don's theory seems sensible. Which means we may never know who did it. But if that's the case, hopefully they've fled and won't return."

"Speaking of returning to Taylorsford, I found out something interesting from Richard just the other day." I turned to Aunt Lydia. "Remember that boy who lived with Paul Dassin for several years? You said his name was Karl Klass, right?"

"Yes." My aunt's fingers caressed her pearls again. "What of him?"

"He did come back. Or at least someone claiming to be him contacted Richard to set up a meeting. Richard's a little worried he might be angling for a piece of Paul's estate, so he asked me to accompany him on his visit. To have a witness to whatever's said, I guess."

My aunt flinched as if she'd been stung by that bee. "Are you sure that's a good idea?"

"Don't worry. It can't be anything that shady. Even if the guy has a different name now, he's quite respectable. In fact, it seems he moves in the highest social circles."

"That doesn't sound like Karl," Aunt Lydia said. "He was always so rough around the edges."

"Apparently he smoothed them out. Seriously, you'll never guess who it is."

"Kurt Kendrick." Sylvia's eyes sparkled with the obvious pleasure she took in divulging this information.

Aunt Lydia yanked on her necklace so hard the clasp sprung open, leaving the strand of pearls dangling from her fingers. "Surely not." She shoved the jewelry into her dress pocket and shot Sylvia a sharp glance. "And even if so, how did you know anything about this?"

Sylvia swept her hand through the air in a dismissive gesture. "Oh, I've been to a few of his parties. We share some mutual friends. But I didn't want to blow his cover since it seemed he wasn't interested in being remembered in Taylorsford. Not as Karl Klass, anyway. But now that he's contacted Dassin's great-nephew, I suppose he's decided to reveal the truth at last." She narrowed her eyes. "I thought you would've recognized him from that photo in the paper, Lydia. I realize he's in his early seventies now, but he still looks like he could man a longboat. The Viking. Remember, that was his nickname?"

"Yes, because he was so tall and broad-shouldered and fair."

"And still is, although his hair is white now, instead of blond. But those blue eyes are just as striking as ever." Sylvia patted her lacquered hair. "I was only six when he took off for parts unknown, but I remember being dazzled even then."

Aunt Lydia sniffed. "He was a hooligan. Dragged Andrew into all sorts of trouble."

"So you should be glad he disappeared when he did. For Andrew's sake, I mean."

"No, because it hurt Andrew and broke poor Paul's heart." Aunt Lydia glanced at me. "Karl just took off when he was eighteen. Never contacted Paul or Andrew or anyone in Taylorsford again, as far as I know. Paul could never locate him, no matter how hard he tried. Karl just vanished. I think Paul always worried that he was dead in a ditch somewhere."

"People always did seem to disappear on Paul Dassin. Not the luckiest individual, was he?" Sylvia turned to look at the back of the house. "I think you need a paint job on the trim, Lydia."

I assumed that was the end of the talk about Karl Klass or Kurt Kendrick or whoever he was, at least as far as Sylvia was concerned. I wanted to ask more questions, but one look at my aunt's tense face locked my lips. Anyway, I knew I'd have a chance to learn more about Taylorsford's prodigal son soon.

Sylvia lifted her sharp chin. "You don't want to let that go too long. I have some professionals I could recommend."

Aunt Lydia shifted her weight from foot to foot. "Thanks, but I don't know when we'll be able to afford a full paint job. Not a cheap proposition."

"No." Sylvia focused her gaze back on my aunt. "You know, if it ever becomes too much of a burden, my offer to buy the place still stands."

There it was. The real reason for her visit. "I don't think Aunt Lydia is interested in selling—ever," I said forcefully.

"I just hate to see the family home fall into disrepair." Sylvia patted her short hair with one hand. It didn't move, which verified my suspicion that it had been heavily lacquered with hairspray. "And it's much too large for one person to rattle around in."

Said the woman who owned multiple large homes.

"Two," I said. "Two people."

Sylvia's aristocratic nose twitched as she looked me up and down. "Ah, yes, two. But you won't live here forever, will you? I imagine you'll eventually marry, or move in with someone, or whatever it is you young people do these days."

I couldn't help myself. "You never married, or . . . whatever."

Sylvia stared at me like I had just burped in public. Or worse. "Well, I suppose I should be running along. Thank you for allowing me to see the garden, Lydia. And don't let me keep you from your weeding, Amy. Seems like a rather messy task to me, but I suppose *you* probably enjoy that." Her gaze ranged over my ragged ensemble. She sniffed before turning away and walking to her car.

"That was a bit rude," Aunt Lydia observed as the sedan backed out of the driveway.

"Who? Me or her?"

"Both," said my aunt, but she grinned. "Don't worry. You can't say anything to Sylvia that I haven't already considered. She's always been a bit of a pain. Obsessed with the family heritage, you know. That's really why she wants the house, not because she wants to live here. She'd probably renovate it into some froufrou monstrosity and turn it into a bed-and-breakfast."

"Called 'Baker House,' to perpetuate and glorify the family name?"

"Yes, which is not my name or yours. So I guess she thinks she has more of a right to everything connected to it." Aunt Lydia shaded her eyes with one hand and stared at the back of the house. "The trim does need painting. But I'll be damned if I'll ever sell this place to Sylvia Baker. I'd let it tumble down before that."

"It won't. We'll take care of it."

Aunt Lydia smiled. "Of course we will. Now don't work too long in this heat." She patted my arm. "I'm going in, but I'll bring you some water here in a minute. You look far too flushed." She turned away but glanced over her shoulder and gave me a wink before heading toward the back porch. "Unless that's simply the residual blush from spending time with our new neighbor."

I swore loudly, but Aunt Lydia just laughed and disappeared into the house.

Chapter Nine

The following Saturday, I almost made it out of the house without Aunt Lydia cornering me. Almost.

"I see you managed to dress up a bit for your visit with Karl," she said as she stood between me and the front door.

I glanced down at my black linen slacks and copper-colored silk blouse. "I have to work today too, you know."

Aunt Lydia crossed her arms over her chest. "Sure, because you wear outfits like that to the library every day."

I inched my way to the left, hoping I could slide by her and reach the door. "Are you saying I don't dress well enough for my job?"

"No, but you don't usually wear your best blouse or heels."

"Not that high, though," I replied, lifting my foot slightly to show off the kitten heel on my shoe. "And okay—I do think a visit to Kurt Kendrick's estate requires a little more dash than my usual style."

Aunt Lydia dropped her arms to her sides, her fingers still clenched tight. "I don't like it, Amy."

"So you've said. More than once."

"And yet you still don't want to listen, do you?"

"Look, I know you don't approve of Kendrick, or Karl Klass, as you call him. But Richard is going to be with me the entire time. And I really do want to see that house and the art . . ."

Aunt Lydia turned aside to stare at one of Uncle Andrew's paintings. "An art dealer and collector. Not the sort of thing I would've ever pictured as Karl's career."

I stepped up beside her. "He wasn't interested in art when he was young?"

"Not that I could tell. Andrew was, of course. He always loved to sketch and paint. But Karl never expressed any interest in it, at least not in my presence. Of course, I wasn't around him that much."

"Just enough to know that you didn't like him." I laid my fingers on her arm and squeezed, forcing her to look at me.

Aunt Lydia shrugged off my hand. "He was a wild child. So handsome, and he knew it. Very smart, according to Paul, but he didn't bother to apply himself at school. I guess I shouldn't judge him since most of what I know about him is hearsay. But I do. He was a bad influence on Andrew. Convinced him to skip school and blow off his homework and heaven knows what else. Also, there were the drugs."

"Weren't a lot of kids into drugs back then?" I fiddled with the gold bangle encircling my wrist.

"Yes, but not a lot of them dealt drugs."

"Oh." I considered this information in light of Kurt Kendrick's later wealth. "You think he made his fortune that way, don't you?"

"I do. I mean, it only makes sense. He ran off when he was eighteen, the day after he graduated from high school. Just barely graduated too, from what Andrew told me. Anyway, Karl had no money, no college degree, and no real skills. Other than his looks and charm and, I guess, his shrewd mind. So my speculation is that he continued and expanded his career as a drug dealer. How else could he have accumulated enough wealth to get into the art game? That usually takes a big investment at the start."

"Maybe so, but he could've gone straight after only a few years. I mean, once he made enough cash to get into dealing art instead of drugs. He's in his early seventies now. He might have shaken off any criminal connections years and years ago."

Aunt Lydia touched the gilt frame on one of the paintings. "Perhaps."

"And he may have never been involved in anything illegal. You don't know for sure that he was."

Aunt Lydia slid her hand around the frame until her fingers came to rest on a small bronze plaque bearing the name "Andrew Talbot." "No, I don't. Not for certain. But I know he sold a wide variety of illegal substances when he was a teenager. It just seems like a logical leap to imagine him continuing in that trade, at least until he was rich enough to leave it behind."

"Andrew told you that?"

"Yes." Aunt Lydia cast me a quick glance. "He had a problem, you see, off and on. Nothing that was obvious to others, but of course I knew." She looked back at the painting, lines furrowing her forehead. "It was Karl who introduced Andrew to drugs. I don't care what else he's done in his life or who he's become. I will never forgive him for that."

"Well, I don't intend to become his friend, trust me. I'm really doing this so I can see the inside of that house and the artworks. Also as a favor to Richard."

Aunt Lydia's face brightened. "Yes, that will be nice. You two can get to know each other a little better."

I held up my hand. "No matchmaking. This isn't a date, and I don't see things going in that direction. But I do want us to be friends."

"Of course," my aunt said, looking me over again. "But it is a very nice outfit. Shows you off to your best advantage. And you never know . . ."

"Enough," I said, rolling my eyes. "Now I'd better go, or I'll be late for work."

"All right," Aunt Lydia said as she followed me to the front door. "But maybe suggest stopping after your visit for a bite to eat or something? Tell Richard I haven't been to the store, and there's not much in the house . . ."

"Bye, see you later." I stepped onto the porch and closed the door while she was still making suggestions as to how I should entice Richard to take me to dinner.

*　*　*

Richard did check me out when I walked to his car after locking up the library later that day. His appraising gaze swept from my head to my feet and back again.

"Hello," he said as he jumped out of his vehicle. "Nice of you to match your outfit to my car." He grinned as opened the passenger-side door of his copper-colored sedan. "Ready to meet the elusive Mr. Kendrick?"

"I guess. Ready to take a good look at his house, anyway." I lifted my right foot onto my left knee and slipped off my shoe so I could massage my toes. "Sorry, long day on my feet in these things. I usually wear flats."

"No worries." Richard slid back into the driver's seat and gave me a smile. "I know all about aching feet, trust me."

"I bet you do." I cast him a quick glance as I fastened my seat belt. "At least you never had to wear toe shoes like the poor ballerinas. That must be torture."

"No, never had to do that, and yes, from what I hear, it is."

"I've read stories about it. How their feet bleed and all that." I stared out the window as Richard pulled into the street. "It looks so beautiful when they dance, but it must be painful."

"I don't have to deal with female dancers who have that issue, thankfully."

I turned my head to study his profile while he kept his eyes focused on the road. "Oh? Do you only work with contemporary dancers? You specialize in modern dance, I know, but I bet you studied ballet at some point."

"Of course. I even still take some classes from time to time. It's good training. But I perform and choreograph contemporary dance, so ballet is never my main focus."

"And you teach only contemporary?"

"Definitely. Not skilled enough in ballet to teach that to anyone. Well, I suppose I could handle the basics, but I think it's best to leave the real training to the specialists." Richard lifted his right hand off the steering wheel to fiddle with some controls on the dashboard. "I also occasionally teach jazz dance classes or even a bit of show dance. You know, Broadway-type stuff. I've dabbled in that in the past."

"You've danced in some shows?"

"Yeah. Not my favorite thing. I mean, the dancing is fine, and some of the choreography is fantastic, but it's the same thing night after night. Not the way I like to work. But after I left my first company job, I had to pay the rent somehow." He flashed me a smile and flexed his arm. "I had a few offers, but I didn't want to be reduced to being supported by some sugar momma."

I blinked and plucked at my blouse, which suddenly felt like it was plastered against my skin.

"Is it too hot in here for you, or is the temp okay?" Richard pointed at the dashboard. "I can turn down the AC if you want."

"It's fine," I replied, turning my head toward the side window. "Oh, look, there's the road you mentioned in your text. Where Kendrick lives, I mean."

"I think it's still quite a ways up the mountain, but yeah." Richard turned the car onto the narrow gravel lane.

The car bounced over the rutted road for several minutes before Richard spoke again. "What about you, Amy? Did you always want to be a librarian?"

"No, not always. When I went to college, I wasn't really sure what I wanted to study, to tell you the truth. I liked a lot of things—history, literature, art history . . ."

"Art history, huh? It seems my instinct to bring you along was spot on. Your knowledge might prove helpful in dealing with this Kendrick fellow."

"Maybe. That's what I majored in, actually. But when I graduated from college, I decided I didn't want to continue in that field, so I started looking around at graduate programs that fit my academic background. Library work seemed perfect, especially since I'd always loved books, so that's where I ended up. I thought I would specialize in art librarianship, but . . ." I bit my lip. No use getting into why I was working in Taylorsford instead of a university library.

Richard shot me another bright smile. "You ended up here instead. Which isn't so bad, all things considered."

"No, it isn't. Ah, there's the sign." I tapped my window. "Highview. That's the name of the place."

"Stone pillars topped with urns, a name, and all," Richard said, pulling up in front of a metal gate. "Obviously someone with money lives here." He lowered his window and leaned out to press the buzzer on one of the pillars. A voice squawked something, and Richard spoke his name into the intercom.

The gate swung open. "And then there's this automatic gate," I said. "Also something I'd only expect to find at an expensive estate. Although I guess if you fill your home with valuable art, you have to take precautions."

"Guess so." As Richard drove on, the gate shut behind us.

This road was paved, its blacktop surface mottled with shadows cast by a canopy of leafy branches. Azaleas and rhododendrons created a solid wall of green at the base of the hardwood trees that lined the driveway.

We rounded a corner, and sunlight flooded the car, forcing me to blink. As my vision cleared, I stared at the house and let out a little gasp. Set in the middle of a large clearing surrounded by forest, it was one of the most beautiful homes I'd ever seen. The three-story central section was constructed from variegated fieldstone that must have been pulled from local fields. Tall windows, their glass wavy as only hand-blown glass could be, were sunk into the mottled gray stones. Two-story wood-framed wings, painted a pale-jade green, extended from both sides of the central structure. Smaller windows flanked by black shutters gleamed against the wood siding, and a lacy veil of ivy covered the largest of the stone chimneys.

Richard parked in the circle of blacktop at the end of the driveway. A smaller lane, probably leading to a garage, curved behind the house. A covered porch featuring Grecian-style pillars and a pediment shaded the front door, which was painted a deep forest green. Filling the space between a whitewashed picket fence and the front porch, a cottage garden blazed with color. I climbed out of the car and ran to the gated arbor.

"It's gorgeous." I unlatched the gate and stepped into the garden. "Look at these plants. All either native to the area or antique varieties."

"Well, when you have a lot of money, I guess you can have whatever you want." Richard moved close to me and gazed over the garden. "But it is very nice."

"Lovelier than some perfectly manicured lawn." I tilted my head to stare up at the fieldstone facade. "The house too. It has that slightly rundown but comfortable quality. Like an antique that's more valuable because of its dings and dents."

Richard studied the house with interest. "It does have a certain bohemian charm. Although I'm sure it's actually in perfect shape."

"Not perfect, I'm afraid," said a cultivated male voice. "But it won't collapse on your heads, I assure you."

Richard and I turned as one to face the speaker, a man so tall his thick head of white hair almost touched the lintel of the open front door.

"Welcome," said Kurt Kendrick. "Won't you come inside? I promise I don't bite." He grinned, displaying a mouthful of very large, very white teeth. Which, along with his imposing figure and words, reminded me of a drawing from one of the library's picture books.

An illustration of the big bad wolf.

Chapter Ten

"Thanks again for the invitation." Richard bounded up the porch steps as Kendrick headed back inside.

"Come in, come in," said the older man, waving us forward without looking over his shoulder.

I followed Richard into the house, closing the door behind me. "Do you need to lock this?"

"No, it's set to lock automatically." Kurt Kendrick turned to face us. "I have excellent but rather unobtrusive security. Have to, really, in my business."

Dismissing my fanciful image of him as a fairy-tale wolf, I decided Cousin Sylvia was right—he did resemble an elderly Viking. He was a large man, but his size was composed of bone and muscle, not fat. He wore his thick white hair a little longer than was fashionable, and his blue eyes were bright as delft pottery. His rugged face, though lined, was still attractive. I could see how he might have set hearts on fire when he was young. A smile twitched my lips. If he'd had the power to dazzle Sylvia as a child, he must've been quite something.

Kendrick scrutinized us with equal intensity. "Richard, I can see your kinship with Paul. You look very much like him, though obviously younger and fitter. Paul was a bit of a couch potato, really." He turned his laser-sharp gaze on me. "And this must be Amy Webber. Definitely one of Rose Baker Litton's descendants. Same amazing eyes, although"—he tapped the side of his nose—"much kinder."

"I look like my mother," I said, sharply enough that Richard side-eyed me.

Kendrick seemed more amused than offended. "Ah, yes, Deborah. She did have those big dark eyes as well. Of course, she was a small child the last time I saw her. She was only seven when I left Taylorsford. Now shall we head to the living room? We can converse a little more comfortably there."

Distracted by an array of beautiful objects, I kept falling behind as Kendrick led us through the high-ceilinged front hall. I stopped dead at one point to admire a set of branched candlesticks, their gleaming surface only slightly dimmed by a patina of tarnish. They resembled pictures I'd seen of silverwork by Revere. I had to clasp my hands behind my back to keep from lifting the candlesticks to check for the maker's mark. They sat on a heavy oak sideboard, old enough to feature dovetail joints. It also showcased a collection of vibrant porcelain that looked suspiciously like pieces from the Ming Dynasty.

Because they probably are, Amy. Kendrick is an art dealer and collector. He's not likely to fill his home with cheap reproductions.

When I forced myself to turn away and follow Kendrick into one of the rooms branching off the central hall, I almost stumbled into Richard, who'd stopped short in front of a small pastel in a chipped gilt frame.

"Is this a Degas?" he asked, his voice slightly hushed.

I moved beside him to study the drawing, which showed a young dancer adjusting the ribbons on her toe shoes.

"Yes," Kendrick called out from the other room. "Picked that up some time ago. Nice little piece, although not his best work."

Richard looked over at me. *Not his best work?* he mouthed, arching his dark brows.

I widened my eyes and put my finger to my lips. "Impressive all the same," I said, walking into what Kurt Kendrick called his living room.

It was a comfortable space with leather sofas and upholstered chairs anchored by worn Oriental rugs. A stone fireplace dominated the outside wall.

But it contained so many paintings and objects d'art that it resembled a gallery rather than a room in a normal home. Glancing around, I noted pieces that looked like the work of well-known modern artists as well as some old masters.

"So this is your personal collection?" Richard asked as he took a seat on one of the leather sofas.

Kurt Kendrick sat in a wood-framed chair that bore all the hallmarks of William Morris's nineteenth-century Arts and Crafts studio. "Yes, although I change out a few pieces from time to time. I don't like to sell from my personal stock, but occasionally someone makes an offer I can't refuse." He grinned again.

That wolfish smile. I looked away, staring at a large painting that incorporated delicate floating shapes. It had to be a Paul Klee. Feeling overwhelmed by the understated but obvious wealth surrounding me, I fiddled with the shoulder strap of my small purse. "Sorry, but could you direct me to the restroom? Too much coffee today."

"Of course, dear." Kendrick waved toward the door with one hand. "At the end of the hall on the right."

I fled the room just as Richard asked the art dealer something about his life with Paul Dassin. *Perhaps it was best to allow them privacy for some of that family related conversation anyway*, I thought as I slipped into the small but elegantly appointed washroom.

After I washed my hands, the continued sound of running water baffled me until I realized it was coming from outside. I stood on tiptoe to peer out the room's high, mullioned window. It offered a view of the backyard and, as I'd suspected, a detached garage. Just outside the wood-framed garage's open doors, a man was washing a car.

A black Jaguar.

My heels hit the tile floor with a thump.

So it was Kurt Kendrick's car that had been parked near the archives' building the day Doris Virts was murdered. Of course, there was no way to know if he'd been the driver, since he might have a chauffeur, but still . . . I pulled out my cell phone to send a text to the number the detectives had instructed me to use if I remembered more information. But as my finger hovered over the send key, I hit delete instead. Maybe it would be better to send an anonymous message to the tip line. The sheriff's office should check out this clue, but I didn't necessarily want them questioning me or Richard, especially after our visit to the possible suspect's home. And I certainly didn't want Aunt Lydia to know Kendrick might be involved in Doris Virts's murder. She already disliked him and was likely to track him down and accuse him to his face. Which could either be extremely embarrassing or dangerous, depending on whether Kendrick was complicit in the crime or not.

I splashed some cool water on my flushed face before heading back to join the others. Slipping into the living room, I sat in the first available chair, a wingback upholstered in houndstooth-patterned wool.

"So Paul actually knew Eleanora pretty well?" Richard asked after acknowledging me with a nod of his head.

"Oh, yes." Kurt Kendrick stretched out his long legs, his expensive leather loafers plowing a row through the pile of the rug. "When she was in jail, he visited her every day. At first to collect information for his newspaper. But then, apparently, as a friend."

"More than a friend, if what I've heard is true," Richard said.

Kendrick shrugged. "On his part, perhaps. Paul never said that Eleanora reciprocated his feelings, although he was pleased that her health actually seemed to improve while she was awaiting trial." Kendrick turned to me with a smile. "Sorry, I don't mean to exclude you. I was just filling Richard in about some information on his great-uncle's involvement in the Cooper trial."

"Paul told you all this?" I clutched my purse in my lap to hide the shaking in my hands.

"Yes, he loved to talk about it. Ad nauseam, really. But I suppose it was one way he could still feel close to Eleanora. He loved her, you see. So much that he never looked at another woman, as far as I could tell."

Richard slid forward on the sofa seat. "You said Eleanora's health improved when she was in jail? That seems odd."

"Perhaps it was just getting over the initial shock of her husband's death. But yes, Paul always claimed that she was very thin and weak when he first met her, right after she was incarcerated and awaiting trial."

"And she seemed healthier in jail?" Richard rubbed at his jaw with the back of his hand, his expression puzzled.

"Over time, anyway. I think Paul liked to believe it was because of his friendship and support. Gave her the strength to fight, he said." Kendrick examined me with narrowed eyes. "Are you all right, Amy? You seem a bit tense."

"I'm fine." I spoke slowly so I could keep my voice steady. "So Mr. Kendrick, did Paul Dassin ever say why he thought Eleanora left town after the trial? Most people claim it actually proved her guilt, even though she was acquitted. I mean, it is odd that she fled so quickly and left all her inherited property behind."

Kendrick settled back in his chair but kept his eyes on me. "Paul told me she probably just wanted to leave all the bad memories behind. She came from some mountain community, you know. Little place called Chestnut Gap. Paul always assumed she went back home. He said he could understand that. Why wouldn't she prefer to go back where she had family and was loved and respected instead of staying in Taylorsford, where she was hated?"

"Not hated, surely." Richard tapped his fingers against the buttery leather of the sofa. "She was acquitted, so the town must've understood she wasn't guilty."

"Oh, no, they still thought she was. Believed it was Paul's articles that swayed public opinion outside of town and influenced the jury in the town where they held the trial."

"That's what I've always heard too," I said, fighting my desire to blurt out something about the black Jaguar.

Kendrick continued examining me in a way that did nothing to ease my nerves. "Yes, your family in particular, Amy. Especially your great-grandmother."

"You must've known her. Was she as difficult as everyone says?"

"Difficult?" Kendrick's bushy eyebrows disappeared under the thick fringe of hair falling over his forehead. "She wasn't difficult. She was a bitch." He held out his hands. "Sorry if that offends you, but it's the truth."

"No, not at all. My mom says the same thing." I took a breath to slow my breathing. "You didn't like her, I take it?"

Kendrick's smile tightened into a grimace. "She didn't like me. I guess she was around fifty to fifty-five when I knew her, but she was still a looker and quite the grande dame. She was also very sure her opinions were always right and had no hesitation about meddling in other people's affairs. She must've told Paul he was making a mistake taking me in at least a thousand times. Called me a ragamuffin and a delinquent and a good-for-nothing. To my face, you understand. She was nothing if not direct."

"Sorry," I said, looking down at my hands.

"You're not to blame for your ancestors. Heaven knows I don't want to be blamed for mine."

I glanced up to meet his searching gaze. "You were sent to the orphanage when you were twelve?"

"Yes, after being shuttled between various relatives for a few years. My mother died when I was born, you see, and soon after, my father embarked on a successful slow suicide by drinking himself to death. So I was bounced from grandparents to aunts to cousins until finally they all decided they'd had enough and shipped me off to the orphanage. That didn't last long either. I wasn't much for rules, you see."

"But Paul took you in," Richard said, raising his voice to draw Kendrick's attention. "And cared for you for six years. But you still ran away at eighteen and never contacted him again. Why?"

Kendrick met Richard's stern gaze squarely. "I needed something more. Paul was a good man, but what else could he give me? My family, despite not wanting me around, still refused to allow Paul to adopt me, so I had no hopes of an inheritance. He wouldn't cut out his *real* family, you see."

These last words were spoken with so much force that Richard sank back against the sofa cushions and took a breath before speaking again. "So you thought it was better to just strike out on your own? Make your own fortune, which obviously"— Richard gestured toward the paintings—"you have."

"Something like that. And I didn't really want to burden Paul anymore. Not with me or my . . . business ventures."

I eyed Kendrick and tightened my grip on my purse. So maybe Aunt Lydia was right about the drug dealing. And perhaps, to his credit, Kendrick didn't want Paul connected to him while he engaged in more serious criminal activities. "You also left without a good-bye to your best friend, or so my aunt claims."

Kendrick turned his brilliant blue gaze on me. "Ah, Andrew. Yes, I left him behind as well. Although not forever. We did have some contact in later years, not long before his untimely death." He laid two fingers to his nose again. "Lydia doesn't know that, my dear, and I'd appreciate you not mentioning it to her. I'd rather explain all that to her myself one day, if she'll let me."

"If you insist." I couldn't read anything in his expression, but the hair on my arms lifted. This man was not someone to mess with, whatever his guilt or innocence.

"I do." Kendrick rose to his feet. "Now might I suggest a little tour of the house? From the way she's been examining the works in this room, I suspect Amy would like to see more of the paintings and other pieces."

"Yeah, sounds great," Richard said. "Although we don't want to take too much of your time."

"Nonsense. I have an hour to spare. I would even invite you to dinner, but sadly, I must go out later. Business," he called out as he headed for the hall, "at least mine, never takes a holiday."

The tour would normally have enchanted me, as Kendrick showed off his collection of pieces by artists whose works I had studied only from photographs and other reproductions. But all I could think about was that black Jaguar parked out back.

So when he finally ushered us to the front door and bid us good-bye, I rushed to the car while Richard was still shaking Kendrick's hand.

Richard shot me a questioning look as I typed my anonymous message to the sheriff's office tip line.

"Warning your date you'll be late?" Richard asked as I hit the send button on my phone.

I was too preoccupied to attempt a clever response. "No date," I said, focusing my gaze on the side window as we headed back down the long driveway. I considered telling Richard about the Jaguar but decided against it. There was no sense in dragging him any further into my investigations. I also had no desire to taint his new relationship with his great-uncle's former ward, especially if Kendrick did turn out to be innocent.

Richard tapped me lightly on the arm. "If you'd like to stop for a bite to eat . . ."

"No, thanks. I just want to get home, if you don't mind," I replied, still staring out the side window.

"Of course," Richard said in a way that made me turn to look at him.

"I'm really tired is all."

"Understandable. Another time." Richard's tone was perfectly pleasant, but he kept his eyes on the road and only made small talk for the remainder of the drive.

When we reached our street, I decided a white lie was in order. I'd just say Richard had had some prior engagement or something. I certainly couldn't tell Aunt Lydia that he'd been the one to suggest dinner and I'd refused.

I'd never hear the end of that.

Chapter Eleven

After a few weeks, the furor over the murder died down, although wild speculation flourished like honeysuckle on farm fences.

I listened to it all, making mental notes based on everyone's theories, but said little in response. I also didn't tell Aunt Lydia much about my visit with Kurt Kendrick, avoiding any mention of his comments concerning Uncle Andrew. Instead I blathered on about the house and the art until Aunt Lydia's eyes glazed over and I knew she wouldn't question me again.

Straightening in my diner seat, my delicious homemade egg salad sandwich reduced to crumbs on my plate, I idly swirled my now-cold coffee with a teaspoon as I listened to my aunt discuss the murder with Zelda Shoemaker and their close friend Walter Adams.

It was Monday, Walt's day off for the week. Since he had less than one year until retirement and a mountain of comp time, his boss had suggested a four-day workweek. Walt had certainly earned the shorter hours. He'd worked at the Government Accountability Office, better known as the GAO, in DC for over forty years, driving the two-hour round trip every day before the MARC rail line improved his commute.

"I just wish the investigators would come up with something," Aunt Lydia said. "It's unnerving, thinking of a murderer in our midst. Everyone looking at each other like, *'Are you the one?'*" She pointed her fork at Zelda and Walt, who laughed.

"I was at work," Walt said. "Squinting at a computer screen like always." He leaned back, tipping up the front legs of his chair. Chrome with a crimson faux-leather seat cushion, the chair was too short for his lanky frame. He was over six feet tall and, according to my aunt, had scarcely gained a pound since high school.

Aunt Lydia, Zelda, and Walt had been friends since grade school, when they'd ridden the same bus. The fact that Walt was one of the few African Americans living in Taylorsford at the time seemed to have no effect on their friendship. Until they were teens, that is. Sent to a large high school that drew in students from all over the county, they went their separate ways for a while. "There was a lot of racial tension around that time," my aunt had explained. "It really wasn't safe for Walt to hang out with two white girls. We still occasionally met in secret, though. Just to catch up on things."

Now the three friends met at the Heapin' Plate for lunch once a week. I occasionally joined them when Sunny volunteered to take charge at the library.

"And I have an alibi too. I was working at the county food bank. Lots of people saw me there. Not that I would shoot someone in the head, anyway. Not when poison's so much easier." Zelda grinned and tapped her finger against the red Formica tabletop.

I flashed her a smile before allowing my gaze to wander. The Heapin' Plate was an eclectic mixture of late nineteenth-century class and nineteen-fifties kitsch. The building had once been a general store and retained its tall plaster walls and pressed-tin ceiling. But Doris and Bethany hadn't followed that style in their decorating, opting for chrome-edged round tables, yellow-checked gingham curtains, and metal ladder-back chairs. Separating the eating area from the kitchen was a massive oak counter capped with a thick slab of marble. It was a remnant of the building's previous incarnation. The rest of the store's original antique furnishings had been stripped and sold—by Sylvia Baker, of course—before the building was rented to the Virts.

"Say what you like, I don't buy that stranger-passing-through-town theory that Don Virts keeps mentioning." Zelda shook her head, bouncing her cap of crisp blonde curls.

With her wrinkle-free face and rosy cheeks and lips, Zelda looked younger than her sixty-five years. Of course, her dyed and permed hair added to this illusion, although Zelda went no further with youth-enhancing alterations. She was a short full-figured woman whose zest for life lit up her tea-brown eyes. I had it on good authority that Zelda, a widow, was pursued by several of the older men at her church.

She always laughed at this and swore she'd never marry again. Many people took this as a sign of her devotion to her late husband. But Aunt Lydia had told me in confidence that there was another reason.

Zelda and Walt were in love. And had been ever since grade school.

Of course, given the time in which they'd grown up, they'd never dated. They'd both married other people and were, to all appearances, happy. Zelda, who was childless, had reveled in her job as town postmaster. She'd loved knowing everything about everyone and had only retired because her superiors, who'd wanted to "modernize" the post office, had forced her out.

Walt, whose wife had died five years ago, also lived alone since his four children worked in jobs scattered all over the country. "I guess that's the least terrifying option," he said after taking a sip of his iced tea. "Hard to believe someone in your hometown would murder your mom."

"There's been murders here before."

I glanced over my shoulder and up into the face of Clark Fowler.

His years as a signalman on the railroad showed in Clark's lined face, but his dark eyes were bright as those of a hawk. And as unblinking.

"Hi, Clark. Have a seat." Aunt Lydia motioned toward the empty chair next to her.

"Thanks, but I'm just here to pick up some takeout." Clark circled around so that he was facing me across the table. "But heard ya talkin' and had to chime in."

"What murders?" Walt asked. "That Cooper case was never proven, and the orphanage deaths were a tragic accident. You know that better than anyone, Clark."

"Not an accident. Not by a long shot."

"What do you mean?" Walt's chair legs hit the linoleum with a clang as he leaned forward.

Zelda laid her hand on Walt's arm. She was probably signaling him to hush. It was hard to believe that Walt hadn't ever heard one of Clark's rants about his mother's death, but I supposed it was possible. His crazy work schedule and tendency to bury himself in his woodshop when he had any free time might have prevented him from encountering Clark Fowler's conspiracy theories until now.

And after all, I hadn't heard about it before the discovery of that file in the archives, even though I'd spent time in Taylorsford since I was fifteen.

Clark thrust his bony fingers through his belt loops, hitching up his loose jeans. "My mother never killed those kids with bad mushrooms. No, sir. She was plenty sick before that, and so were they. They died of some illness caused by somethin' out there on that farmland. Somethin' in the soil, or water, or air. Town just didn't want to admit to it. Negligence was what it was, pure and simple."

"What a load of nonsense."

Everyone swiveled in their chairs. Mayor Bob Blackstone stood in the doorway, brushing some imaginary lint from his charcoal-gray sleeve. He was a man of average height, whose muscular frame seemed poised to burst through his fitted suits.

The conversations filling the diner ceased, and all eyes followed Bob as he strode over to our table, smoothing his slicked-back brown hair. Although he was only forty-six, he always looked like he had stepped off the set of some fifties' television courtroom drama. "Clark Fowler, you've been spreading that lie for years. Isn't it about time you accepted reality?"

"You mean your reality?" Clark dropped his hands to his sides and straightened as much as possible, given that his shoulders were hunched by arthritis. "I know it was your dad and his cronies who covered stuff up. Put the blame on my mother, God rest her innocent soul."

"No one blames her. It was an accident," Bob replied calmly.

Bethany Virts—short, wiry, and dark haired like her older brother, Don—popped out from the kitchen, clutching a white paper bag. "Mr. Fowler, I have your order." She held up the bag and shook it slightly, as if enticing the old man to turn away from the mayor.

Clark paid no attention to her. He stepped around the table to face off with Bob Blackstone. "I know that story about mushrooms was a cursed lie. My mother knew the difference between poisonous 'shrooms and the edible kind. She grew up in the mountains, learned all 'bout herbs and wild plants—just like that Eleanora Cooper, whose name's been smeared for decades too. And by the same people."

"No one is accusing your mother of anything. It was an accident, pure and simple. My father knew that, as did everyone in town."

"Your father was in on the cover-up. Mighty convenient for him and the others not to be blamed. And what happens? Why, the orphanage disappears, along with the truth, and you eventually get to scoop up the land for a thin dime. And now"— Clark fixed Bob with his piecing glare—"you get to sell it off for a mighty nice chunk of change. Shenanigans is what I call it. Shady deals and shenanigans."

I looked over at Aunt Lydia and raised my eyebrows. *Shenanigans*, I mouthed at her, but she just pressed two fingers to her lips and shook her head.

"If you don't mind"—Bethany's high voice broke through the sudden chatter filling the room—"I'd rather you not talk about this in my diner."

I looked over at her, noticing her thin face had turned as pale as the bag she clutched. She set it down and slumped against the counter.

"Yes, really, people," Aunt Lydia said, raising her voice so she could be heard above the din, "give the poor child a break. She just lost her mother."

Clark wheeled around and pointed a gnarled finger at Bethany. "Don't play the innocent—you don't want to hear this 'cause your grandpa was probably in on it too. Douglas Beckert was just as guilty as the rest, and I bet your mother knew. That's why she was killed. She knew her daddy helped cover up the truth 'bout all those deaths at the orphanage, and with her mind goin', someone was afraid she would spill the real story."

Bob Blackstone leapt forward and grabbed Clark Fowler by the forearm, spinning him back around. "Leave that girl alone. You can believe whatever you want, old man, but don't attack innocent people based on your wild theories. Or do I have to call Deputy Tucker on you again?"

Clark yanked his arm free and stepped back, his breath wheezing from his lungs. "I've been silent long enough. You've seen to that, you and your father and the whole mess of big shots who think they run this town. Well, I'm tellin' you now—I'm not puttin' up with it no more. I've got some information, yes, I do. And I'm going to make it public just as soon as I can. Then let's see how that blasted development deal of yours works out. It won't, if I have anything to do with it, I swear."

Bob raised his arms and curled his fingers as if he were about to make a fist. Walt shoved back his chair until it screeched and jumped in between the two men.

"Enough of this. Bethany's suffering, and all you two can do is argue and fight. You should be ashamed."

I glanced at Zelda. Her eyes were shining with unabashed pride.

"This is none of your business," Clark snapped.

"I'm making it my business. Now you grab your food, pay Bethany, and go. We don't need a fight between two grown men who should know better."

Bob Blackstone dropped his arms but cast Clark one last angry glare over Walt's shoulder. "I'm not going to lower myself to fight someone who's obviously mentally disturbed. But I'm warning you, Clark Fowler—spread any more rumors or inter-fere with my business dealings in any way, and I'll make you pay." He turned on his heel and stormed out of the diner.

Clark muttered to himself, something about "liars and thieves."

Walt laid a gentle hand on the older man's shoulder. "Go home, Clark. Cool off. I'll grab your food. I'm sure Bethany won't care if you just put it on your account." He crossed to the counter and grabbed the bag.

Bethany looked up as Walt slid some money across the counter. She shook her head, but he just pressed his fingers against the back of her hand.

"Here, you have your lunch." He handed the bag to Clark. "Head on out now, okay?"

Clark gazed sullenly up into Walt's pleasant face. "All right. Got no quarrel with you." He shuffled to the front of the diner but turned at the door. "But there is somethin' these town leaders have been hidin' for a long time, I just know it. Every one of them that was on that town council back in the day is guilty. And that includes your friends' grandparents too, Walt Adams. All them Bakers and Littons and Shoemakers and Beckerts and the whole lot of them." He hoisted the bag of food close to his chest and turned to shove his way through the half-open front door.

Walt sat back down at our table. "I guess that was our entertainment for the day."

"You handled that well," Aunt Lydia said.

Zelda just smiled. As I leaned over to pick up a dropped napkin, I noticed she and Walt were holding hands under the table.

It was sweet and sad all at the same time. They still didn't think that they could be open with their affection. Old habits died hard, especially if you'd been raised to fear exposure.

"But that stuff Clark Fowler said about a cover-up, is that possible?" I asked, straightening in my chair. "Because I'm helping someone with research about the Cooper murder case, and I wonder if it does tie in somehow."

Aunt Lydia and Zelda shared a conspiratorial glance.

"Oh, that's right, your new neighbor," Zelda said. "The good-looking one. Richard something."

I shot Aunt Lydia a furious glance. "Richard Muir."

"Yes, a dancer of some sort. And single, I hear." Zelda smiled brightly.

I blotted my lips with my napkin to muffle a swearword. "He is also a choreographer and a full-time instructor at Clarion. And Paul Dassin's great-nephew. Which is really why I am helping him. He wants to research the Cooper case. Thinks that Eleanora got a bad rap."

"I think she probably did." Walt's expression was thoughtful. "Being an outsider and all."

Zelda looked over at him, her bright eyes shadowed under lowered lids.

"Richard Muir is a very nice young man," Aunt Lydia said. "Although he hasn't managed to accept that dinner invitation I extended a couple of weeks ago."

"He's been busy filling in for someone who was injured and couldn't teach a summer workshop at the university. But I know that he's free now because he called today." I cursed silently when Aunt Lydia offered one of her cat-in-the-cream smiles. "Yes, *called*. But mainly because he wants to come by the library tomorrow for some more research assistance."

"Be sure to invite him to dinner again," Aunt Lydia said.

Zelda sat back and slid one finger of her free hand around the rim of her water glass. "You know, we were all so young back in 1958, when that orphanage tragedy happened. Six or seven, right?"

"Walt and I were six," Aunt Lydia said. "You were seven."

"Right. So we don't really know much about it. Not like some of the older folks in town might."

I dropped my napkin over my empty plate. "What are you thinking, Zelda?"

"Oh, just that maybe Lydia and Walt and I could do a little research of our own. Talk to some of our parents' friends. The few who are alive, I mean. And some other people who would've been old enough at the time to really understand what was going on. I know everybody, or at least where they live. Had to, at the post office. I can make a list."

"But we'll have to be careful." Walt lifted his and Zelda's entwined fingers up to the tabletop and immediately released her hand. "We still don't know who murdered Doris. What if there's something to what Clark Fowler said? About her knowing some secret, I mean?"

"That's true. You probably should keep any investigating low key." I considered mentioning my suspicions about Kurt Kendrick, but a little voice in my head warned against it.

Think, Amy. If Kendrick is involved, do you really want Aunt Lydia or Zelda and Walt digging into his business? With his possible ties to illegal activities?

I pushed back my chair and rose to my feet. "This has been very interesting, but I need to get back to work. Poor Sunny hasn't had a lunch break yet, and it's past one-thirty." I grabbed my purse and fished out some money. "Here, this should cover my lunch and the tip."

"Too much," Zelda said.

"No, it isn't. And as for this detective project of yours"— I frowned—"I don't want you putting yourself in harm's way for me."

Zelda waved me off with one hand. "It's not for you, my dear. It's for your delightful new neighbor. And my own curiosity."

Ah, there was the crux of it. "Okay." I studied the three people at the table. Walt looked concerned, Zelda excited, and Aunt Lydia surprisingly subdued. "I know nothing I say will change your minds. Just be careful."

"Of course," said my aunt. "And I'll do my best to keep these two out of trouble if I can."

"We have Walt to protect us," Zelda said, patting his hand.

I met his concerned gaze. "But he can't watch over you every minute. He'll be at work a lot of the time."

"Oh, all we'll be doing is talking to people," Zelda said. "What harm could come from that?"

"I don't know," I replied. "But I just have this feeling that maybe there was a kernel of truth to Clark Fowler's wild ramblings. And if that's the case . . ."

"You and Richard Muir could be in danger too," my aunt said firmly. "So let's all agree to be careful and not do anything foolish."

"Agreed," said Zelda and Walt in unison.

"Agreed," I said. I noticed Aunt Lydia drumming her fingers against the tabletop. She appeared hesitant about this turn of events. That was odd. She was typically the first one to leap headlong into a new adventure. But something was holding her back this time.

I held her gaze for a moment before I turned and left the diner, but if she was hiding any more secrets, I couldn't read them in her eyes.

Chapter Twelve

I spread the files that I'd pulled from the archives across the large wooden table that dominated the center of the library workroom. Despite reopening the library, the state investigators still didn't want the archives used as a work space. However, they did allow me to grab specific files or boxes and carry them into the library—once they'd vetted the materials, of course.

Since Richard had scheduled a research session, I'd assembled all the information I could find on the Cooper murder trial. Fortunately, this was not something the investigators deemed important to their own case.

"Here he is," Sunny said, ushering Richard into the work-room. "Now"—she pointed her finger at him—"don't you keep Amy past six o'clock. She got into work very early to pull all this material for you."

He held up his hands, palms out. "I swear I won't take advantage of the library director. I need her for my research, after all."

"Oh, as for taking advantage"—Sunny winked at Richard—"depends on what you mean by that."

I glared at my assistant. "Don't you have story hour today?"

"Yes, indeed. I have a date with *The Very Hungry Caterpillar.*" She tossed her blonde hair behind her shoulders. "A charming fellow, if a bit of a pig."

Richard smiled. "And if I were a small boy, I would be entranced. By the reader, if not the story."

Sunny wrinkled her nose adorably. "Only if you were a small boy?"

"Well, I confess you remind me of my first crush. My kindergarten teacher, who was a beautiful blonde just like you."

"I'll accept that." Sunny placed one finger against her delicate jawline. "I do have my youthful admirers."

"No doubt," Richard said. "Older ones too, I bet."

"A few." Sunny cast him a beaming smile before leaving the workroom.

"Here's what I dug up on the Cooper case." I motioned toward the table. "Surprisingly, not as much as I expected, but maybe that's because the trial was held elsewhere. It may not even be as much information as you already have from your great-uncle's research."

"Might be a different perspective, though." Richard crossed to the table and sat on the work stool next to mine. "I have Paul's articles but nothing from other journalists or the local paper."

I cast him a glance as I opened one of the archival boxes. "Sunny is a real catch, you know."

He raised his eyebrows. "I can see that. Surprised she's still single."

"She's rather picky." I fanned out some newspaper clippings in front of Richard. "And there aren't a lot of eligible men in this area. Sunny sticks around because of her grandparents. They raised her after her mom, who was single and living with them at the time, took off one day and never returned. They have this organic farm, you see, and Sunny helps them manage that."

"Sounds like she's a good granddaughter." Richard picked up one of the acid-free transparent sleeves containing a clipping and studied it intently. "And she is quite lovely. But"—he glanced over at me—"I don't think we'd work out. No spark, you see."

"How can you tell?"

"We ran into each other in the shopping area near Clarion after one of my rehearsals last week. Sunny was buying shoes or something. Anyway, we figured we might as well take advantage of the opportunity and grab a bite to eat. Had a nice time, but we agreed there wasn't anything there beyond friendship. So you can cease with the matchmaking. I know it's coming from a good place, but it isn't really necessary. Although I can tell you come by it naturally." He shot me an amused look. "Runs in the family?"

So he'd noticed Aunt Lydia's efforts. Of course he had. She wasn't exactly subtle.

"Yeah, sorry about that."

"Didn't bother me." He squinted as he peered at one of the documents. "More evidence that people back then did call Eleanora a witch. At least if this letter from one of the town matrons is to be believed. Interesting."

I fiddled with the elastic tie on the archival box. "Aunt Lydia did want me to reissue the dinner invitation. Hope that's all right. I mean, we are neighbors. I'll talk to her about cooling off on the matchmaking, though."

He turned to me. "Dinner sounds great. And I don't actually mind all such efforts. Depends on the other party, doesn't it?"

A dinging from the front desk alerted me that a customer was waiting. *Saved by the bell, literally.* I jumped off my stool. "Sorry, I need to get that since Sunny's doing the reading program."

"Sure." Richard had his head down. Probably trying to hide his amusement at the flush creeping up my neck. "You do your job. I'll be right here, reading through this stuff and taking notes. Oh, and Amy"—he lifted his head and looked me up and down—"there really does need to be a spark to make it work. Matchmaking, I mean."

"So you're saying you're in no danger, no matter what Aunt Lydia does?" I called over my shoulder as I stepped out of the room.

"I didn't say that."

I spun on my heel to meet Richard's wicked grin.

"Actually, I think I might be in a lot of trouble," he said.

"Excuse me, can I check these out now?" called the person at the desk. I closed my mouth, which had dropped open at Richard's last comment, and turned to see one of our regular patrons holding up a stack of books.

I rushed over to the computer. "Sure, sure. Just put them down on the counter."

A short line had formed behind the first patron, which was fine since it prevented me from glancing back into the workroom. After checking out books to several people, I busied myself by straightening the reshelving carts before compiling some statistics from our library circulation system for my report at the monthly town council meeting.

While this wasn't busywork, it did keep me occupied and out of the workroom.

After about thirty minutes, Sunny bounded up to the desk. "I'm back. Caterpillar successfully transformed into a butterfly, and children happily entertained. So if you need to go help Richard with his research . . ."

I straightened some library flyers. "I'm sure he's doing just fine on his own."

Sunny stepped behind the desk. "Hey, Richard," she called into the workroom. "I can spare my boss now if you'd like another pair of eyes on that material."

"That would be great," he called back.

I shook my finger at Sunny. "Enabler."

She brushed her hair back with one hand. "Who, me? I'm just suggesting you assist a library patron, that's all."

"Uh-huh." As I walked into the workroom, Richard looked up.

"Did you know"—he waved a clipping envelope at me—"that Eleanora's hometown no longer exists? At least, I can't find any mention of it on current maps. Remember? Kurt Kendrick told us it was called Chestnut Gap. Well, I found that name mentioned in this article, but when I searched online with my phone, I found no matches, at least not in this area."

"You won't." I crossed behind him and took the offered clipping. "I found the town listed in another article and did a little Internet sleuthing earlier."

Richard tapped his phone with one finger. "So it just disappeared into thin air. What was it, Brigadoon?" He grinned. "Danced in that show once back in college. Never wanted to see a kilt again."

I cleared my throat, banishing the image of Richard in a kilt from my mind. "No, nothing quite that fanciful. Chestnut Gap was settled by Scotch-Irish immigrants back in the eighteenth century. And was wiped out by logging operations around 1926. Apparently some lumber company bought up the land, claiming the townspeople didn't have proper deeds or papers establishing their ownership."

Richard swiveled on his stool and looked up at me. "Was it the Baker Company? That was your family's business, wasn't it?"

"At that time, yes, although it was sold by Rose's brother, William Baker, not long after. But fortunately, that's one sin I can't lay at my family's door. They weren't involved in the Chestnut Gap take-over."

"Well, it kind of explains why no one came looking for Eleanora after she disappeared. And maybe why she never showed up in Taylorsford again. She probably went back home, then moved with the rest of the town a year later."

"Yeah, but"—I sat on the stool next to Richard—"to leave the house and land behind and never make a claim on them? That's odd."

"True. Apparently, according to my parents, that's the thing Great-Uncle Paul never understood. Eleanora was Daniel's rightful heir. Why not claim what was hers? I bet that was one reason Paul bought the property when it fell into receivership."

I smoothed the surface of the envelope before sliding it back into the storage box. "You think Paul was holding it for her, hoping she'd return one day?"

"Yeah, I think he probably was."

"A very romantic gesture. Poor guy, I guess he really was in love."

"Well, if we take Kendrick at his word, apparently Eleanora was Paul's one true love, and he vowed to remain devoted to her alone. I can believe that since my family never heard of another woman connected with Paul in any way." Richard picked up a handful of papers and clippings. "I'm done with this lot if you want to refile them."

As he handed them over, his fingers brushed my hand, and I felt a zing of energy.

"Static," I said, refusing to meet his eyes. "This building's humidity controls are nonexistent."

I carefully placed the rest of the items back into the storage box before glancing up to meet his smile. "One thing I couldn't find in my research and Kendrick never mentioned—if he loved her so much, why didn't Paul Dassin travel to this Chestnut Gap place and try to find her? After the trial, I mean."

Richard shrugged. "I don't know. I guess the fact that he loved her doesn't mean she loved him. I've always gotten the impression that Eleanora was totally devoted to her husband, even after his death. So maybe my great-uncle thought it wise to give her some space."

"That makes sense. And if he did try to find her later, she'd already disappeared again. Sad."

"Yeah, and they didn't have the Internet or other simple means to trace someone. People *could* disappear back then. Well," Richard added thoughtfully, "they actually still can, if they are determined enough."

"But it's not so easy these days. Sometimes I wish it was." I snapped the elastic loop back over the button on the acid-free box. "Like when I left Clarion. I guess you heard about that incident. Everyone did."

"No, but I was traveling a lot last year." Richard spun on his stool to face me. "So why did you leave?"

"Oh, well . . ." Damn, why had I brought this up?

"If you'd rather not say, it's fine."

"No, it's just a little embarrassing. But maybe you'll understand, considering your former fiancée married someone else and all." I placed my hands in my lap, fighting my urge to clench them together. "Okay, so I caught my boyfriend with another woman. At a party. And I made a scene. In front of several deans and other administrators."

"Wait"—Richard leaned forward—"you're the woman who threw the glass at that reception?"

I rubbed a fold of the soft fabric of my tunic top between my thumb and fingers. "See, you did hear about it."

"I just heard it was Charles Bartos's girlfriend." Richard tipped his head to the side. "That couldn't have been you."

"It was. We'd been dating for over a year at that point. I thought it was serious."

Richard studied me with narrowed eyes. "Hard to imagine someone like you hooked up with a guy like Bartos."

I swallowed hard. Of course he wouldn't expect it to be me. Why would someone like Charles—handsome, famous, and wealthy Charles—be dating someone like me?

"You know Charles?" I gripped my knee with one hand to still the sudden tremor in my leg.

"Not well. I only know he's the biggest pompous ass on campus." Richard reached out and gently pried my hand from my knee. "Bartos played for one of my student recitals once. Only once, despite the university's desire to promote cross-discipline programs."

"Why?" I allowed my fingers to relax in Richard's warm grip.

"He yelled at my dancers because they wanted to rehearse the piece a few more times than he thought necessary. Made a couple of them cry. Never apologized. I sized him up as a total jerk then and there. Honestly, you're well rid of that egomaniac."

I met Richard's sympathetic gaze. "I thought maybe you couldn't see him dating someone like me because I'm not . . . an artist or famous or anything."

"Are you kidding me? You're far too good for him. He and that blonde in his trio make a better match. Both narcissists. They deserve each other."

"Oh." I was so shocked that I just sat there while Richard continued to hold my hand.

"Seriously, Amy, you can do better." He gave my fingers a squeeze before releasing them.

Just in time, as Sunny dashed into the workroom, her eyes very wide.

"There's been another murder," she said with a quaver in her voice. "Brad came in to update us on the Virts investigation and got a call."

I jumped up and ran out of the workroom with Richard on my heels.

Brad was barking orders into his phone. "Get a full forensics team out to the Fowler place immediately. I don't care how short staffed we are; this is a priority."

"What did you just say?" I grabbed the edge of the desk to steady myself.

Brad ignored me, but the next words he spoke into his cell phone rang in my ears, loud and clear: "And make sure the coroner examines the body before anything is moved."

"Bob Blackstone," I blurted out.

Brad held the phone at arm's length and stared at me. "What?"

"It's probably nothing. I mean, I'm sure it is . . ."

Brad leaned over the counter. "If you know something, tell me."

I released my grip and stepped back, almost falling into Richard, who placed his hand on my shoulder to steady me.

"They had a fight yesterday. Well, not a real fight. But an argument. In the diner."

Brad's gaze bored into me. "A fight? Bob Blackstone and Clark Fowler?"

"Yes, over that old orphanage tragedy. Mr. Fowler was making accusations. Something about Bob's dad and others on the town council at the time covering up the truth."

"Did Blackstone threaten Fowler?" Brad's intense scrutiny made me lean back against Richard, who tightened his grip on my shoulder.

"Well, sort of. Yeah, I guess he did. But I doubt he meant it that way . . ."

"You let me decide that. Clark Fowler is dead, and it doesn't look to be due to natural causes." Brad turned away, speaking into his phone again before glancing back at me. "Others saw this fight?"

"Sure. Bethany and everyone in the diner. Aunt Lydia was there if you need another witness. And Walt Adams and Zelda Shoemaker."

Brad headed for the door, calling over his shoulder, "Stay put, at least until one of my deputies can get the basic details on the diner altercation. Shouldn't take too long, but if you could just wait here for a half hour or so . . ."

"Sure," I said as he headed out the door.

"Looks like we all might have to stay past closing hours today," Richard observed, dropping his hand.

"Well, not you. Or Sunny. You guys weren't at the diner." I pressed my palms against the circulation counter and bent forward. Of all things, to be caught up in another murder investigation. I breathed deeply, trying to calm my racing heart.

Sunny leaned in and covered one of my hands with hers. "We're staying with you, though."

"And I'll make sure you both get home safely. I don't want either one of you to walk on your own, not with this new murder," Richard said.

"Well, I have my car, and the farm is some ways outside of town." Sunny tapped her nails against the counter as she studied us. "But Amy walked. So you should stay long enough to escort her home."

"Happy to." Richard laid his fingers over my other hand.

Facing the prospect of another interview with law enforcement was so daunting, I didn't try to pull away, not even when I caught Sunny's sly smile.

Chapter Thirteen

We were able to leave the library a little before seven, though only after one of Brad's men asked me to detail the incident in the diner three or four times. He probably would've demanded a fifth recounting, but Richard stopped him, stating that he surely had enough information, and anyway, the sheriff and his deputies knew where I lived.

Sunny had closed up the building at six, so I only had to make sure the front door was locked before Richard and I headed toward our homes.

We walked in silence until we reached the final block. "So Fowler was killed last night." Richard was walking so fast that I had to jog to keep up with him.

"Shot in the head, just like poor Doris Virts."

"Which means it might be the same killer." Richard glanced at me. "Can't really see the connection."

"Unless Mr. Fowler was on the right track. About some cover-up, I mean."

"It's possible." Richard stopped and shaded his eyes with one hand. "Is that your aunt on your porch? With the front door standing wide open? Not a smart move these days." He strode off toward the house, leaving me to follow.

"Amy!" Aunt Lydia crossed to the railing and leaned against it, waving her hand. "And Richard. Thank goodness you're both home."

"What's going on?" I moved beside Richard, who had paused at the bottom of the porch steps.

"I'm not sure." Aunt Lydia's skin appeared as thin and fragile as the pods of the honesty plants growing in our garden. For the first time, I could see her true age on her face. "But someone broke into the house while I was out."

Richard bounded up the steps to take Aunt Lydia by the arm. "Did you see them?"

She shook her head. "No, but the door was slightly ajar. And I know I locked it when I left for my garden club meeting."

"Have you gone in?" I climbed the steps and crossed to the front door, peering into the front hall without touching the doorknob.

"Not yet. I was afraid someone might still be inside . . ." Aunt Lydia patted the hand Richard had laid on her arm. "I'm all right. Just didn't want to walk in by myself."

"Can't blame you for that." Richard released her arm and stepped aside. "Have you called the sheriff?"

"Yes, but they're all tied up right now. Said it might be some time before anyone got here." She shot me a questioning look. "Something about another murder?"

I raised my eyebrows. "Zelda hasn't given you the scoop on that yet?"

"No, she was at garden club with me. I just gleaned a few tidbits from things the dispatcher said."

"Clark Fowler." Aunt Lydia swayed slightly, and I grabbed her arm. "Deputy Tucker was in the library when he got the call, and I stupidly mentioned the argument in the diner. That's why I'm late. Had to answer questions again."

Aunt Lydia pressed the back of her hand to her forehead. "What is this world coming to?"

"Do you want me to take a look around?" Richard asked. "I won't touch anything."

"Yes, but I want to come with you. There's no telling what time a deputy will get here, and I can't sit on the porch all night." Aunt Lydia shook free of my grip and turned to follow Richard into the house.

I trailed them, careful not to bump into the half-open door. Everything looked fine in most of the rooms. But the library was another matter. Fortunately, the door stood wide open, so we could step inside without touching anything.

It was clear that the room had been searched, and not by anyone interested in disguising their actions. Drawers hung precariously from the desk, their contents spilled out across the floor. Numerous books had been yanked from shelves and tossed aside. Leather-bound volumes mingled indiscriminately with brightly colored paperbacks in piles on the floor, while the books left on the shelves had tipped and fallen on top of each other.

I put my arm around Aunt Lydia's shoulder. "Don't worry. We'll clean it up."

"Can't touch anything yet." Richard picked his way through the papers, ledgers, and office supplies littering the worn Oriental rug that covered the center of the room. He stood over the desk and stared at an object on the oak top. It was a framed picture—its glass smashed and one end of the frame ripped off, as if someone had been looking for something hidden behind the photograph.

"That's my picture of Paul," Aunt Lydia said. "But it was on one of the bookshelves, not the desk."

"Whoever searched the room must've thought it would make a good place to hide something." Richard pushed the frame to one side with his keys. "But what?"

"I have no idea. It's not like I have any real valuables. And what could you hide in a framed photo?"

"Papers, maybe?" I suggested. "Letters?"

"If this were a movie, it would be a will. But"—Richard pocketed his keys and gave Aunt Lydia a sympathetic look— "this is no movie."

"No, it's all too real." I shivered. Two murders in our quiet small town, and now this? I wanted to flee and huddle on the sofa in the sitting room with a bottle of wine and some mindless television.

Pull yourself together, Amy. Your aunt needs you. She's the one who should be pampered now, not you.

"Let me check the rest of the house," Richard said. "First, the back porch. If nothing's been disturbed, you two can wait there."

I shook my head. "Not sure you should wander around on your own. What if the intruder is still here? Shouldn't we wait for the deputies?"

Richard pushed past us and strode down the hall. "Pretty sure whoever it is has fled by now. If not before your aunt got home. Anyway," he called over his shoulder, "I think your aunt could do with a stiff drink, so let me at least check the kitchen."

Aunt Lydia made protesting noises, but I just tightened my hold on her and led her down the hall. Richard poked his head out of the kitchen and pronounced it all clear, then led the way onto the back porch.

"Here, catch your breath for a moment," he told Aunt Lydia as he helped her into the cushioned wicker chair. He looked up at me. "Maybe Amy can get you some water or something?"

"Sherry." My aunt sat up, her back not touching the chair. "A very large glass, please."

* * *

Richard checked over the rest of the house and pronounced it clear of any "vandals or Visigoths" before two deputies—part-time officers, judging from their lack of full uniforms—showed up.

We were questioned by the younger of the deputies, who'd said his name was Jeff and kept fiddling with his badge as if he couldn't quite believe he was authorized to do anything. The older deputy introduced himself as Martin before heading for the library to collect evidence.

"It wasn't a break-in, though, was it, ma'am?" Jeff asked. "No broken windows or forced doors. Front door left open, but no sign of the lock being tampered with or anything. Seems like someone just walked in."

My aunt rubbed at her temples with her fingers. "I thought I locked up—I really did. But maybe I forgot."

"But wouldn't someone have noticed? I mean, it's the front door. Anyone on the street could've seen the person coming and going." I paced one end of porch, walking in circles around Uncle Andrew's old easel.

Jeff scratched at the light stubble on his chin. "I suspect no one was on the street at the time. Or leastwise, there hasn't been anyone who's come forward to say anything yet, and with us driving up with the sirens and all, you'd think they would have. Of course, we'll knock on doors to double-check that with your neighbors later, but so far, no one's volunteered information."

"And you don't have security cameras." Richard, who was seated on the glider, looked over at me and shrugged. "Don't take that as a slam. I don't either."

"No, I never thought we'd need such a thing." I stopped in front of the easel and crossed my arms over my chest as Richard continued to stare at me.

"I never used to lock my doors, you see." Aunt Lydia sighed. "I only started recently, after Amy kept pestering about it. Perhaps I did forget."

"Looks like it, ma'am. Unless someone other than you or your niece has a key."

Aunt Lydia shook her head. "No, I've never given a key to anyone except Amy."

Richard stood. "You know, while you're here, I think I'll go check my home. It's just next door, and if someone was hitting houses in the neighborhood . . ."

"Good idea," Jeff said. "But don't enter if you see any signs of forced entry, like any doors or windows open. Come get one of us first."

Richard called out, "Back in a minute," as he left the room and strode toward the front door.

"This has been the strangest day," Aunt Lydia said. "First a murder, then this. I guess your department is really stretched."

"We are, ma'am. Truth is, I only get called in when there's a lot going on. I mean, this isn't my full-time job. I work over in Bellville at the feed plant. But I do live in Taylorsford. Wife grew up here."

"Oh, and who is she?"

"Angela Frye, before she married me."

"Ah, one of Roger Frye's grandchildren, I bet. The farmer who worked the old Trask place?"

"Yes, ma'am." Jeff looked up from his small tablet as Martin entered the room. "Find anything?" he asked, pocketing his stylus.

"Can't tell yet. Gathered up some stuff." Martin held up an evidence bag. "But couldn't get any prints off that picture or the desk. Nothing recent, anyway. Looks like our thief used gloves."

"If you find something specific missing, you'll have to let us know," Jeff told my aunt.

"Of course," she replied.

Martin shifted the evidence bag from one hand to the other. "The weird thing is that the thief left some items that seem valuable to me. I mean, if someone was looking to pawn stuff for drugs or something, you'd think they'd have made off with some of those silver frames and candlesticks or that laptop sitting on a side table."

"Appears they were looking for something in particular." I crossed to stand behind Aunt Lydia and gripped the top edge of her chair. "Not stealing whatever they could put their hands on."

I considered this information in light of my recent research. It did match the theory of someone killing people to keep some damning information secret. But why would they search for anything in my aunt's house? As far as I knew, there was no connection between Aunt Lydia and Bob Blackstone or Don Virts. I couldn't think of anything that would link them, unless someone thought Doris had blabbed information about the land deal to Aunt Lydia. But even so, that wouldn't be information that would be written down, and my aunt surely had no other secrets that would elicit this type of break-in.

As far as you know, Amy. I stared down at my aunt's narrow shoulders, which did not touch the back of her chair. *But it seems she hasn't always told you everything . . .*

There was still Kurt Kendrick, a.k.a. Karl Klass—a wealthy man who might have connections to people willing to break into a house just to send a message. Someone who might have the money and connections to hire a professional thief to make a burglary look like an amateur break-in.

I gnawed at my lower lip. It often seemed to come back to Kendrick—a man linked to Aunt Lydia through his friendship with her late husband. A secretive millionaire who'd hinted that he'd been in contact with my uncle without Lydia's knowledge. It was not out of the realm of possibility that he'd asked Andrew to stash incriminating documents or other contraband for him. Maybe, with the sheriff's office snooping around and questioning why his car was at the scene of a crime, he'd sent in a mercenary to retrieve any such evidence. Even if his criminal actions were in his past, exposure of Kendrick's secrets could shine an unwelcome light on his current business activities.

I rolled my shoulders to shake off the shiver that this thought produced. Of course, I was probably being fanciful. But there was something about Kurt Kendrick that lent itself to such imaginings.

"Yeah, appears someone was looking for something specific," Martin said, pulling at his tight shirt collar. He was wearing a wrinkled uniform shirt with jeans and a tie, which I suspected was not something he wore often from the lopsided way it was knotted. "Think we'll head out now if that's all right. Got plenty of photos and other evidence, so you can go ahead and clean up if you want."

"Maybe tomorrow," Aunt Lydia said. "I think for now I want to grab something to eat and just relax in front of the television. But"—she offered the deputies a gracious smile—"thank you so much for your assistance."

"Of course." Jeff bobbed his head. "Happy to help."

"We'll pass all this along to the sheriff and Chief Deputy Tucker," Martin said. "One of them will get back to you as soon as they can."

"No problem." Aunt Lydia rose to her feet, gripping her cane with both hands. "I'll let my niece show you out."

"Just keep a lookout. And lock your doors," Martin said before heading down the hall, his partner on his heels.

I thanked them again, opening the front door. As they stepped onto the porch, I noticed Richard on the steps, waving his keys.

"My house is fine. Still locked tight when I got there, and nothing moved or messed with inside. Looks like the thief wasn't canvassing the neighborhood."

"Good." Jeff tapped his badge. "Just give a call if you notice anything else in the area." He nodded at Richard and me, then headed toward the street.

Martin fished in his shirt pocket and pulled out a business card. "Contact info's on there if you need it, miss. Take good care of your aunt now," he added, pressing the card into my palm before following his partner onto the sidewalk. They headed across the street, obviously following their plan to check in with the neighbors.

"I will, and thanks again," I called after them.

Richard was still standing on the steps. "What a day. I think I need some reinforcement." He looked me over. "Seems you could too. Care for a drink? I have plenty of wine over at the house."

I shook my head. "I should stay here. Can't leave Aunt Lydia alone."

"What was I thinking? Of course you need to stay with her tonight. Rain check, then?"

I examined his face—handsome even in the garish glow of the porch light. I knew I should say no. I didn't need this complication in my life, especially not with everything else that had happened recently. But he had been so helpful and kind to Aunt Lydia . . .

"Okay."

Richard smiled. "Thursday night at eight?"

I took a deep breath. "Okay."

He turned and took the steps two at a time, calling back, "It's a date!"

Oh, God, it was. I walked back into the house, closing the door and throwing the dead bolt with so much force that it rang like a bell.

Chapter Fourteen

The following day, the library was filled with people asking questions—but not about books or research. They were more interested in news about Clark Fowler's murder and details on the incident at my aunt's house.

"I just want to hide in the workroom," I told Sunny after the twentieth time describing the break-in to an inquisitive patron. I sighed, already tired from cleaning up my aunt's library early that morning.

Sunny patted my hand, which was pressed so hard against the top of the circulation desk that my knuckles were blanched. "So do it. I can cover for you."

"I don't know. Feels like throwing you to the wolves."

"Hyenas are more like it. Wolves are actually pretty nice." Sunny grinned.

Trust my nature-loving friend to know that. I returned her smile and straightened. "I'll take your word for it."

"Anyway, that's how it is in towns like this. You haven't lived here that long, but you must've seen how everyone gets into everyone else's business. Speaking of which, I'm glad to hear nothing was taken from your house. Don't think I said that before the deluge of questions this morning."

"Thanks. Yeah, seems like the thief was looking for something but didn't find it. Or, if they did, it was something neither

Aunt Lydia nor I knew existed." I frowned. I certainly hoped my aunt was as innocent as she appeared. It seemed so, since I'd asked some questions as we cleaned and she hadn't said anything that led me to think otherwise.

"Weird. Well, I'm just glad you were both out at the time." Sunny twirled a strand of golden hair around one finger. "I've been trying to convince the grands that they need to lock their doors, but they keep resisting. Maybe this will do it."

"Hopefully."

"Speaking of older relatives—one of yours was in the library yesterday while you were at lunch. With all the other stuff going on, I forget to mention it." Sunny's bright eyes were shadowed under her lowered lashes.

"Oh, who was that?"

"Sylvia Baker."

"Really? Never seen her darken our doors before."

"Me either, but she showed up breathing fire."

I frowned. "Over what?"

"Something to do with the archives. She wanted to be let in to look for some papers or something and was really pissed when I said no." Sunny made a face. "I mean, the sheriff's office hasn't cleared us to allow anyone in yet. Not like I could disobey their order, even for her. But man, was she ever mad."

"You could've pulled stuff."

"Offered, but that wasn't good enough. She just snapped at me and stormed out, saying something about funding." Sunny shrugged. "Which isn't totally her call, whatever she thinks."

"Sadly, that's how Sylvia is—convinced she can run the town just because she owns a lot of property. Anyway, don't worry about saying anything bad about her to me. I've only seen her a few times in recent years. We aren't close, even if we are family."

"I know. I just don't like to be rude. But if anyone deserves it, that woman does."

"For sure."

"And the archive . . . where's my mind?" Sunny pulled an overstuffed manila folder from a nearby shelf and laid it on the desk in front of me. "I forgot to mention that Brad returned this file earlier. Said there wasn't anything of use in it. Not even as much on the orphanage tragedy as he expected."

"Oh?" I opened the folder and gently lifted the brittle newspaper article and set it aside, revealing a short stack of typed town council minutes. I scanned a few pages, noting nothing of interest until the name *Douglas Beckert* caught my eye. A possible connection, since he was Doris Virts's father and had served on the town council in the late 1950s. I picked up that portion of the minutes and read through the section containing his name.

But it was nothing of importance—just a mention of the town reimbursing him for some business he conducted with the Carthage Company on their behalf.

"Nothing useful?" Sunny asked.

"Not so far, but I'll have to dig into it more later when we aren't so busy."

I tapped my fingers against the pitted oak top of the circulation desk. I'd never heard of a Carthage Company operating in the area, but it had probably been out of business for years. I straightened the papers and closed the folder. Maybe Aunt Lydia would know more about it if I could remember to ask her.

As I placed the file back on the shelf that held any pulled archival materials, I glanced over at the front doors. "Uh-oh, there's Zelda, making a beeline for the desk."

"Looks like she's on a mission. Can't believe she doesn't have the whole story yet, but you never know."

Zelda reached the desk, breathing hard. "Hello, dears. Let me just catch my breath." She leaned against the counter. "Have some news for you, Amy, if you have a minute."

I looked her over, noting her flushed cheeks and mussed curls. "Sure. You heard about the break-in and poor Clark Fowler, I guess?"

Zelda fanned her face with one hand. "I did, but this has nothing to do with Clark, tragic as that is. Or the problem at your house. Already talked to Lydia and some others about all that. No, this has to do with our little investigation."

"What investigation?" Sunny asked, widening her blue eyes.

"Oh, it's silly." I shot Zelda a sharp look. "Just some historical stuff Zelda and Walt were looking into. Related to Richard's research."

"Okay." Sunny bit her lower lip. "Didn't mean to pry."

"It's nothing, my dear," Zelda fanned vigorously. "Walt and I are digging into the past for some information Amy thought might prove useful." She stopped her hand in midmotion. "Might even help your little group's effort to halt the subdivision, come to think of it."

Sunny was suddenly all attention. "Really? I'd like to hear more about that."

"Be happy to share if Amy agrees." Zelda glanced at me.

"It's fine," I said. "But maybe we should talk in the workroom. We can leave the door open to keep a lookout for patrons who need assistance."

"Oh, I'll cover the desk," Sunny said. "Just fill me in later."

I thanked her and invited Zelda to walk around the desk and into the workroom.

"So what did you find?" I asked as I pulled the door closed behind us.

156

Zelda perched on one of the stools. "That Clark was right, for one thing. About Eloise and some of the children probably being sick before the mushroom incident, I mean."

"So there might have been another reason for the deaths?" I stopped short as I stepped on a pencil that had rolled from the table onto the floor. Picking up the pencil, I noticed the dust clinging to one of the table legs. The workroom could stand a thorough cleaning. I sighed as I stood up. One more thing that needed to be done . . .

"Possibly." Zelda smoothed her zebra-patterned skirt down over her knees. "I mean, it's just hearsay, but some of the older folks we've talked to remember Eloise Fowler feeling poorly long before she died. Old Mrs. Croft, who worked the drug-store counter back in the day, recalls Eloise buying some stom-ach medications and complaining of nausea and cramps and other problems. Mrs. Croft didn't think much of it at the time, although she says she also noticed that Eloise had lost a consid-erable amount of weight over a few months."

"That is interesting." I tapped the pencil against my palm, my mind racing. Perhaps Daniel Cooper hadn't been the only person to die of poisoning in Taylorsford. But he'd passed away in 1925, and Eloise Fowler and the children hadn't died until more than thirty years later. If Eleanora had left town soon after the trial, she couldn't have been involved in the orphanage case. Which meant maybe there had been someone else who'd wanted Daniel dead and then killed the others. But why? Unless it was a psychopath, of course. A serial killer . . . I banged the pencil against the edge of the table, shattering the lead.

Zelda eyed me for a second before continuing to speak. "And the Reverend Kilpatrick, who's in a nursing home now but still has all his faculties, told us he was concerned over the health of the orphans several months before their deaths. He went out to lead a Bible program that summer and felt many of the children were far too thin. Claims he even questioned Eloise about whether the town leaders had given her enough money for groceries."

I dropped the broken pencil into an old cigar box that held other pens and markers. "Had they?"

"She said so, but who knows? Might have been afraid to say otherwise—worried about offending the town council and losing her job."

"I guess that's possible. I still worry about that." I tried to end this statement with a little laugh, but it came out more as a nervous squeak.

"Oh, don't you fret. Everyone knows you do a great job with hardly any funding."

"Well, not everyone," I said. "By the way, speaking of common knowledge, what do you know about Kurt Kendrick? I guess you heard he's really Karl Klass, Paul Dassin's former ward?"

"Yes, I heard that." Zelda brushed some invisible lint from her dark blouse. "I wasn't terribly surprised, to tell you the truth. That he was not quite who he said he was, I mean. Never did trust the man. He had some business dealings with my late husband, you see."

I stepped closer to her. "Really? What sort of business?"

"Well, you know Steve owned a moving company, right? Anyway, not long before he passed, he took some jobs with Kendrick. He said the pay was incredible for what he had to do."

"Which was?"

"Just transporting a few art pieces, or so Steve claimed. He did say it was different from his usual moving jobs. He had to take more precautions, for one thing. The pieces were packed up in cases with all sorts of protective wraps and such, so he didn't see what they were, but he had to drive extra careful so he didn't jolt them or anything."

"You didn't like it?"

"No, I didn't, because it always seemed like the timing was odd. Late at night or early in the morning. And Steve wasn't allowed to talk about it. Supposedly so no one would try to hijack his truck. I guess the artworks were really valuable, and Kendrick was worried someone would try to steal them. Anyway, Steve moved stuff between Kendrick's gallery in DC and the estate out here. Back and forth, it seemed like." Zelda lifted her shoulders as if shaking off a chill. "It just never felt right to me, is all. Not anything I could put my finger on. And once, when business was bad, he offered Steve a private loan. Said it was to tide us over, but I told Steve *no way*, and that was the end of that."

Zelda leaned forward. "Just between you and me, I've heard that Kurt Kendrick did lend money to others in town, even when the banks refused. Don Virts, for one. He had a bad credit history, and the only way he got his practice set up in town was with a private loan from Kendrick."

I swallowed a swearword. Now here was a smoking gun. If Don had borrowed money, a lot of money, and hadn't repaid it, perhaps Kendrick had sent a message through some hired goon? Maybe killing Doris had been his way of threatening Don to pay? Sending a message that the rest of Don's family would also be at risk unless he coughed up the cash? I shook out my clenched fingers and forced a casual tone. "Aunt Lydia thinks Kendrick must've made his money illegally. His original stake, I mean. She said maybe he's gone straight since then, but she suspects he started out by running drugs."

Zelda nodded. "Wouldn't surprise me, to be honest. Although I'm not sure he's such a choirboy now. Like I said, I always felt there was something not quite right about those deals he struck with my husband. Even Steve seemed a bit nervous, although he liked the money. But he often mentioned that Kendrick's assistants packed guns and looked like thugs."

"Bodyguards or private security, I guess."

"Yes, I suppose." Zelda placed one finger to her chin. "Anyway, Mr. Kendrick was nice enough when Steve died. Sent me a check for work Steve had supposedly done for him right before the accident. I wasn't sure that was the truth, but I wasn't about to look a gift horse in the mouth."

"I can't blame you for that," I said right before a loud bang from the direction of the circulation desk made me jump.

"I demand to see the director!" shouted a man's voice. I spun around and pushed my way through the door, Zelda on my heels.

Dashing out of the workroom, I came face-to-face with a furious Bob Blackstone, who was leaning across the desk, shaking his fist at Sunny.

"What's going on?" I took a deep breath to calm my racing heart. Yes, this was the mayor and basically my boss, but I wasn't going to tolerate anyone bullying my staff. "Mr. Blackstone, there's no need to yell. Whatever your problem, let's discuss it calmly and quietly. This is a library, after all."

"It's you I want to talk to, anyway," Bob replied, lowering his voice and dropping his hand to his side.

"Well, here I am." I lifted my chin to meet his angry gaze.

"Not for long, though, if I have anything to say about it. You're a town employee, you know. You need to watch your mouth and think before you start spreading rumors."

So this was about me mentioning the argument in the diner to Brad. I should've known. "I wasn't relaying any rumors. I just told the chief deputy what I saw."

"And set him and his boys on me. They've been hounding me ever since, practically accusing me of Fowler's murder. I had to call my lawyer to get them off my back."

"If you have nothing to hide, it will be cleared up soon enough," Zelda said, wrinkling her nose as she eyed Bob.

"You stay out of it, Zelda Shoemaker," Bob said. "What are you doing behind the desk, anyway? Sticking your nose in where it doesn't belong, I bet. I know that's your favorite hobby."

"Volunteering," Sunny and I said in unison.

Zelda snorted and stepped out from behind the desk to face off with Bob. "None of your business, Mr. Mayor. What should be your business is this crime wave that's struck our town. Two murders and a break-in within a month? I'd think you'd be concerning yourself with that problem, not harassing young women just trying to do their jobs."

"If they stuck to doing their jobs, everything would be fine. But this one"—he pointed at me—"is too busy throwing innocent people under the bus for crimes they didn't commit. Someone"—he cast another suspicious glance in my direction—"even tried to implicate Mr. Kendrick by saying his car was seen by Ms. Fields near the archives' building the day Doris was killed. But I've gotten word that the sheriff's office looked into it and already exonerated Kendrick. As they will me, soon enough."

I bit the inside of my cheek. So Kurt Kendrick had been cleared of any suspicion. Well, maybe the authorities were convinced, but I wasn't. Not yet.

"And I'm just trying to do my best for this town too," Bob said, "with no thanks from Miss Flower Child over there and her tribe of hippies, or whatever they are, who spend most of their time trying to prevent honest businessmen from conducting legal transactions."

Sunny brushed back her hair with one hand. I couldn't be quite sure, but I thought she thrust up her middle finger as she did so. "If you mean that subdivision project of yours, yes, I do mean to prevent it. As do a lot of other people, and not all of them 'hippies,' as you said. We're holding a protest a couple of days from now on the old Cooper place, by the way. Thought you should know."

Bob flushed as red as a ripe tomato. "Just try it. That's my land. I'll have you arrested as trespassers."

"Not if we stay on the road behind the fence. That's public access. And Mrs. Tucker gave us permission to use the edge of her land that connects with your property. So I don't think you can stop us, Mr. Mayor."

"Jane Tucker, Brad's mom?" I asked, blinking rapidly. Talk about awkward, especially if Brad had to arrest any protesters.

Sunny shrugged. "She supports our movement. Not that surprising. She doesn't want a bunch of houses springing up next door to her family home."

"Truth is, nobody wants all those houses except you, Bob. And whoever is bankrolling you," Zelda said.

"Nobody's bankrolling me," snapped Bob. But he shifted his gaze, looking past Zelda to stare at a "Reading Transforms" poster on the wall behind the desk. "I'm working with developers on the project, but it's just me making any investment."

I'd always heard you could tell someone was lying if they wouldn't look you in the eye, so I was pretty sure this was not the truth. "Whatever the situation, Mr. Blackstone, you really can't blame people for being less than thrilled with your project. A lot of folks think that land should be turned into a park. Something we don't have. Something that would benefit everyone."

Bob turned his intense gaze on me. "Something that would cost money to maintain. A drain on town resources. Just like this library."

Zelda stepped forward and shook her finger at Bob. "You may be the mayor, but you can't make decisions without the town council's approval. So don't be threatening to do anything to this library. You want to see protests, you'd surely see some then, I promise you."

"Don't worry, Zelda. I won't touch your precious library"—he glared at me—"no matter how much I'd like to. But I would appreciate it if town employees stopped suggesting I had anything to do with Clark Fowler's death. That's a damned lie." He yanked down his jacket sleeve so hard, a button popped off and flew onto the circulation desk. Bob grabbed it up before Sunny or I could move. "Didn't like the guy, but I'm no killer, whatever some outsider might think."

Outsider. There it was. Because I wasn't born here. Because I hadn't lived here all my life.

But Bob Blackstone plans to bring in a lot more outsiders, doesn't he? So look him in the eye and smile. I don't care how much your stomach knots up. Don't you dare let him intimidate you.

"I only told Deputy Tucker what I saw and heard. The honest truth. Never claimed I thought you were guilty of anything. That's not for me to say."

"You're right it's not," Bob Blackstone said before turning his glare on Sunny. "As for you and your friends—go ahead and protest. Won't make a damned bit of difference."

Sunny pressed one finger against her lips for a second before replying. "I guess we'll see."

"Yeah, we'll see all right." Bob turned on his heel and strode out of the library.

"How'd he get elected, again?" I asked as the front doors slammed.

"Hell if I know," Sunny replied.

"Laziness." Zelda shook her head. "No one willing to run against him and his family name, and everyone figuring it doesn't matter anyway. No one wanting to step up and fight for change. See what it gets us?"

Sunny thrust back her narrow shoulders. "I'm willing to fight."

Zelda looked her up and down and smiled. "Maybe you should run for mayor next election."

"Maybe I will," Sunny said, her eyes sparkling.

I almost said something about losing my assistant but stopped myself in time. It wasn't such a bad idea, all in all. The town could use someone like Sunny.

"I'll vote for you," Zelda said. "Heck, I'll be your campaign manager, if you want."

"Sounds like a plan," Sunny said. "But first, we have to stop this development."

"No, *first* we have to shelve some books." I pointed at a couple of full book carts. "Unless Zelda wants to be trained to be a real volunteer."

Zelda grinned and patted her curls. "Think I'll run along now. Got a hair appointment."

"Sure you do," I said with a grin of my own. But I quickly sobered as I thought of everything she'd told me. "I do appreciate what you've found out from your interviews. Sounds like some of it might actually tie into current events."

"Could be." Zelda turned to go but paused to look back at Sunny and me. "The thing is, if it does, such knowledge might be dangerous."

Sunny placed her hands on her hips and tossed back her hair. "In my experience, lack of knowledge is what's really scary."

"Spoken like our next mayor," Zelda called out as she headed for the front doors.

"You've done it now," I said as Sunny grabbed one of the full book carts. "Zelda is going to nag you to run for office until you do. And my aunt will probably join the effort."

"I don't mind." Sunny pushed the cart out from behind the desk. "I think it's a brilliant idea. Don't you?"

"I think I'd better start looking for a new library assistant," I said.

Chapter Fifteen

Dragging myself home after work that Thursday, I considered calling Richard and cancelling our eight-o'clock date. I wasn't in the mood to make small talk or deal with anything that required being pleasant. But I'd made the mistake of mentioning Richard's invitation to Aunt Lydia, so I was stuck. If I didn't go over to his house and visit for at least an hour, I'd never hear the end of it.

"Is that what you're wearing?" Aunt Lydia examined me and pursed her lips.

"Sure, why not?" I'd thrown on an old pair of jeans and a worn *NSYNC concert T-shirt. Battered sneakers completed my ensemble.

Disapproval wrinkled Aunt Lydia's brow. "It's a bit . . . inelegant."

"Well, Richard's seen me in my gardening outfit, so this is a step-up."

"I just thought perhaps that lovely little sundress . . ."

No, no, and no. I knew which dress she meant. The one she'd bought for me because she'd said the peach fabric went perfectly with my coloring. The one with the low-cut neckline that made me look more like a waitress at Hooters than a librarian.

"I don't think it's that kind of get-together." I glanced in the mirror hanging over the front hall sideboard and tucked my shoulder-length hair behind my ears, displaying the gold and coral earrings Aunt Lydia had given me for my birthday. "Besides, I'm wearing nice jewelry. That elevates the ensemble, as the fashionistas say."

Aunt Lydia tapped her cane against the hardwood floor. "I don't believe the earrings accomplish quite as much as you think."

"It will have to do. I'm late as it is."

"Very well, if you can't be bothered to look nice, I suppose I can't be bothered to worry about it." My aunt lifted her cane and waved it at me. "But you'd better not run back home in a minute or two, or I'll know you didn't make any effort at all."

I walked to the front door and paused, patting my pocket to make sure I had my keys. "Really, Aunt Lydia, this is just a friend thing. You know, good neighbors and all that. Don't try to marry me off to the poor guy." I opened the door and stepped onto the porch. "And don't forget to lock up behind me."

Aunt Lydia met me at the door. "You don't have to keep reminding me. Not that feebleminded yet." She fiddled with the doorknob for a second before looking me right in the eye. "And Amy?"

"Yes?" I said as she pulled the door almost shut.

"He'd be lucky to get you."

The lock clicked, and the dead bolt slid into place. I stared at the door for a moment before shaking my head and making my way down the porch steps.

The evening air was warm and laced with the scent of the roses that draped the fence between our two houses. I walked the short distance slowly, considering how I should react if Richard decided this was actually a serious date and not just a casual get-together.

But why would he? It was true that he'd flirted with me—I wasn't so ignorant I couldn't see that. But perhaps he flirted with every woman of a certain age.

And maybe he just wanted a friend in a town where he, like me, was considered an outsider.

I squared my shoulders and swiftly climbed the steps of his front porch. Pressing the doorbell, I decided I was going to enjoy this evening, talking with a neighbor. Making a friend. I could use a few more of those myself.

Besides, I had Zelda's information to share.

Richard opened the door. I was instantly grateful for my instinct to wear something low key. He was dressed casually as well, in a loose gray T-shirt and some type of black workout pants. His feet were bare.

Yes, casual, just like me. Although he looked *good*.

Far too good for your own good . . .

"Hello, come in," he said, waving me inside. "Hope you don't mind just some snacks with the wine. I planned to make something but got called to campus to cover a studio today."

"No problem." I followed him into the living area of his front room. "I've eaten dinner, so I don't need much."

"You're in luck, because it isn't much. Just crackers and cheese to go with the wine. Have a seat." Richard gestured toward the sofa.

I settled into the soft cushions with relief. It had been a long day, and I'd been on my feet for most of it.

Richard hovered near the sofa for a moment, adjusting the placement of a tray full of various cheeses and crackers before straightening and looking at me. "Now, white or red?"

He clutched his hands together at his chest. A tense gesture. Surely he wasn't nervous?

No, come on, Amy. This guy has probably had women lined up ever since he was a preteen.

"White is fine. I like both, but in summer . . ."

"Yeah, lighter in the heat. Okay, just a minute. Be right back." Richard left the room so fast, I almost laughed.

He really was nervous. Which was hilarious—and terrifying.

I wasn't sure I wanted him to care so much. And yet, I wasn't sure I didn't.

Which was what really scared me.

I sank down into the sofa, hunching my shoulders. If I were smart, I would get up and leave now. That would be the safest option, all in all.

"Here you are." Richard returned with two full glasses. He handed me one and sat next to me.

"Thanks." I took a long swallow of my wine, not looking at him.

"Glad you could come by. To be honest, I get a bit tired of spending evenings alone."

"Guess that's one disadvantage of living out here. Hard to arrange casual get-togethers with campus colleagues or friends." I took another deep drink, then frowned as I held up my wine and realized I'd already downed half the glass.

"I don't mind that. I see those people enough when I'm at Clarion. It's nice to escape to a totally different environment, to tell you the truth."

I glanced over at him, noticed that he was studying me, and took another swig of my drink. "So I never really found out what happened with your fiancée," I said after what felt like minutes of silence. "Not that it's any of my business . . ."

"Oh, it's fine." Richard set down his wine glass and leaned back against the sofa. "It was for the best. Meredith—that's her name, by the way—came to her senses before I did, that's all. She was a dancer too."

"I thought that might be the case." I placed my now-empty glass on the coffee table.

"More?" Richard asked.

I shook my head.

He tipped his chin, staring at the ceiling. "Two dancers who met during a summer tour with a company. Not a new story." Richard lifted his left arm and placed it across the back of the sofa, right behind my head.

"You knew each other for how long?" I slid forward to grab a slice of cheddar and a cracker.

"Three years. Yeah, I know. Should've figured out we weren't right for each other sooner, but"—Richard sighed—"we were always on tour. Or I was teaching or off on some choreography gig. We rarely lived together in one place. Never shared an ordinary, everyday life."

I glanced over at him. "And that was a problem?"

"Yes, apparently." Richard grabbed up his drink and took a long swallow before absently swirling the wine in the glass.

"So what happened?"

"Reality." Richard shrugged. "Meredith was upset when I agreed to take the position at Clarion. Got the news around January, and she was gone a week later. After she unsuccessfully tried to talk me out of accepting the job. I argued that I loved teaching and wanted to concentrate on that and choreography, but she thought I was making a mistake. Didn't understand why I would give up performance opportunities while I was still young enough to dance. Asked me why I wouldn't build on what little fame I had to keep performing now and wait to teach later."

"From what I hear, you had more than a little fame."

Richard took another drink before answering. "Of a sort. I mean, I'm fairly well known in the dance world. But I'm not a household name or anything."

"Few dancers are."

He cast me a warm smile. "True. Anyway, right after I accepted the position at Clarion, Meredith took off for New York to dance in an off-Broadway show. Said it would only be a few months. Then I got the call, though not from her. From a mutual friend who'd attended her spur-of-the-moment wedding to an old flame. An old flame who *is* a household name." Richard finished off his wine and set the glass down with enough force to rattle the wooden coffee table. "That's when I realized what Meredith had known before she left—that she didn't want to settle down in some little university town. She didn't want the dance instructor; she wanted the performer, the guy who could get her into parties, the 'name' she could flaunt to her friends in the know. Unfortunately for her, that's only part of who I am. A part that I am less and less interested in. But apparently it was the only part she wanted."

"Sorry." As I sat back, I realized I was leaning against his arm. "Sorry," I said again and slid forward.

"You don't have to move."

I looked over at him, noting his pensive expression before settling back against his arm. "You're better off in the long run. Breaking up before the wedding is a lot easier than after."

"No question. I lucked out. Meredith and I weren't a good match. Just like you and that Bartos guy. Not compatible in the long run. And it certainly *is* better to know the truth sooner rather than later. Anyway"—he turned his body slightly until he was leaning over me—"I'm glad you're single. Makes things simpler for me."

I scrunched into the corner of the sofa. "Simpler how?"

"Not having to compete with some other guy. Unless I've totally misread the situation, of course."

"No, but . . ." I straightened, determined not to let his proximity unnerve me. "Well, you hardly know me. We've just met."

"True, but"—he reached out and gently tapped my lips with two fingers—"the spark is there. At least for me."

I considered lying and rejected that tactic immediately. We were always going to be neighbors. And no matter what happened, I also wanted us to be friends. "Yes, there is something. But"—I scooted to the front edge of the sofa—"I might want things to move a bit slower."

He sat back, his gray eyes examining me in a way that made my fingers twitch. "Fair enough. I can be patient. And hopefully our little research projects will give us time to get better acquainted."

"I do have some news to share. About the past, I mean." I stood and crossed to the bookcase and studied the short row of archival boxes for a moment before turning to meet Richard's interested gaze.

"Something related to the murder trial?"

"Not exactly. But it does put that whole orphanage tragedy in a new light." I described the information Zelda had shared with me. "I mean, it doesn't necessarily tie in with the Cooper case, although I have wondered if there could possibly be a connection. Some type of serial killer who only strikes every decade or so? Okay, that's a stretch, but Zelda's information might have some bearing on the recent murders. What if Clark Fowler was on the right track and that's why he was killed?"

"Yeah, that confrontation in the diner." Richard lifted his shoulders at my look of surprise. "I put two and two together from what you told Brad. Didn't seem like the mayor would get so worked up over some guy's comments unless they'd hit a nerve. I figured there might be a grain of truth in Fowler's claims."

"Hmm . . . you seem to be taking to this small-town 'everyone is into everyone else's business' thing rather well."

He grinned. "I'm a quick study."

I had to fight my urge to run back to the sofa, drop down beside him, and give into what I knew in my heart I really wanted.

But . . . *You promised to be more careful after last time, Amy.*

I strolled over to the edge of his dance floor instead. "Did Sunny also tell you about the protest planned for tomorrow? It will be right next door."

He rose to his feet. "She did. I don't mind. Might even have joined in, but I won't be around. Have to go into the city for a physical."

He crossed the room to stand in front of me.

"Really? Wouldn't think you'd need one. You look like you're in pretty good shape." I bit the inside of my cheek when I noticed his amused expression.

"It's for insurance. For the new job. It'll be blood tests and the whole lot. A pain, but what can you do?"

Standing there in a casual pose that was still somehow elegant, Richard exuded an energy that made heat rise up the back of my neck. I turned away and focused on the smooth expanse of dance floor. "I hope you realize this is going to make it difficult for you to sell this place in the future."

"Not a problem. I have no intention of ever selling this house." He circled around until he was facing me again.

I crossed my arms over my chest. "You might meet someone who wants to live elsewhere."

Richard leaned in, brushing my jawline with the back of one hand. "I doubt it. The girl I have my eye on would probably be happy to stay in Taylorsford. She has family here."

"This isn't exactly what I meant by slowing down."

Richard moved away, crossing the room in a few graceful strides. "I think we need some music."

"For what?" I walked over to the wall of mirrors but kept my eye on Richard as he fiddled with the controls on the sound system.

"Dancing, of course." He turned around and held out his arms. "Best way to get to know someone."

"Oh, no"—I leaned back against the polished wooden barre and grabbed it with both hands, locking myself in place—"that's not happening."

Music filled the room. Some type of Latin dance music.

He walked toward me. No, not walked. Even though it was just simple steps, his movements turned it into a dance.

I tightened my grip on the barre. "I'm hopeless at it."

"What, dancing? Nonsense."

Words floated over the music. *Sway with me . . .* I knew this song. My parents had taken ballroom dance lessons once and cha-chaed to that tune. But their version had been sung by a woman—Rosemary Clooney. This was someone else.

I allowed my mind to dwell on this puzzle, distracting from the sight of Richard closing in on me while executing moves that were perfectly matched to the music.

And sexy. Far too sexy.

"Michael Bublé," I announced.

"Do you mind? I have a dance mix on the playlist. This just came up first."

Sure it had. Like those words didn't matter.

"No, but . . ." I shrank back as Richard reached me. "I really can't dance. Seriously."

Richard glanced down. "Your foot is tapping."

It was. I pressed my toes into the sole of my shoe before I looked up into his face. "It's the music."

"It's your body's response to the music. You should trust that, you know." Richard placed his hands on my hips. "You want to move, you know you do. So move. Who's looking?"

"You," I said but dropped my grip on the barre.

"And I don't care, so . . ." He pulled me onto the floor.

I grabbed him just to keep from tripping. He grinned and gently lifted my hands, placing one on his shoulder and the other at his waist.

"Now just follow my lead."

"I'll step on your feet."

"No, you won't."

He guided me in a simple circle around the floor. Nothing fancy—just steps forward and back and an occasional glide. It was really almost as easy as walking. I caught myself swaying slightly to the music.

"See"—Richard pulled me closer—"you can do it, if you just stop worrying about what you look like or what anyone else thinks."

As his lean body pressed against mine, I felt warmth envelop me like water in a heated pool. He dipped me slightly, and the muscles of his thigh rippled against my hip. I gasped and stumbled.

He caught me and set me on my feet as the song died away, only to be replaced with something equally seductive but much slower. "There you go, overthinking again," he whispered in my ear.

I forced myself to stand completely still. "This playlist, you've used it before, haven't you?"

"No"—his fingers caressed my skin, sliding from my ear to the hollow of my throat as he met my questioning gaze—"but I did create it earlier today. Deliberately, I confess."

"To seduce me?"

"Yes. Is it working?"

I knew I should tell him no, but that was a lie. "Maybe."

His smile lit up the room. "Good. Now just one kiss, and I will stop. I don't want to move too fast either. I just want to . . . pique your interest."

I couldn't help but smile in return. "Oh, is that what you call it? Hook the fish, then give it some line?"

"Exactly." He placed his hands on either side of my face, cupping my chin in his palms. "But only in the case of a very special fish, worth the time it takes to reel it in."

His lips were inches from mine. I dug my toes into my sneakers and locked my knees to prevent them from buckling. "Have you caught a lot of fish this way?"

"A few. But ended up throwing them back. Don't think I'll want to do that this time."

I pressed my palms against his chest, trying vainly to maintain some sort of equilibrium. "You can't know that yet."

"I know," Richard said and leaned in to kiss me.

Just like with the dancing, despite my best intentions, I couldn't resist. My arms slid around him, allowing him to pull me so close I could feel his heart rapidly beating against my chest. I moaned softly as my lips opened up under his. It was a terrible betrayal by my own body.

And totally, absolutely wonderful.

When he released me, I just stood there like an idiot for a moment.

"Well, that seals it," Richard said, tapping my nose. "Keeping this fish for sure."

I probably did look like a carp as I opened my mouth and closed it again without saying anything.

"Now, more wine? I promise we can sit and discuss the driest possible historical research like two platonic friends for the rest of the evening."

"Um, no, I'd better go," I said when I finally found my voice. "I appreciate the wine and cheese and . . . everything, though." I forced a feeble smile and dashed across the room.

Richard followed, meeting me at the front door. "Didn't mean to chase you off. I really do want to honor your request to slow things down." He traced my lips with one finger. "It's just—well, I can't seem to help myself where you're concerned. And that scares me too. Because it's never happened before. I've always been the one in charge, in control."

I met his searching gaze and read the honesty in his eyes. "You haven't done anything wrong. Nothing at all." Throwing caution to the winds, I leaned forward and kissed him before opening the door. "Reel me in, mister, but just allow me a little play on the line."

He laughed as I stepped onto the porch. "Absolutely. Anything for such a prize catch," he called after me as I skipped down his stairs and onto the sidewalk.

Aunt Lydia was waiting in the sitting room when I entered the house. She'd obviously nodded off in front of the television but straightened and rose slowly to her feet when I popped in to say goodnight.

"You had a good time?"

My lips still tingled from the memory of Richard's kisses. "Yes, very nice." I kept my tone light and headed swiftly for my upstairs bedroom.

Aunt Lydia thumped her way over to the foot of the staircase. "So what did you two talk about?"

"Fishing," I said, then bounded up the steps before she could ask anything else.

Chapter Sixteen

Sunny had begged off work the next day—a Friday, fortunately, which meant the library closed at five o'clock. She claimed she needed to organize and attend the protest, so I was stuck working to the end of the day and locking up the library.

By the time I got home, cars blocked the road beyond Richard's house. I spied Brad Tucker's cruiser and assumed he was in charge of security.

I dropped off my purse in the house and confirmed that Aunt Lydia was not home before heading back outside. Walking past Richard's house, I stepped into the midst of the protest.

It was as calm as I would expect of anything Sunny had organized. Her group, holding up signs condemning the development or asking that the land be preserved as a town park, were clustered off to one side. Facing them, Brad Tucker and some other deputies stood quietly, not making any moves to stop their chanting.

I spied Aunt Lydia standing next to Zelda and Walt and made a beeline to join them.

"Hey," I said. "How's it going?"

"Peacefully, so far," Walt said. "Both sides remaining civil."

"Good." I slid between him and Aunt Lydia. "Strange, I don't see Sunny."

"She was here earlier," Zelda said, "but she slipped away for a bit."

"Probably just needed food or a bathroom break," Walt said. "I think she's been here since early morning, so that's understandable."

"Well, sure." I turned to Aunt Lydia. "You doing okay?"

"Just fine," she said, but she laid her hand on my arm and leaned into me.

A breeze wafted over us, carrying the scent of orchard grass and honeysuckle. I gazed out over the fields beyond the low fieldstone wall separating the edge of the road from the old Cooper farm.

I pictured Daniel Cooper working those fields with his mule and plow. Would he have wanted a mass of houses springing up in his fields like toadstools instead of his carefully cultivated crops? I didn't think so.

As I surveyed the crowd, I noticed Sylvia Baker standing off to one side between the deputies and the protestors. That was odd. I wondered why she'd shown up. It wasn't like her to mix with the townsfolk except when she was lobbying for something.

Of course, if she was a silent partner in Bob Blackstone's development project, her presence would be more understandable. I narrowed my eyes and studied the tall slender figure with her cap of silver hair. She wore a linen pantsuit that probably cost more than my monthly salary.

"Uh-oh," Zelda said. "Here comes trouble."

I turned and glanced in the direction of her pointed finger. A large black sedan had pulled up behind Brad's cruiser.

Bob Blackstone stepped out of the sedan along with a white-haired man in a navy pinstripe three-piece suit. A moment later, Don Virts appeared, climbing out of the back seat of the car.

They approached us, walking three abreast.

"The law and the profits," Walt said.

It took me a moment to catch his play on words. "Oh, yeah, absolutely," I said, giving him a smile.

Brad Tucker pushed his way through the crowd, adjusting his hat to the proper angle. "Can we help you, Mayor Blackstone?"

Bob pulled a cloth handkerchief from his pocket, pressed it under his nose, and sniffed loudly. "Yes, you can disperse this crowd."

"Afraid I can't." Brad surveyed Bob and the other men, his expression sympathetic but implacable. "These people are within their rights to protest. They're on public land or have permission from the landowner to gather here. I'm afraid I can't do anything but make sure no one engages in illegal activities."

Don clutched his arms against his narrow chest. "Don't seem to be doing much about that from where I stand."

Brad pushed his hat away from his forehead. "These people have the right to protest, Dr. Virts. I have no authority to stop them."

"My lawyer may have something to say about that." Bob Blackstone motioned for the white-haired man to step forward. "We have an injunction."

"Can't see what that would be based on." Brad shifted from foot to foot, obviously uncomfortable with this turn of events.

"The law, obviously." Bob drew up to his full height, dwarfing Don, who stood next to him. "Now I know you'd prefer not to hear this, given your girlfriend's involvement, but we can prove that this is an illegal assembly."

Brad scratched at the back of his neck. "I don't have a girlfriend, and how can you prove that?"

The white-haired man stepped forward, waving some papers. "Mr. Blackstone owns this land and is entitled to evict trespassers."

"But the protesters aren't on his land. They are standing on public access property, or fields owned by someone else, who has given them permission to be here," Brad said.

"Ah, but"—the lawyer flourished his sheaf of papers once again—"we have proof that the property lines are incorrect, and instead of standing on Mrs. Clifton Tucker's property, some of them are occupying my client's land."

I released Aunt Lydia's arm and moved forward as all eyes turned toward Brad and Bob. "That can't be true," I said. "There are land plats in the library archives showing all the original property lines. Nothing's changed for decades, so if this was ever in dispute, why wait until now to say so, Mr. Mayor?"

"Once again, this is none of your business, Amy Webber." Bob Blackstone's glare was so fierce, it made me stumble backward. Walt stepped up to grab my arm and steady me as we rejoined Aunt Lydia and Zelda.

Brad cast me a grateful smile before turning his attention back on the mayor. "As Amy says, that's ridiculous. My family has owned this land for generations. We know where our property lines are drawn."

"Apparently not," snapped Bob Blackstone. He yanked down his jacket sleeves before continuing in a smoother tone. "I had another survey done just recently. Seems your family has been encroaching on my property for some time."

If Bob hoped to rattle Brad, he had miscalculated. The chief deputy straightened and stared down at the mayor. "Doesn't matter. I'll just ask some of the protesters to move to the side of the road so they are off what you claim as your land, and they will still be within their rights."

Bob's heavy eyebrows knitted together. "I want them gone."

"Can't do it," Brad said.

I looked at him with new admiration. Whatever his faults, it was clear Brad Tucker was a stickler for protecting civil liberties.

Don Virts stepped forward until he was standing toe-to-toe with Brad. "So you'll protect these troublemakers but not a law-abiding citizen? You didn't have any trouble harassing me about my own mother's death. And for your information, I think I know what really happened in that case."

"If you do, you should make a report at the office, not here." Brad took two steps back, clenching and unclenching his hands as if fighting the urge to punch Don.

"It was some drifter," Don continued as if Brad hadn't spoken. "I ran into him a few days before my mom's murder, hanging around the back door to the office. Looking for drugs, I suspect. Asked for a handout, but I chased him off, and he threatened me. Said he'd find a way to make me pay for refusing him." Don lifted his chin and stared up at Brad with a belliger-ent expression on his foxlike face. "There's your murderer, I bet. My mom and Clark Fowler too. Probably asked for money from both of them and got angry when they said no."

"That would be convenient," Brad admitted. "But why didn't you tell us about this drifter before?"

"Didn't think of it. I get a lot of bums hanging around the office. They know dentists have drugs on hand, you see. Didn't even connect it until just today."

Brad tapped his boot against the gravel surface of the road. "Well, you'd best come into the office and make a full report. But that, interesting as it may be, has nothing to do with what's happening today."

Bob Blackstone turned his gaze from Brad to glower at me and my companions. "And of course, the rumormongers are out in full force. I suggest you double-check their information before you act on it next time, Deputy Tucker. If you don't want a lawsuit filed against the county, I mean."

Brad shot a quick glance in my direction. "The sheriff's office doesn't work off of rumors, Mr. Mayor. We had solid evidence of your confrontation with Clark Fowler."

"And now you also have my solid alibi for the night he was killed."

"Yes." Brad drew out the word as if he was reluctant to agree. "It seems to check out."

"It was that drifter," piped up Don Virts. "Just you wait and see."

"That's neither here nor there"—Brad crossed his arms and stared down his nose at the three men in front of him—"in terms of this protest. So why don't you gentlemen climb back into your car and head over to the sheriff's office, where you can make whatever statements you wish to make."

"I want you to take a look at this first." Bob motioned toward his lawyer, who was still clutching the pile of documents.

"All right, but let's move out of the way." Brad strode toward Bob's car, forcing Bob and his entourage to follow him.

As the four men huddled together, staring at the paper work, a voice rang out behind me.

"Nice to see you again, Amy."

I spun on me heel to face the speaker.

Kurt Kendrick, who seemed to have materialized from nowhere but must've been simply hidden amid the crowd of onlookers, brushed back the thick fall of white hair from his forehead, smiled at me, and nodded at Zelda and Walt before allowing his gaze to rest on my aunt. "Hello, Lydia. It's been a long time."

My aunt's face blanched pale as a calla lily, but her extended hand was rock steady. "Quite true, Karl. Although I suppose I must call you Kurt."

Kendrick clasped Aunt Lydia's hand for only a second before dropping it. "As it's my legal name now, that's probably best."

"Surprising to find you here of all places, Mr. Kendrick. Wouldn't think an environmental protest would be your thing." Dwarfed by Kurt Kendrick's height, Zelda had to tip her head back to look up at him.

"Well, I'm actually more concerned about Paul Dassin's legacy." Kendrick ignored my aunt's loud sniff of disapproval as he focused on Zelda. "I'm sure he would've hated the idea of a subdivision. No doubt he would prefer this land to become a town park named in honor of Daniel Cooper. What do you think, Mrs. Shoemaker?"

"I didn't really know the man well, but I suppose you're right." Zelda glanced up at Walt. "Did you ever meet Mr. Dassin, dear?"

Walt shook his head. "Saw him around town occasionally, but I didn't know him. I was so busy with work back then, and he seemed to keep to himself."

Aunt Lydia fixed Kurt Kendrick with her most imperious gaze. "He was a homebody. And rather depressed in his later years. Especially after you left town and never bothered to communicate with him again, Karl."

I studied the rigid set of her jaw. She wasn't going to forgive Paul's former ward. Not any time soon, anyway.

"I'm sorry for that, but I had my reasons."

"No doubt." Aunt Lydia looked Kendrick up and down. "So now you want to protect his legacy? Well, better late than never, I suppose," she said before turning her back on him to speak with Zelda and Walt.

As the protestors' chants mingled with other side conversations, I coughed to draw Kendrick's laser-sharp glare off my

184

aunt. "So you support the efforts to fight the development, Mr. Kendrick?"

"Please, call me Kurt." He flashed me a toothy smile. "Yes, I do. I suppose I should actually have a word with Ms. Fields at some point since she's the primary organizer of the protests."

My stomach lurched as I remembered the information that Aunt Lydia and Zelda had shared concerning this man. If Kendrick *was* involved in shady deals and had criminal connections, he might also have a dangerous motive for seeking out Sunny. It was impossible to read his mood in his carefully composed face, which just made me more nervous. Sure, maybe he did want to talk to Sunny, but not about her environmental causes. She was the only eyewitness to his black Jaguar being at a murder scene, after all. Despite receiving clearance from the sheriff's office, he might still have an interest in silencing any future testimony.

"I don't think I'd try that today," I said. "She's pretty busy. Maybe stop by the library sometime next week, when we can both chat with you."

Kendrick looked down at me, his blue eyes shadowed under his pale lashes. "Of course. A much more sensible plan. I'll do that. Although it won't be next week. I must leave the country tomorrow for a buying trip, and I'll be gone for quite some time."

He looked away, and I followed his gaze to the men clustered around Brad. As if he sensed someone staring at him, Don Virts turned his head and took two awkward hops backward.

With Kurt Kendrick examining him like predator eyeing his next meal, Don's expression betrayed an emotion that raised the hair on my arms. It was fear, pure and simple.

Zelda's words came back to me. Don had borrowed money from Kendrick. Had he ever repaid it? Or had Doris been murdered for a debt her son couldn't repay?

Think about it, Amy. Or maybe it was two different killers. One person who murdered Doris to send Don a message, and then Don himself killing Clark so there wouldn't be any more issues with Bob Blackstone's development deal. A deal that might provide its investors, including Don, enough money to pay off old debts.

A swearword escaped my lips.

Aunt Lydia turned to face Kendrick and me. "Everything okay, Amy?"

"Sure, just stepped on a sharp rock," I replied, lifting my foot. "Thin soles, not made for gravel roads."

She looked me over before lifting her chin and staring at Kendrick. "So Kurt—as I suppose I must call you—are we to see more of you around town now? Have you decided to grace Taylorsford with your presence after isolating yourself for several years?"

"Perhaps, although I don't live here most of the time. And I must travel quite a bit for my work."

"Oh, yes, buying and selling art now, aren't you? Not what I would've expected, if I'm honest. But I hear you've made quite a tidy sum." Aunt Lydia tipped her head to one side as she examined him. "Pity Andrew never lived to see you succeed in the art world."

"Yes, that is a pity." Kendrick looked over her head as he spoke, his expression blank.

But if I could hear the anger rumbling under his words, so could Aunt Lydia. She straightened and thrust back her shoulders. "He talked about you for many years, you know. Wondering where you'd gone and if you were okay. His best friend, who just disappeared one day without a good-bye. But I must tell you—eventually he just stopped mentioning your name. I guess he finally forgot you."

"Perhaps he did." When Kendrick turned his gaze back on Aunt Lydia, his eyes blazed blue as the heart of a flame. "Perhaps that was for the best."

Aunt Lydia didn't even blink. "I certainly thought so."

I examined my aunt and the art dealer. They would've made a beautiful couple—both tall and handsome with distinctive features set off by their white hair and blue eyes. But the gaze they fixed on one another didn't look friendly. No, not at all. In fact, it resembled a mongoose staring down a cobra.

The three of us stood in uncomfortable silence until a loud "No" rang through the air.

"I'm not leaving without speaking my piece." Bob Blackstone strode toward the protestors, leaving Brad, Don, and the lawyer behind.

"Think I'll head out," Kendrick said. "Nice to see you again, Amy." He walked away without speaking to Aunt Lydia again.

As Kurt Kendrick mingled with the crowd clustered near the trees, Bob Blackstone faced off with the protestors. "Now listen here, you lot," he shouted over their chants, "I have something you need to hear."

They quieted down, lowering their signs. "All right," said one young woman. "Say what you're going to say."

While Bob outlined the merits of his development to the skeptical crowd, his lawyer and Don Virts stayed back at his car and consulted their phones. So much for his backup.

I glanced over at Sylvia, wondering if she would join Bob Blackstone or stay silent. But she remained at the edge of the crowd. In fact, she was also on her cell phone, chatting away. Some business matter, probably.

As I watched, Sunny strolled out of the woods that rimmed the Tuckers' farm. I assumed she'd probably stopped in at Brad's mother's house to rest or use the facilities. Head down, she walked up behind Sylvia and paused.

Sylvia grimaced and gesticulated with her free hand, leading me to surmise she was arguing over some contentious deal. Then as if sensing a presence behind her, she turned on Sunny with a furious expression. Sunny backed away, obviously apologizing.

"Uh-oh," I told Aunt Lydia. "Looks like Sunny's getting an earful."

"Sunny can handle herself," Aunt Lydia said, but she frowned as my assistant jogged over to meet us.

"Hey," I said with a smile.

Sunny didn't smile in return, which was odd. She twisted a lock of her hair around her finger and muttered a quiet "Hello."

Aunt Lydia laid her hand on Sunny's arm. "Sorry, I saw you were being harangued by my cousin. I hope she wasn't too rude."

"No, no, it isn't that." Sunny glanced from side to side as if determining who was nearby. "I just . . ." Stopping short as footsteps crunched through the gravel behind us, she gazed at the protestors. "Is that the mayor?"

"Yep, and it looks like your friends are getting a bit tired of his pontificating," Walt said. "Can't say I blame them."

"The mayor has some good points," said a cool voice.

I turned around. "Hello, Sylvia. Surprised to see you here."

"I do live in Taylorsford." She adjusted the leaf-patterned silk scarf at her neck.

"Occasionally," Zelda muttered.

I thought Sylvia might react to that, but she just tugged down the sleeves of her jacket.

"Sorry, we cut you off. What were you saying?" I asked my friend.

Sunny brushed back her hair but kept her hand up as if to block her face from scrutiny. "I'll tell you later. Need to rejoin my group." Her stack of bangle bracelets jingled merrily as she waved her arm in the direction of the protestors. Before she turned away, her gaze swept over Aunt Lydia, Zelda, Walt, and me. Strangely, she avoided glancing at Sylvia.

They probably had exchanged some choice words when she'd walked up behind my cousin. I knew how sharp Sylvia's tongue could be and how little of such treatment Sunny would gracefully endure.

Once Sunny rejoined her friends, she led them in chanting louder protests against the mayor, who finally stopped talking and backed off.

Muttering something that sounded like obscenities, Bob Blackstone strode down the road to rejoin his lawyer and Don Virts, who were now leaning against the hood of the black sedan.

Zelda gave Sunny the thumbs-up gesture and shouted, "You go, girl! Stand up to the man!"

Aunt Lydia looked at Walt and smiled. "Still the same old Zelda."

"Yes, isn't it wonderful?" Walt replied.

I studied my aunt and her old friends for a moment. It was good to see that Aunt Lydia would never truly be alone, no matter what happened.

And what do you think is going to happen, Amy?

I shook my head. Nothing, of course. And even if it did, I would be right next door . . .

No, I couldn't think like that. I had to let things play out without a lot of useless dwelling on what-ifs.

I was happy to be distracted when my cell phone buzzed in my pocket.

It was a message. From Richard.

Need to stop by tonight to talk to you both, it said.

So much for abandoning my tendency to overthink things. I took a deep breath and plastered a smile on my face. As Zelda began to chant along with the protestors, I moved to her side and joined in, much to the amusement of Walt and my aunt.

Chapter Seventeen

I changed my top three times before deciding on a white peasant blouse trimmed with vibrant embroidery.

It was the best match for my favorite pair of shorts, which were rust-red cotton with a wide elastic band at the top. They were comfortable without looking sloppy, which meant I wouldn't get the side-eye from Aunt Lydia.

Glancing in the antique standing mirror that filled one corner of my bedroom, I also admitted that the shorts showed a good bit of leg. I grinned. Something else that would please my matchmaking aunt. I slid my feet into a pair of open-backed sandals, noticing as I moved that the peasant top revealed more cleavage than I'd planned.

I turned to grab another blouse from the wardrobe as the doorbell chimed, and Aunt Lydia yelled, "Richard's here."

Shoving my hair behind my ears, I left the bedroom without changing my blouse. I reached the top of the staircase just as Aunt Lydia ushered Richard into the house.

"I'm thinking sitting room," she said as she led him down the hall. "More comfortable, and you look like you've been through the wringer today."

Richard glanced up as I clattered down the stairs. "Hi, Amy."

"Hi." A sudden wave of shyness made my greeting come out as a squeak.

His gaze swept over me, lingering on my bust and legs. "Nice outfit," he said with a wink.

Aunt Lydia paused and turned her head to look at me. "Yes, it is. You should wear shorts more often, Amy. You have lovely legs."

I flushed pink as a sunset, but she just walked into the sitting room, her silver head held high.

Richard waited for me to catch up with him. Leaning in, he whispered in my ear, "Your aunt is right, and I'm an expert on legs."

I elbowed him. "Stop it. Don't give her more ammunition."

He grinned and stood aside to allow me to walk in front of him.

Aunt Lydia was already seated in her favorite chair, leaving us the sofa and a hard-backed rocker. I headed for the rocking chair as Richard slumped onto the sofa, but Aunt Lydia waved me aside. "If you share the sofa, we can talk more easily."

I sighed as I sat beside Richard. "My aunt likes to order people about, as you can see."

"I think she has the right idea." He draped his arm around my shoulders.

Aunt Lydia settled back in her chair and beamed.

I gazed up into Richard's face, frowning when I realized Aunt Lydia was right. He did look tired. Lines I hadn't noticed before bracketed his mouth. "So what's this news you felt compelled to share?"

"It's from that physical I had for insurance purposes. No, don't worry. I'm fine. But lucky. Those required blood tests might have saved me from some serious complications."

Aunt Lydia tapped her cane against the rag rug covering the floor. "Oh, dear, what's wrong?"

"Iron. Too much iron."

I sat up, dislodging his arm. "What?"

"In the water. You know I've been using Daniel Cooper's well. Fixed it up a bit, but didn't really have it tested, because I'm an idiot, apparently." Richard shifted on the sofa, sliding a little closer to the edge. "I thought, where's the harm? It's just water, and it looked and tasted clean. So I just had the pump updated and left it at that. I thought I was smart, saving money. But it seems my great-uncle had the right idea in switching to the town system."

Aunt Lydia drew a circle on the rug with her cane. "Your well water has too much iron in it? Not surprising—there's a lot of minerals and such in the groundwater around here."

"Maybe so, but the iron levels in my water must be extreme based on my bloodwork. No other logical explanation for it."

"Too much iron is harmful?" I'd never heard of such a thing. In my experience, people took iron supplements to *improve* their health.

"Very, according to the doctors I talked to." Richard leaned forward, resting his hands on his knees. "They told me excess iron can build up in the body over time and cause serious complications. You wouldn't even know what was happening until you started experiencing symptoms like stomach cramps, vomiting, and weight loss. If not caught in time or diagnosed properly, it can even kill you. Which is why I'm lucky. The blood tests identified it before I got sick. A few weeks to flush the excess out of my system, and I'll be fine."

"But you can't use the well, obviously." Aunt Lydia rose to her feet and crossed to a side table where her picture of Paul Dassin, in its new frame, sat among a cluster of family photos.

"No. I suppose it could be filtered, but I'm not taking that risk. It's back to town water for me."

"That would be safest," I said, sinking back against the sofa cushions.

"Yeah, but you see"—Richard looked up to meet my aunt's piercing gaze—"it got me thinking."

I sat up with a start. "You said vomiting and other stomach upsets and weight loss?"

He nodded. "Just like the story you told me about Eloise Fowler and those children at the orphanage."

"So it wasn't really mushrooms. They would've had a well too, right?"

"And not that far from mine. Same water table, probably."

I jumped to my feet. "The orphanage opened in 1957, and the deaths were about a year later. The timing fits—they were slowly being poisoned by iron in the water, and no one knew."

"Or did they?" Aunt Lydia stared at the photos on the table. "Maybe that's what Clark Fowler meant when he was raving about a conspiracy."

I crossed the room to stand behind her. "But your father, and Bob Blackstone's father, and Doris Virts's dad were all on the town council then. You think they knew and let those children die? Surely they wouldn't have allowed such a thing."

"No"—Aunt Lydia turned around, her blue eyes filled with unshed tears—"they wouldn't have allowed that, not if they'd known ahead of time. But they might have covered it up if they found out afterward. To protect the town."

"Oh." I couldn't think of anything else to say. Turning aside, I pressed my hand against the back of my aunt's chair.

Richard rose to his feet. "It's possible, if you consider the trouble it might have caused. Lawsuits or other court actions could've forced the council to pay damages to Clark Fowler, if no one else. Might even have left the town bankrupt."

"And destroyed all Lee Blackstone's hopes of running for higher office," Aunt Lydia said.

I dug my fingernails into the suede fabric of the chair. "Could Bob Blackstone know this? He's been so adamant about expanding the town water system to serve his subdivision. Wonder if this is why?"

"Might be." Aunt Lydia ran her fingers across the top of a silver frame that held a photo of her parents—sitting on the back porch of this house with my mother and aunt nestled in their laps.

I could see she was deeply troubled by this news and moved to stand beside her. "He certainly wouldn't want any development company to know. There's no guarantee town water will be available for a while. If they want to start building right away, the developers will have to provide wells and septic tanks."

Richard crossed the room to join us. "That's a big gamble. What if the new owners fall ill?"

I shrugged. "Maybe the mayor figures if he can get the developers to buy the property now, he can pocket the money before they realize the problem."

"To be fair," my aunt said, "it might take them a while to draw up their plans, so Bob could be banking on having time to expand the town system first."

I crossed my arms over my chest. "Or he's willing to gamble and hope for the best."

"But no developer would purchase that property if they knew the truth." Richard laid his hand on my shoulder. "Unless Blackstone could immediately offer them access to town water, and there's no guarantee of that anytime soon. His current buyers would back out. They wouldn't take that risk."

I dropped my arms to my sides and gazed at my aunt's averted face. "So Mayor Blackstone *does* have a reason to murder someone. I mean, if Doris Virts knew about the cover-up and was rambling, or if Clark Fowler got his proof somehow . . . Although that's also a good reason for Don Virts to kill Clark, I suppose. He probably needs his cut of the money from the deal and didn't want Clark to jinx it. But that doesn't explain Doris's death, unless . . ." I swallowed the words forming on my tongue. I didn't want to mention my suspicions about Kurt Kendrick to Aunt Lydia yet. She already hated him enough to confront him again, and I didn't want to chance that.

Richard squeezed my shoulder. "We shouldn't jump to conclusions. Although I think Brad Tucker should be told. About Bob Blackstone if nothing else."

"Definitely." Richard's body heat warmed my back. It was sensation I liked a little too much. I pulled away from his hand and moved closer my aunt. "This certainly sheds a new light on the past." I picked up Paul Dassin's photo and studied his arresting face. Richard would probably look much like his great-uncle when he was older. Which wouldn't be a bad thing. "There's something else if you think about it. Something that happened before the orphanage tragedy."

Aunt Lydia turned her head to stare at me. "What do you mean?"

I traced the outline of Paul Dassin's face on the glass with one finger. "Richard mentioned symptoms that sound an awful lot like poisoning."

"Daniel Cooper?" Richard stepped forward to flank my aunt's other side.

"It could explain a lot." I set the photo back amid the family pictures. "Like a healthy young farmer falling ill, displaying symptoms that mimic poisoning."

Richard glanced over at me. "And then his bride is accused of murder."

Aunt Lydia leaned heavily on her cane. "Yes," she said in a soft voice. "A young woman who was an outsider, a stranger. She came from an isolated mountain community and practiced herbalism. Not something the people of Taylorsford were accustomed to in 1925. It would have been considered unchristian at the time. So if you think it through, it's not surprising she was accused."

"They wouldn't have known about the excess iron in Daniel's water. They wouldn't have even known to look for it." I linked my arm through my aunt's crooked elbow.

Aunt Lydia's expression remained troubled. "It does explain Daniel's symptoms and his death. But why wouldn't Daniel or his mother have shown such effects before? The family lived on that land for years."

Richard cast me a thoughtful look. "But not in the same house, right? My home was built in 1923. So there had to have been another earlier house somewhere on their land."

"It burnt down, and Daniel built yours to replace it," Aunt Lydia said. "That much I remember from chatting with Paul Dassin when I was young. The family only consisted of Daniel and his mother, you know. His father died in the Spanish-American War when Leona Cooper was pregnant with Daniel."

"Oh, sad." I looked from my aunt to Richard and back again. "But it's weird that the Coopers lived on their land for so long, yet Daniel only fell ill years later. It doesn't take that long for iron-poisoning symptoms to show up, does it?"

"Not from what the doctors told me. Maybe a year to eighteen months. Two years, tops." Richard rubbed at his chin with one hand.

I examined the arrangement of family photos. All that history, captured in black and white. If only those people could speak. "Would the location of the wells make a difference?"

"It could, I suppose," Aunt Lydia said, pulling free from my arm to press her palms against the table. "I know people on the other side of town who've had to dig wells. One family hit water with no problem, while their next-door neighbors' project kept spewing up nothing but sand. Properties were close together too."

"So we need to investigate where the old house was located. I bet it's in the archives somewhere. Remember, Aunt Lydia, I was just talking about the collection of land plats earlier today? I think that's where we should start." I turned to Richard. "You up for a little research tomorrow morning? If we go in early, we'll have the place to ourselves before the library opens at ten o'clock."

"Sure," he replied, "but if we're doing that, I'm heading home now to grab dinner and then get some sleep. It's been quite a day. Thank you for hearing me out, Lydia, and Amy"—he leaned in to kiss my cheek—"see you tomorrow." As he reached the hall, he spun on his heel to face us again. "Oh, wait. I almost forgot. I have a conference call I need to be on tomorrow morning." He lifted his hands. "Weird timing because it's international. I'll have to do that from home, so can I meet you at the library, say, around nine-thirty?"

"Sure," I replied, giving him a little wave.

After a glance at Aunt Lydia, who just arched her eyebrows, I ran into the hall. I caught Richard at the front door and grabbed his arm. "That wasn't a proper good-bye," I said as he gazed down at me.

"Well then, I'd better remedy that."

I lost all sense of time after that and was shocked when he abruptly pulled away.

"Perhaps I'd better go on home now." He stroked my bare shoulder. "Your aunt will wonder what we're up to."

"I bet she can guess," I said, my voice strangely hoarse.

Without another word, Richard reached out and gently tugged my sleeves back over my shoulders.

I was lost then, and I knew it.

Charles would've simply turned away or pointed out the rumpled condition of my blouse, expecting me to take care of it even if he'd been the one to muss me in the first place.

But Richard fixed my blouse and smiled and kissed me softly on the lips one more time before leaving the house.

I locked the door after him, fumbling with the dead bolt three times before I finally slid it into place. As I wandered dreamily toward the sitting room, a rustling from the parlor made me stop dead.

Something crashed to the floor. Creeping over to the open door, I peeked into the shadowed room and spied books scattered across the rose-patterned wool rug that covered most of the hardwood floor. I stepped into the parlor to investigate.

The books were from a small collection housed in a curio cupboard that sat next to a chair Rose Baker Litton had imported from England. Strangely, one of the curio cabinet's glass doors hung open. I rubbed at my nose, fighting an urge to sneeze, and knelt beside the chair.

Such an ugly chair. Who in their right mind would have shipped it across the Atlantic? The horsehair-stuffed velvet seat had faded from its original black to a coppery brown. Its dark wood back was carved into a fantastical motif that managed to look threatening as well as uncomfortable.

I glanced up at the carvings. Of course, vines and roses. A rather narcissistic folly, like the entire parlor. A room devoted to roses in honor of the woman who had decorated it. At least the chair's carved vines were realistic enough to include thorns.

Just like Grandma Rose, my mom would say.

I rubbed my arms with both hands. It was colder in this room than anywhere else in the house. Which was weird because Aunt Lydia had closed off most of the vents to preserve energy. But perhaps it was just the heavy damask drapes insulating the room against the summer heat.

The fallen books were all slim volumes in leather bindings. They probably contained poetry or the daily homilies so popular in the early twentieth century. As I placed them back into the curio cabinet, my fingers stroked the smooth crimson leather of one of the volumes. I hated lingering in that room but couldn't overcome my curiosity—show me any book, and I'd want to browse its pages.

Before I could open the volume, Aunt Lydia called out to ask if I was all right. I shoved the book into the cabinet and closed the fragile glass door, confirming it was securely latched. Jumping to my feet, I left the parlor and met my aunt in the hall.

"So he gave you a proper good-bye, did he?"

I met Aunt Lydia's amused gaze. "Yes, very proper."

"I doubt it, but that's just as well," said my aunt as she turned and headed down the hall. "Now let's fix some dinner. Sadly, none of us can live on love."

I trailed her into the kitchen. "No one said anything about love."

Aunt Lydia shook her head. "No one has to. All anyone has to do is look at your face." She lifted a saucepan from a pewter hook on the wall. "Fortunately, Richard has that same look in his eyes, so I'm thinking you're safe."

I pressed my fingers to my mouth, where I could still feel the sensation of his lips on mine. Hopefully, Aunt Lydia was right, but I wasn't so sure.

"I don't know. When he's with me, I feel one way, but when he isn't . . ." I opened the refrigerator and stared blankly at its full shelves. "It just seems weird he would choose me of all people."

Aunt Lydia placed the pan on a burner and grabbed a cutting board. "While you're standing there with your forehead all wrinkled, venting the cold air from the fridge, I need celery, a tomato, and a green pepper. Also an onion and some garlic from the bin. And Amy"—she shot me a sharp glance—"you do know what your problem is, don't you?"

"I'm insecure?"

"Well, yes, but worse than that, you overthink things. Just let life happen once in a while, why don't you?" She pointed at the cutting board with a knife as I dumped the vegetables on the counter. "It's like how I don't exactly know what I'm going to make of all this, but I'm confident it will be something good."

"Okay, okay." I stared at the ingredients. "We need pasta, don't we?"

"Yes, we do. See how easy that is?" Aunt Lydia gave me a wink.

I shook my head. "But this is just cooking. Love is a little more complicated."

My aunt handed me the knife. "Only if you make it so. Now chop."

Unable to think of a good retort, I took out my aggression on an onion, dicing it into tiny pieces.

Chapter Eighteen

Alone in the library the next morning, I paused at the circulation desk and looked over the quiet main room.

Sunlight spilled through the tall windows, casting patterns across the beige carpet. Despite the dust motes dancing in the beams, there was no musty smell like in my aunt's front parlor. Instead, the lemon scent of furniture polish mingled with the heady aroma of paper, book glue, and bindings—a combination that always made me smile. I loved the smell of books. Although I appreciated the value of computers and online research, nothing could replace the magic of rows of books filling shelves. So much information, so much wonder, so many new worlds, all contained within the library's four walls.

Grabbing the 1958 folder from the archives refiling shelf, I flipped it open and stared at the paper that mentioned Douglas Beckert and the Carthage Company. What could he have bought in his own name that the town would've felt compelled to reimburse? Drumming my fingers against the typed minutes, I decided to figure out what the Carthage Company did, now or in the past.

I looked up the company name on the Internet, limiting it first to the state and then to this general area. Only one mention fit all the criteria, and amazingly, the company still appeared to be in business. I pulled up their website, not sure what to expect, and the description of their services caught me by surprise. This was not just a another hint—this was a vital clue.

The Carthage Company: Experienced Professional Water Testing for Commercial Organizations, Industrial Sites, and Homes, it said.

I scanned through their website, confirming that they were a high-tech lab equipped to test wells, ponds, reservoirs, city systems, and other water sources. Founded in 1950, they'd been in continuous operation since that time.

Jotting down their phone number, I glanced up at the wall clock. Nine o'clock on a Saturday, which might mean no one would answer my call. But I had to give it a try.

I reached someone on the fourth ring.

"Sorry," said the woman on the other end of the line, "I was in another room, and I'm the only one here right now."

"No problem," I told her, then identified myself as the Taylorsford library director before launching into questions about the company's records.

"Oh, we keep them," the woman, who introduced herself as Jenny, said. "You never know when there might be an inquiry based on some real-estate transaction, or a lawsuit, or something like that. But we don't store the older records here. Those are paper files, and there just isn't room. Our offices got very cramped about ten years ago, so we sent everything dated before 2000 to an off-site archive—Iron Mountain's facility in Pennsylvania. Ever heard of it?"

I assured her I had and asked what it would take to get a copy of a specific report from that secure storage facility.

"Well, you'd need the approval of the original person or organization who commissioned the testing," Jenny said. "Like, if you are calling about a report requested and paid for by the town of Taylorsford, you'd need to send us a letter on official stationary, signed by the mayor, someone on the town council, or whoever can approve such things. You can scan and e-mail the letter, but it does have to be on official stationary and signed. Then we would make the request to Iron Mountain on your behalf."

"I see." I considered this for a moment. "But you have a database of all the reports, I assume? At least listing who commissioned or paid for the tests?"

"Yes, but it's private information. I mean, I can't give out names of people or organizations over the phone to just anyone."

"No, of course not," I said and thanked her before hanging up the phone.

I pondered this information. If, as I suspected, the Taylorsford Town Council had commissioned the Carthage Company to run a test on the orphanage well water, it was clever of them to have placed it in Douglas Beckert's name. That way, no future mayors or council members could request the report unless Beckert approved. His death many years ago rendered such an inquiry doubly difficult.

Clever and duplicitous, I thought as a series of knocks resonated from the workroom.

Richard. I jogged into the workroom and opened the staff door.

"Hi." He leaned in to kiss my cheek before stepping inside.

"How was the interview or whatever?"

"Oh, fine." Richard followed me to the circulation desk, where he kicked off his shoes. "Forgot to clean them after my last run, so there's some mud caked in the treads. Better if I go sock-footed so I don't soil your carpet. Do you mind?"

I shook my head and led him into the reading room. "Not until we open. Shoes required, you know. But you can just head out the back door before then."

"Planning to get rid of me already?" Richard's grin faded as he studied my face. "You look serious. Found some critical info?"

"Yes, in a way." I detailed my phone conversation and theories concerning the Carthage Company.

"So that pretty much clinches it—the town council probably instituted a cover-up, just like Clark Fowler said."

"Looks like it. Now, as to the property lines and the wells . . ." I waved my hand over one of reading tables, where I had placed a large document, anchoring each end with an archival box. "Here's a copy of the land plat that includes the Cooper and Tucker farms from around 1900. Originals are held at the state library, but we have copies of some."

"Interesting." Richard stepped up to the table.

I moved beside him, and we leaned over, our heads close together as we traced the property lines and other markers with our fingers.

"Don't see that Bob Blackstone has any case," Richard said, his finger pressed against one section. "The Tucker property clearly extends to the tree line, and it's the same today."

"The edge of the woods could've changed, I suppose, but the mayor's assertion sounds questionable to me. Just Blackstone trying to muddy the waters, I bet. And look"—I tapped my thumb against one spot—"there's the symbol for land that will perk."

Richard glanced over at me. "What?"

"Perk. Like coffee. Means you could dig a well there and likely find water."

"You know this how?"

"I've had to read these things before." I pointed a finger at myself. "Researcher, remember?"

"Lucky for me." Richard leaned in to give me a swift kiss on the lips before turning his attention back to the property map. "So this symbol, is that an existing well?"

"Yeah, looks like the only one on the Cooper lands. There's another one, see, but that's on the Tucker property."

Richard straightened and took a couple of steps back, surveying the entire plat. "Then the original well was the one I showed you when we walked through the woods."

"Yep, and I bet the original house wasn't far off." I traced a line with my finger. "See here, there's the symbol indicating a building. On the other side of the woods."

"It is a narrow band of trees at that point." Richard rubbed at his eyes. "Sorry, everything's gone a bit blurry. Didn't sleep well last night."

I stood back from the table and examined him. "I guess not, after getting that medical news."

"That wasn't the problem," he said, giving me a look that made me blush.

I turned away and lifted the boxes off the plat, allowing it to roll back into a loose cylinder. "We still need to do more research, but at least we've determined the location of the original well, which undoubtedly explains why Daniel didn't fall ill until he built the new house and dug yours. Somehow there must be just enough difference in the groundwater between the two. One had the excess iron problem, and the other didn't."

Richard nodded. "And if the true story matches my great-uncle's novel, Daniel's mother was already ill with some type of cancer, so her death within months of moving into the new house wasn't unexpected."

"Which meant it was just Daniel who was affected. Although, wait—remember what Kurt Kendrick said? About Eleanora's health improving in jail?"

"Yeah. Great-Uncle Paul hoped it was because of his attentions, but it wasn't." Richard rubbed at his chin with the back of his hand. "She got better because she wasn't in her house.

I guess she hadn't been living at Daniel's that long before, so she recovered fairly quickly once she wasn't drinking the tainted well water."

"That must have been it." I glanced up at Richard's thoughtful face. "It's funny, if you think about it. Kendrick's bad behavior saved him. Getting swiftly kicked out of the orphanage and Paul taking him in not only gave him a fresh start, it also prevented him from falling ill or dying."

"He does seem to have extraordinarily good luck."

"Yeah, but so did my family, since they chose to hook into the town water system. Not sure why they did, but I'm glad. And obviously the Tuckers' water is fine."

"But the orphanage well was not." Richard gazed at the rolled document. "Of course it wouldn't be on this plan, but I wonder where that building was located?"

"Somewhere affected by the iron contamination, obviously. Maybe my aunt, Zelda, or Walt can tell us more."

"Kurt Kendrick would know for sure."

"But he told me he was traveling to Europe today and would be gone for some time."

"Okay, so we'll have to ask the others next time we see them." Richard glanced up at the wall clock. "Speaking of time, it's already nine fifty. Don't you need to open the library in a few minutes?"

I shook my head. "It's actually Sunny's turn to cover Saturday. I told her I'd switch, but since she was out yesterday, she wanted the hours. Anyway, we always have volunteers on Saturdays, so she said she'd be fine." I frowned. "But she should be here by now. She likes to get in at least twenty minutes before opening, and it's not like her to be late."

"Could something have happened to her? Car trouble or something?"

I yanked my cell phone from my pocket. "Hold on, I'm going to check with her grandparents."

Carol Fields answered my call, sounding baffled when I asked to speak to Sunny. "She's not here. Didn't come in last night, but we didn't worry because we got a text message saying she wouldn't be back home until today."

"That's something, I guess." I tucked my phone under my ear, bending my neck to hold it in place, and picked up the two archival boxes.

"Yes, but"—Carol sounded troubled—"she also said she was crashing at your place."

"What?" I had to juggle to keep from dropping one of the boxes. "But she didn't. I mean, she didn't even ask us if she could."

"Really?" Carol's voice wavered. "You think I should I call Deputy Tucker? It's not like Sunny to make stuff up."

That was the most disturbing thing. Sunny's grandparents, former flower children who'd once lived on a commune, were the last people to be concerned about Sunny staying over somewhere, even at some guy's house. If that had been the case, Sunny would have told them.

She had no reason to lie to Carol and Paul Fields. None whatsoever. And anyway, I'd never known Sunny to lie, even with good reason.

I dumped the archival boxes on the circulation desk. "Call Brad Tucker. I'm sure it's nothing serious, but if her car ran out of gas or something . . ." I knew I was making stuff up just to reassure Carol, but I didn't know what else to say.

Because if Sunny had run out of gas, why would she send that text? Or why not send another one? Why hadn't she called for help?

Visions of Sunny's bright-yellow car tumbling into some deep gulley flooded my mind. "You call Brad. I'm going to look around town, see if I spy her car anywhere," I told Carol before asking her to call me with any news.

"What's up?" Richard crossed to the circulation desk.

"It's Sunny. She's missing."

"What?" Concern filled Richard's eyes. "How can Sunny be missing? She was leading that protest just yesterday."

"Well, she's not here, and she'd never ditch work without telling someone. And her grandmother said she sent a text saying she wasn't coming home and was staying with me last night, but she couldn't have because we never saw her . . ."

"Whoa, whoa, slow down." Richard reached me and gripped my shoulders. "So no one knows where she is right now?"

"No." I swallowed the lump in my throat but couldn't halt the tears filling my eyes. "And she wouldn't have lied. She's the most truthful person I know."

"Okay." Richard pulled me close. "Relax." He adjusted his hold until my head pressed against his shoulder. "Now let's consider what we should do. Have you called the sheriff's office?"

"I told Mrs. Fields to call Brad Tucker. Figured he might help even if it isn't declared official business yet."

"Good thinking." Richard tipped up my chin with two fingers. "I do have my car. So maybe we should take a drive around town and see what we can find. What do you say?"

"Definitely. I'll open the library and just put one of the volunteers in charge for the day. They can at least cover basic services. And one of them can lock up if I give them a key. I mean, they can't do everything Sunny knows how to do, but at least they can check out books." I sniffed back a sob.

Richard kissed my forehead before releasing me. "Don't worry. We'll find her."

"I hope so." I rubbed at my tear-stained cheeks with the back of my hand as Richard pulled a tissue from his pocket.

"Here, this might help." He leaned in and wiped my face, then stood back and surveyed me. "A little better."

"Gee, thanks," I muttered.

He grinned. "I doubt either of us looks spectacular right now. But we can't worry about that. Go open up and talk to your volunteers. I'll throw on my shoes, and then we'll hit the road."

I almost blurted out that he looked fantastic, as usual, but pressed my lips together instead.

As Richard balanced elegantly on one foot and then the other to slip on his shoes, I considered my feelings for him. Everything was moving so fast. Maybe I should slow things down a bit, even if I didn't really want to. Although Richard had been nothing but sweet so far, so had Charles early on. Perhaps, just to be safe, I should keep things on a more casual level, at least for a little while.

I slapped my thigh with my hand. What was I thinking? This was not the time to be concerned about personal issues. Richard had a car and had offered to drive me around to look for Sunny. Whether or not our relationship would grow into something more substantial was not important. I had to keep such concerns to myself. There was only one thing that mattered right now.

Whatever else happened, we had to find Sunny.

Chapter Nineteen

We drove out to the edge of town, stopping at each of the businesses that sprawled from the curve in the road beyond the town limits' sign to a crossroads that separated the strip malls from farmland.

There was no sign of Sunny's car, and none of the shopkeepers we talked to had seen her. Our last stop, at a car dealership that promised financing to everyone despite poor or no credit, was the most depressing. The owner was far too interested in the possibility that Sunny might be the victim of a third murder. He expounded upon this theory for several minutes before Richard grabbed my hand and pulled me outside.

The door slammed behind us. I sighed and climbed back into Richard's car. I was despondent by this point, my thoughts bouncing between different versions of disasters that could have befallen Sunny, each one worse than the last.

Richard slid into the driver's seat, but before starting up the car, he tapped my arm and pointed to a nearby historical marker. "Merritt's Crossing?"

I shook off my morose silence to explain that the crossroads had been named after the Union leader who had opposed the famous Confederate unit Mosby's Rangers.

"Interesting," Richard said. "So this area wasn't totally under Confederate control?"

"Oh, no, not at all. It was really a mix. Parts of this and surrounding counties supported the South, and other parts supported the North. Side by side, really. It must have been very confusing. And then there were the Quakers. They didn't fight for either army, although they gave medical aid to injured soldiers."

"From either side?"

"Yes, or so they say." I stared out the window as we turned around and headed back toward Taylorsford. "Still no sign of Sunny's car."

"It's possible she drove into the city, although that would be a little odd after spending all day at the protest. But we don't know."

I dropped my head into my hands. "I'm so worried."

"We'll find her," Richard said firmly. "Sunny's such a bright spirit, I can't imagine her light being extinguished so soon."

I lifted my head and peeked at him through splayed fingers. "Are you secretly a poet as well as a dancer?"

He laughed. "Hardly. Now while we keep searching for that very yellow car, tell me about your life before Taylorsford. Did you grow up in this area?"

I peered out my window, still hoping to catch a flash of canary yellow. "No, I grew up farther east. Still in Virginia, but closer to the ocean than the mountains. Not on the beach, though. Nothing so glamorous. We lived in the suburbs in a very typical house. Just an ordinary family." I pressed my forehead against the glass, mulling those last words. "Well, maybe not that ordinary."

"What does your dad do?"

"He's in computers. Programmer since back in the days of COBOL and BASIC. His name's Nicholas, but everyone calls him Nick. He's a sweetheart. Not much for talking, but he listens really well."

"Great skill to have." Richard drove the car down one of the few side streets in the historic section of town. "And your mom?"

"Debbie. Well, Deborah, of course. She's a marine biologist. Studies crabs. For real." I tapped my finger against the car window. "They're actually out of the country right now. Traveling around Europe on a second honeymoon. Hopefully having a blast. They've been planning this trip for ages."

"And you have a brother?" Richard focused on the road with occasional glances out his side window. Like me, he was obviously still hoping to spy Sunny's car.

"One brother—Scott. He's two years younger than me and works in computers like my dad."

"Also a programmer?"

"Nope. Cyber security. Yeah," I said when I spied Richard's surprised expression, "Scott works for the government. Has top security clearance and all that."

"So a family of scientists. Not sure how well I'll fit in."

I sneaked a glance at him. *If he wasn't seriously interested, he wouldn't be planning to meet the family. That's not something Charles ever mentioned.*

My cotton shorts stuck to the leather as I nervously shifted in my seat. I discreetly tugged the material free and concentrated on keeping my voice steady. "Oh, they're not that intimidating. Except when Scott and Dad discuss computer stuff. That's like trying to decipher a foreign language. I use computers in my work, but I'm nowhere near their level. When they get going, I just sit back, smile, and nod."

"That would be me too. So I'm curious—Lydia said your mom wouldn't visit Taylorsford. Or was it just the family home?"

"No, although that's a big part of it." I slouched against the passenger door. "As you heard from my aunt, my mom didn't get along with Rose. Says her grandmother was mean. Quite a dictator, according to Mom."

"So your mother left home as soon as possible?"

"Yeah, Mom couldn't get away fast enough. Once she went off to college, she never came back. Which wasn't fair, if you ask me. Pretty much left Aunt Lydia in the lurch, especially after Rose fell ill and succumbed to dementia." I allowed my temple to rest against the cool window glass. "It was weird when I was a kid. Aunt Lydia would visit us, and everything would be great, but then near the end of her visit, there'd always be an argument between my mom and her about Great-Grandma Rose. Mom would never budge, though."

Richard glanced at me, curiosity gleaming in his gray eyes. "You never met her—Rose, I mean? Because, if I'm doing the math right, she must have lived until you were in your early teens."

"I was fourteen when she died. But no, never met her. My mom wouldn't even let me visit Aunt Lydia until after Rose passed. I think Mom worried about exposing me to someone with dementia. And apparently my great-grandmother got pretty mean at times. Not that it was her fault, of course. But anyway, Mom claims the house always creeped her out, especially after Rose died." As I spoke these words, I gasped and straightened in my seat.

My mother *had* returned to Aunt Lydia's house. Once. How could I have forgotten that?

Richard shot me a concerned glance. "What is it? You've gone white as a sheet."

I turned to look at him. "I was wrong. Mom did go back. We were all there, once. For Rose's funeral." I clasped my hands in my lap. "Haven't thought about that in forever. Blocked it out, I guess. Which is really odd 'cause it was the first time I ever visited the house. You'd think I'd remember that clearly, but"—I tipped my head back so I could look up through the sunroof—"I don't. It's all hazy. I vividly remember visiting Aunt Lydia every summer after but not much about that first visit."

Richard placed his right hand on my left leg. "Well, funerals can be traumatic sometimes. For kids in particular. Especially if there was an open casket and lots of distraught adults."

"No, it wasn't that." I searched my memory. "It was after the actual funeral. A day or two later. Something happened, and I remember someone screaming. My mother. She was yelling and crying and tossing things in suitcases. I can't remember why—only, I think something happened to her, or she found out something, or . . ." I pressed my hand against my forehead, forcing back some other memory. Something cold, something dark. "I don't know. It's all hazy. I just remember my dad and my aunt tried to calm Mom down, and she"—I blinked rapidly as tears welled in my eyes—"she struck out and hit Aunt Lydia in the face. So hard it left a red mark. And then we left. We just left, Dad and Mom and Scott and me. And my parents never came back."

Richard stroked my bare knee before placing his hand back on the steering wheel. "Well, that's pretty traumatic, I'd say. You visited, though, so it couldn't have been anything too terrible. Or your mother wouldn't have allowed you to come back."

"No, I guess not," I said, staring at my clenched fingers. "Mom said it had nothing to do with me, I remember that much. Whatever it was." I lifted my head and offered a weak smile. "She claimed it was just something that affected her. Not sure what that means or why I never questioned her about it, to tell you the truth. Guess I was secretly afraid it would lead to a discussion that would prevent me from visiting Aunt Lydia again."

"Now that you're an adult, maybe you should talk to your mom again. Figure it out. It's not good keeping secrets like that in a family. Now"—Richard shared a comforting smile—"on a lighter note, any nieces or nephews? Sadly, that's something I'll never have, since I'm an only child. Unless I marry a girl with siblings, of course."

"No." Something bright caught my eye, and I snapped my head to the right, but it was just a bank of yellow flowers. I slumped in my seat, focusing on the dashboard. "Anyway, Scott is gay. Not that he can't get married, or even have a child through adoption or surrogacy or something, but he's between partners right now."

Richard cast me a questioning glance. "Your parents are okay with it? Him being gay, I mean."

"Oh, sure. They're very open-minded about stuff like that."

"Good." Richard said this so forcefully, I turned to stare at him.

"Your parents wouldn't be okay with it?"

"God, no." He rubbed at his chin. "And so many of my dancers have a hell of a time. Thrown out of the house, financial support cut off, and so on. I've seen too many wonderful people break down during rehearsals or studio because they aren't accepted by those who supposedly love them." He frowned. "Always worse after holidays."

I eyed him, noticing the lines bracketing his mouth. There was obviously more to this, but I didn't want to pry. "That stinks."

"It does. But fortunately, the dance world is pretty accepting. Most of the arts are. It's one thing a place like Clarion really has going for it, at least in its conservatory programs. A refuge for some."

"Some," I said, recalling my self-imposed banishment. But that was my own fault. My temper, driving me to act like a two-year-old.

And your insecurity, Amy. Making you overreact when Charles showed his true colors.

Insecurity, just like I told Aunt Lydia. That's what was hounding me, making me question any new relationship. Even though Richard had given me no reason to doubt his intentions. I straightened and turned my body toward him as much as I could while still strapped in. "I need to ask you something, and I want you to answer me honestly."

Richard's eyebrows rose up to the fall of his dark hair. "Just so you know, I try to always speak truthfully."

"I'm sure you do, but"—I gripped my hands together—"this might be a sticky subject."

Richard shot me a sharp glance. "Are you about to tell me you're already married or something?"

"No, nothing like that. It's more about how I look."

"Oh? What's sticky about that? I like how you look."

"I mean, you're a dancer."

"True."

"So you're very athletic and physically fit and all."

"Goes with the territory."

"Yes, but"—I twisted my hands until my nails bit into my palms—"I'm not."

Richard glanced at me again, his expression surprisingly serious. "Oh, is that what this is about?" He refocused his gaze on the road. "I guess you haven't seen much of my work, have you?"

"No," I mumbled, scuffing my sneaker against the car mat. No, I hadn't bothered to look him up online. Which told me something about myself.

More concerned with your own hang-ups than finding out about someone else, aren't you, Amy? Now who's the narcissist?

Richard placed his hand back on my leg. "You might want to do that. There are some videos online. Check out a dance performance called *Dimensions*. It's my most famous piece of choreography. So far, anyway."

"All right. But I don't see what that has to do . . ."

"Check it out, then we'll talk." He gave my bare knee a squeeze before lifting his hand. "Why don't we head back to your aunt's house? I think we've exhausted our options, at least for now, and I need something to eat, or at least some water, before I attempt to drive farther afield."

"Okay, makes sense." I settled back against the smooth leather of the seat and stared up through the sunroof at the clear sky. Depression washed over me again. There was a murderer loose in Taylorsford, and I couldn't figure out whether to focus my suspicions on Don Virts, Bob Blackstone, or Kurt Kendrick. Or maybe I was just spinning theories and none of them were involved. Maybe it was some stranger. I shivered. In a way, that would be worse because it would mean Sunny's disappearance might be something entirely unpredictable.

I glanced at Richard. "I don't have a sister, you know. But I felt Sunny filled that spot."

"She still will," Richard replied, tightening his grip on the steering wheel. "Nothing is going to happen to her. I won't allow it."

"And you can control such things?"

Richard flashed me a grim smile. "Maybe not, but I will certainly try."

I settled back in the passenger seat. "And I will certainly let you."

*   *   *

I apologized to Aunt Lydia for leaving for hours without really telling her where I was, but she waved off my words.

"You had more important things to worry about."

"Yeah, but we didn't find any trace of Sunny." I handed Richard a glass of water before pouring one for myself.

"The news is all over town now." Aunt Lydia sat across from Richard at the kitchen table. "Walt and Zelda headed out to take a look around a little while ago, and I heard even the mayor has joined the search. All volunteer, of course, since the sheriff's office can't do anything official yet."

I flung up the hand holding my glass, slinging water across the floor. "The mayor? Bob Blackstone is out looking for Sunny?"

"Why, yes. Zelda said he found out she was missing when he saw Walt and Zelda searching the old Lutheran cemetery. You know, the one where Daniel Cooper is buried, across from the library. Bob stopped and asked them what they were doing, and they filled him in."

"Damn, damn, damn." I yanked paper towels off the roll so hard the standing metal holder fell onto the butcher-block counter.

"What's wrong?" Aunt Lydia pushed back her chair. "Why shouldn't Bob Blackstone join the search?"

"I think Amy's concerned that Blackstone could be involved in Sunny's disappearance." Richard knelt beside me as I mopped up the spilt water. "Let me get this. Grab some more towels and toss them this way." He patted my hand and slid the damp wad of paper from my fingers.

I stood and righted the towel holder before tearing off more sheets.

"I can't believe that," Aunt Lydia said. "Bob may be some-thing of an opportunist, but he's surely no kidnapper."

"How do you know?" I tossed the extra towels to Richard. "He's the one with the best motive to harm Sunny, isn't he? She and her friends stand between him and a lot of money if they succeed in stopping his development plans."

Richard rose to his feet, balling up the wet towels. He threw them across the room and they sailed into the trash can like a perfect three-pointer. "It does make sense, unfortunately. Black-stone seems to be connected to all of this. He had that alterca-tion with Clark in the diner. Maybe he decided to silence him permanently."

I crossed to Richard's side. "And if Doris Virts did know about the iron problem on his property, he could've killed her too."

Lines crinkled Aunt Lydia's forehead as she gazed up at both of us. "He does have motive, but I just don't see it. He doesn't have the temperament. Now Karl . . . I mean, Kurt Kendrick, on the other hand, is exactly the sort of person I would suspect."

You and me both, I thought. Brad and the rest of the sheriff's office might be convinced that Kendrick's black Jaguar was sim-ply at the wrong place at the wrong time, but I wasn't so sure. *But Kurt Kendrick is in Europe right now, Amy.* Well, that's what he'd told me, but I had no guarantee it was the truth. What if he'd only said that so no one would consider him a suspect in Sunny's disappearance?

"I don't know," Richard said. "Kendrick isn't hurting for cash, but maybe Bob Blackstone needs that development project more than we know. People will do a lot of horrible things where money is concerned. No matter their temperament."

I lifted my cell phone from the counter. "I'm calling Brad Tucker and telling him to find Bob Blackstone right now."

"Amy, think for a minute." Aunt Lydia grabbed her cane to steady herself as she rose to her feet. "You've already implicated the mayor once, and he produced a solid alibi. What if this is another false accusation? You could be fired. He is your boss, after all."

I punched in the numbers to the chief deputy's line. "I don't care. I'm not taking any chances."

I reached Brad, who assured me that he would locate Bob Blackstone as soon as possible. "Doubt he's involved," he said, "but it won't hurt to make sure."

I tapped the phone against my palm as I met Aunt Lydia's expectant gaze. "He said he would check on the mayor. But he also said he'd found no trace of Sunny or her car." I lowered my head.

Richard put his arm around my waist and pulled me close. "At least Deputy Tucker is taking this seriously."

"He's in love with Sunny." Aunt Lydia lifted her shoulders. "No need to look so surprised, Amy. I have eyes, you know."

"And your informant, Zelda."

Her lips twitched. "Yes, and Zelda. So are you two going out again? I'd advise against that. It's getting late, and you've been running around since the early morning. Might be best to allow Brad and the others to continue the search. I'm sure we'll get a call if anyone has news." She crossed to the counter before turning to address Richard. "I can throw together something if you'd like to stay for dinner."

"Oh, Richard can't stay," I said before he could reply.

He released his hold and spun on his heel to face me. "I can't?"

"No, remember you said you had to get back home? Some business call?" I met his questioning gaze with a lift of my chin.

His eyes blazed with something that looked like anger. "Strange, I'd forgotten." Richard turned to Aunt Lydia. "Sorry, apparently I have to run. But thanks for the invite."

Aunt Lydia frowned and examined me. "Another time, then."

"Of course. And I expect one of you to call with any news of Sunny." Richard touched my arm. "Amy, would you mind walking me out? I want to make sure you lock your door immediately behind me. Can't be too careful these days."

I opened my mouth to protest, but Aunt Lydia's expression stopped me. "Of course," I replied, forcing a smile.

I trailed Richard to the front door, where he turned on me.

"What the hell was that about? I didn't mind staying for dinner, but apparently you don't want me here."

"I think we should cool things down a bit." I examined my fingernails, studiously avoiding his gaze. "We've spent so much time together lately, maybe we should take a little break."

"Because . . . ?"

I looked up into his face. His somber expression clearly indicated his disappointment. "Because I think things are moving a little too fast."

Richard lifted his hands, palms out. "You need to stop this, Amy. This is your anxiety talking, not you."

"Of course I'm anxious. Two people murdered and Sunny missing . . ."

"That's not what I mean. You're freaking out over our mutual attraction. And I do think it's mutual, whatever you say."

"Maybe so, but we have to be realistic."

"Why?" Richard cupped my chin with his hand. "Why do we have to be anything? Why can't we feel what we feel and forget all the other nonsense?"

I stared into his beautiful gray eyes. "I just don't want to be hurt again."

"Then you don't want to live." He released my chin and slid his fingers down my neck in a soft caress. His hand came to rest just above my left breast. "Because you can't protect your heart and really live. Because really living means taking a risk."

"But how many times?" I cursed the tremor that had invaded my voice.

"Over and over, if necessary."

"Not sure I can do that."

"I think you can. I think you're stronger than you know." Richard leaned in and kissed my lips. A gentle, lingering kiss that sent heat radiating throughout my body.

I pulled away. "I'd better go."

"All right. But I will be back. I'm not giving up on this. I've waited too long to find you." Richard opened the front door and stepped onto the porch but looked back at me before he made it to the stairs. "Promise me one thing."

"What?" My grip tightened on the doorknob.

"Watch that video. *Dimensions*, remember? Watch it and then come talk to me."

I owed him that much, at least. "I promise."

He pressed his fingers to his lips, then held his hand out toward me. "One more kiss. My promise to you that I am not playing games." As he turned away, the porch light turned his skin sallow and made him appear, for once, older than his thirty-five years. "See you soon," he called over his shoulder as he took the stairs in two leaps and jogged toward his house.

Chapter Twenty

As I wandered toward the kitchen, Aunt Lydia called to me. "I'm back here," she said. "And I want to talk to you."

Great, here comes the lecture. I stiffened my spine and marched onto the back porch, holding my head high.

Aunt Lydia sat in the rocker, cradling a glass of sherry between her hands. "I poured you one. It's on the side table. Grab it, and sit your butt down, and listen to me, young lady."

I picked up the glass and sat in the wicker chair, crossing my legs at my ankles.

Like a little schoolgirl, waiting for instruction.

I uncrossed my legs. "I know you think I was rude."

"Yes, because you were. But that isn't what I want to tell you." Aunt Lydia took a sip of her sherry. "I'm not about to get into whatever is going on between you and Richard. That's your business."

"Thanks." My eyes widened in surprise. I'd been so sure she was going to lecture me about ushering Richard out of the house. "So what do you want to talk to me about?"

"Your great-grandmother." Aunt Lydia straightened until her back did not touch her chair. "I know you've heard things from your mother, and they aren't untrue. In fact, Debbie was right more than she knew."

I scooted to the edge of my chair. "Right about what?"

"That Grandma Rose was intentionally cruel, not just afflicted with dementia. Of course, she couldn't help that part, but I always wanted to believe that her illness was the reason she acted the way she did. I mean, the primary reason. But now"— Aunt Lydia took a long swallow of her drink—"I'm not so sure."

"What changed your mind?"

"Things we've learned recently. Things you and Richard have uncovered. Like the whole situation with the well water. You see, my father was on the town council back in 1958 during the orphanage tragedy. And he talked to his mother quite a bit. They were close, you see. My dad was an only child, and his father was a distant sort, not much for talking. Especially, heaven forbid, talking about *feelings*. So my father always shared any personal concerns with his mother."

"Okay." I wasn't sure where this was going, but Aunt Lydia looked so serious, I knew it must be important.

"Anyway, if the town council did know the real reason why Eloise Fowler and those children died, and they covered it up, then my father would have been part of the conspiracy. Which would've torn him to pieces. He was a kind man, always trying to do the right thing. He would have suffered greatly if forced to keep such a secret."

"You think he would have confided in Rose, just to have someone besides your mom to talk to?"

"Yes, undoubtedly. Which would explain certain things I've never really understood before."

"Such as?"

"Such as why Grandma Rose changed dramatically after that time. Oh, she was always stern and self-centered. But she didn't become erratic until after the orphanage tragedy. Of course, I was only six when that happened, but I do remember how Grandma changed. I used to be in awe of her, but she could be fun sometimes, playing card games with me, or teaching me piano, or allowing me to use a touch of her powder or lipstick to play dress-up."

I gestured with my hand, sloshing the liquid in my glass. "But she was different after '58?"

Aunt Lydia stared down into her sherry. "Yes. Retreated from most public gatherings, except for church. Didn't want to interact with me or many other people. Jumped at loud noises as if she expected something bad to happen at any moment. Started muttering to herself a lot."

"That could've been the start of her slide into dementia. The early onset of it."

"Perhaps, but"—Aunt Lydia slid her finger around and around the rim of her glass—"there was more to it than that, I think."

I studied my aunt for a moment. Her head was bent over her hands, an uncharacteristic pose for someone with her ramrod posture. "You think she put two and two together like we have and realized that Daniel died of iron poisoning, just like Eloise and those orphans?"

"Yes, I think perhaps she did." Aunt Lydia straightened and finished off her sherry in one swallow. "She was so convinced Eleanora had murdered Daniel that she actively fought to have Eleanora convicted. Produced the herbal and talked about the torn-out pages, of course, but she did even more than that."

"More? What more could she do?"

"Oh, spread a lot of rumors about Eleanora practicing witchcraft and so on."

"How do you know that?"

Aunt Lydia's knuckles turned white as she clutched her empty glass. "Some of her friends used to visit us when she was ill, and they told me things. I mean, Grandma Rose didn't recognize them half of the time, so they talked to me instead."

"She was in love with Daniel, right? I figured that out from my research, just reading between the lines."

"Yes, and she swore that Eleanora Heron had used enchantments of some kind to lure Daniel into marriage. But that was nonsense. Sure, Grandma Rose loved Daniel, but he never loved her. He was ten years older, for one thing. He liked her well enough, from what I heard, but thought of her more like a little sister than anything else. Any romance was all in Grandma's head. At least that's what her contemporaries told me."

Examining my aunt's tense face, it dawned on me that this was one of the secrets Aunt Lydia had kept from me—one of the reasons she hadn't welcomed my investigation into our family history. She had good reason to suspect Great-Grandmother Rose's motives for testifying against Eleanora. I supposed it was hard for my aunt to admit the depths of her grandmother's jealousy and duplicity, even now. It certainly didn't paint a pretty picture of Rose.

I pointed at Aunt Lydia's glass. "More?"

"No, better not. Help yourself if you wish, but I'll never sleep if I have more."

I shook my head. Not that sleep was probably in the cards for me, either way. "I'm fine too."

"Of course, Grandma Rose was furious when Eleanora was acquitted. Vowed to find new evidence to somehow bring her to justice."

"But she couldn't be tried for murder again. Double jeopardy."

"I know, and I guess Grandma Rose realized that pretty quick. Anyway, her friends told me she stopped talking about the murder after Eleanora left town. Although she never forgot. She even put money in a trust at the Lutheran church to pay for the perpetual upkeep of Daniel's grave. I found that out later when I was dealing with her finances."

"Such a sad story," I said before finishing off my drink and standing up. "Here, let me take your glass into the kitchen with mine. You rest. Sure you don't want something to eat?"

Aunt Lydia placed her other hand on my wrist as I took her glass. "No. And just set those on the side table." She looked up into my face, her blue eyes very bright. "Stay. There's more I need to tell you."

I placed the two glasses on the table and stared out at the garden, now sepia-tinted by the twilight. "More? What do you mean?"

"Grandma Rose swore that Eleanora tore pages from the herbal, pages that contained recipes for poisons. It was the harshest evidence against Eleanora, but it didn't convict her. Thank goodness, because I believe Rose lied. There were no pages ripped out by Eleanora, not for any reason."

"Then who . . ." I turned, resting my hip against the table. "Rose tore out the pages? And did what?"

"Hid them, I think."

"Why?"

"To strengthen the case against Eleanora, I suppose." Aunt Lydia absently rolled a fold of her silk blouse between her thumb and forefinger. "I think she fabricated it all. Everything she told the court about Eleanora."

"Because she hated her for stealing Daniel's affections?"

"Yes, but also because she honestly believed Eleanora killed him. I'm convinced she believed that with all her heart, at least until 1958."

"When the orphanage tragedy produced another possibility."

"Yes." Aunt Lydia sighed deeply. "Maybe she doubted her earlier certainty then. Maybe she even felt guilt for treating

Eleanora so badly, although she never said so. But she did say some strange things at the end . . ."

"When she wasn't in her right mind."

"True, but there were things she said in her ramblings that never made sense to me. Not until now. It's why I wanted to talk to you tonight. To let you know that maybe your mother had reason to flee this house and never return."

I stepped away from the table and stood in front of my aunt. "Mom? How does she tie into it?"

"Do you remember Grandma Rose's funeral?"

"Yeah, although I seem to have blocked some of the events out of my mind until recently."

"I'm not surprised. It was probably traumatic for you and Scott, seeing your mom like that. Debbie's always been so steady, so logical. But that day, she was hysterical. We had to call the doctor, who fortunately agreed to come to the house to give her a sedative."

I sank back into the wicker chair. "What happened?"

"I'm not quite sure. She'd gone up to Grandma Rose's room to get a photo of our parents that sat on the nightstand. But she was up there so long, your father became concerned. He went upstairs and discovered your mother, curled up in a corner of the bedroom, weeping. When he tried to get her to leave, she became hysterical, screaming about darkness and bugs and not being able to breathe. It was totally unexpected and irrational. Not like Debbie at all."

Dark and cold. I recalled it now, my mother's words. Something dark and cold.

Aunt Lydia leaned forward. "Now I wonder—did Debbie see something or find something in that room, something that made her realize that Grandma Rose had been lying all along?

That our grandmother was a perjurer who had attempted to get an innocent woman convicted?"

"But why would that upset Mom so much? She hated Rose anyway. Wouldn't she have been happy to prove she truly was an evil woman, not just a selfish, cold one?"

Aunt Lydia settled back in the rocker. "I don't know, but it's the only thing that makes sense. Maybe Debbie found those lost pages from the herbal? I can't explain it; I just feel she discovered something that shook her to her core. Because, you know"— Aunt Lydia lifted her hands—"even if you hate a relative, they're still family. And some people feel an ancestor's shameful acts can taint them too."

"But Mom would never think that way. She's too practical."

"Maybe so. She sure wasn't that day. Anyway, she doesn't remember anything. I've asked her plenty of times, and she always claims the entire day is a blur. She says the only thing she knows for certain is that she won't return to this house."

"Perhaps I should ask her." I weighed this option. It made me nervous to contemplate discussing anything so irrational with my pragmatic mother, but it was definitely a long-overdue conversation. "But I think I'll wait until next time I'm home. Don't think I want to have that conversation over the phone."

"No, you'd better have that talk face-to-face." Aunt Lydia met my gaze and expelled a short breath. "I know Debbie would never say such a thing, but I've sometimes wondered if she saw a ghost."

I straightened in my chair. "Seriously? Why would you think that?"

"Because of some things I have experienced in this house." Aunt Lydia studied me intently. "You haven't ever felt anything odd when you were here? A blast of cold air in the middle of summer, or drapes moving without any wind, or some shadow you only see out of the corner of your eye?"

"No, of course not." My voice sounded shrill even to my ears. I could tell my aunt was not convinced. She probably knew I wasn't being entirely honest. I had felt peculiar prickling sensations when I was in the front parlor. Like something wasn't right. Like someone was hidden just out of sight, watching me.

But my mother's practical voice invaded my thoughts, making me dismiss such ideas as nonsense. "Don't tell me you have. I thought Richard's house was supposed to be haunted, not this one."

"I know it doesn't make any sense. Not in any logical way." Aunt Lydia gripped her knees with both hands. "Weird things happen, but when I think about them later, it feels like a dream or just my overactive imagination. Because even though I believe in the possibility, this is the wrong location for ghosts. Nothing's happened in this house to warrant a haunting. Nothing I know about, anyway."

I tipped my head to the side and looked her over. "Exactly. Besides, I've never heard you even hint at experiences with mysterious phenomena. You've always been honest with me about everything else—why not tell me about your fears of ghosts and ghoulies and things that go bump in the night?"

Aunt Lydia released her grip and waved one hand through the air. "Oh, you were just a teen when you first started visiting me. I know how heightened everything can feel at that age. I didn't want to put silly thoughts in your head, and I certainly didn't want to frighten you. I figured if you experienced anything similar, you would tell me. Then I would've talked to you about it, if only so you didn't feel alone. But since you never said a word, I assumed you hadn't felt anything odd." She pressed her hand against the arm of the rocker. "That it was all in my head."

"All in your head." I examined the deep lines bracketing her taut lips. "That was part of it too, wasn't it? Great-Grandmother Rose eventually lost her mind, and you were afraid . . ."

"People would think I was going the same way. Yes." Aunt Lydia sighed. "That's something that definitely haunts me, ghosts or no ghosts. I witnessed Rose's decline, her slide into oblivion. The idea that I could end up just like her is terrifying."

There it was—the real reason my aunt had refused to ever speak about any peculiar happenings in her house. "I don't think there's any chance of that. You are one of the sanest people I've ever known. I'm sure there's a logical explanation for anything odd you've experienced in this house. Like doors not hung properly, rusty hinges, hidden cracks that let in blasts of air, or stuff like that. It's an old house and not in the best condition." I stood up. "You are not going mad, no matter how many shadows you see. I would wager a million dollars on that."

"Good to know." Aunt Lydia shook her shoulders as if casting off some burden and reached for her cane, which she'd propped against the rocker. "I believe I will make us dinner now. Even if it's just soup and sandwiches, we need something." Balancing her weight over the cane, she rose to her feet.

"I can help with that. But tell me," I added as I followed her to the kitchen, "what was it that Rose said later in life that made you suspicious about her involvement in the Cooper case? In her ramblings, I mean."

"Oh, just random things . . ."

The doorbell chimed, and we both jumped.

"News," I said and hurried to open the front door.

Brad stood on the porch. He swiftly removed his hat and bobbed his head. "Hello, Amy and Mrs. Talbot."

"You found Sunny?"

He shook his head. "No, sorry. But it's turned into an official case now, so that will give us more resources." He twisted the brim of his hat between his hands. "I came to tell you about Bob Blackstone. Since you called me, warning about him and all."

"What about Bob?" Aunt Lydia appeared beside me.

"I did find his car. Up on Logging Road. But I don't think he had anything to do with Sunny's disappearance."

I stepped into the open doorway. "Why not?"

"Because his car was totaled, and he's in pretty bad shape. Apparently someone ran him off the road, although what anyone else was doing up on that old gravel road, I can't imagine."

"Is he all right?" Aunt Lydia tapped her cane against the metal doorsill.

"Not really. Fortunately, he could still talk a bit when I got there. He told me he was run off the road by some vehicle he didn't recognize. He lost control of his car, and it rolled into a ditch before it hit a tree. By the time the rescue squad arrived, Bob had lapsed into unconsciousness."

"My goodness." Aunt Lydia grabbed for my arm. "What next?"

"Is he going to be okay?" I asked, covering my aunt's hand with my own.

"Not sure. He's in the ICU right now, still unconscious. Bad head injury. Doctors might have to induce a coma to help his brain heal or something like that." Brad shook his head. "This just gets weirder by the day."

I clutched the bottom of my T-shirt with my free hand. "I'm sorry I suspected the mayor, but he just seemed to be a possible link to everything."

Brad shifted his weight from foot to foot. "Actually, it was lucky you called me. If I hadn't been out searching for him,

Blackstone could've died in that car. That's not a road many people use anymore."

"Which makes it even odder that someone else was there, unless . . ." I gazed up into Brad's solemn face. "He was being followed, wasn't he?"

"Looks like it. Which just adds a new wrinkle. And we can't ask him to clear up anything for some time. So now I've got to see if my team can puzzle it out without all the facts."

I almost mentioned Kurt Kendrick but remembered that the sheriff's office had cleared him. Although I had other reasons to suspect Kendrick, my theories were all based on hearsay and intuition. I had no real evidence to share. Not yet, anyway.

"I know you'll do your best." I offered Brad a smile. "You always do, it seems to me."

In the porch light, it was impossible to tell if Brad was blushing, but he did clear his throat before speaking again. "Part of the job."

"Thank you for coming to tell us this." Aunt Lydia released her grip on my arm and motioned toward the back of the house. "Would you like some coffee before you go?"

"Thanks, but no time. Gotta get back out there." Brad shoved his crumpled hat back on his head.

I reached up and flipped the bent brim down. "There. That's better."

He was definitely blushing. Poor guy. I made a mental note to talk to Sunny about giving Brad another chance. He really was a good guy under it all.

But Sunny had to be located first. Safe and sound. And Aunt Lydia was right—Brad and his team were probably our best chance to find her.

"We won't keep you," I told him. "Just let us know if there's any news about Sunny."

"I will," he said with a tip of his hat. "Good night, ladies."

I echoed Aunt Lydia's good-bye and added, "Please know you have our support and trust. If anyone can find Sunny, I believe you can."

That seemed to finally crack the ice between us. Brad offered me a warm smile before turning and heading for his cruiser.

Chapter Twenty-One

The next day was another Sunday. I toyed with the idea of attending church and even took the unusual step of blow-drying my hair rather than letting it air-dry. But after examining my face in the mirror and noticing the dark shadows under my eyes, I decided I wasn't up to answering the sincere but intrusive questions I was sure to face about Sunny's disappearance.

Besides, there was weeding waiting for me in the garden.

That's what I told Aunt Lydia, anyway, when she appeared in the kitchen in an aqua silk dress and beige pumps.

"Suit yourself." She spread some cream cheese on the bagel that she'd heated in the toaster oven. "I'd skip it too, but I'm supposed to be reading the lessons, so"—she waved the butter knife at me—"must fulfill my responsibilities."

"As you always do. Admirably," I replied while pouring syrup over my toasted frozen waffles.

"Just remember to take your cell phone while you're working in the garden. What with everything going on, I don't think any place is safe these days."

"I will. And I'll even be extra cautious and lock the back door."

"Good." Aunt Lydia examined me as she sipped her coffee. "You look tired. Not surprising, I guess. Maybe you should just rest today."

"No, I need to be doing something, or I'll spend the entire day fretting and waiting for a phone call from Brad. Maybe I can sweat off some of my anxiety over Sunny. And nothing clears my mind like working in the garden."

"Okay. Although, I might suggest something more tasteful than those denim cutoffs and that T-shirt." She squinted. "What does it say? Something about time . . ."

"'Wibbly wobbly, timey wimey.' It's a *Doctor Who* reference."

"Oh, that show." Aunt Lydia pursed her lips. "So very strange. Anyway, the shirt's ratty looking, whatever it says. And who knows if you might run into someone . . ."

I waved my fork at her. "Nothing about Richard, please."

Aunt Lydia ate her bagel in silence. She didn't speak again until she stood and carried her plate to the sink. "I really don't understand you sometimes, Amy."

I finished off the last bite of my waffles. "Don't feel bad. I don't understand myself a lot of the time either."

Turning and leaning back against the deep porcelain sink, Aunt Lydia huffed. "Sorry, but I must say something. I know I only met him once, but it was pretty clear that Charles Bartos was bad news. Now don't make that face at me. I saw how you behaved when you were dating him—always starving yourself because *Charles* thought you were getting a little pudgy. Not wanting to plan things with me or your friends because *Charles* might call. Always worrying whether your hair looked right, or certain clothes made you look fat, or whatever. Totally submerging your own personality to please a man who, frankly, wasn't worth the powder and shot it would take to blow him up. Let's face it: you allowed Charles to treat you like dirt for months before he finally dumped you for that violinist. Put up with all his nonsense without a peep, but now you want to give Richard the cold shoulder for heaven knows what reason. I just don't get it."

"Learned from my mistake." I dropped my gaze and furiously stirred my coffee. "And don't want to make another one."

"Okay, fair enough. But I don't think Richard is a mistake. That Charles fellow, yes. I could tell in an instant what he was. Nothing but a raving narcissist."

My spoon clattered to the table as I stared at her. "Why didn't you say anything?"

Aunt Lydia's stern expression softened. "Would you have listened?"

I took a deep breath before answering. "No."

"That's honest, at least. Oh, look at the clock. I must be off." She crossed to me and laid one hand on my shoulder. "Of course you should take as much time as you need to figure things out, dear. Just try not to drive Richard away while you're at it. Because even if you don't want to date him, I think he'd make a very good friend."

"You're right." I patted her hand before she withdrew it. "In fact, there's something I need to do this morning before I go outside."

Aunt Lydia paused in the archway. "Oh, what's that?"

"Watch a video online." Seeing her raised eyebrows, I added, "Richard asked me to. One of his choreographed pieces. Not sure what's up with that, but I promised I would see it."

"So you must. Our family prides itself on keeping its promises."

"I know." I smiled at her before she turned away. "Go on. I'll lock up as soon as you leave."

"Make sure you do," she called back to me as she disappeared into the hall.

I waited until I heard the door open and close before I walked out of the kitchen and down the hall. After securing the locks, I ran upstairs and brushed my teeth before heading into the library and grabbing my tablet from its charging station.

Carrying the tablet into the sitting room, I sank into the comfort of the suede sofa and searched for the dance video Richard had mentioned.

Dimensions, he'd called it. I entered the title and his name. A link to the video popped up immediately.

It was an amazing piece. Set to the song "In the End" by Snow Patrol, it incorporated dancers of all shapes and sizes, including some large people who moved more gracefully than I expected. Beginning as a series of repeated gestures and movements, the piece grew into an astonishing tapestry. All of the dancers performed the same steps at one time or another, but their distinctive physiques lent those repeated movements a unique quality that lifted the piece above most contemporary dance I'd seen.

As I glanced at the description under the video, I noticed a link to an interview with Richard. I clicked on it, hoping it would give me a deeper understanding of what this choreography meant to him.

I watched the interview once in stunned silence, then had to dash to the bathroom to grab a box of tissues before watching it again.

Turning off my tablet and laying it on the side table, I stared blankly at the dark television screen hanging on the far wall. After several minutes of reflection, I jumped to my feet and ran into the hall, where I snatched my house key from the ceramic bowl on the side table. Shoving my feet into a pair of sneakers I'd dumped by the front door, I left the house, somehow remembering to lock up before hurrying off the porch.

Standing uninvited at Richard's door, I leaned on the bell.

He opened the door after only the second ring, wearing gray workout pants and a loose white T-shirt. As usual when he was at home, his feet were bare.

"Amy, anything wrong? You look like you've been crying. Not bad news about Sunny, I hope?"

"No." I took a deep breath. "May I come in? I need to talk to you."

"Sure." Richard looked puzzled as he stepped back to allow me to enter the house. "Have a seat," he added as he locked the door. "Hope you don't mind if I grab my coffee from the kitchen before I sit down. It's made, but I haven't poured any yet. Not sure I can be coherent without it."

"Of course I don't mind." I plopped onto the sofa. "Take all the time you want."

"Do you want some?" he called out as he headed for the kitchen.

"No, I'm fine." I leaned back against the sofa cushions, fighting an urge to leap to my feet and pace the room.

Richard returned, carrying a steaming mug. He balanced the coffee cup on a short stack of dance magazines on the coffee table and sat next to me. "So what's this all about?"

I looked up and over his shoulder, focusing on the bookcase that held Paul Dassin's research. "You know how you told me to watch your dance thing online?"

"'Dance thing'?" Richard quirked his eyebrows. "Oh, you mean *Dimensions*."

"Yes. Well, I did. And your interview too."

Richard sat back, stretching his arm across the seat behind my head. "I see. What did you think?"

"It made me cry. Ugly cry, which is why I look like such a mess. But I had to come and talk to you right away, because"—I sniffed back another sob—"because . . ."

"Because?" Richard lowered his arm onto my shoulders.

"Because I have been so stupid, making assumptions while all the time you've had that in your past, and I had no idea, and here I was, wanting to put the brakes on anything between us just because I was scared and insecure, and . . ."

"None of that," Richard said, pulling me close. "It's not something everyone would know. Not a household name, remember?"

"Yeah, but your friend . . . she was a very close friend too, wasn't she?"

"Karla? Yes, she was." Richard adjusted his arm so I could lay my head against his shoulder. "We started out in dance together in an after-school program when we were just kids. When we were both accepted into the conservatory, we were so thrilled"—Richard caressed my arm with his free hand—"so excited to continue to learn and work together. We used to partner all the time. Set solo choreography on each other, practiced duets, challenged one another . . . it was never romantic, although I knew her body as well as my own. And I loved her more than anyone. She was my muse."

I tilted my head to look up at him. "You said in the interview she was the best dancer you'd ever known."

Richard's pensive expression brightened at the memory. "She was. Had the most incredible aptitude. Beautiful technique too, but it was more than that. Karla could interpret emotion better than anyone I've ever seen, before or since. She got to the heart of a piece, pulled out its essence, and displayed that through every little movement. Even the tiniest flick of her hand could tell a story or express more emotion than other dancers using every trick in the book. She was a marvel."

"But you also said she was tall and big-boned."

"Like a glorious Amazon." Richard stared at the ceiling. "That's what I called her. My amazing Amazon. She always liked that"—he dropped his chin toward his chest—"until she didn't."

I slid my right arm behind his back, hugging his waist. "Until she couldn't get into a company. That was the problem?"

"Yeah. She was perfect just as she was, but she stopped believing that. You see, she and I always dreamed about dancing for specific companies. We talked about those troupes incessantly, studied their videos, and attended their performances whenever we could. So as graduation approached, we made our list and spent extra time training for those auditions. It was such hard work, but also an exciting, glorious time, and then"—Richard leaned in, resting his head against mine—"Karla was rejected by every one of them."

I lifted my hand from his waist and smoothed his dark hair. "Because of her size."

"Because they couldn't see past it. They didn't notice her innate talent, her drive, her technique, her expressive ability, her utter brilliance. All they saw was her height and build. *Not right for us*, they said, but Karla knew what they meant. Not the right size or shape. That was all that mattered in the end."

I had heard this already from his online interview, but it didn't matter. I knew he needed to say it again.

He needed to say it to me.

"I told her it didn't matter." Richard straightened. "I said we'd start our own company, or I'd create solos for her, or something. We'd find a way. But she confessed that one of the people auditioning had pulled her aside to suggest she go into teaching and give up performing. Told her that she'd never make it in the professional dance world. It would be impossible, given her build. That was a lie, but Karla believed it."

Sensing the sudden tensing of his body, I pulled back my arm and slid away.

. He turned to face me, his eyes shadowed with pain. "That was the worst of it, you see. She believed that lie more than she believed in me."

"She left you a note?" I had to concentrate to keep my voice calm.

"In the studio where we always practiced. Where we'd shared so much joy. Yeah, there was a message for me, taped to the barre. Not a suicide note, thankfully, but still a good-bye." Richard sucked in a deep breath.

"Which involved you in the investigation into her disappearance."

He nodded. "That's how I knew what could happen after we found Doris Virts. With the deputies and all their questions and procedures."

"So Karla left dancing completely?"

"And my life. She told me not to look for her—she was going to disappear and would never dance again. Of course, I did try to find her but without success. I suppose she changed her name or something." Richard rubbed his jaw with the back of his hand. "She eventually contacted her family to let them know she was okay. So at least the investigation into her disappearance ended. But her family wouldn't tell anyone from the dance world where she was. Not even me."

"That had to be heartbreaking."

"It was, especially since I felt partially to blame. You see, I *had* gotten into one of our dream companies." As Richard lowered his hand into his lap, his fingers clenched into a fist.

"It was about her, not you."

Richard's glance pierced right through me. "I did learn that in time. Anyway, at first I thought I'd see her again. I couldn't picture a world where she'd give up dance completely. She loved it too much. So I always imagined running into her at a dance event, or a performance, or finding out she was teaching at some studio. But I never have. I guess she made good on her promise."

"Which is very sad for the dance world, as well as for you."

"It is." Richard closed his eyes for a moment. "The note wasn't the only thing, you know. She also left a message for everyone who walked into that studio. She covered the mirrors in lipstick, using harsh words like 'too big,' and 'fat,' and much, much crueler phrases. She wrote it all out—her hatred for those who told her those things. And worse, her hatred for herself."

He hadn't said that in the interview, only that his friend had run away and left the dance world. "I'm sorry, so sorry," I murmured, feeling like there was nothing else to say.

Richard grabbed me by the shoulders. "So you understand why I don't want to hear nonsense about body size and all that?"

I nodded. "I also get why you created *Dimensions*. You wanted to prove them wrong, didn't you?"

He slid his hands down my arms. "In a way. But more importantly, I wanted to demonstrate that all bodies are beautiful, that all movement is magic, and that there are so many different ways to express reality—so many different ways to *see*. I wanted to show them how to see."

"So now that's your mission in your work?"

A smile flickered over his face. "Yeah, it's what I do."

"Beautifully, I might add."

"Thank you." He took hold of my hands. "I really am attracted to you. Honestly."

I ducked my head. "Sorry I've been so silly. I get insecure, you know?"

"You shouldn't." Richard looked me over. "You're beautiful just as you are."

"Ratty T-shirt and all?"

His hands slid over my shirt. "I like it. It's soft."

"I think that's more me than the T-shirt."

"Even better."

"Your coffee is getting cold," I said, trapping his hands in mine.

"Don't need it. You've woken me up. I drink too much coffee anyway. Maybe I'll switch to Amy in the morning."

I chuckled. "Okay, that's a new one."

Richard grinned. "I'm a creative guy, remember?" He pulled me closer and whispered in my ear, "One day, I'd like to show you just how creative I can be."

"One day, I think I'd like that," I replied before he kissed me.

We stopped talking for quite some time after that.

I finally slid away from his hands and staggered to my feet when I heard a clock somewhere in the house chiming the hour. "Better go. Aunt Lydia will be coming home from church soon."

"Like she cares." Richard flopped back and stretched his legs across the length of the sofa.

I tugged down my rumpled T-shirt. "I didn't leave a note or anything. She thinks I went out to weed, and when she doesn't see me in the backyard . . ."

"Yeah, okay, you'd better go. But first, come here and give me a good-bye kiss." He held up his arms.

"Uh-uh," I said, heading for the door. "I do that, and I'll never get out of here."

"Damn, my evil plan thwarted again."

"But not forever. I mean, you do know where I live." I could hear his laughter as I left the house.

I smiled, pleased I could make him laugh.

Because you really want to make him happy, don't you, Amy?

Why, yes. Yes, I did. I shoved my hair behind my ears. Nothing wrong with that. He deserved to be happy.

Just as I did.

I walked back to Aunt Lydia's in a daze, pausing at the fence between the houses to admire the climbing roses. As I stroked the velvet petals of one particularly lovely bloom, a car horn sounded behind me.

Turning slowly, I watched a silver sedan pull over in front of me. I peered into the car. "Sylvia, what are you doing here? Aunt Lydia's still at church."

The passenger-side window rolled down automatically. Sylvia leaned across the seat. "I came to find you, not Lydia. I heard you were searching for your friend. I might know where she is."

"Sunny?"

"Yes, Sunshine Fields. I was out checking on some of my mountain property, and I thought I spied her car. It's a bright-yellow Bug, right?"

"It is," I said, jogging over to my cousin's car.

"I saw it off to one side like someone had just pulled off the road for some reason. Didn't stop because I hadn't been told Sunshine was missing until I got back into town just now. But when I heard about that, and what her car looked like, I thought I should come and find you."

I leaned in the open window. "Did you see anyone in the car?"

Sylvia patted her lacquered hair with one hand. "I believe there was, but like I said, I didn't think anything of it at the time. I simply concluded that someone had pulled over to check a map or something. But when I heard the news . . ."

I yanked open the front passenger-side door. "Can you take me back there?"

"Certainly. That's why I came by. I thought you might want to help me check it out."

I jumped into the car. As I slammed the door, I realized I'd still left no note for Aunt Lydia. But I could call her, or call Richard and ask him to tell her where I'd gone.

Because if there was a chance to find Sunny, I had to take it.

"Very well, let's go." Sylvia punched buttons to roll up my window and lock the door.

I buckled my seat belt before sliding my cell phone from my pocket.

"What's that for?" Sylvia stared at my hands as if she'd spied something vile.

"Oh, just thought I'd call Deputy Tucker. He's been out looking for Sunny, so he'll want to know about this lead." As I punched in numbers, I noticed Sylvia reaching for something in her oversized purse.

A gun. I stared at the cold metal cylinder pointed at my heart.

"Hand over the phone, and buckle your seat belt," said my cousin. "We're going for a little drive."

Chapter Twenty-Two

As I strapped myself in, I slipped my hand to the side and fiddled with the passenger side front door handle. It wouldn't budge. Sylvia obviously had engaged the automatic locking mechanisms and had no intention of allowing me to open the door or the window. *She must be unhinged*, I thought with a swift glance at my cousin's sharp profile.

There was no way I could open the door, at least not until Sylvia released the locking switch or opened her door when we reached our final destination.

If you reach it.

Trapped in the confines of the car with Sylvia and her gun, I knew force was useless. I needed to talk myself out of this situation if I could. "What are you doing, Sylvia? Surely we don't need such protection searching for Sunny."

"It's not for protection," said my cousin. "It's to make you behave." She placed the gun in her lap. "Just remember I can grab this pistol and shoot you faster than you can make any move on me." She tapped the steering wheel with one polished fingernail. "And I will warn you—all things considered, I'm a pretty good shot. So don't get any stupid ideas."

Sylvia tossed her bulky purse over her shoulder and into the back seat as she revved the car engine and pulled away from the curb. She pushed the car far over the speed limit before swerving onto a little-used side road and continuing to press her foot hard against the pedal.

"I'm terribly confused," I said after excruciating moments of silence in which I contemplated my cousin wrapping the car, and us, around a tree. "Why are you doing this?"

"Just tying up loose ends," Sylvia said airily. She kept one hand on the gun, which did nothing to alleviate my fears of her losing control of the car. "Clearing up a few things before I take an extended vacation."

I stared at my hands, wondering whether grabbing the steering wheel was worth the risk. Probably not. At the speed we were going, we were likely to end up in a deadly crash. Or Sylvia would actually be able to lift the pistol from her lap and shoot me. "So is that the gun you used to murder Doris Virts and Clark Fowler?"

"Who says I murdered anyone?"

"They're dead, and you have a gun. And I think maybe you have a motive."

"Oh, and what would that be, Nancy Drew?"

"You invested in Bob Blackstone's development project and then somehow found out about the excess iron in the water table." I clenched my fingers until the knuckles turned white. "You were afraid that Doris or Clark, who somehow knew about the iron problem, would spill that secret."

"Warmish." Sylvia stared straight ahead, jutting out her sharp chin. "I admit I might lose a little cash if that deal falls through. But there was more to it than that."

I considered all the facts I'd assembled so far. Any knowledge of the tainted wells, which might derail the development deal, would also expose the town council's actions back in 1958. "Okay, so you somehow learned the truth about the orphanage tragedy and knew it would prove our family's complicity in the cover-up."

"Much warmer," Sylvia said, lifting her black pump off the gas pedal and slowing the car as we turned onto a narrow side road.

We were headed into the mountains. Somewhere off the beaten track, although we were still on a paved road. "But that's just history. I mean, it was a terrible thing, and yes, our family members were partially to blame, but why does that matter so much now? It's all in the past."

Sylvia narrowed her eyes. "Which you have no respect for, it seems, despite your profession."

"I appreciate history, but I don't believe the sins of the father—or mother—must be visited on the children. What they did, they did. What does that have to do with us?"

"Everything, if you have any concern for our family name. Oh, wait"—Sylvia tightened her grip on the steering wheel—"it isn't your name, is it? You aren't going to carry it into the future. I'm the only true Baker left. And that name is still worth something, even far beyond Taylorsford."

"Name or no name, it's still my family." I untangled my fingers and gripped my knees with both hands. "I can see why it won't put the Bakers in a particularly good light, but what does that really have to do with us? How can that hurt us except by puncturing our family pride?"

Sylvia shot a quick glance at me. "You don't get it, do you? The family name is important to my business interests as well as my sense of pride."

I stared at her, my mind racing. There was something here I hadn't considered. Something outside of all my theories. "That's ridiculous. How can past indiscretions, which you had no direct hand in, affect your financial dealings now?"

"Because I do business in parts of the world where one's family name is still much more important than it is in the United States. With people who, despite their own rather sketchy practices, prefer that their investors have no scandals that could be exploited by the media or other interested parties."

"Not sure I understand that."

"Well, of course you don't." Sylvia cast me a disapproving glance. "You don't know much about the financial world, do you? You're just a naïve child, sitting in your ivory tower surrounded by books."

"So you're saying family skeletons might rattle your business partners?"

Sylvia shifted in her seat. "An apt assessment," she said after a moment of silence. "But yes, anything that makes me appear less than a squeaky-clean businesswoman from an impeccable family could prove detrimental to my partners. And me, as well. You see, such things might draw the interest of the media, who would be thrilled to crank out stories about past scandals. Which could turn a spotlight on me, my bank accounts, and business transactions. Not something my partners are eager to have happen."

"Because you're laundering money for criminal interests through your real estate deals? Or otherwise cooking the books?" I studied my cousin's haughty profile. "You don't want bank examiners, or insurance adjustors, or the IRS taking too close a look, I suppose."

"Well, at least unlike a few other people in our family, you aren't stupid." Sylvia's fingers clenched on the steering wheel. "I did conduct some business under aliases in order to protect the Baker name for use in more critical deals. But I tried not to do that too often, although a fake name or two does come in handy now and then."

251

Aliases, deals, and, no doubt, doctored books and shell corporations. My cousin had been busy. I pressed my throbbing temple against the cool window glass. "Did you always know? About the tainted wells, I mean."

"No. Actually, you have Dr. Virts to thank for that. You see, I'd never have been forced to such extremes if he hadn't seen fit to blackmail me. And poor Bob Blackstone as well."

Blackmail? I straightened in my seat. The facts clicked together in my mind like jigsaw puzzle pieces. Of course. Don Virts, who needed money to repay Kurt Kendrick, must've found out about the orphanage cover-up from his mother. Her father, Douglas Beckert, had been on the town council at the time.

Douglas Beckert, who was reimbursed by the town for water testing done by the Carthage Company.

"Doris told Dr. Virts about the test the town council secretly commissioned after the deaths at the orphanage, didn't she?"

Sylvia shot me a look of astonishment. "My, my, you have been busy. Yes. Although Doris was only a child at the time, she overheard her father ranting about some lab results. He was quite distraught, which is why it stuck with her over the years. She remembered that some private company had done the testing and her father had originally paid for the tests. She dutifully kept this secret because her father had demanded her silence. But then, when her mind started to go . . ."

"She confessed it to her son."

"Well, according to Don, she mistook him for her long-dead father, but yes, she rattled on about it once in Don's presence. He realized what it meant right away. Took his mom to the library shortly thereafter. Encouraged her to look at materials from the 1950s, which gave him the opportunity to peek at a particular folder when he arrived to pick her up." Sylvia shook her head. "Don is so paranoid sometimes. He thought sending

Doris would look less suspicious than if he asked to see files connected to the orphanage affair. As if anyone would have put two and two together over something like that."

Click, went another puzzle piece. Yes, Sunny had mentioned that Doris had used the archives to look at materials from the 1950s. I also remembered how Sunny had claimed she'd left Doris once, just for a few minutes, under the watchful eyes of her son.

Very observant eyes, indeed, that had undoubtedly seen what I had also spied in the town council minutes—the mention of the Carthage Company in connection to a reimbursement to Douglas Beckert.

So it was Don Virts who'd shoved that file into the wrong cabinet. He'd probably been in a rush when he heard Sunny returning to the building, although his panic would've been based on his own sense of guilt since Sunny wouldn't have made any connection between the file and his planned crime.

Sylvia sniffed. "I must admit that Don was rather resourceful. When he contacted the company that conducted the tests, he pretended to represent his family and was able to get a copy of the report. Still had some Beckert family stationary, which helped his claim. Clever of him, I must say." There was a tinge of admiration in Sylvia's tone.

"So he has a copy of the report that proves the town council knew about the iron levels, even if only after the fact."

"And thus, proves the cover-up." Sylvia tapped her fingers against the steering wheel. "Unfortunately, Don knew I was likely to do anything to protect the family name, since I'd forced him to retract some comments he'd made about the Bakers during town council meetings in the past. Actually, I considered simply doing away with Don once he embarked on his scheme to blackmail me over my family's involvement in the orphanage cover-up. That is, until he informed me he'd left an envelope in his home safe to be opened in the event of his death. Unfortunately, not only did it contain the copy of that report; it also detailed where the original was held at some high-security archive."

"Iron Mountain," I said, which earned another sharp glance from Sylvia.

"So there I was, having to pay off Don. So unpleasant." Sylvia's lips thinned, accentuating the deep lines bracketing her mouth.

"You could've just exposed his blackmail and allowed the truth to come out. Maybe it would've hurt your business interests and family pride, but wasn't it time Taylorsford took responsibility for the orphanage tragedy? Not to mention the whole well-water thing could finally clear Eleanora Cooper of any wrongdoing, although I don't suppose you care about that."

Sylvia inhaled so quickly, she coughed. She cleared her throat before speaking again. "So another bit of deduction? Just couldn't keep your nose out of it, could you?"

I rolled the hem of my T-shirt between my hands. "There were too many odd things. It was driving me crazy. I had to find answers."

"Well, I'm afraid I can't allow your armchair-detective obsession to continue, my dear. It really is too bad. If you'd just minded your own business, you wouldn't be in this situation."

"If you hadn't murdered people, neither would you," I snapped before I could stop myself.

Sylvia appeared unfazed by my outburst. "It wasn't what you think. I felt no personal animosity toward either Doris or Clark. I just had to silence them so they couldn't spill their secrets. I was afraid of other people putting the pieces together. I have a reputation as a society hostess, philanthropist, and patron of the arts, you know. There are media outlets who'd love to broadcast an exclusive exposing dirt on our family and, by association, me. Sadly, I've made a few enemies among some of the paparazzi over the years. And despite their uncivilized behavior, some of them can be quite clever." She glanced at me, flashing a smile that held no humor. "Just like you, my dear."

"So Doris wasn't raving, after all. You were following her?"

"Yes. I wanted to make sure she didn't start talking to the wrong people. She almost blabbed to the authorities, you know, not long before I silenced her. I heard she made it to the sheriff's office and demanded to speak with a deputy before Bethany tracked her down and took her home." Sylvia turned the car onto a gravel road. "I told Don he should insist she live with him and his family instead of with that sister of his. Just so he could keep an eye on her. 'Lock her in her bedroom, if necessary,' I said."

I shivered as the unemotional tone of Sylvia's voice clashed with her words.

"But no, he couldn't be bothered. So I had to keep an eye on her after that. And shut her up for good, when I had the chance."

I was jolted from side to side as Sylvia drove her car over the washboard ruts of the gravel road. The woods that lined the road were thick with evergreens and oaks. I sank into my seat, imagining one heavy gust of wind crashing the low-hanging branches into the car.

"But Clark Fowler . . ."

Sylvia waved her left hand. "Oh, him. I had no real plan to kill him. He'd been spewing his conspiracy theories for so long, and no one believed them, so I thought there was no harm in it. But then Clark had that run-in with Bob Blackstone, and I was afraid Bob's subsequent anxiety might drive him to confess Don's blackmail scheme to the authorities."

"And I guess you preferred to let Bob live, at least until the development deal went through," I muttered.

Like my aunt, Sylvia's hearing was not in the least impaired. "Exactly. So I went to have a little talk with Clark Fowler instead. Just a chat. Of course, I carried my gun in my purse as I always do. For my own protection."

"I guess Clark didn't want to be told to stay quiet."

"No, so I had to silence him."

I looked up at her stoic profile. She was so calm and logical—and yet completely mad.

Foolish me, I'd always thought that a person with serious psychological issues would be easy to identify. Now I realized that I was wrong. Although Sylvia had struck me as cold and self-absorbed, I would never have imagined her a sociopath. Yet here she was, calmly chatting about murdering people for no more reason than preserving her family name and protecting a few business deals.

"I thought perhaps Kurt Kendrick was involved, but he wasn't, was he?"

"Kurt? No. Although he does conduct business with some interesting partners. As I said, he and I share some mutual friends."

I clutched my upper arms with both hands to still my shaking. So I hadn't been completely wrong about Kendrick. Just as Zelda and Aunt Lydia expected, his hands were not entirely clean. But it seemed in this instance he was innocent of any wrongdoing, unlike my murderous cousin, Don Virts, and—to a lesser degree—our illustrious mayor.

I turned my head to stare out the window. The wild woods had given way to a field of overgrown shrubs and grasses, indicating that the area had once been cleared. A mountain farm, I thought as we rounded a corner and drove into a parking area fronting an old barn.

Sylvia stopped the car before the open barn doors. "Now stay put," she said as she lifted her gun and stepped out of the car, locking the doors behind her with her key fob. She waved the gun at me and walked through the barn doors and was swallowed up by shadows.

The second Sylvia disappeared from my view, I frantically unbuckled my seat belt and wiggled my door handle. It still wouldn't budge. I clambered over the center console to reach the driver's side. Yanking that door handle freed the lock. Kicking the door open with my right foot, I stumbled out of the car and ran.

If I could reach the woods, I might have a fighting chance. Sylvia had the gun, but if I could get to the trees, she wouldn't have a clear shot. She had the advantage, but she was only one person.

It was one against one. Although the gun was a problem. *A problem, Amy? A problem?* The hysteria I couldn't release bubbled up in my throat, almost choking me. But I couldn't focus on that. I had to get away.

I had almost reached the tree line when Sylvia's shouts rang in my ears. I just lowered my head and ran faster.

Right into the arms of the short, wiry man who stepped out of the woods.

Don Virts. Where the hell had he come from? It was as if he'd materialized from the trees, like some forest gnome.

"Hold up there, missy," Don said, wrapping his arms around me. Despite his small stature, he was surprisingly strong. "You're not going anywhere."

Unable to move my arms, I kicked his shins. He swore and jabbed his elbow into my ribs, knocking the wind from my lungs.

"You took your time," Sylvia said as she strolled up to us, the gun held casually at her side. "You ditched your car somewhere secluded, I hope."

"Other side of the woods, next to the Fields girl's car."

"Good." Sylvia tossed her car keys at Don. "Here, hold onto these for a minute while I keep our nosy librarian in check."

As Don released his hold on me to grab the keys from the air, I tumbled to the hard ground. I looked up into Sylvia's cold face and knew my next escape attempt would require better planning if I wanted to avoid being her third victim. She had leveled the gun until it was pointing directly at my forehead. "Stand up," she commanded.

I rose slowly, my eyes on the gun.

"Now march into the barn. And remember, I've got my pistol trained on you."

Walking with measured steps, I crossed the graveled lot and entered the barn. Hearing two sets of footsteps behind me, I knew Don was trailing Sylvia.

Ordering me to halt once I was inside the barn's wide center aisle, Sylvia pressed the barrel of the gun against my shoulder. I glanced to my right and spied a shiny new dead bolt on a weathered wooden door.

Don moved closer, stepping around us to push back the bolt. Sylvia lowered the gun to her right side and reached for my shoulder with her left hand.

I took the opportunity to twist away, hoping I could somehow drop to the ground. Sylvia's hold on the gun had loosened, and if I could trip her up . . .

Sylvia released a string of expletives that I was shocked she even knew. She grabbed me by my upper arm and yanked me around to face her with a strength that must have been born of desperation and adrenaline. As she swung at me wildly, she dealt me a blow with her right hand. The one that still clutched the gun.

I stumbled backward. Staring at my attackers, a wave of nausea overcame me. I gagged and pressed my hands against both temples as if that action could still my rattled thoughts and stop the ringing in my ears. Don grabbed me by the shoulders and turned me around before yanking my arms down and holding them behind my back. As soon as Sylvia opened the door, Don shoved me forward, sending me sprawling onto a hard wooden floor. It was all I could do to turn myself over as the door closed and the dead bolt slammed shut.

Dust motes danced in the air above my face, or maybe it was the stars flickering in my eyes from that blow to my head.

Trapped. I was trapped again. I blinked rapidly and thrust up one hand, as if I could grab hold of one of those stars. As if I could reach something, anything, that could free me from this makeshift prison.

Chapter
Twenty-Three

Fingers clutched my upraised hand.

"Richard," I muttered, tightening my grip.

The dusty scent of old hay and grain rose up in my nose as the person kneeling next to me shifted. "No, sorry, just me."

I sat up with a jolt, scraping the bare skin on the back of my legs against something. Pressing my hand to the surface, I realized the rough wooden boards were peppered with bits of straw.

"Sunny!" I turned my head, sending stabs of pain from ear to ear. As I stared at my friend, her face wavered like she was trapped behind old glass. But it was my eyes, blurring everything. "Are you okay?"

"Not really." Sunny's normally bright voice sounded hoarse.

As my vision cleared, I examined her more carefully. Her silky hair lay in ropey tangles across her shoulders, and her lips were chapped to the point of bleeding. "You've been here the whole time?"

"Yes."

"So since Friday, right after the protest?" I released Sunny's hand and pushed several strands of hair out of my eyes.

"Yes, and so far only Sylvia and Don have come around. I hoped it was Brad or another one of the deputies when I heard the commotion outside, but then the door opened, and Sylvia held her gun on me as Don Virts shoved you in here." Her deep breath caused a rattle in her throat. "They locked the door again, of course. I wasn't fast enough to do anything to stop them."

I touched her bare forearm, noting the red marks fading on her wrists. "We've been searching for you."

"I know. I heard them talking. They were worried. Especially about Brad."

"And they should be. He's pulled out all the stops to look for you." I allowed my gaze to wander around our small prison. A high barred window allowed in enough light to see our surroundings but offered no avenue for escape. I rubbed at my temples. Our makeshift cell appeared to be an old storage room. There were burlap sacks piled on the floor and wooden posts jutting out from the plank walls. *For saddles*, I thought, although there were none in the room. But a frayed rope halter and a moth-eaten horse blanket hung from hooks in one wall. So a tack room no longer in use. I refocused on Sunny's tired face. "You realize Sylvia Baker and Don Virts are in on this together?"

"Yeah, knew they had to be because they both kidnapped me. It was after the protest ended. Most everyone else had left, although Don Virts was still around. He volunteered to help me collect any trash left on the property, then offered me a bottle of water. I guess it was dosed with some kind of drug, a roofie or something, because after a little while, I started to feel dizzy, and then I guess I stumbled over my own feet and passed out." Sunny rubbed at her forehead. "I don't remember anything about being put in a car, but I imagine Don helped Sylvia with that. But then he must've taken my keys and driven my car, because when I woke for a moment, all I saw was the back of

Sylvia's head. She was the only one besides me in her car." Sunny held out her hands. "I was tied up, so I couldn't escape, and anyway, I was so groggy I passed out again until we arrived here."

"I don't have any idea where *here* is—do you?" I wiped sweat from my forehead. It was hot and stuffy, wherever it was.

"No. Just that we're in the mountains somewhere off the beaten track. I glimpsed this old barn as the two of them hauled me out of the car, but that's all."

"I heard Don say he hid your car where no one could find it."

"And took my phone."

"Yeah, I figured that." I slid one hand into my pocket. "Mine's gone too, of course." I took hold of Sunny's dry fingers. "One of them sent a text to your grandparents. Said you weren't coming home Friday night. That you were spending the night at my house. So no one wondered where you were until Saturday when you didn't show up for work."

"They think they're pretty clever, I guess."

"Well, smarter than me because I really got it wrong. I thought Kurt Kendrick was the mastermind. I did suspect that Don and Bob were involved, but I never thought my cousin was mixed up in the murders in any way. Yet she was the one who killed both Doris and Clark."

"Well, that's not something you would expect."

"No. I mean, Kendrick supposedly has some underworld connections, so I thought he might've had you kidnapped because you saw his car at the archives that day. But apparently that was just a coincidence."

"Don't beat yourself up—you pieced most of it together. You nailed the part about Don and Bob being involved. Sylvia Baker was the wild card. Who would've thought she was capable of killing people with no remorse?" Sunny pulled her hands free

and tried to spit onto the wooden floor. But no bubble of mois-
ture appeared on her cracked lips. "Sorry, I'm so dry. Feel like I
have cotton stuffed in my mouth."

"Didn't they give you water?"

"Yes, but I've stopped drinking it. Think there's something
in it. I kept drifting in and out of consciousness for a while.
Couldn't have been the initial drug, so I guess they've been dos-
ing me since." She moved her leg, revealing a thermos sitting
on the floor near her hip. "I didn't drink any more water after I
figured that out, and my head cleared right up."

"But you can't go without water indefinitely." I examined the door to the tack room. The thrown bolt was visible
through the cracks between the wallboards.

"I don't think they mean to keep me indefinitely," said
Sunny. "Or you, I'm afraid."

I stared at her. "What do you mean?"

"Face it, Amy. They mean to kill us sooner or later. Not sure
why they haven't yet, to be honest." As Sunny lifted her hand to
rub at her eyes, her fingers trembled. "I heard them conspiring.
When I walked up behind Sylvia Baker at the protest, she was
talking to Don on her phone. I knew it was him because she stupidly said his name. Right after she mentioned something about
taking care of Bob Blackstone just like the others. I didn't put
it together right away, but I guess Sylvia thought I'd heard too
much and figured I might mention something to Brad, so . . ."

"She and Don grabbed you." I pressed my back into the
rough boards of the wall behind me. "Because they killed Doris
and Clark Fowler. Well, Sylvia pulled the trigger, but Don
helped cover it up."

"I figured. Otherwise, why be so worried about what I
might've heard?"

I touched my left temple and grimaced. There was a painful knot right above my ear. That blasted gun. But at least Sylvia hadn't decided to shoot me. Yet. "It all sprang from Don's blackmail of Bob and Sylvia."

"Really? What would Dr. Virts have on them?"

As I outlined what I'd heard from Sylvia and a few of my own theories, Sunny looked puzzled, then angry.

"But why grab you? I was the only one who overheard them plotting on their phones."

I shrugged. "Sylvia knows we're close, so I guess she was afraid you'd told me something. And I was nosing around, you know, discovering information. She might've been worried about that, although I'm not sure how she would've known . . . Anyway, I think there's another less-conscious reason. Something to do with my inheritance of Aunt Lydia's house. Maybe I'm the one who sounds crazy now, but seriously, Sylvia can't be in her right mind if she thinks murder is the proper way to get ahead in life." I scooted closer to Sunny and put my arm around her shoulders. "I'm so sorry you're caught up in all this. Can't believe someone in my family is to blame."

"Not your fault." Sunny laid her head on my shoulder. "You and Lydia don't even have a relationship with Sylvia. She might as well be a stranger."

"I know, but it's still family." I considered what Aunt Lydia had said about my mother. Had Mom really been traumatized because a grandmother she despised had turned out to be even more evil than she thought? It was possible. I sure felt guilty about Sylvia's actions, and I hardly knew her.

I heard the scuff of shoes on gravel and froze.

Sunny lifted her head. "I think they're right outside," she said softly, then touched her fingers to her lips.

"Want to see if I can hear anything," I whispered back before crawling to the tack room door.

I pressed my ear to the solid door, then slid over to the adjoining wall. The chinks between its boards offered a better listening post. I tried to see anything through the cracks but only spied feet.

"Don't want your gun," Don Virts said, kicking a few stones with his loafers.

"Take it," Sylvia commanded. Her black leather pumps were scuffed, probably from chasing me down. "Somebody has to get rid of those girls, and it's not going to be me."

I shivered as if drenched by a bucket of ice but held up my hand when Sunny mouthed, *What are they saying?*

"Oh, I see. You have no trouble putting a bullet in my mother or Clark Fowler but can't shoot the two young women who could wreck all our plans?" Don kicked some more gravel. "What're you going do with that gun, anyway? You don't plan to hang onto it, I hope."

"Why shouldn't I? It's not registered to me. I acquired it through, shall we say, back channels. In fact, it's the very one I want you to use. No way to trace it to either of us."

"You are a cool customer, aren't you? I bet you just sauntered away from those murder scenes without any care for blood spatter or anything else too."

"Don't be ridiculous. I took precautions. Wore gloves and cheap raincoats and ditched them in a trash bag I carried in my handbag. I could stuff all that and the gun in my purse, and no one would ever question me, because who notices an older woman carrying a large handbag?"

"Bold as brass." There was a tinge of admiration in Don Virts's voice. But fear too. Definitely some fear.

"I knew no one would suspect me. Why would they? I am a harmless woman. A pillar of society. A contributor to many worthy causes."

"And my bank account, which is also worthy." Something snide had crept into Don's tone.

"You flatter yourself. You are a worthless blackmailer, nothing more. You couldn't even manage to kill Bob Blackstone. It's quite likely he'll recover, and what then?"

I motioned for Sunny. "Sylvia's talking to Don about the blackmail," I whispered when Sunny moved next to me.

Anything else? Sunny mouthed. I shook my head, not wanting to frighten her with Sylvia's murderous request of Don.

"One of us will have to shut him up permanently before that happens." Don tapped his loafers against the ground. "He can't be allowed to reveal I was blackmailing him. That would blow everything wide open."

Black heels spun, spitting out a shower of gravel. "What's that? Who's there?"

"I don't see anything."

"There, in the trees. A shadowy figure." Sylvia's voice, usually so clear and firm, cracked on that last word. "Is someone watching us? Did you bring along an accomplice?"

Don snorted. "No, certainly not. I wouldn't want to deal with yet another person in something as distasteful as this. It's bad enough I have to work with you. And anyway, there's no one there."

"Very well, I suppose my eyes deceived me." Sylvia's voice regained its typical cool tone as the black pumps turned to face Don's loafers. "And as for selecting your compatriots wisely, you must admit you were foolish in your choice of Bob as a blackmail victim. He had no stomach for murder, did he? Happy to buy your silence about that iron contamination on his property but not willing to keep his mouth shut when he figured out who was behind the murders. A weak man, in the end. The kind who'd roll over if the authorities questioned him more than once. You should have thought of that."

"He wouldn't have figured it out if you hadn't forced me to help you kidnap the Fields girl. That's what made it all click in his mind, or so he told me when he threatened to go to the sheriff's office with what he knew."

Sylvia laughed, a harsh squawk that held no humor. "So you decided to just run him off the road instead of confronting him face-to-face? That was a coward's trick. But of course, taking advantage of your own mother and her secret was pretty low too."

"But you're the one who killed her." Don's last words ended on a whine. "Why'd you have to go and do that, anyway? From some of her ramblings about being followed, I figured you might be watching her, but I never thought you'd resort to murder."

"That was your fault. I had no choice once I knew I couldn't trust you to keep her quiet. 'Take her into your own home,' I said. But no, you didn't want to have to deal with her, so you left her with your sister. Where, at any time, she could have experienced a lucid moment and told everyone the truth."

"Yes, the truth. Don't forget that. It *is* the truth. What the town council did, covering things up. It was your father and grandfather along with the rest."

"Your grandfather was in on it too, or you'd never have known. No, Dr. Virts, I don't think you can claim any pride in this matter. Especially since you decided to ask me for more hush money rather than turn me in."

"You're a fine one to talk about scruples," Don said. "But then, I knew your family pride would force you to pay. Couldn't bear to see your name dragged through the mud, could you?

The almighty Bakers, founders of the town. And you, swanning about like a fine lady, always acting like your ancestors were some kind of aristocracy when they were lumber barons who lucked into some valuable land and probably stole the rest."

"Don't speak about my family that way." Sylvia's voice cut through the air, sharp as a tin can's lid. "You have no right to judge them."

"Don't I? I think I can judge all I want. Look what they've produced—a murderer who's cold as the cash she loves to accumulate. More concerned with perpetuating the family name than human life. And for what? You have no husband or children, so who comes after you? Lydia's niece and nephew are the only heirs to the mighty Baker heritage, if not the name. Is that the real reason you want to kill one of them? To end your illustrious family with you?" Don's tone dripped with sarcasm. "That would be a shame. She can be a nosy little thing, but at least the girl isn't a heartless bitch like you."

"Shut up!" Sylvia screeched. "You shut your mouth!"

"Or what? Don't forget I still know things. And I'm your best alibi. Me and my clever story about the drifter."

"Stupid, not clever. Easily disproved."

"I don't think so. Anyway, I'm not dispatching your relative for you or that Fields girl either. You want them dead, you kill them."

"Don't forget that they can implicate you as well."

"Doubt they'll get the chance. I trust your murderous instincts. I'm sure you won't let them live. But just remember"— the loafers scattered gravel as Don turned aside—"you'll eventually have to track down the boy too if you really want to do it up right. Kill off the final stumbling block to your claim to be the last of the Bakers."

"You stay here."

"I have your car keys. So no, I don't think I will stay." The loafers walked away.

"Yes, you will. Permanently," said my cousin.

Sunny and I fell back on our heels as a gunshot reverberated through the clear summer air.

Chapter Twenty-Four

Had Sylvia actually shot Don Virts? A gust of wind rattled through the barn, followed by a shriek from Sylvia and another gunshot. Although strangely, this one sounded like she was firing into the distance.

Into the woods, where she thought she saw someone lurking before. As Sunny and I clung to each other, certain we would be next, I entertained the momentary hope that someone *was* there, but logic told me it was unlikely. Sylvia had just been spooked by a random deer or bird or something.

"Hear that?" Sunny asked after a minute or two. "A car, pulling away."

"But who's driving?" I released my grip on my friend and scooted back over to the wall. Standing so I could press my eye to one of the wider chinks, I peered out.

There was a body lying on the gravel driveway. A prone form, topped with dark hair.

"Don's on the ground. Not sure if he's dead or alive." I bit my lower lip. "Wonder what that second shot was for? It didn't sound the same."

"Don's obviously hurt, so Sylvia shot him. Maybe twice?" Sunny jumped to her feet and joined me, pressing her forehead to the slatted wood wall so she could peer outside. "No sign of her car, so she must've left."

"Why, I wonder?"

"Maybe she freaked out and just made a run for it."

"She blasted two other people at close range, but shooting Don Virts in the back freaked her out? Not likely." I turned to face Sunny. "But for whatever reason, she's gone for now. So we have to try to get out of here."

"How? There's a lock on the door."

I stared between the boards at the thrown bolt. "Yes, but"—I wiggled one of the boards—"if we could tear away some of these, maybe we could actually reach the latch."

Sunny slapped her hand to her forehead. "Stupid me. Why didn't I think of that?"

"Because you were drugged most of the time." I pulled harder on the board. "We need an object that will pry this out or break it. Think there might be something metal in here?"

"Horseshoes, maybe?" Sunny crossed to the other side of the tack room in two strides. "I'll check over here. You take that side."

"Okay." I dug through a pile of burlap sacks and popped open a battered crate, but all I found was mouse droppings. Or rat droppings? I wasn't sure which they were; I was just relieved I hadn't encountered the actual animals.

"Snake skin," Sunny said. "Big one too. But fortunately the snake seems to have moved on."

"Hopefully," I muttered.

We dug around for a few more minutes, turning up nothing useful but a rusty metal flask that broke in half when Sunny slammed it against one of the boards.

But that made me think . . . drinking bottle. "The thermos!" I shouted as Sunny snatched it off the floor.

"Great minds," she said, waving the silver metal thermos.

"It might be heavy enough," I said. "We can take turns—one keep a lookout while the other hits at the board, and then switch off."

"This is the spot." Sunny tapped her fingers on a section of the wall near the door. "Already has a crack in it, see?"

I examined the rough board. There was a long split, running from one side to the other. "Perfect. All right, let's give it a try. You watch for Sylvia, and I'll take out my aggression on that board."

It took several rounds of each of us hitting at the wood to splinter it. It cracked the thermos as well as the wall, but we finally broke the board enough to pull the bottom section free, creating an opening just wide enough for a slender arm to slide through.

Sunny pressed her body tight to the wall. "Almost have it."

I peered through the higher chink, afraid I'd see Sylvia's car pulling up at any moment. "Do you need help?"

"Yeah. Take hold of my waist and keep me balanced. I'm going to try to shove the bolt back and might need to get on tiptoe to reach."

I grabbed her waist, gripping the sweat-dampened fabric of her cotton sundress with my fingers, and held on tight as she lurched forward.

"Got it!" She slammed the palm of her hand against the bolt. It slid back, and the door immediately swung open, the rusty hinges squealing in protest.

We looked at each other for only a second before dashing out into the open center aisle.

The barn obviously hadn't been used in some time. The straw bales stacked at the far end of the aisle were brown with mold. Glancing up, I could see why—a section of the ceiling was missing, and the barn roof was open to the sky.

"Sylvia must've bought this property in a bankruptcy sale," I said, wiping bits of straw from my denim shorts.

"Seems likely." Sunny swayed slightly.

I gripped her arm. "Steady."

"Sorry. Guess I'm still woozy from those drugs."

"And dehydration, probably. We need to get you to the hospital."

Sunny leaned against me. "First, we need to get out of sight. Sylvia could return any second."

"You're right. Let's head for the woods. We can follow the road but stay hidden in the trees. As soon as we reach someplace with a phone, we'll call Brad and send the authorities after Sylvia."

"Shouldn't we check on Don?" Sunny's face expressed her distaste for this task, but she resolutely strode over to the dentist's prone body. He lay facedown in the gravel. The back of his shirt was soaked in blood. I doubted he could be alive, but Sunny was right. We had to know.

Kneeling down, Sunny laid her fingers against his neck. "No pulse. I guess he's gone." She stood, wiping her hand against her dress. "So dirty already, it doesn't really matter," she said when she caught my eye.

I glanced at the road. "We probably should get moving."

Sunny nodded and motioned toward the trees. "Thank goodness I wore my good sneakers to the protest."

I lifted my foot. "The soles of these are like rice paper, but what the hell. I'd walk barefoot to get away from here."

"Then let's make tracks." Sunny shoved her hair behind her shoulders and headed for the trees.

I followed, listening for any sound of Sylvia's car. But all was quiet as we plunged into the shadowy woods.

*   *   *

We walked for what felt like miles, keeping the road in sight but staying behind the tree line. By the time we reached a paved road, I had worn a hole in the bottom of one sneaker, and scratches had etched my bare arms and legs. But we hadn't seen Sylvia's car, which was a relief.

The fact that we hadn't seen *any* vehicles was less appealing. I could tell Sunny was rapidly running out of steam. No wonder, if she hadn't had anything to eat and little to drink for almost two days.

"Here, let's stop for a minute," I said, guiding her to a birch tree. I leaned against its smooth trunk, allowing Sunny to rest her head on my shoulder.

"Must find a phone," she muttered.

"And we will. But I don't want you collapsing on me. I can't carry you, even if you aren't that big."

Sunny lifted her head and looked out toward the road. "I'll make it."

"Of course you will, but take a minute to catch your breath." I gently pushed a tangled lock of her hair behind her ear. "You know, you really would make a great mayor. You're smart, and fair, and determined."

"Some would say stubborn," Sunny replied with a wan smile.

"Nothing wrong with that. Might be a positive trait in a mayor. Fight the good fight and all that."

"I am seriously considering it." Sunny straightened and patted my hand. "Now let's keep moving. I won't get to be anything if Sylvia finds us."

"Right. So encouraging," I said but managed to twitch my dry lips into a smile.

We set off again, following the paved road. When we came to a road sign indicating its name, Sunny let out a little *whoop* before slapping her hand over her mouth.

"Oak Level Road—I know where that comes out," she whispered between her splayed fingers. "Connects with Old Ford Turnpike."

"Which bisects Main Street. Hallelujah," I said.

Obviously revitalized by this discovery, Sunny squared her shoulders and picked up her pace. "We should come upon a house or two soon."

"Hey, slow down. You're still not in shape to jog," I said, following her as best as I could.

She stopped short, causing me to step on her heel. "Sorry." I placed my hand on her shoulder to steady myself.

"Shhh . . ." Sunny turned her head, her finger to her lips. "Car."

My fingers dug into her shoulder. "Sylvia?"

"Not unless she's switched vehicles. It's sort of a maroon color. Look, can you see it?" Sunny pointed toward a break in the undergrowth.

I squinted. The vehicle was a dark-crimson SUV, moving slowly. "It's Walt's car! Come on, we have to flag them down!" I ran, ignoring the throb in my head as my feet pounded the hard ground. Batting aside the thorny branches of some wild shrub, I made straight for the road.

Sunny was right on my heels. "Hey, hey!" she shouted, waving her bare arms over her head as we stumbled onto the grassy shoulder.

I reached the edge of the road, shrieking, "Stop!" at the top of my lungs.

The SUV screeched to a halt a few yards beyond us. Both the driver and passenger doors flew open, and Walt and Zelda jumped out.

We ran toward each other like actors in some romantic commercial. But this wasn't a blooming meadow, it was a hard-surface road, and if Sunny and I looked anything like Walt and Zelda, it resembled clumsy jogging more than graceful leaping.

But that didn't matter because we were safe.

Walt wrapped his arms around Sunny as she faltered and almost fell to the pavement. "Thank God," he said, holding her on her feet. "You're okay. You're okay."

Zelda reached me and hugged me so tight I coughed. "Lydia will be so happy to see you!" She released her hold and slid her hands down my arms to my wrists. Holding me at arm's length, she examined me. "You look like you've been rode hard and put up wet. But Lydia won't give a flip about that for once. She's been so frantic, I thought she was going to have a heart attack."

"Come on. Let's get you in the car." Walt guided Sunny to the SUV and flung open one of the back doors. He helped her inside while Zelda put her arm around my waist and led me to the vehicle.

"You were out looking for us?" I asked as I climbed in beside Sunny.

"Yes, everyone is." Zelda slid into the passenger-side front seat and turned to face us. "When Lydia got home from church and you weren't there but the house was locked up tight, she called Richard Muir to find out if he'd seen you. Of course, he said you'd left his house and headed home some time before. So that set off all the alarms." She studied us, her full lips trembling. "Poor dears, you look so rough. Walt"—she added as he started up the car—"go straight to the hospital. These girls need to be checked out immediately."

I almost protested, then thought about Sunny and nodded. "We think Sunny was drugged. And she hasn't had any food or clean water for quite a while."

"And Amy was bopped on the head with a gun," Sunny said, laying her head back against the leather upholstery. "We're going to mess up your car, Walt," she murmured.

"Not a problem," Walt said, shooting us a quick smile in the rearview mirror. "Just glad we found you. Now tell me, what the hell happened?"

"It was Sylvia Baker," I said, "and Don Virts. They were in on it together, although only Sylvia actually killed anyone."

"Well, I never." Zelda fanned herself with her hand. "Always disliked the woman but would never have imagined her a murderer."

"I think she was counting on that," I replied, finally allowing my aching limbs to relax into the soft leather of the car seat.

Zelda dug through her purse and whipped out her cell phone. "I must call Lydia."

I straightened a little in the seat. "Can you call Deputy Tucker or the sheriff's office first? Sylvia fled in her car, so they need to know to look for her. And she told me something about using aliases. They should know about that right away."

"Sure, dear." Zelda tapped an icon on her cell. "Preprogrammed," she said, holding the phone to her ear. "Can't be too careful."

"What about Dr. Virts?" Walt asked.

"Dead," Sunny said. "Back at the barn where they held us. It's off that old gravel road that intersects with this one somewhere higher up."

"Logging Road." Walt's face in the mirror was thoughtful. "That's where they found Bob Blackstone's car. Must be connected."

"Yeah," I said. "I think we'd better inform the sheriff or Deputy Tucker about Sylvia before we explain everything to you, but it is connected."

Zelda handed her phone back to me. "Here. Got Brad Tucker on the line. Maybe you should talk to him directly."

I took the phone and cleared my throat before speaking to Brad.

He listened without speaking while I filled him in on what had happened to Sunny and me and what we'd heard from both Sylvia and Don. When I finished my story, he asked several questions about Sylvia's car, what I might have seen of her gun, and where his team would find Don's body.

"And Sunny is safe?" he asked for the umpteenth time after I provided all the requested information.

"Yeah, just dehydrated. And we think she might have been drugged with something, so she's a bit groggy. Walt and Zelda are taking her to the hospital."

"Meet you there," Brad said before hanging up.

I glanced over at Sunny, whose eyes were closed. "He's very concerned about you."

"I'm official business," she said. But she smiled.

"Now call your aunt," Zelda said.

"Yes, ma'am." I popped my hand up in a mock salute, only to touch the side of my head and wince.

"Hard to believe Sylvia Baker is behind all this," Walt said. "Although I always did think her obsession with family heritage was a little extreme."

"Just a little," I agreed. "But her motive was also tied up with her business interests, which apparently are not all entirely legal. And it was Don who started it all, as you heard. If he hadn't blackmailed her . . ."

"And Bob," Zelda said, glancing over her shoulder. "Your aunt. Call." She shook her finger at me.

I punched in our landline number, hoping Aunt Lydia was at home.

She was. Her relief at hearing my voice was palpable, but once she determined I was okay, she demanded to speak to Zelda. To arrange to meet us at the hospital, no doubt.

"Call Sunny's grandparents," I requested.

"I will, right away. And Richard. He's out searching, you know."

"I'm sure. All right, here's Zelda, and"—I choked up as the enormity of the day's events hit me—"I love you."

There was a slight pause before Aunt Lydia replied, "I love you too." Her normally clear voice was shaky. "Now let me talk to Zelda."

I handed the cell phone to Zelda and wiped tears from my cheeks with the back of my hand.

She passed me a wad of tissues as she took the phone. "Hello, Lydia. Yes, she'll be all right. Just having a good cry. As she should, poor lamb."

Sunny opened one eye and looked over at me. "We're about to be managed," she whispered.

I nodded, dabbing the tissues to my eyes. Yes, Zelda and Aunt Lydia and the Fieldses would no doubt take charge once we reached the hospital. Which was something I actually welcomed at this point.

And Richard would probably want to take care of me too. Which was, surprisingly, also okay by me.

Chapter Twenty-Five

After a CAT scan and a few other tests, I was allowed to leave the hospital. Of course, the tests—honestly, the *waiting* for the tests—had taken most of the night. By the time I was sent home with strict instructions to rest quietly for several days, ribbons of rose were threading the clouds sailing above the mountains.

The doctors had insisted on keeping Sunny for a couple of days to flush the drugs from her system, as well as to rehydrate her and get her electrolytes back in order.

"So I'm still trapped," she'd told me when I'd asked the attendant pushing my wheelchair to stop by her hospital room.

"But at least this time people are looking after you, not planning to kill you."

She dug around in the eggs on her tray with a plastic fork. "You sure about that?"

I laughed and told her I would be back to visit her soon. As the attendant wheeled me from the room, we almost ran into Brad, who was hovering in the hallway.

"Go on in," I said. "She's back to her old self, it seems."

He tugged at his collar. "That might not be so good for me."

"Give it a shot." I laid my hand on his forearm for a moment. "I know she appreciates everything you did to try to find her."

"It was official business," he replied, not meeting my eyes.

"Uh-huh. Well, take your official self in there and talk to her." I squeezed his arm before releasing it. "I should thank you too."

"You're welcome," he said, finally returning my smile. "But I can't claim all the credit. I have a good team."

"And they have a good leader." I made a shooing motion with my hands. "Now go talk to Sunny."

We had to take the elevator to the main floor to meet up with Aunt Lydia, who was talking to the hospital cashier about insurance and other matters.

"Where are Walt and Zelda?" I asked when the attendant rolled me up next to my aunt.

"I sent them home soon after we got here. Walt has to work today, you know."

"Just wanted to thank them again, but I'm sure I'll see them soon." I shifted in the wheelchair and glanced across the room. There was a solitary figure slumped in one of the waiting area's chairs. "Oh, Richard's here."

"Yes, and he was stuck in that uncomfortable chair all night. Once I called, he rushed home and picked me up and drove me here. But only family is allowed back in emergency area, so he couldn't see you. Which didn't make him very happy, I must say."

Richard lifted his head. I waved, and he jumped to his feet and crossed the floor in a few long strides. As soon as he reached the wheelchair, he grabbed the chair's arms, leaned over, and kissed me passionately on the lips.

"Now none of that. She's supposed to remain quiet for a few days." Aunt Lydia waved a folder of hospital forms at Richard.

"I'm not going to disturb her rest." Richard released his grip on the wheelchair and stepped back.

"Well, a kiss like that would disturb mine," Aunt Lydia said and smiled.

I smiled too. Because Richard was, ever so slightly, blushing. He held up his hands. "I will be good."

"In that case, I think you should come over tonight," Aunt Lydia said. "We never did have that dinner, you know."

"I'd love to. But are you sure you want to fix a meal after this?"

"Oh, I'll just make one of my vegetable lasagnas. I can throw those together in my sleep."

"And might have to," I said, which earned a grin from Richard.

Aunt Lydia tucked the folder under her arm. "It will be fine. Richard, if you'll pull your car around, we'll get this young lady home, and then all of us can finally get a few hours of sleep. But set your alarm because we expect you on our doorstep at six o'clock tonight."

"I promise," Richard said, holding his hand to his heart. He headed for the hospital entrance's revolving door as Aunt Lydia instructed the attendant to push me outside.

"I will tell you this, Amy," she said as we waited under the main door canopy. "If you don't want him, I might have to make a play. I mean, I know I'm a good deal older, but"—she winked at the attendant—"I'm not dead yet."

The poor man choked on a cough, then muttered something about allergies.

When Richard pulled up to the curb and got out, I was hiccupping so hard from laughter that he had to rub my back to calm me down before I could climb into the car.

* * *

As soon as we got home, Aunt Lydia put me to bed. "Sleep," she said. "I'll do the same, at least for a few hours."

I sat up as she plumped the pillows behind my head. "Sylvia is still out there somewhere, isn't she?"

"Yes, but Brad told me they think she may have fled the country. Or is trying to, anyway. They found her car at the city airport in the long-term lot. No sign of her yet, though."

"Glad I gave Brad that tip about Sylvia using aliases. I hope that helps their search." I shook my head. "It's unbelievable to think of her killing people just to protect a few business deals and keep some family secrets buried."

"Not really. She loves money and was always obsessed with the family name. I guess exposing her grandfather and father's involvement in the orphanage cover-up was something she couldn't tolerate. Or, from what you've told me, something that some of her business partners wouldn't accept." Aunt Lydia stepped back and studied me. "I'm just glad she lost her nerve before she killed you. Or Sunny."

"I don't know if that's what it was." I chewed on a fingernail. *Not totally convinced she fled due to losing her nerve after killing Don, are you, Amy? It was almost like something scared her off. Like she did see something—or someone—in the trees and shot at it to protect herself.*

But there hadn't been anyone else there, at least not that Sunny or I had seen, so I wasn't going to mention my silly notion to Aunt Lydia. Especially since I knew her concerns over unexplainable occurrences.

"Brad said they assigned a deputy to our street?"

"Yes, she's been driving around the block ever since we got home. They also posted someone near the Fieldses' farm."

"Good." I leaned back against the pillows. "Okay, I'll try to sleep. Not sure I can, though."

"I bet you will." Aunt Lydia paused at my bedroom door. "Just close your eyes and clear your mind."

"Yeah, that's the hard part," I replied as she left the room.

But I did fall asleep, waking only when Aunt Lydia reappeared at my door and softly called my name. "Almost six o'clock," she said. "Well, it's really five thirty, but I thought you might want a little time to dress before Richard gets here."

"Gonna be casual," I said, sitting up and rubbing at my eyes.

"Of course, dear. Just come down when you're ready."

I stared at the door. Aunt Lydia must've really, really been scared when I went missing. She wouldn't be so accepting of my laid-back clothing choices otherwise. Especially not when we were expecting company.

I threw on some lightweight navy yoga pants, tucking the spare cell phone Aunt Lydia had provided into one pocket. From my closet, I chose a gauzy yellow tunic decorated along the hem and neckline with small sunburst medallions. Sunny had brought it back with her from a trip to India. Somehow, it felt appropriate to wear something she'd given me. I didn't bother with shoes.

By the time I walked into the kitchen, Richard was already at the counter, slicing a loaf of Italian bread while Aunt Lydia pulled her lasagna from the oven.

"Smells wonderful," I said as my stomach growled. Of course, I hadn't eaten anything except some hospital Jell-O since my frozen waffles the day before.

"Doesn't it?" Richard walked over and wrapped his arm around me. "I almost brought wine, but then I remembered your poor head." He gently kissed my temple. "It's probably not the best choice to drink on top of a slight concussion."

"A wise decision," Aunt Lydia said. She set the casserole dish on a rack on the counter. "Need to let it cool for a bit, but go ahead and have a seat at the table. Forgive me for not setting up in the dining room, but with just the three of us . . ."

"We never eat in the dining room," I told Richard as I pulled out my chair. "It's like the front parlor. Nice to look at, but no one ever uses it."

"This is better, anyway. More comfortable, I bet." Richard replied, sitting next to me. He leaned back in his chair, raising the front legs off the floor. "By the way, what do you plan to do about the library? I guess there's no one to run it with you and Sunny out of commission."

"Just keep it closed for a few days. People should understand, given the circumstances. I hope to get back in there on Wednesday, anyway."

Richard laid his hand over mine. "Don't push it."

"I'm sure I'll be fine by then." I glanced over at Aunt Lydia, who was still bent over, both hands gripping the counter next to the stove. "Speaking of feeling fine, are you okay?"

"Sure, sure." She turned around.

"You've gone pale as a ghost." Richard dropped the front legs of his chair and leapt to his feet.

"I'm fine," Aunt Lydia said, but I could tell this was a lie. Her eyes were glassy, and beads of sweat dotted her upper lip.

"No, you're not." I jumped up and ran to her side. "What is it?"

"Pressure," she said, clutching her hand to her left shoulder. "Felt like a weight on my chest." She waved Richard back. "No, no, I don't need help. It's mostly gone now. Probably just heartburn. Too much sampling of that spicy sauce."

Richard gripped her right arm. "You need to go to the hospital."

Aunt Lydia managed a little smile. "Just came from there."

"And should go back. Amy, call nine-one-one."

"No, absolutely not." Aunt Lydia straightened. "I am feeling much better, and I won't be dragged off on a stretcher. I will go if you drive me, but no ambulance."

Richard looked dubious. "All right, if that's the only way to get you there, I'll drive you. But we leave now."

"Ruined dinner," Aunt Lydia said, but she allowed Richard to take her arm and escort her out of the room.

"Don't worry about that." Richard looked back at me as he led Aunt Lydia to the front door. "What do you think you're doing?"

"Coming with you, of course."

"No," said Aunt Lydia.

"No, you're not. You're going to stay here and rest, as the doctor ordered. Don't argue"—Richard held up his free hand, palm out—"you know it's best. Otherwise you'll be stuck in one of those horrible waiting-room chairs, and no one can rest in those, trust me."

"But Aunt Lydia . . ."

"Richard is right," she said firmly. "You stay here. The deputy is outside, cruising the neighborhood, so you'll be watched over. Just lock up after us and then grab something to eat. I'm sure you're starving." She fixed me with one of her most imperious stares. "It will honestly help me more, knowing you're resting here."

"All right," I said stepping close enough to kiss her on the cheek. "But call me immediately with any news. You too," I said, pointing my finger at Richard.

"We will." Richard pressed his palm against my shoulder. "Get some rest. I'll call as soon as I can."

He hurried Aunt Lydia out of the house. I stepped out onto the porch and watched his car pull away before I went back inside and locked the door behind me.

As I walked back toward the kitchen, something crashed behind me and made me spin around. The front parlor again. I took a deep breath before crossing to the parlor door and flicking on the lights.

A figurine lay in pieces on the rose-patterned rug. I stared at it, recognizing the item as one that always perched on top of the glass curio cabinet—the figure of a young woman drenched in frothy ruffles and ribbons. A rose-bedecked young lady with white hair falling in curls about her shoulders, holding a now-shattered shepherdess hook. I crossed to the cabinet and knelt down. One door hung open, and a couple of the leather-bound books had once again spilled onto the floor.

I picked up the top book. It was the slender maroon volume, now covered in fragments of porcelain. I brushed off the bits of shattered figurine, then held the book by the spine and gently shook it to remove any fragments from inside.

A folded packet of paper fell from the book and onto my knees.

I stared at it for a moment. Standing slowly, I brushed porcelain dust from my tunic and pants before I unfolded the pages with trembling fingers.

Because I knew what this was. I'd seen paper like this before.

The lights in the parlor flickered. I clutched the packet to my breast and ran out of the room, pausing under the hall chandelier. As I stared at my hands I realized I held two or three pages, pressed together. I used my fingernail to gently pry the pages apart.

The handwriting on the front was familiar—a distinctive, spidery script. Eleanora Cooper had written this. I held the first page closer to my eyes.

It was a remedy for aching joints. I peered at the second page. A salve for burns. The third page was the same, harmless, instructions—this recipe detailing how to create a pain reliever from willow bark.

The missing pages from the herbal, written in Eleanora's hand. Yes, they existed, as Rose Baker had claimed. But they had nothing to do with any type of poison.

I flipped the first page over and gasped. There was additional writing on the reverse side, but in another hand. A bold script that looked nothing like Eleanora's delicate handwriting.

I did what the law would not, it said. *I obtained justice for Daniel.*

It was signed with a large, sweeping, capital *R*.

I pressed the pages to my heart. I knew what I held.

A statement of guilt. A confession, signed by my Great-Grandmother Rose.

I leaned against the wall under the stairs, the pages clutched in my shaking hands, staring blankly at the paintings that lined the opposite wall.

Eleanora Cooper had not come back to claim her house and lands because she could not.

She couldn't return to Taylorsford because she never left.

I focused on one of Uncle Andrew's lovely landscapes as my mind spun with ideas about where Rose could have hidden Eleanora's body. Because Rose had murdered her rival, I was sure of it. But how could a girl of seventeen have committed such a crime and covered it up for the rest of her life? How had no one guessed her secret until now?

Footsteps shook me from the whirlpool of my swirling thoughts. I turned toward the sound. "Aunt Lydia?"

But why were the footsteps coming from the back of the house?

"Richard?" I called out, my voice shaking.

"No, sorry. It's me," said my cousin Sylvia.

Chapter Twenty-Six

I backed away as she moved forward. "How did you get in here?"

"Oh, your Great-Grandmother Rose gave her brother, William, a key to this house, and it's been kept in my family. Passed down to my father and then me. And Lydia never did change the locks."

"You were behind the break-in. The sheriff's office thought Aunt Lydia must've left the door open, but she didn't. And I suspected Kurt Kendrick, but he had nothing to do with it either."

"No, that was me. I was searching for something but broke that stupid picture frame and then had to mess things up to make it look like a real thief had done it." Sylvia was holding her right arm at an odd angle. She tugged down the cashmere sweater draped over her lower arm. "Anyway, why do you think I would need Kurt's help for anything? We are acquaintances, nothing more. Honestly, I don't require some man to fight my battles. And Kurt is not someone I'd mess with, to tell you the truth. There are rumors . . . Well, never mind. I have more important matters to consider. Like how to slip out of town and the country without drawing any unwanted attention. Such an annoyance, but easily dealt with. Just like you, my dear."

"There's a deputy in a cruiser out front," I said.

"Which is why I came in the back. Same key, you know." Sylvia's smile thinned her lips into a straight line. "You're pretty clever, aren't you? Breaking out of that tack room somehow and getting away."

"Sunny and I worked together."

"I'm sure. She's a little too smart for her own good as well. But none of that matters now. I've made my escape plans, and they are much more clever than you could ever imagine."

"You left your car at the airport."

Sylvia tipped her head to one side as she studied me. "Yes, that was part of it. I rented another one under an assumed name. I already had an alias set up, as I mentioned before."

"Just in case you decided to murder someone?"

"No." Sylvia drew this word out as if speaking to someone who didn't quite understand the English language. "For previous business dealings. It came in handy a couple of times, especially for some tricky international deals."

"I see. For all those shady transactions you've brokered before. It does make sense, now that I think about it. All that money you've accumulated from deals no one in town was involved in or really understood. So you have a false passport, I suppose."

"Oh, at least one." Sylvia shrugged back the sweater, and I spied what she was hiding.

Her gun.

I held up the pages of the herbal like a shield.

As if they could somehow protect you from a bullet, Amy. Yeah, brilliant.

But Sylvia did drop her arm and seemed to forget the gun. Her eyes focused on the pages as if she could ignite them with her gaze. "You found them."

"Yeah, the missing pages. The ones Great-Grandmother Rose claimed contained recipes for poisons when she accused

Eleanora Cooper of murdering Daniel." I lowered the papers and pressed them to me.

"The ones she tore out and hid. Wrote a confession on them too, didn't she? Yes, I know all about it." Sylvia allowed the gun to dangle from her crooked fingers. "I visited Rose, you see. Many times. Lydia wasn't always around."

"Using your key to get into the house." I inched a few steps to the left, incrementally closer to the front door.

"Exactly. At first I just wanted to hear all the old family stories. Someone needed to preserve that history." Sylvia shrugged. "Lydia always seemed so disinterested. Too wrapped up in her torrid love affair with that painter. Oh, didn't you know what a passionate thing Lydia was back in the day?" Sylvia clucked her tongue. "Shameful, the way they carried on."

"They were married."

"Yes, but still . . ." Sylvia patted her hair. "I've had my share of lovers, but there's a time and a place. Lydia and Andrew seemed to feel that place was anywhere."

An image of Richard filled my mind, and I knew I would feel the same as my aunt. Especially if we were an established couple.

You have to live long enough to make that happen, Amy.

Yes, I had to live. Somehow. I held out the herbal pages. "Is this what you want? Go on, take them. It's just history now, anyway."

"Is it? Rose killed Eleanora, you know. Ah, you guessed that already. Well, I prefer not to have one of my ancestor's murderous actions exposed, if you don't mind."

The irony of this brought a sharp retort to my lips, but I clamped my mouth shut. Sylvia was already burning with some strange insane passion. No use adding fuel to her fire.

"How do you know she killed Eleanora? I never would've imagined that. Before I saw this, I mean." I stretched out my arm. "Here, take them."

Sylvia snatched the pages from my hand. "She told me. Rose rambled quite a bit, but in the midst of all the nonsense, there were moments of lucidity. And once, when I think she mistook me for her mother, she confessed. Not how she did it. She never said that. Just talked about getting justice, but then she cried that maybe it hadn't been and moaned about guilt, as well as something about a prison. 'Cold and dark,' she said."

Cold and dark. The words my mother had used when she'd fled this house after Rose's funeral. I shivered. "That was after the orphanage tragedy. After she knew she might've been wrong about Eleanora."

Sylvia stuffed the pages into her pocket. "Poor thing, she really seemed to suffer. Started at shadows like she saw ghosts. Kept saying she felt betrayed because she thought she'd done the right thing. She couldn't believe she'd been wrong but was terrified she had been. And so on. A tortured soul, in the end."

I slid a few more inches to the left. "So it wasn't just protecting your illegal deals and your investment in the mayor's development. It wasn't simply hiding the family's involvement in the orphanage cover-up either—you wanted to make sure no one found out about Rose."

"Yes. Didn't want people putting two and two together. Orphanage well and Daniel Cooper's well—not a big leap."

"No, it isn't. Richard's been using Daniel Cooper's old well. He had to have some medical tests, and the doctors found seriously elevated levels of iron in his blood. It wasn't hard to figure out the entire story from there."

"You see"—Sylvia swung the gun up, pointing it at me—"much too clever, little girl."

"But you can't just disappear. People can't, these days."

"Maybe not without a lot of money. But I have a lot of money, and most of it is in foreign banks." Sylvia took several steps toward me. "The kind of banks that are very, very protective of their clients."

My hip bumped into the side table that sat against the staircase wall. Acting on instinct, I grabbed the ceramic bowl and threw it at Sylvia, knocking the gun from her hand. As she shrieked a string of swearwords, I spun on my heel and made a run for the front door.

Sylvia ignored the gun and leapt to her feet. I slid my cell phone from my pocket, hoping I could punch in 9-1-1 before she reached me.

She was fast though, faster than I expected. She clutched my arm and slammed my hand against the table, sending my phone sailing into the opposite wall.

I tripped her, sending her sprawling. Before I could do anything besides scoop up my phone, Sylvia sat up, holding her head. My kick had sent her smashing into the wall. She was groggy and incapacitated. But not for long.

Run, Amy. Time to run.

I headed for the back porch. The garden would hide me for a while. At least long enough for me to make a call.

Shoving my way through the unlocked back door, I took the stairs two at a time to reach the ground. Hopping over the gravel as it bit into my feet, I dashed into the heart of the garden, where the waving fronds of chamomile and plate-sized borage leaves would hide me from immediate view.

The back door swung open. Sylvia stood on the top step, surveying the garden. Light spilling from the back porch glinted off the gun in her right hand.

Stupid, Amy, you should've grabbed that gun. Too late now. I swore at myself and tapped my phone. It didn't light up. Frantically pressing the power button, I realized it was broken. That smash against the wall had been more destructive than I'd imagined.

Sylvia must've spied the movement of my hands or shadow. She dashed down the main pea-gravel path as if pursued by devils.

Or ghosts. She's probably created a lot of ghosts, I thought and had to bite my lip to stifle a burst of hysterical laughter.

I circled around the flowerbed, hoping Sylvia would keep to the main path, but when a dark figure loomed before me, I knew she'd cut off my escape. I flung out my hands in a panic.

She grabbed me and spun me around to pull my arms behind my back. "I'd blow your brains out right now, except I don't want to draw the attention of that deputy out front. So come along, back into the house, and let's discuss this matter in private."

"I'm not going anywhere with you!" I twisted and looked up into Sylvia's face, then shrank back. Her eyes had gone blank, and her lips were curled away from her teeth like a rabid animal. I pulled one hand free and raked my nails across her cheek. She grunted and thrust me aside, her fingers catching on one of the sunburst medallions on my tunic. It popped free and sailed into a tangle of dark foliage.

That was how it happened, I thought as I shoved Sylvia with more force than I thought possible. *That was how Eleanora's brooch was lost in the garden.*

Because Eleanora must've struggled too. Hit back against Rose. Fought for her life.

Sylvia swore under her breath as she tumbled to the ground but kept her grip on her gun. I wanted to pry it from her fingers but stepped back instead. Grabbing the gun was a foolish risk, particularly now, when Sylvia's anger might drive her to use it indiscriminately.

But I had to do something. I knew once she regained her footing, she would come for me again. Running to the front of the house and flagging down the deputy was my first choice, but the open stretch between the house and gardens would make me a perfect target—especially if Sylvia was now willing to shoot and damn the consequences.

There was only one avenue of escape. I had to head for the woods and take the path Richard had shown me. Maybe I could circle around the side of his house and reach the road without giving Sylvia an opportunity for a clean shot.

My bare feet would be ripped to shreds by the rough path, but I would grit my teeth against such pain. It was better than a bullet.

I reached the trees just as I once again heard the crunch of hard-soled shoes on pea gravel. Sylvia was close on my heels.

I dove into the woods, searching desperately for the path. Batting aside blackberry vines, I finally found it. I was limping by this point, but I forced my body forward.

Pain cannot stop you. Keep going, no matter what. You must.

Behind me, thin limbs and dead leaves crackled. I knew what that meant. Sylvia was close. Too close.

Run, Amy. Don't think. Run.

I flew through the arbor, my feet barely hitting the ground. As I reached the far side, I heard Sylvia calling.

"Amy, you really can't get away, you know."

The hell with that. I dashed out into Richard's yard.

But I hadn't considered the illumination of his back porch spotlight. There was a crack like a large branch breaking, and something whistled over my head.

A bullet. I zigzagged as Sylvia took another shot. Although she apparently wasn't quite the crack shot she thought she was, I couldn't stay out in the open. It was too dangerous, with the yard so open and brightly lit.

I choked back a sob and veered right, heading back into the woods.

My big toe caught on the edge of a low stone wall. I stumbled forward, my arms outstretched, beating at the empty air.

The well. I fell onto my hands and knees. The rotten wood boards groaned and gave way, plunging me down.

Down into the cold. Down into the dark.

Chapter
Twenty-Seven

I fell, the boards still beneath me, and hit bottom with a jolt.
The well was dry, but a thick layer of silt cushioned the
boards as they crashed to the bottom, protecting me from serious
injury. The silt shifted under my weight, and I panicked, imagining sinking into that dark mass of dirt and debris. But thankfully the boards, which were lashed together, had pressed tightly
against the sides of the well, preventing them from tipping. After
a moment, the boards settled like a raft on a calm sea.

Sitting up, I uncurled from the ball I'd instinctively tucked
into as I fell. I tested my limbs, leaning against one side of the
well and touching the other side with my toes. I winced. My left
ankle throbbed and appeared to be swelling. Glancing down
I realized that the pain radiating up my arm was due to my
right wrist, which was twisted at an odd angle. I attempted to
open and close my right hand, and my fingers barely moved.
Great—at least one sprained ankle and a broken wrist. Not
much chance I could climb out under my own power.

Not that it would've been likely anyway. As I glanced
upward, I noted the moss-slicked stones as well as the distance
between me and the circle of sky. Even someone in top physical

shape would have had difficulty climbing out without a ladder or rope.

As I stared longingly into the violet twilight, a shadowy form obscured my view. Sylvia, leaning over the opening to the well.

"Just like fish in a barrel," she said, pointing her gun at me.

"No, no, no," I said in a voice that was far too calm for the situation. It was shock, turning an unimaginable situation into something like a slow-motion dream.

As Sylvia leveled the gun at me, I closed my eyes, hoping it would be over quickly. *Just let it be over. Let it be done.*

A gust of wind whistled over the well, knocking Sylvia backward. The gun fired, but the bullet sped heavenward, rendered harmless by its unexpected trajectory.

That was odd. All had been still before that sudden gust. There was not even a breeze stirring the leaves this evening. It was as if the gust had appeared out of nowhere, like invisible hands shoving Sylvia aside and throwing off her aim.

I said a little prayer of thanks while Sylvia swore loudly. "Lucky girl," she yelled. "I'm out of ammunition." She peered down at me. "Or maybe not so lucky. If no one finds you in time, I'm afraid you'll be wishing for a bullet before the end."

She laughed and turned away. The clear evening sky once again filled the circle above my head, and I heard her footsteps grow fainter and fainter.

Wish for a bullet? No. Because I knew someone would find me. Somehow. Someone had to find me.

Sirens pierced the evening air. I straightened and began to scream for help. Surely they would hear me. They would hear, and discover me, and pull me out of this dank stinking hole.

But then I heard the sound of a car speeding away. The sirens followed and faded.

They were chasing Sylvia. Who would never tell them where I was. Who was leading them away.

Continuing to scream was probably fruitless, but I had to try. I yelled for help over and over, until my voice grew so hoarse, it was simply a raspy whisper.

Exhausted, I slumped against the damp stone wall. Groundwater seeped through the stones, soaking the back of my tunic. Cradling my injured wrist in my lap, I examined my circular prison.

The stones were old and worn smooth. No decent foot or handholds even if I could bear the pain of my ankle and wrist long enough to attempt a climb. I looked closer, noticing the vegetation that had wormed its way between the stones, creating a lattice. I grabbed one slender snaking vine and tugged until it broke off in my hand. Well, that was no use. The vines were certainly not strong enough to hold my weight.

Maybe there was something down in the silt that could help. A chain from an old bucket, perhaps. That was unlikely, but I had to consider every option.

Yes, think. Analyze and plan. No matter how futile, it was important to keep my mind occupied. Otherwise, I knew I would lose it.

I sucked in a deep breath, almost choking on the acrid scent tainting the air. *Minerals*, I thought. *Iron, copper, and other minerals, dissolved in the groundwater. Seeping into the rock and dirt.*

Pressing my back into the stones behind me, I gingerly slid my left hand between the edge of the boards and the wall and thrust it into the silt.

I gagged as my fingers explored the thick muck. It was deeper than I expected—I couldn't reach the bottom of the well, even when I leaned over and thrust my arm in up to the elbow.

But my fingers hit something hard. A sharp object, slick as glass. Perhaps there really was something I could use to do . . . something. I yanked my arm back, and it pulled free with a sucking sound. My fingers still clutched the thing they'd encountered. I lifted my hand up to examine the object in the faint light spilling into the well.

And screamed again. Repeatedly, until I finally lost my voice completely.

It was a bone. A human bone, bare of any flesh, worn smooth by time and the elements. A finger.

Glued to the bit of finger by a thick glob of mud, a simple gold band still glimmered beneath a patina of silt.

Using deep breaths to calm myself, I laid the bone in my lap. I stared at the ring for some time, considering whether to remove it to check for any inscription.

But of course, I didn't have to. I knew whose ring it was.

I knew that I'd discovered the answer to the final question.

I had found Eleanora Cooper.

* * *

Time passed like episodes in a dream—disjointed and submerged in shadows. Pain washed over me in waves, but I almost welcomed it. The throbbing in my ankle and burning ache in my wrist told me I could feel. And if I could feel, I was still alive.

I drifted in and out of consciousness for a while, dreaming of dancing with Richard, only to wake to the reality of my cold dark prison.

Cold and dark. Great-Grandmother Rose had spoken those words when she was old and wracked with guilt. I now knew why. Because she'd left Eleanora Cooper in this terrible place. But dead or alive? I rather hoped Rose had tossed Eleanora's lifeless body here, but something whispered that Eleanora had plunged into this well as I had, fleeing her pursuer. It only made sense. Eleanora had fled a murderous Rose, only to tumble into an already abandoned well.

And Rose had left her here. To die. Alone.

In the cold and the dark.

I touched my forefinger to the ring on the skeletal finger. A wedding ring.

No longer terrified, I now felt only pity for a woman who had tragically lost her young husband only to be accused of his murder by her husband's friends. People who'd never accepted her. Who always thought the worst of the stranger, the outsider.

She had suffered through Daniel's illness and his death and then a trial. Acquitted, she'd been attacked by her neighbor's daughter and had died, slowly and horribly.

And alone. I allowed my tears to fall, afraid to raise my filthy hand to my eyes. Eleanora hadn't even been granted the grace to be buried beside her beloved husband.

No wonder Great-Grandmother Rose had lost her mind when she learned what had happened at the orphanage. She had thought killing Eleanora was justified until she'd heard that well water could kill as effectively as hemlock or cyanide, though more insidiously. Such knowledge would've planted the seed of doubt, and the guilt would have grown, wrapping around her like a vine, poisoning her mind.

Rose was not to blame for the dementia that had plagued her later years, but I wondered if her true break from reality had started much earlier. She'd carried the terrible secret of Eleanora's death for years until she was told another secret with the power to shatter her carefully constructed palace of justice. A hidden truth that had forced her to face her guilt, if not confess it.

I stared up at the circle of sky above my head—the same sky Eleanora would've seen as she died. The same stars winking against an indigo sweep of heaven.

"I'm sorry," I whispered. "I'm so sorry."

Something blotted out the sky for a moment, and a light shone down, blinding me.

"She's over here!" yelled a voice.

A blessed voice. A miraculous light.

I lifted my left arm and waved it as hard as I could. "Hello, hello," I croaked.

"Amy!" shouted another voice. One I knew and loved.

"Richard," I said, although I knew he could not hear me. My voice had come back enough for me to make actual sounds, but it was still so shattered it wouldn't carry my words to the surface.

"Hold on, we're bringing a ladder," the first voice said. Brad, that's who it was. Deputy Brad Tucker on official business. Doing his duty.

But also being a friend.

A flexible plastic and metal ladder was tossed down one side of the well. "Can you climb?" asked Brad.

I shook my head and waved my left hand again.

"All right. Don't worry. Someone's coming down to get you," Brad said before shouting, "No, not you, Muir. One of the firefighters. They're experienced with this sort of thing."

A tiny smile quirked my lips. I could visualize Richard protesting this command.

Sirens again split the air. An ambulance. Of course, they'd have to transport me to the hospital. This time that thought was comforting rather than annoying.

The firefighter who climbed down to me was young with biceps that bulged beneath his tight shirt. Thank goodness, because I needed someone who could lift me.

He clung to the bottom rungs of the ladder, studying the situation.

"Think we need the chair," he called up to the others. "She's not going to be able to climb, even with my help. And I'm afraid to step down on that wood. It's barely holding her weight. No way it supports both of us."

"Hi," I croaked.

"Hi." The firefighter offered me a comforting smile. "Just hang in there. We're getting another piece of equipment, but we'll have you out of here soon." He bobbed his head. "My name's Ethan, by the way."

"Thanks, Ethan. I'm Amy."

"Yeah, I know. We've been searching for you for hours, ever since your boyfriend called the chief deputy because you weren't answering the phone at your house."

Aunt Lydia. I had totally forgotten about her trip to the hospital. "My aunt . . ."

"She's fine, and from what I hear, very eager to see you."

"We thought she was having a heart attack, you see," I murmured.

"Naw. Some kind of angina or something, they said. Probably gave her meds. Kept her for observation overnight, I heard. She's okay, though."

"That's good," I said. "That's really good."

Another object was lowered into the well—a seat like a child's swing, attached to ropes and pulleys. Ethan leaned forward and grabbed the ropes to steady the seat.

"Now," he said, "here comes the tough part. Do you think you can stand long enough to climb onto that? I'll strap you in and guide you up, but I don't think I'd better step down on those boards. Might send both of us to the bottom."

"I can do it," I said, although I wasn't sure.

You must, Amy. You've stayed tough so far. Be strong now.

I stared at the bone in my lap. Taking hold of the edge of my tunic with my left hand, I wrapped it up over the skeletal finger, securing it by stuffing it into the top edge of my bra. I didn't think it mattered anymore how much skin Ethan saw. To his credit, he appeared unfazed by my action.

"We could come back for whatever that is later, you know," was all he said.

"No, too important." I struggled to my feet, pressing my left hand against the wall and hopping on my right foot.

Somehow, I was able to climb onto the seat with Ethan's help to balance me. He strapped me in and shouted to the others to pull me up.

Ethan climbed the ladder, keeping pace with my ascent so he could make sure my chair didn't bang the sides of the well.

I looked up, watching the circle of sky grow bigger and the stars brighter until we breached the top of the well.

Temporary lights flooded the area, creating rainbow halos around every person and object. I blinked as an army of people encircled me. They lifted me off the chair and strapped me to a backboard.

One of the rescue workers tugged my tunic free of my bra, spilling the skeletal finger across my midriff.

"What's this?" they asked in a hushed voice.

Brad Tucker was standing at my shoulder. I motioned him closer with my good hand and pointed to the bit of bone. "Eleanora Cooper."

He instantly understood. He barked an order for someone to hand him an evidence bag. He carefully lifted the finger and slid it into the bag, then turned to another deputy on his team. "Leave the ladder," he said. "We have some more work to do down there."

I held my left hand to the stiff brace at my neck. "Hard to breathe."

"Yeah, but they need to keep you immobilized, at least until you're fully checked out."

I closed my eyes as the rescue workers tipped the backboard and slid it into the waiting ambulance. As one of the workers strapped down the board to a stretcher, a man jumped into the back of the ambulance.

"Hey," said the woman inside the ambulance, "what do you think you're doing?"

"Riding along," Richard said. "Got permission from the chief deputy."

The EMT waved Richard back. "He's not really our boss," she said, hooking me up to an IV.

"Please let him stay," I whispered as the worker leaned in to check my pupils.

"All right, if he stays out of the way." The EMT stepped aside and sat on the adjacent stretcher. "Ready to go," she called to the people outside.

As the ambulance doors slammed shut, Richard perched on the built-in seat on my other side.

"Sorry, can't turn my head," I muttered.

He stood and leaned over me, brushing my lips with a kiss.

"Sit," said the rescue worker. "We don't need another patient."

Richard sat back down but laid his hand on my shoulder and kept it there for the entire ride to the hospital.

And even though I couldn't really reply, or laugh, or even see his face, Richard kept me entertained with stories about the funny stage disasters he had experienced during his dance career. Including the time his tights had caught on a nail and ripped open, exposing his bare backside to the entire audience.

"Some of them were appreciative, at least," he said. "Got the best applause of the night."

That prompted a hearty chuckle from the EMT.

Chapter Twenty-Eight

I spent three days in the hospital, which was two more than I thought necessary. But Aunt Lydia overruled all my suggestions that I was fine and should be released immediately.

She had backup from the doctors, Sunny, and even Richard, who listened to my complaints without saying a word. Of course, he didn't have to argue with me. Aunt Lydia had that covered.

On the second afternoon, Aunt Lydia said she had to run some errands, and Richard volunteered to drive her, leaving me alone. As I flipped aimlessly through various television channels, I heard an unexpected voice say, "Hello."

Kurt Kendrick walked into my room, cradling a tasteful but obviously expensive bouquet of orchids.

"Amy, so happy to see you were not too bruised and battered by your ordeal," he said, setting the flower arrangement on the side table.

I stared at him with suspicion. "Thanks for the flowers, but I thought you were in Europe."

"Well, you see"—he pulled up a chair and sat down, his long legs bumping up against the metal bed frame—"my plans went completely haywire. My business is a bit erratic that way. Sellers change their minds, and sometimes buyers can't make up theirs."

His grin was disarming, but I remained on guard. "Surprised you felt a need to visit me. Especially when you've just arrived home from overseas. You must be tired, and it's not like you know me that well."

"Don't I?" Kendrick leaned in and clasped my uninjured hand. "I suppose I may feel a connection that's not reciprocal. But having spent time around your family in the past . . ." He lowered my hand onto the hospital blanket and sat back. "You do resemble Rose, you know, and never more so than now, with those dark eyes shooting daggers at me."

I choked back a swearword before replying. "I may look a bit similar, but I'm nothing like her."

"No, that's very true. You are much nicer and not in the least bit insane." His brilliant blue eyes studied me intently. "You thought I was involved, didn't you? In the death of Doris Virts, at least."

I sank back against my pillows. "Yes, at first."

"Because of the car."

"Partially. Also, people told me things . . ."

"Ah, people." Kurt Kendrick ran his fingers through his thick hair. "Like your aunt, I suppose. And perhaps Zelda Shoemaker?"

I stared down at my clenched left hand, refusing to meet his eyes. "Just people. Anyway, you do have a reputation, Mr. Kendrick."

"Oh, I have several."

I glanced up to meet his amused gaze. "So why was your car there that day? That's one puzzle piece I still can't place."

"Just a coincidence, actually. Those do happen in life, if not in your books."

"I know, but it's a strange one, you must admit."

"Not really." Kendrick rested his chin on his tented fingers and examined me.

As if you were one of his art objects, Amy. I used my good hand to push myself up and stiffened my spine, not allowing my back to touch the pillows. "So explain it to me."

"And now you have the look of Lydia about you. Only the expression, of course, but I can see it clearly. Very well," he said, ignoring my sniff of disapproval. "I was parked there behind your library for a specific reason. A perhaps not-entirely-innocent reason. However, it had nothing to do with Doris Virts. I'm not sure why you would ever connect me to her murder anyway, since I didn't even know the woman."

"I thought since Don owed you money . . ."

Kurt Kendrick waved his hand through the air as if shooing off an annoying insect. "Oh, that. Yes, Virts owed me some money. But I assure you I wouldn't kill his mother over it. Or anyone, for that matter. That isn't the way I do business, despite what your aunt may think."

"She believes you made your first fortune running drugs."

"Does she? Well, suppose I take the fifth on that one—would you think me beyond redemption?"

I stared at his craggy face, noticing no change in his cheerful expression. "Not necessarily. But you still haven't told me why you were parked near the library the day Doris was murdered."

"It was a private art deal," he replied. "The seller didn't want to meet me in public or at my house. So we arranged a pickup at a neutral location, and I parked on the side road near the library so we could discuss the terms of the sale."

"You often conduct business in your car?"

"Not often, no. But this seller had good reason to be careful."

"Because the piece was stolen, or what?"

"My dear, surely you don't expect me to answer that."

I narrowed my eyes as I continued to study him for any signs of anxiety. There were none. Obviously, whatever Kurt

Kendrick was up to, he had no fears of being caught. "Guess not. But how did you explain this little art deal to the sheriff's office? I know they cleared you, so you must've told them something."

"I did, and they did, and let's just leave it at that, shall we? Now"—Kendrick pushed back his chair and rose to his feet—"I should probably go. I don't want to tire you."

"I'm fine," I said but decided against asking him to stay.

"Just wanted to check on you and wish you speedy recovery. And Amy"—he leaned forward until he was looming over me—"perhaps it would be best if you confined your investigations to library-related research in the future. You can see where digging into things you don't understand might prove dangerous, I hope?"

He straightened but continued to stare down at me, no longer resembling an aging but still charming courtier from a Baroque painting. Now he appeared as stern and cold as some Old Testament prophet carved in marble.

I shrank back into my pillows and swallowed hard before I replied. "I don't expect there'll be any reason to do so. Not unless we have another sudden rash of murders in Taylorsford, and I can't imagine that we will."

"I should hope not," said Kurt Kendrick, and he smiled once again. "Take care, Amy. And when you can, try to convince that aunt of yours to forgive and forget, will you? I would like to invite both of you to dinner some time." He waved a quick good-bye before leaving my room.

After he'd gone, I studied the orchids he had brought. They were beautiful, but I couldn't help but note how the blossoms resembled the mouths of tiny beasts.

Chapter Twenty-Nine

On my third evening in the hospital, Aunt Lydia and Sunny kept me company as I glumly stared at a plate of what the hospital referred to as *dinner*. Richard had visited that day but left early for a Skype interview about one of his recently choreographed pieces.

"All I have is a sprained ankle and a broken wrist," I said, sitting up straighter in the hospital bed. Making a face at my tray, I stirred anemic peas into a small mound of runny mashed potatoes.

Sunny cast me a sympathetic look. "The food's the worst, I know." She ran her fingers through her now silky hair. She'd been released from the hospital two days before but was already back at work, managing the library in my absence.

"And dehydration, and possible aggravation to that previous blow to your head, and being exposed to heaven knows what germs down in that muck. You had some fever until today, you know. They weren't about to release you before they determined that it was just caused by exposure and inflammation and not some deadly pathogen from that well." Aunt Lydia extracted her cell phone before she snapped shut her purse. "The doctors say tomorrow and not a minute before. Now that we've settled that, I'm going to call Zelda and see if she has any more details on Sylvia."

"Oh, don't bother." Sunny looked up from her examination of the cards attached to the flowers on my windowsill. "I know all about it."

I glanced at her, raising my eyebrows. "Brad filled you in?"

"Maybe. Anyway, the latest is that Sylvia has finally confessed to everything. When they caught her, at first she refused to talk, but when she was told Bob Blackstone had regained consciousness and told the sheriff all about the cover-up and Don's blackmail, she spilled everything. Brad said it was like she had some mental break or something, because she started raving about the need to protect secrets and how no one would ever understand how hard she'd worked to preserve the family name."

"I just can't believe my cousin killed three people over a minor land deal and some historical secrets. Information that couldn't really affect anyone still alive." Aunt Lydia shook her head. "And then tried to flee to South America. You'd think it was a Bogart movie or something. Criminal mastermind on the lam."

"But they caught her before she could take that private plane to wherever, thanks to Amy alerting the authorities to check all her accounts for aliases." Sunny flashed me a smile.

Aunt Lydia opened her purse and tossed in her cell phone before pulling out a tissue. "To be perfectly honest, it's a little scary, thinking that there must be a murder gene in our family."

"The only person I want to kill is whoever cooked this," I said, pushing my food tray to the side.

Sunny lifted the card from an arrangement of yellow chrysanthemums and waved it at me. "Speaking of Brad . . ."

"You know that gift is just a friend thing," I replied.

"Better be. You break Richard's heart, and you'll have to answer to me."

I made a noncommittal noise.

Sunny stuck Brad's card back with the mums and surveyed the collection of flowers and blooming plants. "Which one is his, by the way? The orchids?"

A flush heated my cheeks. "No."

"The roses, of course," Aunt Lydia replied before I could say anything more. "Aren't they beautiful?"

Sunny touched one velvety crimson petal. "And expensive. Wow, guess he really is a goner."

"Look, don't jump to conclusions. It isn't that serious yet . . ."

Aunt Lydia and Sunny both laughed.

After she collected herself, Aunt Lydia dabbed at her eyes with the tissue. "As a matter of fact, Richard told me to bring you to his house tomorrow as soon as you're released. He's going to show me some of his choreography through some sort of streaming thing. Yes, I asked him to, so don't raise your eyebrows at me, young lady. He's also going to fix us both some lunch. Said he thought I might appreciate the break. Which I do." She smiled at me. "It's been rather exhausting running back and forth on top of arguing with a stubborn patient. Not to mention, I've also been eating hospital food. In the cafeteria, but still . . . not ideal."

"Yeah, I guess not." I held up my left hand. "Mea culpa. In other words, thank you both for putting up with me. I know I've been a bit grumpy."

"A bit," Aunt Lydia agreed.

Knowing she was right, I decided to overlook that comment. "And thanks for making sure Mom and Dad didn't take the first flight home. I'd hate to ruin a trip they've planned for years."

"I told them I was looking after you." Aunt Lydia cocked her head to one side. "I haven't mentioned Richard to them, by the way. Thought maybe you'd want to broach that topic."

"Yeah, in time," I said.

Sunny and Aunt Lydia shared a conspiratorial glance.

"You shouldn't wait too long," Sunny said. "They'd probably want to know before the engagement."

"Engagement? We just met," I snapped, then slumped back against the pillows as I surveyed my aunt's amused face. "Sorry, grumping again."

"It's okay. Blame it on the medication," Sunny said. "That's what I did. Seemed to work." When she tossed her head, her hair shimmered in the light like a golden veil. "Convinced Brad, anyway."

I shot her a rueful smile. "Girl, you could probably convince Brad the moon was made of Styrofoam."

"I know," she said. "Isn't it delightful?"

* * *

The following day, Aunt Lydia drove me home. Or rather, to Richard's house. He met us at the car as soon as my aunt pulled into his driveway. Putting his arm around me, he helped me navigate the porch stairs.

"See"—I leaned into him as I lifted my cane slightly—"Aunt Lydia and I match."

"I see. I also see that I will have no dance partners today." Richard caressed my shoulder. "So you must endure watching other people perform my choreography."

"Not you?" I asked as he guided me into the house.

"Maybe a bit of that too. If you can stand it." Richard led me across the room and helped me settle onto the sofa.

"You moved the coffee table."

Richard scooted an ottoman in front of me. "So you can prop your foot. Here, I'll help lift your leg."

314

Aunt Lydia watched this little scene from the edge of the seating area, amusement dancing in her blue eyes. "May I take the armchair? Looks comfortable enough."

"Of course." Richard raked his hands through his hair. He was flustered again, which was, I had to admit, rather adorable.

Before Aunt Lydia sat down, she surveyed the rest of the room. "Dance studio. Different, but sensible. Are you planning to teach here?"

"No, I don't think so. I get enough of that at work. This is for me." Richard crossed to the bookcase. He plucked an object from the shelf that held Paul Dassin's photograph. "Thought you might want to see this," he said, handing it to Aunt Lydia before he sat beside me.

"Ah, the brooch Amy told me about. Finally." Aunt Lydia shot me a look before settling back against the chair cushions. "Poor Eleanora. All she wanted to do was help people with her herbal medicines."

"Brad told me they are going to inter her bones in a grave right beside Daniel," I said. "I know it's silly, because if they are anywhere, it isn't here, but I think they'd both like that."

"I'm sure they would." Richard placed his right arm around my shoulder and drew me to his side.

Aunt Lydia stared up at the high ceiling, apparently studying the wrought-iron light fixture. But I knew she was actually thinking about the same thing that had been on my mind for days—Rose.

"She said so many strange things in her later years," she mused. "Grandma Rose, I mean. I didn't think anything of it, other than how her mind had slipped into some twilight world where time and words had little meaning." She lowered her head and stared directly at Richard and me. "But now I can see a pattern."

"She wanted to confess, I think," I said. "Sylvia claimed she actually did once, when she mistook her for someone else."

"Yes, I can believe that." Aunt Lydia curled her fingers around the gold brooch resting in her palm. "She did ramble on about the 'cold and dark' quite a bit. And about guilt. I thought she meant Eleanora's guilt, but now I suppose she meant her own."

"But why would Eleanora visit Rose after the trial?" Richard asked. "She knew Rose was her enemy."

"I think I've figured that out. I found a letter once when clearing out Rose's things. Again, I thought little of it at the time. But now"—Aunt Lydia leaned forward—"it holds more significance."

"Something Rose wrote?" I snuggled closer to Richard, allowing my still-sore body to relax.

"No, something she received. A letter from her mother, written when her parents took her brother to tour military academies. William was fifteen and wanted to attend an academy for his last few years of high school. Thought of joining the service, I suppose, although he never actually did. Anyway, the letter was dated a few weeks after the conclusion of Eleanora's trial. Rose's mother wrote the usual pleasantries, but she also urged Rose to make peace with Eleanora. Suggested she invite her over to the house and make her apologies."

"So Rose was alone at the house during that time?"

"Yes. She was seventeen, which was considered adult in those days. Anyway, the rest of the family was gone for weeks, traveling from one school to another. Rose was home alone, taking care of the house and garden."

"And she did invite Eleanora over, but not to apologize," Richard said.

"Apparently." Aunt Lydia sat back and unclenched her fingers, exposing a glint of gold. "It's the only way I can imagine Eleanora's brooch turning up in Rose's garden."

"I don't think Rose meant to kill her," I said slowly. "Maybe she just wanted to hurt her, like Rose felt she'd been hurt. But then things got out of hand, and Eleanora fled into the woods."

"And tumbled into the abandoned well, just as you did. And like Sylvia, Rose left her victim there, all alone, to die. She must have considered it fate, doling out proper justice. She used to mutter about fate and justice quite a bit in her ramblings." The lines bracketing Aunt Lydia's mouth deepened. "So Amy, there *was* a reason for our house to be haunted. I know you're a skeptic, but I believe the ghost of Eleanora was trapped in the house where her ordeal began. A lost soul, intending no harm, but struggling over the years to convince someone in our family to give her the justice she deserved. Perhaps she haunted Rose, who went mad but still refused to confess the truth. Then she tried to reach Debbie and then me." Aunt Lydia sighed. "But none of us would listen. It took you to reveal the truth."

"But not due to a ghost's requests." I adjusted my cast until its weight was better supported on my knee. "It was just the right circumstances at the right time. Although I admit that if anyone had a reason to haunt our family, it was Eleanora."

"You think so?" Richard asked. "I wonder."

I glanced up at him. His intense gaze was fixed on the ceiling, but it seemed as if he was looking inward.

"Well, whatever else we disagree on, I think we can all acknowledge that it's a tragic story for everyone involved."

"Yeah, a ballet scenario, for sure," Richard looked down and gave me a little smile. "And on that note, allow me to inflict my choreography on you while I fix lunch." He kissed my left temple before he stood and grabbed a remote from the side table. He waved the remote at Aunt Lydia as he crossed to the rack of audiovisual equipment. "You asked for it."

"So I did." She laid the brooch on the side table next to her chair.

Once Richard turned on the system and queued up his videos, he left the room to fix lunch.

"That's him, dancing, isn't it?" Aunt Lydia asked at one point.

"Yeah, that's him," I replied, tearing my gaze off the television screen just long enough to glance at her.

"Hmm . . ." Aunt Lydia tapped her fingers against her lips. "Just like my Andrew. Sexy as all hell."

"Aunt Lydia!" I fanned my face with my good hand.

She just settled deeper into the chair and grinned.

*　　*　　*

Aunt Lydia left after lunch, claiming she needed a nap.

"No, you stay, Amy. Richard can bring you home later," she told me as she headed for the front door.

"She arranged that so we'd have time alone," I said after the front door closed.

Richard sat beside me on the sofa. "I knew I liked her. Now I think I love her."

"Don't tell her that. She might decide to fight me for you."

He chuckled. "Not sure I can juggle the two of you. But it's tempting."

"You're so full of it."

Richard tugged me closer, until I was settled snuggly against him. "If I'm full of anything," he said, tracing my lips with his fingers, "it's love for you, Amy Webber."

Cradled in his arms, my sprained ankle and broken wrist carefully protected, I sighed and closed my eyes.

"Then kiss me, you romantic, you."

Which he did. Extremely well and for quite some time.

Chapter Thirty

A month later, after the Virginia Department of Forensic Science completed its analysis of the bones found in the well, Eleanora Cooper was laid to rest beside her husband.

Aunt Lydia handed out tissues to Sunny, Richard, Brad, Walt, Zelda, and me as we clustered together at the edge of the crowd. We all needed tissues to wipe away perspiration, not tears. It was a hot summer day, and most of the town had turned out for the burial, crowding the old Lutheran church cemetery.

They had come to honor the woman the town had dishonored for long. I knew their remorse was partially due to my ordeal in the well, which made it almost worth it. Finally, Eleanora's name had been cleared. While recuperating, I had written a post for the town website, detailing the truth about Daniel's death as well as the cover-up connected to the orphanage tragedy. With Aunt Lydia's permission, I had also included Rose's involvement in Eleanora's death.

It might've been my family history, but it was the truth, and both my aunt and I agreed that it needed to be told.

I pulled my left arm free of Richard's crooked elbow to wipe the sweat from my upper lip. None of us had worn black, feeling that this was not truly a sorrowful occasion, but my pale-pink linen dress was still sticking to my thighs. I pocketed the tissue and plucked my dress away from my legs before clasping Richard's right hand.

"So many flowers," he said as Zelda stepped forward to prop a wreath of lilies against the base of the headstone.

"A lot of people needed to make amends," I replied.

He tightened his grip on my left hand. "That they did."

I had it on good authority—Zelda's, to be precise—that Kurt Kendrick had paid for Eleanora's coffin and the new headstone set over both her and her husband's graves. Etched into the smooth gray stone was the inscription, *Daniel James Cooper, 1898–1925, and Beloved Wife, Eleanora Heron Cooper, 1900–1925.*

The generous gift had done nothing to mollify Aunt Lydia. "Well, he has plenty of money to throw around," she'd said when I'd told her what Kendrick had done.

After the brief service, Richard and I lingered with Aunt Lydia, Walt, Zelda, and Sunny until most of the other people had left the cemetery. Brad made his apologies, saying he needed to supervise traffic, before telling Sunny he'd see her later.

"Date?" I asked.

"Could be," she replied with a sly smile.

Inhaling a deep breath of the honeysuckle-scented air, I released Richard's fingers and held out my hand to Sunny. She passed me a bunch of flowering herbs tied with golden ribbons before handing Richard a matching bouquet.

I clutched my flowers in my left hand. My ankle had healed, but my right wrist was still encased in a cast, although I'd been assured that it could be removed soon.

Sharing a glance, Richard and I walked forward and bent down to lay one bouquet on the fresh grave and one on the grass-covered one.

"Together at last," I said, straightening.

"Oh, I think they were already together," Richard said as Sunny moved up beside him. Aunt Lydia stayed back, chatting with Walt and Zelda.

"You think so?" she asked.

Richard looked thoughtful. "Can't imagine they'd be separated in the afterlife just because they weren't buried together. I think their love would've overcome something like that."

"Always the romantic," I said, sliding my left arm around his waist.

He leaned over to give me a brief kiss. "Always."

"But I've been thinking." Sunny's expression was unexpectedly solemn. "Considering everything that happened, I'm not sure there weren't spiritual forces at work. There were some weird coincidences, you have to admit."

Richard slid his right arm around my waist so we were locked together. "What are you saying, Sunny?"

"Not entirely sure. I'm aware you guys don't believe in ghosts or anything like that . . ."

I shook my head, but Richard said, "I like to keep an open mind."

"Yeah, so"—Sunny turned to face us directly—"think about it. Amy just happens to dig up that brooch after so many years, and the herbal turns up when everyone thought it was lost . . ."

"And the curio cabinet, popping open to lead Amy to that book." Richard narrowed his eyes. "Twice."

"Now come on," I said, but I paused for a moment before I spoke again. "Something did scare Sylvia away from that barn after she shot Don. Something she saw or thought she saw. And a gust of wind blew off Sylvia's aim when she tried to shoot me in the well. On an evening when there wasn't even a breeze."

Sunny clapped her hands together. "See, it's all very mysterious."

"And you think it was what?" Richard asked her.

"Why, Eleanora Cooper's ghost, of course. Seeking to reveal the truth about what really killed Daniel, as well as the true story of her own death."

I shifted my weight off my left foot, which still occasionally ached if I stood too long. "You think Eleanora protected me too?"

"Sure, why not? She didn't want to see someone else die like she did, so desperate and alone."

"I don't know." I looked up at Richard. "I have trouble believing in ghosts."

"It could just be coincidence." He met my gaze, his gray eyes shadowed under his black lashes. "Probably."

"I still believe it was Eleanora—or even Daniel. Maybe his spirit was seeking justice for his wife and others. It had to be one of them. And no one is going to convince me otherwise." Sunny knelt before the graves and laid her fingers against her breast, over her heart. "Thank you," she said, bowing her head.

She rose to her feet and moved past us, touching Richard's arm. "Think about it. I'm sure that one may be impossible to convince"—she jerked her thumb toward me—"but I know what I'll always believe." She strode off to join my aunt, Walt, and Zelda, who were leaving the cemetery.

Richard and I stood alone before the two graves for a few minutes, our arms still entwined.

"Can you possibly believe that?" I asked him.

"No," he said, drawing out the word, his eyes focused on the headstone.

"Yeah, that's Sunny, though. A darling, but willing to consider some pretty wild theories."

"That's not it." Richard pulled away and looked down at me. His expression was so serious, I sucked in a sharp breath. "It's just that I don't think either Daniel or Eleanora would've ever felt the need to haunt anyone. They were innocent, and they both knew that, even before they died."

"Sure," I replied, curious where he was taking this line of thought. "They loved one another and stayed true, no matter what."

"Yeah, and I like to think they've been together, all this time. Together in a better place than this, not just forever, but also from the moment Eleanora died." Richard lifted his right hand to caress my jawline. "They had each other. There was no reason for them to return to this earthly plane."

"So no ghosts." I leaned my face against his palm.

"Oh, I don't know." He cradled my chin and kissed me once before dropping his hand. "Think about it, Amy. There is one person who had a reason to return, if anyone did. Not saying it happened. I honestly don't know if I could ever truly believe in such a thing. But if it were possible, I think there was someone else involved who had a better motive. Someone who needed to expiate her sins. To find a little grace . . ."

"Rose," I said before swallowing hard.

Richard nodded. "If it was anyone, I think it would've been Rose." He looked up over my head at the clear summer sky. "But even so, now it's done, and she's at peace too. At last."

I pressed my head against his shoulder and felt his heart beating strongly beneath my ear. "You really are the world's greatest romantic, aren't you?" I murmured.

"I am." He tipped up my chin with one finger. "Now why don't we head back to my house so I can properly prove that?"

"That sounds like the best idea I've heard in long time." I kissed him before we turned and left the cemetery, arm in arm.

And if a little breeze caressed our hair, carrying the scent of roses . . . well, that was all right with me.

Acknowledgments

Thanks to
My agent, Frances Black, at Literary Counsel.

You told me I could do it, and I did! My heartfelt thanks for your sage advice, professional expertise, and unwavering support.

My editor at Crooked Lane Books, Faith Black Ross.

Thank you for believing in this book from the beginning and for the edits that improved it exponentially.

Everyone at Crooked Lane Books who helped to bring this book to life.

It may not take a village, but it certainly takes a (talented and hardworking) team!

My critique partners, Lindsey Duga and Richard Pearson.

The writing life would be much more difficult, and much less fun, without you.

My immediate and extended family, especially my son, Thomas.

My friends, in real life and online. Special thanks to all my supportive author friends.

And *not* last, *nor* least, but *best*—my husband, Kevin G. Weavil.

Thanks, as always, for being my favorite beta reader and fan. Love you!